Magical Memories

DONNA FLETCHER

JOVE BOOKS, NEW YORK

MAGICAL LOVE is a registered trademark of Penguin Putnam Inc.

MAGICAL MEMORIES

A Jove Book / published by arrangement with
the author

PRINTING HISTORY
Jove edition / August 2000

The Penguin Putnam Inc. World Wide Web site address is
http://www.penguinputnam.com

ISBN: 0-515-12886-4

A JOVE BOOK®
Jove Books are published by The Berkley Publishing Group,
a division of Penguin Putnam Inc.,
375 Hudson Street, New York, New York 10014.
JOVE and the "J" design
are trademarks belonging to Penguin Putnam Inc.

PRINTED IN THE UNITED STATES OF AMERICA

10 9 8 7 6 5 4 3 2 1

*To a group of special ladies whose
hearts are filled with pure magic*

Diane Sharpe
Susan Blecher
Maureen Russo
Cynthia Anderson
Annette Allen
Harriet Scharneck
Susan Scharneck
Suzanne Brunnegraber
Sally Klaczkiewicz
Diane Hanrahan
Val Luna
Nennette Perry
Michele Petosa
Noreen Szymanski
Diane Reinheimer

*An extra special thank-you to Sally Klaczkiewicz
for working her unique blend of magic.
And to Val Luna for allowing me to borrow her
magical cat "Bear" for this book. He was a delight to
work with!*

One

~

Tempest should have listened to her sister when she warned her not to drive home. A snowstorm had been predicted for several areas in the north of Scotland. Heavy accumulation was expected and driving was not recommended. But Tempest was stubborn, and besides, she was looking forward to driving home just as any ordinary mortal would instead of transporting herself with the snap of her fingers, as was a witch's way.

Her fingers locked tightly around the steering wheel and she squinted in an attempt to see clearly through the windshield, the wipers frantically working to eliminate the build-up of the steadily falling snow.

Her sister Sarina had been right in advising her to wait, insisting the weather would worsen. All the reports on the news stations had warned of hazardous driving conditions as the snow continued to accumulate. And Sarina was rarely wrong, her gift of sight being truly remarkable. But Tempest felt the need to leave immediately following her sister's wedding. While the occasion was a joyous one, and she favored the powerful witch Dagon Rasmus whom her sister Sarina had married, seeing them happy together brought back painful memories and ones that were better left forgotten.

A strong gust of wind whipped around the small compact car, sending it into a slide. It took what seemed like forever for Tempest to gain control of the vehicle though it was a mere second or two, and she soundly chastised herself for being so foolish. If she had listened to her sister she would, at this very moment, be in the warmth and comfort of her cottage enjoying a cup of hot tea before the fireplace.

Dagon, her new brother-in-law, had attempted to coerce her into staying but he learned soon enough that his new sister-in-law possessed a mind of her own and was much too accustomed to looking after herself and was much too willful to take orders from anyone, even a meaningful brother-in-law, though he did insist on providing her with a car he felt would be easy for her to handle.

Tempest smiled while her eyes focused on the dark road and the falling snow that continued to make driving visibility near to impossible. Her thoughts were on the wedding, and a grand affair it had been. Dagon's ancestral home, Rasmus Castle, had been ablaze with light and a multitude of guests. Sarina had looked radiant in a white wool gown and hooded cloak trimmed with gold faerie dust and as was her way her feet remained bare though they sparkled with a hint of gold dust. Dagon wore white as well and looked splendid but then Dagon was a handsome man and his good looks would certainly highlight any garment.

All who attended the ceremony commented on how very much in love the couple were. It could be seen in their glances that so often settled softly on each other or in the simple touch of their hands, their fingers threading together to hold fast or in the way Dagon whispered in her ear and caused her to blush. Their love was strong, their commitment stronger, forging their magical powers and producing the most extraordinary magical feat, a child. Sarina would give birth to Dagon's son in the summer and Tempest looked forward to delivering her first nephew.

The wind blew a flurry of heavy flakes across the windshield and she softly touched the brakes to slow her already snail's pace. The flurries whipped away and once again the road appeared before her eyes though she continued her crawling pace.

The wedding had given her an opportunity to see and speak with old friends, a rare occurrence for her. Sydney Wyrrd, a six-hundred-year-old witch and a former student of hers was there and they spoke of years past, other times, other memories. Memories she more often than not kept locked away. But Sydney had become a good friend, one she found she could safely confide in and that was not easy to do for a witch whose existence dated to the dawn of time.

Tempest had seen and experienced much in her many years. She had made and lost many friends, she had taught and guided many witches and she had loved but once and lost. But that time was better left to memories.

She kept steady and alert eyes on the road knowing that she was but a few miles from a village where she hoped to seek shelter for the night, perhaps even a few days if this snow proved persistent.

Many of the wedding guests had simply transported themselves to sunnier climates or the warmth and safety of their homes. Alisande Wainwright, Sydney's niece, and her husband Sebastian who lived in the States had decided to remain a few days with the newlyweds. Alisande was also pregnant and she insisted that Sarina and her had much to discuss. Dagon did not object; he and Alisande had grown up together, he protecting her mostly from her own antics. Now Sebastian, her husband and a mortal who was growing accustomed to his newly acquired witchcraft, was her protector.

Tempest liked Sebastian Wainwright, especially when she discovered how Alisande had cast the magical love spell on him and he had proven himself worthy of dealing with it and dealing with the fact that in joining with Alisande in the sacred circle he had inherited the powers of a witch.

His tales, travesties and triumphs of learning the craft had brought tears of laughter to her eyes and she found him most delightful. He was a mortal-turned-witch who was strong in character and rich in integrity and one she was pleased to call a new friend.

A forceful wind shook the car and rained a thick flurry of snow across the windshield, momentarily blinding visibility. She kept the steering wheel on course and her sight peeled on the snow-covered windshield. She breathed a hefty sigh of relief when a few moments later the road once again became visible.

The sigh of relief soon turned into a loud gasp when without warning a dark figure appeared in front of her car and she slammed into it with a solid thud. She immediately hit her brakes, as softly as possible and with trembling hands brought the car to a dead stop. She left the engine running, pulled her white knit hat down over her ears and grabbed her knit gloves off the dashboard before opening the car door.

The wind almost ripped the door from her tight grasp, and she fought to close it against the forceful swirls of snow that descended on her like vengeful warriors. She pulled up the hood of the faux fur white coat she wore and was grateful for her sister's insistent demand that she wear knee-high boots. The white ones Sarina had lent her were trimmed in lamb's wool, for which she was presently grateful.

She trudged through the ankle-high snow, keeping close to the car as she made her way forward. She gasped once again when she caught sight of the crumpled body her car headlights highlighted. She didn't waste a moment, but hurried to the felled victim with concern.

"Damn, damn, damn."

Tempest expelled a heavy sigh of relief when she heard his grumbling and was more relieved when he turned over to swear more vehemently. She feared no mortal male, so she approached him without apprehension, though for a brief moment when she caught sight of his face she momentarily halted.

He had the look of a man who had lived hard and dangerously. He possessed harsh, chiseled features and dark eyes that warned all to look the other way. Facial scars only added to his intrigue, one running over the bridge of his nose, one under his left eye along the top of his cheekbone and the other one began on his left jawbone and traveled down his neck, how far she couldn't tell since he wore a dark turtleneck beneath a dark wool P-coat that looked to have seen better days.

And even though he was a good four to five inches over six feet and looked to be of solid build he still did not possess the strength to match her powers. She continued her approach without concern, though with curiosity.

"Damn, woman," he shouted at her in what she was certain was an American accent. "Don't you watch where you're driving?"

"It is snowing if you haven't noticed, not good weather for a stroll along the roadside." She knelt down beside him.

He shot her a look that would probably intimidate most men and frighten any sensible woman, but it did nothing for Tempest. She simply ignored it.

"Tell me where it hurts," she said calmly.

"Why? Are you going to kiss it and make it all better?"

Tempest had dealt with testy men before and was not the least bit intimidated by him. With the snap of her fingers she could put him in his place, but she was not about to allow this barbaric soul to rankle her.

"If you wish a kiss to make it better, I will accommodate you, though I would suggest a ride to the nearest doctor would be a wiser choice."

"You'd kiss a complete stranger?" he all but yelled at her as he struggled to sit up.

She placed a gentle hand to his back to help him. "If a kiss would help, why not?" Mortals simply did not understand the true power of a helping hand or a simple kiss. When given with sincerity, the results proved remarkable.

The stranger ran his hand through his dark hair. Varying layers and lengths fell erratically over his forehead, skimmed his ears and teased the top of his shoulders, proving he was in desperate need of a haircut. He then shook his head, caught her eyes with his and without warning his hand shot out to grasp her neck.

"This is why not." He nearly growled in anger and forced her mouth to his. His kiss was meant to be harsh, meant to demonstrate that he was stronger than she, and could take what he chose, but then he did not know that she was a witch.

Tempest shivered when his raging emotions raced through her. While part of his intentions were to teach her a lesson, another part of him wanted to taste her. He was a man of complex layers, often fighting against himself for what was right.

She took command, knowing that what was needed was a simple, heartfelt kiss that would ease his physical pain and soften his emotional torment. She calmed his rough lips with her gentle ones, softening them until they complied and then with a wisp of her delicate lips she taught him what a kiss was meant to be.

Gentle, nurturing, caring, he felt all that and more and was stunned when he realized that his hand had drifted off her neck and that her hands cupped his face and that her warm, sweet breath faintly brushed his cheek as she eased away from him. He felt spellbound and that startling realization snapped him back to reality.

"Lady, you're nuts to kiss a stranger like that."

"You kissed me," she said accusingly.

"You kissed me back," he argued and attempted to stand, only to cry out in pain.

"Don't move," she ordered sternly, and after dusting off the snow that partially covered him from the waist down, she ran a gentle hand down his jean-clad leg. "Where does it hurt?"

"Lady, you don't have a lick of common sense in your head."

"And you, sir, don't have an ounce of trust in your body. And if you continue to be obstinate and sit here and argue with me we're both going to turn into snowmen. Now for once in your life trust someone."

His eyes narrowed, his nostrils flared and his body tensed. He fought against himself, knowing he had little choice in the matter and his reply was purposely curt. "My right ankle."

He flinched at her tender touch and she frowned. She could tell from her exploring touch that his ankle was indeed broken. If only he had passed out when she had run him down, she could have healed his injury before he woke, but now she could not take the chance of performing a healing. She had no choice but to take him to a mortal doctor.

"There's a village a few miles up the road. I'm sure we can find a doctor there."

"Lady, you—"

Glove-covered fingers pressed to his lips silenced his complaint. "Arguing will serve no purpose. You are in need of medical care. Now please, for both our sakes, be polite and cooperative."

His look warned that compliance was not one of his attributes and he reluctantly acquiesced with a sharp nod.

"Good," she said in a cheerful tone and ignored the man's mutterings. "Now we need to get you in my car."

She reached out to help him up but he shoved her hands away. "I can manage."

Tempest simply took a step back and watched. She was impressed by his maneuvers. It was obvious he was accustomed to physical labor. He had no difficulty in pulling himself up on the front end of her car and balancing himself on his good leg.

His eyes searched the surrounding area before settling on her. "My backpack . . . do you see it?"

Tempest scanned the area and found the large pack on the side of the road, almost completely covered with snow. She retrieved it, noticing that a metal rod was dented and realized the backpack had probably taken the brunt of the impact, sparing the man more serious injury.

"I'll put it in my trunk," she offered and turned to battle the driving wind when she sensed not only his physical pain but an emotional weariness, which touched her heart.

She placed his backpack on the ground and walked over to him, slipping her arm around his waist.

"I don't need—"

"Yes, you do," she said firmly. "Now lean on me, I promise it won't hurt."

He looked down at her and she knew he was sizing her up—all five feet six of her.

"I'm much stronger than I look," she said with a smile that was meant to tease.

He shook his head and reluctantly wrapped his arm around her shoulder. "Lady, you're—"

"Tempest. My name is Tempest."

"Great. I meet Tempest in a tempest."

They walked slowly along the car, fighting against the forceful wind and snow.

"I assure you, sir," she said, her voice raised against the storm. "I did not order this weather."

"Michael," he said, his voice strong. "My name is Michael."

She left him to lean against the car for a brief moment as she opened the back door. With a minimum of difficulty she assisted in helping him into the car, suggesting he stretch out long the backseat so that his injured ankle could rest comfortably. He eased himself along the backseat until his back rested against the opposite door and his legs were stretched out along the seat.

He was obviously battling pain, his face pale, his mouth grim and his eyes squeezed shut.

"I'll get your backpack and a blanket from the trunk for you," she said.

His eyes flashed open. "That backpack is heavy; be careful."

"All your worldly possessions?" she asked, though she knew the answer. He wandered, searching for something, though what that something was, he wasn't certain.

"Every last one of them," he confirmed. "And I don't need a blanket."

"I think you do," she said, shutting the door on his shouts.

With the storm blinding visibility, she was able to use her magical powers, without worry of him seeing her, to move his backpack to the trunk. She then grabbed a blue-and-green plaid wool blanket from her travel case and returned to the car, opening the back door.

He was quiet, though his eyes betrayed his annoyance.

She ignored his lethal look as she spread the warm blanket over his legs and tucked it around his waist. "Much better. I'll turn up the heat for you."

"I'm warm enough."

He drew back when her hand went to his face, though his sudden movement did not stop her. She placed her palm to his cheek and then his forehead, and announced, "Chilled. The heat goes up."

She backed out, checking the blanket along the way, shut the door and was in the front seat in no time. She turned up the heat as she'd promised.

"I'm afraid I'm not a seasoned driver," she said, slipping the car into drive and taking off slowly, confident she wouldn't get stuck in the accumulated snow since she used her powers to clear away the drifts from the car.

"No kidding."

She looked back at him.

"Keep your eyes on the road," he warned. "There's no room back here for any more roadkill."

"I'm sorry," she said softly. "The weather is so bad and visibility near to impossible."

"Just get me to a doctor," he said gruffly. "Then we'll be done with each other."

She nodded and kept steady eyes on the road. "Whatever were you doing out in this storm?"

"Look, lady—"

"Tempest," she corrected.

"Tempest," he said on an annoyed sigh. "I don't intend to

tell you my life story and I'm not interested in any chitchat. The only thing I want right now is a cigarette and a shot of Jack Daniels."

"Smoking and drinking is no—"

"Spare me the lecture, I've heard it all before."

"And you don't care?" she asked, her tone not at all judgmental, but curious. He was a man that was not only searching but hurting and she wondered what had happened in his life to make him so cynical and self-destructive.

"I only care about the moment, and right now my ankle hurts like hell and a shot of JD would work wonders."

The man certainly knew how to avoid giving a straight answer. He obviously intended to portray himself as a loner, a man who needed no one. A man who walked life's roads alone. A man too frightened to love.

A sudden gust of wind whipped at the car and Tempest fought to regain control of the swerving vehicle.

"Don't fight it," Michael yelled at her. "Go with it and then you'll regain control."

She listened to his shouts of advice and in seconds she regained control of the car and she was once again crawling down the snow-drifted road.

"Good work," he said, "now relax your grip on the steering wheel. You're doing just fine."

His encouraging words didn't surprise her. He was harsh in many ways and yet she sensed he cared, though it was difficult for him to show it.

"Are those lights ahead?" he asked.

Tempest glanced past the swishing windshield wipers and the falling snow to spot several faint lights in the distance. "I think you're right. It must be the village."

"Good, wake me when we get there," he said and leaned his head back between the seat and the window to doze.

He made it quite clear that he intended no further discussion with her and if he wanted to be obstinate that was fine with her. She would deliver him to the doctor, make certain he was all right, pay the bill since his broken ankle was her fault, and be on her way, though something warned her it would not be that easy.

They arrived at the village thirty minutes later, near to ten at night. With one stop at a well-lighted house she learned where the doctor was located. The friendly woman had called ahead, so the doctor would be expecting them.

Tempest helped Michael up the snow-laden path to the front door and after explaining the problem to the middle-aged doctor he took it from there, disappearing with a hopping Michael into a back room.

She removed her coat, hat and gloves and took a seat in a cushioned rocker by the heat of the blazing hearth. She was grateful for the warmth of her long white wool skirt and matching hip-length sweater. She ran gentle fingers through her long reddish blond hair, several strands feeling damp from the snow.

She had discovered there was a small inn not far from the doctor's home and that was where she intended to rent a room for Michael for the next few days, feeling herself responsible for his care. She, on the other hand, intended to transport her car back to Rasmus Castle, and then she would simply transport herself home. She was tired and wanted nothing more than a hot cup of tea and the comfort of her bed.

She leaned back and gently rocked herself into a light slumber, not waking until the doctor gently shook her shoulder.

"He's all set," the portly doctor said with a smile. "A good, clean break that set nicely and should heal in about six weeks."

Tempest stretched as she stood. "I'm so glad to hear that and so grateful you where available to help him. How much do I owe you for your services?"

"The gentleman paid me already," he said, pulling his wire-rimmed glasses down to rest on the tip of his nose and giving a little gruff cough. "I'm a bit concerned about the chap. He asked if he could stay here the night and of course I assured him he could, but I worry about what he'll do afterwards. I fear he has no money for lodgings and he insisted you were not responsible for him."

Tempest was not surprised by the news; she half expected it. His backpack actually did contain all his worldly possessions, along with limited funds. He was probably working his way through the area, and a broken ankle meant no work and no money.

"A point we disagree on," she told the doctor. "And one I will tend to. Do you advise travel yet?"

"I'd like the cast I put on him to set for a while and then

he is free to go, though I'd advise you not to attempt to go far in this storm."

Tempest agreed. "The Partridge Inn is our destination."

"Good choice."

"If you don't mind I would like to go to the inn, make arrangements for our stay and then return for Michael."

"He'll be ready by then," the doctor said with a yawn. "Excuse me, the day must be catching up with me."

Tempest slipped on her coat and with a gentle touch of her hand to the doctor's face said, "Rest."

He yawned again, sat down in the rocker and promptly fell asleep.

With a few enchanted words, her luggage and Michael's backpack were deposited in the room where she stood and then with a snap of her fingers she returned the car to Rasmus Castle.

She collected her hat and gloves and sent them on their way with a wave of her hand over the pieces of luggage as she walked toward the back room. Now all that was necessary was to transport Michael to her home.

Two

✦

Michael woke with a start, bolting up from his prone position and hitting his head on the ceiling which sloped down over the bed. He mumbled several angry expletives and rubbed his head while he anxiously took in his strange surroundings.

The room was apparently an attic or dormer-type room since the ceiling sloped down on two sides. A casement window sat tucked between the slopes, a white lace valance and a twig wreath adorned with dried flowers being its only covering. Outside, snow continued to fall heavily, adding to the accumulation that covered at least a quarter of the windowpane, and from the look of the temperamental gray sky, there was no relief in sight.

Michael was suddenly grateful for the welcoming warmth of the small room, and it certainly did welcome. The walls were a pale blue with a border of elegantly scrolled symbols painted in purple and gold. The lettering was completely foreign to him and yet—he shook his head—in a strange way familiar.

An old wooden rocking chair whose woven cane seat looked recently repaired sat near the window; its companion a square wooden table held a lamp, a stack of books and a thick, round candle whose three wicks burned brightly and was probably the reason the room smelled like vanilla.

An oak bureau, four drawers high and wide, sat opposite the bed. An assortment of combs, brushes and bottles along with a small vase of dried purple flowers cluttered the top. In the corner between the rocker and the bureau was a wood-burning stove, small yet adequate for the room.

An assortment of colorful wool rugs placed at varying angles covered a good portion of the old wood floor, and a closet door stood slightly ajar beside a closed door.

With a heavy sigh Michael dropped back down on the soft pillow. Where he was and how he got here he didn't know, but somehow he knew the crazy lady he had met in the snowstorm had something to do with it. The last thing he recalled was arguing with her about taking care of him. She persisted in insisting that he was her responsibility until his ankle healed properly and that she would see to his care.

No amount of arguing would sway her, and damned if she didn't have the patience of a saint. Not once did she grow angry with him, threaten or even attempt to cajole him into agreeing with her. She simply made it known that her way was the best way and the only way, and of course to a man like himself who was independent and determined—well, it just wasn't going to happen.

So how the hell did he get here? And where was here?

He smiled, laughed softly and shook his head. He had a sneaking suspicion of his present location, but couldn't recall getting here. He didn't even remember being helped to the car or into this house and least of all being undressed and left to sleep in his briefs.

And that presented another disturbing question. Who had undressed him and put him to bed?

The crazy lady named Tempest who can't drive worth a damn, and who offers to kiss a stranger to make him feel better after running him down with her car, and who is too damned beautiful for her own good?

He grumbled to himself. The snowstorm hadn't allow for an easy view of her features, and when she spoke with him in the doctor's office he had already been groggy from the pain medicine the doctor had given him, but what glimpses he could recall reminded him that she was a beauty, and beautiful women were nothing but trouble.

He eased himself up in bed, avoiding contact with the sloping ceiling, and without much effort carefully brought his cast-covered ankle to rest on the floor. He had no worry that he wouldn't be able to get around on his own. Hard, physical labor had toned and chiseled his body into a mass of muscles. Brawn was a requisite for sailing on the merchant ships and for surviving the often too dangerous ports, and he had been sailing for the last twenty years, since he was sixteen. He had received an education in hard knocks and while he lacked a formal education, he was no dummy. A crusty old seaman had introduced him to books that challenged the mind, and he had become a ferocious reader. He held no fancy degree, but his knowledge was vast, and he was proud of his accomplishments.

Now all he needed to accomplish was to locate his clothes and a bathroom, and then find out where he was. He noticed that his wallet lay on the small table beside his bed, and he glanced inside it, knowing his last fifty dollars would be there; and it was. He put it back on the table and stood with a groan, placing the majority of his weight on his healthy leg.

"Damned if I'll take charity," he mumbled and hobbled over to the closet. It was empty. He gave the room a thorough glance and finding none of his clothing in sight, nor his backpack, he had no alternative but to take his search outside the room.

He found a bathroom right next door and saw to his immediate needs. He found a new toothbrush still in its wrapper on the sink and assumed it was left for his use, so he didn't hesitate to take advantage of it. Combs and brushes lay in a small basket on a stool and he made use of a comb, little good that it did. His dark hair was in dire need of at least a trim, if not a good cutting, but of late he felt the need to let it grow so it fell in layers, skimming his shoulders, ears and forehead. Fortunately, a dark-blue velvet robe, suspiciously his size, hung on the back of the bathroom door, so he slipped it on and cautiously proceeded to investigate his surroundings.

He discovered two closed doors and was about to investigate the one furthest from his room when the scent of bacon and eggs caught his attention. His stomach growled and he agreed with its protest. Changing his direction, he carefully descended the narrow staircase.

He came upon a parlor, medium in size, a fire crackling in

the stone fireplace, overstuffed furniture that welcomed, candles that flickered softly, plants that thrived in dozens of pots and hanging baskets, some flowering and others assorted shades of healthy greens. And books in stacks and on shelves and while he itched to explore their contents, his nose and grumbling stomach took charge and forced him to follow the delicious scent that by now had acquired a strong hint of cinnamon to it.

But it wasn't the mouthwatering aroma that hit him full force when he walked into the kitchen. It was the woman who hummed a lively tune while icing cinnamon buns.

"Hungry?" she asked him, momentarily taking her eyes off her task to smile at him.

He didn't answer directly; he couldn't. She was far more beautiful than he had remembered, and he was annoyed that he found himself speechless. She wore a pale-yellow knit dress that hugged her curves, and a crocheted vest in a darker yellow covered her breasts that looked to be just a bit more than a handful. And while he had always put more stock in a woman's body than in her looks, he couldn't help but be captivated by her beauty. He swore that if an angel could step down from heaven she would possess such a stunning face. Her complexion reminded him of peaches and cream—soft, smooth and sweet. Yet if asked to describe her, the one word that would come to mind would be *serene*. Her beauty held a strange peacefulness, as though a man could simply lose himself within her by just glancing at her face.

And her eyes? He shut his own eyes, the image of hers ingrained in his memory. They were the strangest color green—pale yet bright, young yet old—and he swore they possessed the knowledge of the ages. She was without a doubt a remarkably intelligent woman. And then there was that mass of long, blond hair streaked with red that caught the eye like flickering flames. It was partially pinned and tucked up, and yet several strands fell freely around her face and down her neck. The untidy style was completely seductive, and he winced at that disturbing thought.

"I have your pain pills if you feel you need one," she said softly.

Her gentle voice tingled his flesh, and he silently cursed his libido which he had sorely neglected lately, and which he as-

sumed was the reason for his immediate attraction to this
woman.

He shook his head, more to bring his emotions under control
than to answer her query. "Not necessary," he managed to say.
"But my clothes are. Where would I find them and where
am I?"

She took the plate of buns from the island counter and
placed them on the round wooden table set with a lace cloth
and fine china before answering him. "I washed and stitched
the two pair of jeans you have so that the leg will fit over the
cast. When the cast is removed I'll repair the jeans for you.
All your clothes are in a basket in the laundry room." She
pointed to a door off the kitchen. "I'll bring them upstairs to
your room after breakfast."

"Thanks," he said, grateful for her thoughtfulness and yet
uncomfortable with it. He had always looked out for himself.
He didn't need looking after.

She removed the covers from the pans on the stove, and the
scent of freshly cooked bacon and eggs permeated the air even
more strongly and caused his stomach to grumble loudly.

"Please, sit down," she said, extending her hand toward the
table.

He obliged her with as much haste as the weighty cast allowed.

After placing the platter of eggs and bacon on the table and
adding a basket of hot biscuits, she joined him and answered
his other question. "I am sure by now you realize you are in
my home."

"I assumed as much," he said, and eagerly reached for the
mug of hot, black coffee she had poured for him. There were
many questions he wanted answered, but at the moment his
first priority was satisfying his empty and protesting stomach.
He enthusiastically reached for the platter of bacon and eggs.

"It was the most logical solution." Tempest helped herself
to a biscuit which she generously spread with butter and
honey.

Michael waited for her to continue, though he had a sneaking suspicion that was all the explanation she intended. Still,
he'd give her the benefit of the doubt and wait.

"Biscuit?" she asked and held the basket out to him.

He helped himself to two fat ones while his glance strayed

to her lips, full and plump and oh so inviting. A spot of honey glistened near the corner of her mouth, and the tip of her tongue slipped out to lick it up slow and easy.

"Are you all right?" she asked, her hand moving to rest with a comforting touch on his arm.

He looked at her oddly, as if confused.

"You shivered," she said, explaining her concern. "Have you a chill?"

Her hand moved toward his forehead when he realized just how deeply that innocent lick of the lips affected him, and he drew away from her reach. "I'm fine."

He concentrated on his meal, keeping his eyes off her.

"It is a relentless snow," she said, diverting the conversation.

He looked out the large window in front of which the table sat. Here, as in the bedroom, the window was barely covered. A white lace swag ran along the top and draped down the sides, leaving the outside view unobstructed. And he could understand why. An expanse of snow-covered hills, towering trees and a surrounding field blanketed in pure white stole one's breath and captured the senses.

Though his sensibility quickly took hold and warned him that the roads in this area could barely be passable, especially with the way Tempest drove, his one question was: "How did we get here?"

She was not at all startled by his curt query. She smiled pleasantly at him and patted his arm. "A wish and a prayer."

"You'd need both with the way you drive."

She laughed at his intentional barb. "True enough."

"The roads were passable?"

Tempest placed the last of the eggs and a fat cinnamon bun on his near-empty plate, and spoke truthfully, since she could do no less. "I know a more passable route."

Michael watched her slim fingers gracefully pour herself another cup of tea from the china pot on the table before she chose a smaller bun for herself. He allowed the silence to purposely grow between them and added a hint of suspicion to his voice when he asked, "I don't recall getting in the car."

"I imagine not," she said with ease and added a teaspoon of honey to her tea. "The medicine had taken its toll on you."

"Then however did you get me in the car?"

"A wish and a prayer," she said yet again with a smile.

He simply could not be annoyed with her. No matter how hard he tried, her smile was just too sincere, her voice much too soothing, and her hospitality much too generous. A thought that gave him reason to ask, "Are you always in the habit of bringing stray men home?"

"Are you always so blunt?"

He nodded. "Yes, and are you always so foolish?"

"You think it's foolish to help someone in need?"

He shook his head. "You know nothing about me and yet you bring me, a complete stranger, into your home in the middle of a raging snowstorm, stranding us both here alone."

"I trust you."

He shook his head again. "You don't know me."

"I know enough."

"Really?" he asked sarcastically. "What do you know? Dazzle me with your sixth sense."

Tempest leaned forward, folding her arms to rest on the table, and looked directly in his eyes. "I know you are a man who has spent most of his life alone. You have lived too closely to the edge, all the time searching, for what you do not know. You play fair with those who play fair with you. You hurt no one who hurts you. And you will not allow yourself to care deeply or love, for in your experience it only brings hurt, pain and disappointment. So you run from place to place, searching but fearful of finding."

Michael remained speechless. Her accuracy astonished him and hearing his own doubts and vulnerabilities spoken of by a stranger frightened him. He had always managed to erect a wall between him and the people he met. She was right about him not caring deeply or loving. He had learned at an early age that it didn't pay to love. When you loved someone or even cared for them they eventually went away, and you were left alone, completely alone, and that was a painful lesson for a boy of eight to learn.

He kept direct eye contact with her even though her green eyes held him more spellbound than his dark eyes held hers. "You're so certain I won't hurt you?"

"Positive," she said without hesitation. "I mean you no harm, so therefore you will show me no harm."

He told himself he shouldn't—it wasn't right—but then she was so positive, so sure of herself that he had to demonstrate the obvious. He leaned closer to her, his intentions clear, his lips moist and ready, eager to kiss her.

She laughed softly, and it sounded like a sweet melody drifting around them, and then she leaned forward herself and whispered, "If it is a kiss you wish, just ask."

He stopped, his lips a short distance from hers. "You don't possess a lick of common sense."

"No, I don't," she agreed in a whisper. "But I possess a self-confidence that startles most. Don't you agree?" She laughed, the tender melody wrapping around them as she closed the short distance between them and kissed him gently, a faint brush of her lips over his before settling with care over his mouth and capturing a kiss that stung the senses.

Without thought Michael rushed his tongue over her lips ready to penetrate, deepen the contact, but she backed away from him ever so slowly, and he sensed reluctance. He did not pursue her, though he wanted to.

"You tempt fate, Tempest."

"No, Michael, fate tempts each and every one of us."

He leaned closer to her. "Who are you? You appear in the middle of a god-awful snowstorm, driving like a neophyte and you live here"—he waved his hand toward the large window— "in the middle of nowhere."

"I like my solitude," she answered with complete honesty.

"Yet you generously open your home to a stranger."

"A man in need," she corrected.

"A stranger," he reiterated.

She held her hand out to him. "My name is Tempest, and I am pleased to meet you."

He took her hand with a shake of his head. "Michael Deeds, and the pleasure is mine."

She squeezed his hand with a gentle eagerness. "Now we are no longer strangers. We are friends."

"Acquaintances."

She patted his arm. "I have run you down with my car, helped get you to a doctor, opened my home to you, undressed you and put you to bed. I think we can call ourselves friends."

"Which brings up several unanswered questions. How exactly did you manage to get me into the house, undress me and get me into bed all by yourself?"

Her smile warned of her answer, and he stopped her with

an upheld hand. "Don't tell me. A wish and a prayer."

With excitement she said, "See, you know me already."

"You're beginning to make sense—a frightening thought."

They both laughed and Tempest offered him another cinnamon bun.

"You're an excellent cook," he said, accepting not only the treat but the friendship she so generously offered him. He never really had a friend. He had long ago convinced himself that he didn't need anyone; he had himself. It was strange to think that another person actually cared about him, and stranger still that he liked the feeling.

There was, however, one other detail he had to address. "I can't accept charity. There must be something I can do to repay your generosity."

"How are you in the kitchen?"

He laughed. "I'm not inept, *but . . .*"

"We'll work something out," she agreed graciously. "For now I think you should concentrate on healing that ankle, which means staying off it and resting."

His protest was interrupted by a yawn.

"A nap would suit you well now."

He did feel tired and pleasantly full from the delicious breakfast, but he felt obliged to help her. She had done much too much for him already. "I'll help you wash the dishes first."

She stood and offered him her hand. "No, you will rest as the doctor ordered."

"After I help you," he insisted, ignoring her outstretched hand and standing on his own though he tilted heavily to the left, and if it wasn't for her assistance he just might have toppled over.

"You will rest."

It sounded like an order to Michael, and he never took well to orders. "First I help you."

She smiled and shook her head. "So stubborn."

He was about to agree when her hand touched his face and his eyes grew too heavy to keep open.

Three

The phone rang just as Tempest finished making certain Michael was comfortably situated on the overstuffed, chintz-covered couch in the living room. A dark-green chenille throw kept him warm and a feathered pillow cradled his head.

Few people knew her phone number, which meant only family or close friends called, and of course she always knew the caller's identity. She answered it on the third ring, not at all concerned that the noise would disturb Michael. She had placed him in a healing sleep that would keep him in a restful slumber for the next couple of hours.

"Hello, Sarina," she said with a smile, pleased and not really surprised to hear from her sister. "You are on your honeymoon, aren't you?"

"Yes, of course, but Dagon and I grew concerned when we discovered that the car you borrowed was returned," Sarina said anxiously. "I thought it best to call and make certain everything was all right."

Sarina possessed strong magical powers: she excelled in the ability of sight, seeing and knowing far more than anyone could dream possible. Tempest, however, possessed power that went far beyond the extraordinary, and there were few if any who could match her skills. She could block spells, remove any spell, cast spells and prevent any magical skills from being performed on her. Which was why Sarina was calling. She sensed something was amiss, but could not determine the exact cause.

Tempest spoke truthfully, though omitted certain facts. "The weather proved too much for my inadequate driving skills. I thought it best to return the car and proceed home as quickly and expediently as possible."

"A wise choice," Sarina assured her. "I was worried about you, but Dagon reminded me that you can take care of yourself. Still, I could not help but recall my vision."

The vision was the reason Tempest kept Michael's presence to herself. Sarina had predicted the return of the man Tempest had once loved and who with a mighty spell she had sent away to linger in the void. Time drew near for his return and a second chance, but would the once powerful warlock learn his lesson and succeed in disarming her spell, or would he revert to his old ways and once again call on the dark side to free him?

"Tempest?" Sarina sounded concerned. "Is everything all right?"

Tempest spoke with a depth of wisdom that not many understood. "It is as it should be."

Sarina understood perfectly, though her loving concern remained obvious. "I will phone in a few days."

"See to your new husband," Tempest scolded playfully. "I have work to do."

"I will phone, take care," were her parting words.

Tempest shook her head, smiled and set out to tackle the dishes. She could very well clean up the kitchen with a wave of her hand, and on many occasions did, but there were times she wished to think, and busy hands gave way to clearer thoughts.

She grabbed a white bib apron from a drawer and slipped it over her head, her thoughts as busy as her hands, as she tied the apron strings behind her back and proceeded to clean away the dishes.

Sarina was worried; the forest fairies were worried; Sydney Wyrrd, her former student and dear friend, was worried. And she? She knew nothing would prevent the inevitable. With her own words she had sealed her fate and had no choice but to confront it. But was Michael that predicted fate? Would he set the events in motion that would lead to the ultimate confrontation of darkness and light?

She shivered at the thought. Time would tell and time was what she had right now with Michael. She would come to know him, understand him and determine for herself if he was her fate.

Her own identity she would safely guard, forcing her to abandon some of her magic for the time being, though her rituals she would never forsake. She would not take the chance of stirring his memories; those were his to recall, if indeed he possessed them at all. Time would tell, and time was plentiful.

When she finished cleaning the kitchen she took Michael's clothes to his room and arranged the few garments in the drawers and closet. She had left briefs, worn jeans, a faded navy sweatshirt and white socks that had seen better days in the living room on a chair so that when he woke he could dress.

She stood back, wicker basket in hand, and surveyed the contents of the open drawers and closet. His meager stock of clothing would simply not do. She placed the basket on the blue-and-purple tweed rug near the door and turned her attention to the open closet. She thought a moment, determining what clothing would best suit him and with a wave of her hand filled the small space with two pairs of blue and black jeans, three pairs of wool trousers—one a light gray, one a smoky gray—and the third black. Another hand wave produced four cotton shirts—one black with a thin gray stripe, a solid black, a solid light gray and a solid white one. She added a black wool jacket and a black leather bomber style jacket with a faux fur collar. Shoes came next—a pair of casual black leather shoes, black leather boots, dark-brown workboots and of course slippers, which would be the only ones he could presently wear. But then it would appear odd if she had men's clothing and no shoes, only slippers.

She then turned her attention to the drawers, filling the spaces with wool, knit and cashmere sweaters, keeping the colors to gray, black and white, though she added a navy blue and a solid tan. Sweatshirts were next and they were kept plain and simple, though she thought red would suit him so she added the color from her own curiosity. Socks followed, then white and black T-shirts, and as she waved a finger to add underwear, she stopped.

However would she explain having men's underwear, and new briefs at that, to him, but then his three pairs of well-worn briefs would never do. She crooked her finger and added the briefs, throwing in a couple of grays, blacks and reds. She would worry about an explanation later.

A snap of her fingers closed the drawers, and as she was about to close the closet door she paused, thought a moment, nodded as if her decision was made, pointed her finger to an empty hanger, and suddenly there hung a long, black velvet bathrobe.

She smiled and closed the closet door with a flick of her finger and picking up the basket, she went downstairs.

Now as she chopped and sliced vegetables to be added later to the beef vegetable soup that simmered on the stove she wondered where she had put that old crutch that still looked much like the branch tree it had been carved from.

With a concentrated thought and a wave of her hand the old crutch glided casually into the room to lean against the door frame.

"I'm hallucinating or dreaming while awake."

Tempest jumped, startled by Michael's unexpected presence behind her. He should have slept at least another thirty minutes. He was dressed in the clothes she had left for him, and his hair had been made presentable with a rake of his fingers.

He shook his head as if not believing his own words. "I could have sworn I saw a strange-shaped tree branch float past the living room door while I was dressing."

"Must be those pain pills," Tempest suggested eagerly.

Michael rubbed at his chin. "I don't remember taking any. I don't even remember lying down on the couch."

"You couldn't keep your eyes open," she assured him with a firm nod.

"I do remember growing sleepy."

"You needed your rest." And quick as a wink she changed the subject. "How about a cup of coffee?"

He hobbled over to her. "Sounds good, but it's time for me to pitch in and help."

His dark eyes were soft, his stance relaxed, his manner unguarded. Evidently he wasn't fully roused from his healing sleep since normally his intense dark eyes, rigid stance and ineffable manner warned people to keep a distance, a safe distance from him. She liked this agreeable and somewhat vulnerable man that stood before her offering his help.

"Have your coffee first and then you can help."

"Promise?" he asked softly.

She liked the way his mouth took control of that one word and made it sound like an erotic whisper. But then the possibilities that word held were endlessly suggestive, and of course once a promise was made it must be kept.

She answered just as softly. "Promise."

He raised his hand, his fingers moving slowly toward her face and she found herself holding her breath. When he suddenly jumped with a start, his eyes grew wide and he grabbed for the edge of the counter to prevent himself from falling. "What the hell?"

Tempest didn't have to turn around to see the cause of his astonished reaction. She spotted the culprit sitting behind him on the floor, though explaining to him was another matter.

She turned an unsurprised glance at the shadow on the wall behind her. It was a huge bear, his paws extended, looking as though he was ready to attack. She turned back to Michael and pointed behind him. "My cat, Bear."

Michael eased himself around to look at a black cat of average size licking his paw.

"He thinks he's a bear, and unfortunately when he casts a shadow he resembles one, which enforces his mistaken belief."

Michael stared at the cat who had stopped licking his paw and sat staring back at him with large bright-green eyes. The animal seemed to be sizing him up and after several silent minutes passed, the cat simply walked past him without so much as a purr or a hiss and went straight to Tempest, rubbing himself in and around her legs with a contented purr.

He could live with the obvious snub, though he was surprised. Animals usually took easily to him. He was the one that always fed and cared for the cats on the ship. What he couldn't understand was what had caused his shadow—not the size of it, but the shadow in general. There was no sufficient light to produce a shadow of any size. So where did it come from?

"Let me get you coffee," Tempest offered—anything to change the subject.

"I can get it myself," he said. "Where do you keep the mugs?"

Tempest pointed to the cabinet right behind him. She sensed his misgivings with her explanation, and the healing spell had almost dissipated, returning him to his usual guarded self.

Michael filled his mug and turned to hobble over to the table when he stopped.

Tempest caught his line of vision and winced. He focused on the crutch. However would she explain?

But then he hadn't asked—yet.

She walked over to where it rested against the wall and picked it up to take over to Michael. "It's old, but sturdy. I thought perhaps it would assist you in getting around."

He looked at it oddly and seemed reluctant to take it.

She placed it against the wall. "It's here if you need it."

He nodded and took a seat at the table. It was time he learned who he was dealing with here. She was a stranger and a strange woman at that. She was congenial, helpful, caring and sincere, but she was also mysterious. How could a woman who lived alone, obviously out in the middle of nowhere, open her home to a man without concern for her own safety? Did she know something he didn't? And if so, what was the secret that made her feel safe enough to offer a strange man her home while he recovered?

It was simple enough as to where he would start.

"Tell me about yourself, Tempest," he said. "We're going to be spending enough time together between this broken ankle and the snowstorm. I'd like to know who I'm cohabitating with."

Tempest returned to cutting her vegetables while Bear decided to curl in a ball on the rug by the stove. She anticipated his interest in her and was prepared, though she doubted he was prepared for her answer.

"I am independently wealthy and do pretty much as I please."

"Damn it, woman, what is the matter with you!" he said, his voice raised and agitated. "Are you nuts?"

"No, I'm perfectly sane," she answered calmly.

Her answer brought a gruff laugh from him. "That's a debatable issue."

"Why? Because I'm honest?"

"Being honest isn't always advisable."

"Why would that be?" she asked, scooping up a pile of sliced carrots and dropping them into the pot of bubbling beef soup.

He cupped his coffee mug in one hand, and Tempest couldn't help but notice the length and strength of his fingers, and the few scars that crisscrossed over his knuckles. Life had obviously been a battle for him, leaving him not only physically scarred but emotionally scarred as well. A good reason why he never thought to trust anyone, especially a complete stranger.

"Common sense," he snapped, "which you know nothing of."

She diced a thick potato with ease and smiled. "Instinct."

"What?" he asked confused.

"I rely on my instinct when I meet people, and it has yet to fail me."

His gruff laugh surfaced once again. "You're about how old? Thirty, maybe thirty-two, and you think you know enough about life to rely solely on instinct?"

"I'm a bit older than that and well-traveled."

"The kind of travel that wealth affords," he corrected.

"You're cynical."

"I possess common sense," he argued.

"You don't trust."

"I make a point of getting to know a person first."

"And however do you do that when you obviously don't trust a soul?" she asked with what sounded too much like pity to his way of thinking.

"I ask questions," he answered tersely.

"Which leads to a certain amount of trusting."

"I believe common sense leads to accurate character study."

She laughed softly. "Instinct."

He found himself smiling at the challenging debate she presented. She not only tempted a man's passion but challenged his intelligence. "I suppose instinct helps, but only after assessing a person's character."

"Yet by waiting and assessing you often miss the true essence of a person. It is much simpler to be aware, completely aware, through sight and sound on first meeting, and then you will truly come to know even the most remote person."

He seemed to contemplate her words, his brow drawing together as if in heavy and almost painful thought. "People can deceive."

"Unfortunately true," she agreed, "but it is usually when we are at our most vulnerable."

"Children are vulnerable." It was a statement issued with a harsh regret.

Tempest realized he spoke from experience, and she opened herself completely to his emotions in hope of better understanding him. She mentally prepared herself for the rush of tumultuous feelings that would descend on her, and as she so often did she made her way through the maze of fear, hurt, disappointment, regret and bitterness. But it was the sensation of a little boy's heart breaking that disturbed her the most and made her all the more curious.

She could step inside him and read his life path, but without an invitation to do so she would never intrude on his privacy. And besides, they had plenty of time to come to know one another.

She patiently waited for him to continue, and was not surprised when he turned the conversation back to her. He was obviously curious, and she couldn't blame him. She would give him enough information to satisfy.

"Why do you live in such isolation?"

Her answer was honest as usual. "I enjoy my privacy."

Michael didn't seem to think so. "You're not running away?"

Tempest dropped the sliced potato into the pot. "I have nothing to run from."

"An irate lover or broken heart usually cause people to go off on their own and bury themselves in their sorrows."

She laughed lightly and reached for another potato in the bowl. "It has been some time since I have had a lover." She thought it best not to mention her broken heart. Though it had been hundreds of years, the memories remained painful and were better left forgotten.

Michael threw his hands up in frustration. "Great, now you're letting me know that it's been a while since—"

"I've made love," she finished, her voice light with laughter.

He began his usual lecture. "I'm a complete stranger—"

"Who would never force a woman," Tempest continued for him.

"Right, but I'm also not a eunuch."

"Haven't had sex lately yourself, have you?" Her soft smile did not at all tease but appeared sincerely empathic, which irritated him all the more.

"Is that an invitation?" he asked, focusing dark, intent eyes on her that warned he was serious.

Tempest took a moment to examine the consequences of such action. If he proved to be the one whose return was predicted, the results would set the spell in motion. And if not? Their joining could prove interesting.

Her answer was softly succinct. "Perhaps."

It was his turn to smile, and the audacious turn of his lips hinted at a playful wickedness. "You'll let me know when that *perhaps* turns to a yes?"

"Without delay." Her own smile was equally playful.

His smile vanished suddenly and his expression turned serious. "Why do you trust me? You barely know me. I could be a deceitful character who would use you for his own selfish needs."

"Instincts and awareness," she reminded him and washed her hands before approaching him at the table.

He watched her walk toward him. Her steps were graceful and taken with confidence and not a hint of fear. Her body moved in a fluid motion as if time and space made way for her, and when her hand stretched out to touch his, his glance drifted to her long, slim fingers. Her nails were relatively short and polished with a clear nail polish that glittered with a hint of gold specks, and her skin was a creamy peach that tempted the lips.

His breath caught briefly when her fingers lightly traced the scars on his knuckles.

"You obviously brawled and often, defending yourself and the defenseless. Your convictions are strong and would not allow you to harm the harmless."

Her hand drifted up to his face and the stretch of scars that ran across his nose and under his eye. Her touch was gentle and caring and oh so welcoming.

But her words intruded where he did not want her to go. "As you were once harmed."

Michael grabbed her wrist and yanked it away from his face. "Don't go there, Tempest, you're not invited."

Four

Tempest made no attempt to back away from him; she simply placed a comforting hand on his shoulder, and when his eyes met hers he wanted nothing more than to drown in the solace she unselfishly offered him. He felt an overwhelming gut need to draw her close and press his face against the slight curve of her stomach, wrap his arms around her slim waist, smell the sweet scent of her and forget that life itself existed.

Instead he did what he had done since he was a young child and felt fearful—he erected an invisible wall that would keep her from getting close to him or perhaps keep him from getting close to her.

She stepped back suddenly as if she felt the wall rise up between them, and he let her go, though with a reluctance that disturbed him.

"I think it's time I started earning my keep," he said stubbornly.

He expected her to argue, but she didn't. "As you wish. You can help me in the greenhouse. There's potting to do."

He stood with a wobble. "Never potted plants before, but I learn quickly."

"I'll have you an expert in no time," she said, confidently. "Go through the archway over there into the sitting room, then take the door near the fireplace into the greenhouse. I'll be there shortly."

Michael nodded and attempted to make his way without the aid of the crutch. After a few faltering steps he turned around only to find Tempest directly behind him, crutch in hand. He took it from her with a gruff, "Thanks." And hobbled off in a much steadier gait.

The sitting room was just that—welcoming sofas, chairs, tables, a desk and more bookshelves. No wonder; she was so intelligent, she must have spent all her isolated time reading. The fireplace was old stone and gave the room a satisfying warmth. French doors with ivory lace curtains ran along the back wall, and a peek past the lace showed a screened porch closed up tightly against the winter weather.

Several old paintings in gold frames caught his attention, and he inspected them with a keen interest. On his travels he had visited many museums and had developed an eye for fine art. And he was surprised that a few paintings looked as if they were originals, but then she did say she was wealthy. But it was the picture that hung over the fireplace that caught and held his eye. The scene felt strangely familiar, though that was impossible. He wasn't certain of the period but he would venture to guess from the clothing that it was about the fourteenth or fifteenth century. It was an outdoor celebration, a feast of sorts, with Stirling Castle in the background.

He shook his head and turned to walk away when something stopped him, and he glanced back at the picture. His eye caught a dark figure hovering near the tree close by yet removed from the festivity. He stared at the mysterious cloaked figure, blinked a second to refocus, and when he looked upon the scene again the dark figure was gone.

Another shake of his head, a mumble about being nuts, and he hobbled off with the support of the crutch.

The greenhouse impressed him on first sight. It was a labyrinth of plants. Healthy green foliage spilled over hanging baskets, tumbled out of a variety of different-sized pots, and flowering plants were everywhere. No matter which path he chose to walk along, plants brushed at his shoulders, tickled his head and caressed his cheek, and he couldn't help but smile at their cheerfully eager welcome.

He found an area with a cushioned bench, chair and a table that held a magnificent potted fern. He was tempted to sit but curiosity urged him on, and he was glad he continued exploring.

He discovered the work area. A long narrow bench-like table, waist-high, was braced against the back wall. Two tiers of shelving ran beneath and held all the necessary planting tools, plus containers of all sizes and tubs of soil mixtures, mulch, and what he assumed was fertilizer. A high wooden stool, its long legs painted bright green and the seat top a smiling, brilliant yellow sun stood to the side. Dried herbs hung in bunches overhead, and a large wooden cabinet with several drawers sat to the right of the workbench.

Tempest was obviously an experienced, perhaps even expert gardener. At least there were two things he knew about her. She loved to read and loved plants. He should also add that she was a good cook. She was rather domestic when you added it all together—and yet she just didn't strike him as the domestic type.

"You found where I spend much of my time."

Michael turned to greet her with a smile, and his smile widened when he saw the colorful smock she wore over her yellow dress. It was its own garden of delight. Flowers of all varieties bloomed against a background of blue sky and green earth. It was the perfect protective garment for a gardener.

"You have quite a green thumb," he said, stepping aside as she approached the workbench.

"I feel a connection with the earth." She moved the stool nearer to the workbench and gave it a pat. "Come and sit. I will teach you how to connect to Mother Nature."

He seemed reluctant. "I'm all thumbs and none of them are green."

Tempest laughed. "I think we can do something about that."

Michael joined her, though he remained standing.

"You should really stay off that ankle as much as you can, or at least for a few days. It's only been set, and the broken bone needs a chance to knit properly."

He seemed about to argue then thought better of it, and placing the crutch to the side, he sat on the stool. "Are you a healer besides a gardener?"

She held up her hands. "Everyone has the power within their grasp to heal and grow. The secret to it is the magic of belief. Do you believe, Michael?"

His own answer startled him. "I don't know what I believe in."

"Then it's time for you to learn."

He remained silent, unable to respond. Her question was one that recently nagged at him and was the reason he left his sea life behind. He felt the inexplicable need to explore, and his exploration brought him directly to Scotland. Though he didn't know why, he knew he would find answers here. Of course, first he needed to discover the questions. Perhaps this was his first one.

Tempest gathered pots, tools and seedlings that looked ready to burst from their confined bedding. She ran her hands lovingly over the small green leaves. "These flourishing ladies can help soothe an upset stomach." She held her fingers to her nose.

"Mint," he said with a smile.

She nodded. "Correct, and I don't think they mind your unskilled hands working on them. They are hardy ladies."

"Let's hope so, since my touch is none too gentle."

Her slim hand slipped over his work-worn one. "Then I will teach you how to soften your touch."

He felt a warmth rush up his arm and tingle his flesh. It was a tender and loving warmth given freely, without demands or the need of its return. An unselfish gesture of love, but not the love born of passion; the love of humanity.

He turned his covered hand and entwined his fingers with hers. "You've taken on a hefty chore, Tempest."

She gave his fingers a confident squeeze. "I never take on more than I can handle."

"And you're certain you can handle me?" He squeezed her hand firmly enough to demonstrate his strength.

She leaned close to him. "Never underestimate the power of belief."

He almost laughed. "You believe you can break free of my grasp?"

"Absolutely."

"Then do it," he challenged.

She smiled, raised their locked hands up between them and with tender lips kissed his fingers one by one.

He found her tactic amusing, but refused to surrender until by the third finger his body began to respond to the play of her moist lips against his warm flesh—or maybe his flesh was hot, or perhaps it was the humidity of the greenhouse, or perhaps . . .

He tore his hand away from hers. His temperature was rising rapidly, which was causing another unexpected rise he was not yet ready to deal with, so retreat was his best option.

"You made your point," he admitted. "Foolishly, of course, but . . ." He shrugged as if enough was said, and she should understand.

"Were you never foolish?" Tempest asked and turned to fill the six four-inch pots with soil while waiting for his answer.

Memories brought a smile to his face. "More than I care to remember."

"Enlighten me," she teased and moved to fill a small tin watering can at the sink at the end of the workbench.

"That's not a good idea, and besides, I think I need my full concentration on the chore at hand."

Tempest didn't press the issue, she simply began instructing him on repotting the mint seedlings.

"You don't use gloves?" he asked as he carefully dislodged a hardy seedling from the full bed, paying close attention to her instructions.

"Never," she said and scooped up a handful of soil from the tub beneath the workbench. "Every living, breathing thing needs nourishment. The soil is no different than we are. When our energies connect we nourish each other, and then we grow and flourish. It is a continuous cycle. Birth, growth, passing and rebirth. Mother Nature teaches us this simple fact if we but take the time to look."

Michael added more soil around the seedling. "You make it sound more simple than it is."

"What makes you say that?" she asked, handing him the watering can.

He trickled water slowly around the plant. "You grow these plants in optimum conditions. What of the plants that must brave Mother Nature at her worst?"

"Worst or best, the cycle remains the same. Birth, growth, passing and rebirth. That never changes. It is ever continuous."

"So just like humans, some plants are luckier than others."

"Life doesn't come with guarantees for anyone or anything, Michael."

"I suppose not," he said, and reached for another seedling. "But it's hard when you see some who have so much compared to those who have nothing. It makes you wonder."

She let him finish repotting the mint and worked on an asparagus fern that needed replanting in a larger pot. "You must have come across much suffering in your travels."

"Too much," he said. "The hardest part was knowing there wasn't much you could do. Maybe every now and then you could buy food for those kids in need, but you knew it was only a temporary fix and they would soon go hungry again. I think the worst was seeing the kids starving for someone to care about them, someone to love them."

"You did, if only for a short time. If they hadn't experienced that small touch of compassion they would never know its value. You gave them that."

He shook his head slowly. "That's nothing."

"That's everything. You gave of yourself and they felt it and understood it, and they will never forget it."

He shook his head to protest again, and she shook her own.

"Don't deny the truth, Michael. You yourself have probably experienced that very compassion you gave so freely or else you would never have been able to share it with those children."

"I never knew compassion," he said with disgust.

"Impossible," she argued. "If you never knew it, you could never give it. Someone, somewhere in your life taught you it."

He was about to argue when he stopped himself, paused in thought and softly said, "My mother."

Tempest remained silent and patient. She needed to know about this stranger who so mysteriously entered her life. She wanted to learn of his past, his hopes, his dreams, and she wanted to learn if he was part of her future.

His fingers remained busy planting. "My mother was an alcoholic and a hardworking woman. She worked the early-morning shift at the local diner. It was a busy place, and I guess she made good money because we had a nice, clean apartment, and I always had things. We lived in Hoboken, New Jersey, and we would take the tubes into New York City. She had an eye for a bargain, and we would come home with at least three shopping bags full of clothes, toys and food. She loved to cook, so I never went hungry."

He paused as if he wasn't certain if he wanted to go on, but he did. "She drank mostly at night. She would drink herself to sleep. I think it had something to do with my old man, who

I don't even remember. And if I asked, she would only say he had to go away. I never knew much about him. I don't even recall seeing a picture of him, but then it wasn't that important to me. My mother loved me and often showed it."

He smiled. "She hugged me all the time. I remember trying to squirm out of her grasp, though I didn't try very hard, not even when the smell of liquor overwhelmed me. I'd help get her into bed at night and tuck the covers around her. But no matter how much she drank she was still up at the crack of dawn ready to go to work. She'd make certain I ate a good breakfast, was dressed decently for school, gave me lunch money, then hugged me fiercely, and told me how much she loved me before she dropped me off at Mrs. Garcia's apartment. Mrs. Garcia was a friend and neighbor who walked me to school along with her five children."

Tempest knew the story did not have a happy ending. She felt his pain, sorrow, and the loss of a mother's love as if it were her own, and she held back her tears.

He shook his head. "Ironically, a drunk driver hit and killed her on her way to work one morning. I was eight years old, and I became the state's responsibility, since my mother had no relatives. I was shifted from foster home to foster home. Some weren't too bad and others were nightmares. The last home was brutal. The man was nasty and violent, though he never took a drink. He was just plain mean. He beat the hell out of me more times than I care to remember. Six months into my stay there I turned sixteen and decided I'd had enough of a system that just didn't really give a damn. I ran away. I lied about my age, which was easy since I looked older than I was. I signed onto a freighter, and I've been sailing the high seas until about six months ago when I decided to explore Scotland."

Tempest realized how very much his mother had taught him in the short time they had together. But now was not the time to comment. It had cost him dearly to share a part of himself that he had locked away far too long, and a part of him that had never healed. Words of solace or understanding would do little good right now, so she wisely chose to change the subject.

"Why Scotland?"

He seemed relieved. The taut muscles in his face relaxed,

and his tense hands calmed as he planted the last of the mint seedlings. "My travels brought me here several times. I had the opportunity to explore and found myself fascinated with the land and its people. Aberdeen has a mystical quality about it. Edinburgh is a blend of the old and the new. The various isles haunt the eye, and the mist-shrouded hills leave you breathless. And then there are the people, warm and welcoming." He laughed. "And never at a loss for advice, and good advice at that."

"How long do you plan on staying here?"

He shrugged. "I'm not sure. It may sound strange, but I feel the need to be here. I'm not certain why, I just know here is where I must remain until . . ." He shrugged again. "Until whenever."

Tempest patted the fresh soil around the repotted asparagus fern. "Well until then, those mint seedlings are yours to take care of. And there's seeds that need planting for spring and a few plants that need trimming and repotting."

"You trust me?" he asked doubtfully.

"You've handled yourself well so far, and I think I see . . ." she said, poking at his soil-covered thumb, "a bit of green sprouting right there."

He looked at where she pointed and she smiled.

"You see, you do believe, and that's all it takes."

He smiled himself, feeling good, feeling relaxed, feeling drawn to this mysterious woman who had appeared out of nowhere in a snowstorm and whisked him away.

"We'll finish working here, and then you can rest or help me in the kitchen making an apple pie for this evening's dessert." She touched his hand with the concern of a loved one. "I don't want you doing too much, so please don't hesitate to tell me if you are tired and need rest."

"I'll be a good patient," he said, his own hand reassuring her with a comforting pat.

They worked well together for the next hour. He was an apt student—asking questions, following instructions and learning. But then she learned as well, growing aware of his intelligence, his ability to learn easily, and his need to connect and care for something, anything. Anything that would stop the loneliness that was so much a part of him.

They were both hungry by the time they returned to the

kitchen and while Michael availed himself of the bathroom, Tempest used her magical powers to set the table. He would insist on helping her and she thought he needed rest, so instead of arguing the issue she settled it with a wave of her hand.

Vegetable beef soup was ladled into deep bowls and thick slices of pumpernickel bread waited on the table along with a cucumber salad.

Michael hobbled into the kitchen, cast a glance at the set table but before he could protest he got a whiff of the vegetable beef soup. Without delay he took his seat.

By the time Michael finished his third bowl of soup and the last slice of bread, he was yawning.

"Time to rest," she said.

"What about helping you with that apple pie?" Another yawn attacked him.

Tempest had cast no sleep spell over him and knew his own body was alerting him to the fact that it required time to sleep and time to heal. "I can manage on my own."

"I should help," he insisted, standing and reaching for his empty bowl to help clean off the table. He wobbled slightly and wisely placed the bowl back down.

Tempest reached out and braced her shoulder under his arm, allowing his arm to drape over her opposite shoulder. Her arm went around his waist. "I'll help you to the couch."

This time he didn't protest and followed her lead. He was soon carefully deposited on the big soft couch in the living room, a chenille throw draped over him.

Tempest added another log to the dwindling fire, returning the protective black iron mesh screen in front.

"Don't let me sleep long," he said, his eyes drifting shut.

"Sleep as long as you need to," she whispered and tiptoed out of the room. She went to the closet beneath the stairs and took out her long, white wool cloak, and her white boots lined with lamb's wool. She put both on, grabbed the heavy white wool gloves from the pockets of the cloak and quietly slipped out the door into the swirling snow.

Two hours later Michael woke with a start. He thought he heard the front door open and close, but that didn't make sense. Tempest certainly wouldn't venture out in this storm. He must have been dreaming.

It was almost completely dark, the fire's light lending a soft glow to the room, and he found himself not wanting to stir. He had forgotten the feeling of a home, a good solid home filled with warmth and love, and he wanted to soak as much as the atmosphere as he could. He'd be on his way as soon as his ankle healed. Where to he didn't know, but he doubted it would be as welcoming as this place.

He spotted his crutch by the chair and forced himself to get up. He should have helped her after lunch, but there was still supper. He yawned away the last of the sleep and hobbled to the kitchen. It was empty, though the scent of a baking apple pie permeated the air.

He turned and entered the sitting room, stopping only inches in through the archway. Tempest sat on the pale-green couch with its array of tapestry pillows spread along the back. Her hands stretched out toward the fire as if attempting to warm them.

Her honey-gold hair with its bold red streaks appeared to glisten as if wet, and her cheeks were flushed as though from the cold. He grew concerned.

"Are you all right?" he asked, making his way to her side.

She jumped, startled by his appearance. "I'm fine. Feeling chilled, that's all."

He sat down beside her, resting his crutch next to him, and took her hands in his. "Your hands are ice-cold." He rubbed them with his own. "Don't tell me you've been foolish enough to go outside?"

She could not be dishonest with him, but how did she tell him she had been outside talking with the forest fairies?

Five

~

Tempest shivered, silently admonishing herself. She could easily have cast a protective spell around herself to ward off the cold, but she had been in such a hurry, she had completely forgotten. And that concerned her. She always took precautions. Why hadn't she this time?

She had cast a glance at the woodpile to make certain her supply was adequate, though the fairies had made it known that the storm would end by morning and spring would arrive early this year. But at least her glance had given her a reasonable explanation.

"Wood," she said with a quiver. "I checked the woodpile."

He looked at her oddly, his hands pausing briefly in their vigorous rub. "Not a wise choice in a snowstorm. Unless, of course, the fireplaces are your only source of heat."

She shook her head. "No, I have an efficient heating system." Though she much preferred the heat of the fireplaces. She had allowed too many years to pass before she had updated the cottage to present-day standards. It wasn't that she objected to modernizing the place; she supposed it was nostalgia for a certain period in her life. A period that was better left to memories, as she often reminded herself.

Michael cast a glance around the sitting room, and spying a pale-green and beige wool throw on a chair, he stood. "Stay put," he ordered and without the aid of the crutch he hobbled over to get it.

He returned and wrapped the warm throw around her. "I'll fix you a cup of tea."

"It isn't nec—"

He silenced her with a pointed finger. "Objections are useless, and besides, I make a mean cup of tea."

"Really?"

"You bet," he said and reached for his crutch. He turned his face close to hers and caught the quiver of her lips and heard the slight chatter of her teeth. He shook his head, warning himself not to, telling himself he shouldn't and cautioning himself against being stupid, but then who the hell ever said he was smart.

He leaned closer and pressed his warm lips to her chilled ones. When she made no objections he nipped lightly along the bottom one until it plumped against his own. He moved to the top lip and heated that one to a pleasant warmth, and then he ran his tongue in a delicate line over both before giving her a kiss that caused both their lips to flame hot.

When their tongues started to mate and his body began to respond, he knew it was time to end the kiss before he found himself wanting what he definitely couldn't have. He reluctantly drew away after depositing several faint kisses across her lips.

"Tea," he said as though reminding himself, and leaned heavily on the crutch as he walked out of the room.

Tempest dropped back against the couch with a sigh and a smile. She certainly enjoyed that, and her body was still experiencing the tingling aftermath. She felt warm right down to the bone.

She giggled. His kiss worked faster than a cup of tea. She hugged herself and indulged in the pleasure. It had been too long since her last kiss, but then that was her own fault. She had kept a distinct distance from men, not trusting them or perhaps not trusting herself. She allowed no man to get close because she herself did not want to get close, commit or even love. If she was truthful with herself she would admit that she was fearful of falling in love, fearful of getting hurt, fearful of *his* return.

She glanced toward the fire and whispered a name that had

not crossed her lips in several hundred years. "Marcus."

Had he returned? Had the spell been set in motion?

A single tear spilled down her cheek. She could do nothing but wait and be patient. All would be revealed in time, and only Marcus himself could break the spell. And if not? She would lose him and their love forever.

Tempest wiped the tear away as she heard Michael approach. Surprisingly, he managed to carry the mug of tea and make use of his crutch without any difficulty.

He handed her the mug before easing off his crutch. "Be careful—it's hot."

She took it carefully from him. "Thank you. I appreciate your thoughtfulness."

He sat beside her, his crutch left to rest on the nearby chair. "You've taken good care of me; no reason I can't return the favor. I searched your cabinets for brandy but couldn't find any. It works wonders in chasing away a chill."

"And numbs pain besides helping to soothe restless sleep." She smiled. "And sometimes it's nice just to enjoy a brandy in front of the hearth."

He grinned. "So are you going to tell me where you keep your brandy so I can enjoy a glass?"

"In the pantry off the kitchen. You'll find brandy, scotch, vodka, gin and a variety of wine."

"Your liquor supply surprises me, Tempest."

"I use it to cook with, serve to guests and enjoy myself. I am not a prude, nor do I abuse its enjoyment."

"Neither do I," he assured her. "Though there was a time I almost did. I think memories of my mother kept me from going over the edge, and I was able to keep my drinking in perspective."

"And smoking?" she asked.

He grinned. "Only under pressure do I light up."

"I guess the pressure of being hit by a car would tempt you to have a smoke." She hugged the mug, relishing the heat that permeated her hands. "I want you to know how sincerely sorry I am for running into you with my car."

He didn't want her apology, didn't need it. And he couldn't stand the thought of her feeling badly over the misfortunate incident. "Don't worry about it. The snowstorm was blinding. There was no way you could have seen me on that road."

Tempest disagreed. "I should never have attempted to drive in such hazardous conditions. I don't have enough experience."

"You got us here, didn't you? I'd say you handled yourself well enough. The accident was simply that, an accident. Unpredictable and unintentional. Besides, you have graciously seen to my care. What more could I ask for? Except maybe a ride to the nearest village when I'm healed."

Tempest produced a shaky smile.

Michael took her half-filled mug from her hand. "Let me heat that for you while I get a glass of brandy. You're still chilled."

She didn't pay attention to his chatter as he left. She heard something about help and supper but her mind was busy considering the mistake she had made when she'd returned the car to Rasmus Castle instead of sending it here to her home. Of course he would assume she had a car. How else would she have gotten him here? Another blunder, and one that disturbed her greatly. She did not make mistakes. Mistakes could be costly, and she had learned centuries ago not to make them.

She could transport the car here, but that would be rude without speaking with Dagon and Sarina and asking their permission. She had no doubt it would be no problem, and they would gladly lend it to her, but of course Sarina would expect an explanation. Dagon, on the other hand, probably would not question her, though he would tell Sarina. They didn't keep secrets—a good way to start a marriage.

Well, she had time yet, not to worry now and needlessly. She would speak with Sarina soon enough.

Tempest shrugged off the wool throw and decided to join Michael in the kitchen. He couldn't possibly handle a tea and brandy along with his crutch, and besides, supper needed starting and the apple pie needed looking after. And she enjoyed the thought of his company while she prepared both.

He had found a small serving tray which he was about to make use of when Tempest entered the kitchen.

"I thought you might need help, and I needed to check on the pie."

"It smells good," he said and handed her the mug of tea.

Their conversation turned casual after that. Michael took a seat at the table and sipped his brandy while Tempest worked on supper, and the apple pie cooled on a wire rack. It was a scene of domestic bliss that both seemed to enjoy and that flourished through the evening meal, but quickly changed when Michael entered his bedroom for the evening and discovered the closet and bureau full of clothes.

"Tempest!"

Tempest had barely slipped on her pale pink flannel, ankle-length nightgown when she heard her name echo through the cottage. She rushed to button the three pearl buttons that connected at her breasts and she ran her fingers through her tousled hair, little good that it did.

With her feet bare and her hair messed, she peeked her head around the door into Michael's room. "Something wrong?"

"Where did these clothes come from?"

Another blunder. She couldn't be dishonest with him, so what in heaven's name was she to tell him?

"Don't tell me," he said caustically. "You believed I needed them so you willed them here."

"There's a thought," she said with a smile that faded quickly when his dark eyes warned he was in no mood for humor.

She chose to remain silent. Sometimes it was necessary to leave mortals to their own rhyme and reason.

He was blunt. "Do they belong to a *special* friend of yours?"

His words insinuated that she had a lover and while they did not all disturb her, his annoyance at the fact amused and fascinated her. And given that the clothes actually belonged to him, she could answer honestly, "Yes, they do."

"Won't he mind sharing them?"

Tempest entered the room, her bare feet hurrying to stand on the nearest wool rug. "He's a decent man who shares when necessary."

He obviously fought to contain his annoyance. "Will he visit anytime soon?"

"He's where he needs to be right now."

He practically snapped at her when he spoke. "I have my own things, I don't need his."

She shrugged. "Wear them if you wish to or not. The choice is yours. I just thought you may need a few extra things during your stay here. Your own clothes are among them."

His temper eased. "I appreciate the thought, but my own clothes should be sufficient."

"If not, please feel free to help yourself," she said calmly. "Now, is there anything I can do for you before I retire?"

"No," he answered gruffly. "Good night."

"Sleep well," she said and before turning to leave she hurried to his side, kissed his cheek and wished him, "Pleasant dreams."

The door was closed behind her before he could react, and he was relieved. He didn't know how a flannel nightgown could be sexy but hers was and his thoughts were anything but pure at the moment. And why did she have to go kiss him and stir his emotions?

He pulled off his sweatshirt and threw it on the rocking chair. With an unsteady gait he made it to the bed, unhooking his jeans and sliding them down his legs before he sat down on the bed. With a little effort and a few tugs he had his jeans off. He folded them and laid them on the floor beside the bed. He left his white briefs on and climbed beneath the covers and sighed heavily.

"Damn," he muttered. She was just too attractive, and he'd been here only one day. The doctor said it would take at least six weeks for his ankle to heal. How the hell was he going to last six weeks alone with Tempest and not kiss her, touch her or make love to her? It wasn't humanly possible.

And besides, she wasn't the type of woman that would go for a man like him. He'd be a mere dalliance to her, and he'd had his share of those. Not that he was looking for a permanent relationship in his life, but he was tired of brief flings that left him feeling physically satisfied but emotionally starved.

He draped his arm across his head. Hell, he didn't know what he was looking for. He wasn't even sure why he had chosen Scotland as his exit port. The place always fascinated him, and strangely enough he felt a connection to it, but what he expected to find here, he couldn't say.

Maybe he was hoping to find himself, because he sure felt lost. After his mother died he felt that he didn't belong anywhere. There was no permanency to anything, not a roof over his head or food in his stomach. Not someone to care about him or love him. It was like he had been set adrift on his own, and he had no oars to steer his way. Whichever way the wind blew is where he went. Until he dropped sail and landed here in Scotland.

His eyes grew heavy, and he knew sleep would soon still his jumbled mind, though he didn't care much. It would be good to sleep and not think or dream.

He turned his head and before his eyes drifted shut completely he looked at the strange symbols on the wall and whispered, "Protection."

It was dark, a dark so black that he could not see his surroundings, and yet he knew where he was going. He sensed that he had walked this path many times, and he did not require a light to guide his way. Actually he preferred the darkness, took comfort in it and relished its protective cloak.

His steady steps brought him to the mouth of a cave and before entering he turned to glance into the darkness. He heard the distant hoot of an owl, and then there was complete silence. His presence frightened the forest creatures and they hid and would remain so until his departure. He smiled at that knowledge and with a sweep of his black cloak around him he entered the cave, the darkness swallowing him.

Here again he did not need light to guide his way. He walked the awkward, twisting passageway with a man confident of his direction and in only minutes he came upon a large open area. With a steady wave of his hand torches flamed to life; they protruded from the cave walls that ran at least ten feet high. A stone altar sat in the center of the round-shaped room. A wooden bowl sat to one end, three white candles circled the middle, and a gem-encrusted dagger, the large rubies sparkling bright red in the flames' lights, lay at the other end.

Slowly but eagerly, he reached his hands into the bowl. His fingers worked their way around the smooth, black stones, and he felt their rush of power race over him. He grabbed a handful and dropped them on the altar in the center of the candles. He took a step back, braced his hands on the altar's edge and lowered his head with a groan. His black, shiny, chest-length hair fell like a protective cape in front of his face and brushed the altar.

"Not again," he said in a harsh whisper. "The power should be mine. I am the stronger one."

But the etched symbols on the stones told him a different story, and their portent angered him. He straightened to his full height, casting a shadow that towered to the height of the cave.

*"I will not accept this," he said with a frightening strength
in his deep voice that sent the torches flames flickering. "She
will give me her power, willingly." He smiled, a smile of darkness. "Most willingly."*

*He returned the stones to the bowl, his fingers moving them
around until he scooped a handful up and dropped them on
the altar with a whispered, "Guide me."*

*A pleased smile surfaced on his grim face. "The witch will
surrender to the warlock."*

*He laughed with a deep power that echoed off the cave walls
and down the stone corridors and out into the dark night. The
forest animals shivered as they huddled in their dens, and the
forest fairies took flight to avoid the evil sound from touching
them.*

Michael woke with a start, banging his head on the sloped
ceiling, the strange sound still filling his head. It took him a
minute or two to focus his sight. It was dark, much too dark,
a dark that seemed so heavy it frightened him, and he felt a
shiver race down his spine.

He nestled his head down on the pillow and attempted to
recall the odd dream. It came in fragment, small bits and pieces
he fought to make sense of and forced himself to remember.
But full wakefulness was beginning to take hold of him, and
he realized that as reality intruded, the bizarre dream would
fade.

He rarely dreamed and didn't put much stock in dreams.
There was one dream he would never forget. It was so clear,
so vivid, that to this day he swore it wasn't a dream. It was
right after his mother died. He was staying with Mrs. Garcia
while his fate was being decided. She had made an effort to
seek custody of him, but was told she had too many children
of her own and too little money to provide for another child.
He often wondered how different his life would have been
if . . .

He pushed the thought aside and concentrated on the dream.
His mother had come to him. It was around three in the morning. He remembered because he looked at the glowing alarm
clock on the rickety nightstand next to the bed. Then he
glanced down at the bottom of the bed and there his mother
sat in her waitress uniform, smoking a cigarette. The way he
would always remember her.

Their conversation had been strange. She explained that she had done her part, served her purpose and could do no more for him. He was now on his own. She advised him that life would not be easy for him, but that he would find the strength he needed to face his challenges, to meet his fate. She warned him in a sharp tone, one she used when she expected him to listen and obey, that he should think and choose wisely. That in wisdom came clarity and the truth. She told him how much she loved and admired him, and how grateful she was to be a part of his journey. She hugged him and whispered, "Remember my love for you, and one day it will help you to understand."

His eyes grew misty but he shed no tears. He had cried enough that night so long ago and for many nights to come, until he felt that there were no more tears to shed and that there was no one who cared that he wept.

He shook his head. Why he recalled that dream now he couldn't say, or perhaps it was because on first waking from this dream it had been as clear and vivid as the one with his mother. But he couldn't hold on to this dream. Maybe he didn't want to; maybe it frightened him more than he wanted to admit.

He rubbed his hand over his face and groaned. In an instant he brought the groan to an end and shivered. His groan sounded identical to the one he heard in the dream. Had that mysterious figure been him? Where had he been? What was he doing?

He turned his head, punching his pillow either to soften it or to release some of his frustration—he wasn't certain which, but either way it felt good. He nestled his head and gave a yawn when he once again jumped and hit his head on the ceiling.

"Damn," he said, rubbing what he was certain was a growing lump on his forehead. His eyes searched the room, and he shook his head when he caught sight of the shadow that stretched up upon his ceiling. It was of a bear that looked about ready to strike. He finally discovered the whereabouts of the culprit.

"Bear," he whispered.

The black cat stopped licking its paw and looked at him. A faint light from the half-moon cast upon the pure white snow entered his window; he supposed it was the cause of the shadow. Though the light wasn't very strong, he still couldn't understand how one average-sized black cat could cast the shadow of a bear.

But then things weren't what they seemed to be around here. He wondered if perhaps he had fallen down the proverbial rabbit's hole and was in a completely different existence.

He held his hand out to the cat and at first the cat didn't seem interested. But curiosity appeared to get the better of him, and he sauntered over to the dangling fingers.

Bear swatted at Michael's hand a few times, and when he exchanged playful antics with him, Bear seemed delighted. There was no doubt the black cat was in complete charge of the game and when he tired, Bear simply jumped up on the bed, rubbed himself against his chest, then settled in a cuddled ball against him and went to sleep.

Michael smiled. He had never had a pet and this spoiled and demanding animal simply stole his heart. Besides, it was nice having someone to cuddle with, even a cat.

He yawned again. Sleep was creeping over him and he was grateful. He only hoped there would be no more dreams. His droopy eyes glanced at the wall across from him and he focused on the symbols that ran as a border around the room.

Why were they so familiar? Had he seen them somewhere in his various travels or in the many books he read?

He knew them from somewhere, but where?

His eyes drifted shut and once again he whispered, "Protection."

Six

The snow had stopped and the skies remained gray, making the late afternoon appear more like early evening. A thick log burned brightly in the stone fireplace in the living room, and Michael sat on the couch, his ankle resting on a chintz ottoman whose floral design was nothing less than chaotic.

He had opted to wear his own clothes, a worn denim shirt and his jeans, though he had borrowed the slippers as the cumbersome cast left no other footwear possible. He relaxed now for the first time since morning. Tempest had breakfast cooking when he had entered the kitchen, and the smell of French toast and sausages almost made him lick his lips. After breakfast he had helped with the dishes, and then went to work in the greenhouse, finding he favored working with the plants, and besides, Tempest was a patient teacher. Not to mention that he enjoyed watching her. There was no doubt she was physically beautiful, but something else about her had appealed to him, though he couldn't quite understand or explain it. And stranger still, the nagging feeling was familiar.

He had pointed out some minor repairs the greenhouse could use and suggested that after his ankle healed he could repay her hospitality by making the repairs. She had agreed without hesitation, and it had made him feel that at least he would be of some substantial use.

After a light lunch she insisted that he rest and with a slight twinge reminding him of his injury he decided that it might be a good idea. That was a couple of hours ago, and he had been reading ever since. The book was a history on Scottish witchcraft and he found it fascinating.

Witchcraft dated back to Scotland's earliest days. In the second century, witchcraft enticed King Natholocus to send a messenger to the island of Iona where there was reputed to live a famous witch. The king wished to know the outcome of a rebellion mounting in his kingdom. She foretold of his doom with great accuracy.

Christianity brought the fall of pagan worship, the practice which was based on the cycles of nature. It was actually a practical practice, since survival was dependent upon the growth of crops and the abundance of wildlife. It wasn't until the reign of Mary in 1563 that the Scottish parliament made witchcraft legally punishable.

The witch-hunt sent many practitioners into hiding and forced them to pass on their knowledge secretly until such a time came when it was embraced as a viable practice.

"Interesting book?" Tempest asked and handed him a mug of hot chocolate which he eagerly accepted. She took her mug, shook off her shoes and curled her sock-covered feet under her on the oversized chintz chair opposite him.

"Very much so," he answered, admiring her long, narrow, pale-blue knit skirt and matching turtleneck sweater, not to mention her pale-blue and white polka-dotted socks.

"Scottish Witchcraft." She read the title from the book's spine. "An interest of yours?"

"Not until I picked up this book. Now I find it a bit fascinating," he admitted and sipped at the hot chocolate that tasted as good as he remembered from his youth. He closed the book, placing the jacket's flap in the page he was reading to serve as a bookmark. "Is it an interest of yours?"

"I have many interests."

"I can see from your collection of books that your range is wide, though you do have many on the ancient pagan practices."

"History fascinates me. I don't feel it is portrayed accurately, and therefore it leaves room for debate and interpretation."

Michael found himself drawn to her intelligence. "What makes you say that?"

She hugged her mug in her hands after taking a sip. "History itself proves it. All one needs to do is look at the portraits of powerful people. They are always portrayed as regal characters, dressed stylishly and lavishly, their expressions imperial. If it is a battle scene it is mostly victorious; even a death scene demonstrates how eagerly and bravely lives were given for country and king. If it is a feasting scene it is a lavish ordeal with much merriment. No true suffering, heartache or injustice of the common people are shown. The very people who make a country thrive and grow."

Michael raised the book he had been reading. "Pictures in here portray the suffering and injustice of those tried for witchcraft."

"Look more closely at the pictures. Those doing the accusing or torturing are portrayed as saviors. They are not only saving the innocent, they are saving the evil souls of the damned. And in the end all confess their evil deeds, begging for mercy, and of course they are mercifully put to death. And another soul is saved. Another battle is won. Another victory claimed."

"Obviously it's a period in history you feel strongly about?"

Her smile was filled with sadness. "Power, greed, ignorance and fear breed disaster and cause needless suffering, and the tragic loss of far too many lives."

He looked at her oddly. "You sound as though you speak from experience."

Memories flared and the cries of the tortured innocent souls filled her head. She shook the heartrending images away. "Too much reading," she said with a salute of her mug.

Why didn't he believe her? She spoke with such conviction, and he could easily see the hurt in her eyes. He thought on it briefly before saying, "Have you dated back your heritage to the horrific witch burnings?"

For a second his question surprised her, and then she realized he meant her ancestors and could answer honestly, "Yes, my heritage touches that period."

He grew excited. "Are you a descendant of a witch?"

Another honest answer. "Yes."

His eager interest surfaced with a grin. "Tell me about her, and how you discovered her existence." He waited, but another pertinent question broke his patient silence. "Oh, the symbols upstairs," he said excitedly. "Do they pertain to witchcraft?"

"Some believe so."

"Tell me," he said like an eager child impatiently waiting to hear a tale.

She shared his excitement and thirst for knowledge. "The symbols you refer to are called runes. Many date their inception back to the Germanic tribes, and they are a solid part of Viking history. They have been associated with witchcraft, and the symbols resemble some of the ogam symbols of the druids. If you look closely at history, and the migration of the various tribes you can understand how many of the symbols intermingled. So it is difficult to say where one began or joined with another. Regardless the symbols appeared to be an early form of written communication."

"You have books on runes and ogam?"

"Several that you may find interesting."

"Tell me about your ancestor, the witch," he said eagerly.

Tempest found herself in a quandary. Exactly how much information should she impart, and was she safe in sharing any? She glanced at his eyes, so dark they almost appeared black, though on second glance she could see they were a dark brown and cynical. He didn't trust easily, reserving his opinions and emotions. Who really was this stranger sitting across from her? She needed to know; not only for herself, but for him.

His own excitement kept him questioning. "Did she cast spells? Fly a broom? Turn people into toads? Cavort with the devil?"

Tempest looked at him oddly. "You talk like those who once condemned witchcraft."

"Foolishly," he said with a laugh. "I imagine I'm predisposed to believe in all the nonsense once told to me about witches. I never really stopped to think about witchcraft. It wasn't given much attention in history classes, and most people's image of a witch is the hag so prominently displayed at Halloween."

"Witches look no different than anyone else."

He tapped the book with his finger. "I'm beginning to understand that, and how predominant they were throughout history. It is amazing to realize that monarchs sought out the advice of witches or those with supernatural powers."

"Insightful. Whether it was witches, druids, shamans or masters, it was their extraordinary ability to foresee and comprehend the results of thought and action that learned men sought."

"Did your ancestor help monarchs?"

Tempest nodded. "She was known to give a word or two of advice."

"What became of her?" Michael asked with concern.

"She found it necessary to hide her skills and keep silent her talents."

Michael tapped at the book. "Do you believe there were those who practiced the Craft that intentionally sought to do harm?"

"Are you wondering if evil witches actually did exist?"

"I suppose I am. I mean, think about it . . . usually somewhere along the line there is a basis in fact for everything, so why not a rogue witch who decided to use his abilities for his own pleasure and profit?"

"A warlock," she informed him sadly.

"A warlock is a bad witch?"

"A warlock uses darkness instead of light and practices the Craft for his own benefit. He uses the vulnerable, the misguided, the hopeless."

"So then maybe during these witch burnings the persecutors actually snagged themselves a warlock or two."

"That's highly doubtful," she said confidently. "A warlock possesses a defined power that defies the common man."

Michael put it more plainly. "You mean he's a sly character."

"Sly is an inadequate description."

"That good, is he?"

She finished sipping her hot chocolate before nodding. "All that and more, as they say."

"Do you think your ancestor ever came across a warlock?"

"There is a tale—"

"Tell me," he said eagerly, though a yawn warned of his weariness.

She wasn't ready to verbalize difficult memories, and he truly required rest in order to heal. "Another time. You are tired and need a nap."

"I want to know about her," he said as if the information was necessary to his well-being. "Was this her home? Were the symbols upstairs placed there by her for protection?"

His anxious need and pertinent questions startled her, though she remained calm. "Another time," she insisted and stood, removing the book from his lap and taking the empty mug from his hand. "Nap first, answers later." Much later, if she could help it.

Michael reluctantly relented. "I'll have my answers."

Tempest placed the mugs on a nearby table while she assisted him in stretching out on the couch. "I'm certain you will." She draped the chenille throw over him.

"Wake me to help you with supper."

She brushed his dark uneven hair away from his face and ran a tender hand over his cheek. "I will not deprive you of your kitchen duties."

"See that you don't," he teased. "I'm looking forward to peeling potatoes."

"And carrots," she said with a smile. "Now sleep." She leaned down and kissed his cheek ever so gently, and taking the mugs from the table, quietly left the room.

Michael stared after her. She was a strange yet enchanting woman. Her touch and kiss held not a hint of passion—only pure concern. She actually cared about him and his well-being, and he wondered if that depth of sensitivity wasn't more of an aphrodisiac than passion.

His eyelids drifted closed though he fought against sleep, his mind cluttered and anxious for answers. What was this sudden, relentless need to know about her ancestor? Why did he find this woman who probably lived over hundreds of years ago so fascinating? He wondered what she looked like and if she ever loved, and he wondered what her name was.

"Tempest," he whispered as his eyelids drifted completely shut and sleep claimed him.

Tempest shut off the water and stopped washing the dishes, having thought she heard her name called. When no sound stirred the silence she shrugged and finished the chore. She intended on keeping her hands busy; if she could keep her focus on the chore at hand, she would refrain from thinking and at the moment she wanted her mind silent.

Too many thoughts, too many memories and too many disturbing questions from Michael. Questions she eventually would not be able to ignore. What then?

With busy hands being uppermost in her mind, she hurried off to the greenhouse. Not giving herself a chance to think, only to work, she gathered all the items necessary to make an herbal wreath.

But busy hands don't always silence a busy mind, and while Tempest worked, her mind continually drifted back to Michael. It was difficult to be objective where he was concerned. Over the last two days she had come to understand him better, and the reason for his inability to trust and for the hint of cynicism in his eyes. Life had failed him at a very young age, leaving him emotionally scarred and trusting no one.

She imagined that was when he erected that wall in front of him. The wall she felt every time she attempted to get close, to touch, to care, to comfort. She could sense his uncertainty when her hand reached out to help him, and she felt that heavy, burdensome wall all too often, though . . .

She smiled, recalling his unexpected kiss.

He had lowered his defenses long enough to share that kiss, and she had liked what she felt and sensed. And she wanted very much to get to know that man who kissed her, especially since that kiss had lingered much in her mind.

She shook her head and attempted to concentrate on the wreath, but her mind continued to drift. She wasn't at all surprised when she felt the thin wire slice her finger, and all the way to the kitchen she berated herself for being so clumsy. Of course a little attention and magic applied to the wound would work wonders, but she still should have been more conscious of her actions.

The small piece of cloth she had wrapped her finger in was soaked through with blood when she entered the kitchen. She was about to open the overhead cabinet beside the sink where she kept her herbal remedies for just such occasions, when she felt Michael come up behind her.

She turned and her breath caught. For a brief second he looked darkly mysterious, as if a shadow hovered over him, hiding his true features from her. Then it passed, and he appeared as though he had just stirred from a sleep. He yawned, rubbed at the back of his neck and then ran his fingers through his hair. It was when his eyes became fully alert and he focused on the bloody cloth that he swiftly took action.

"What happened?" he asked, grabbing her wrapped hand.

"I woke you, I'm sorry," she said, surprised his sleep had been disturbed. She had cast a light resting spell on him. He should have slept for at least another hour.

"I woke sensing something was wrong," he said with a shake of his head. "A crazy sensation, but accurate." He unwrapped the blood-soaked cloth and examined the cut.

"Wire," she explained. "I was making an herbal wreath when—"

"This cut needs stitches," he said with concern, and wiped at the blood that continued to flow.

"Nonsense" she said, though a quick glance told her he would have been right in his diagnosis if she were a mortal. "A little ointment and a tight bandage, and it will be as good as new."

"It needs stitches," he repeated, though more firmly.

"No doctor in sight, so a bandage will have to do," she said, attempting to free her hand.

His firm grip told her she wasn't going anywhere. "I can stitch it for you. It will probably only take two or three. I used to stitch the guys on the ship all the time."

"Not necessary," she said with a smile. She knew her own remedy and touch of magic would heal the cut without a trace of a scar. Stitches weren't at all necessary.

"This wound won't heal properly without stitches." He dabbed at the blood that refused to stop flowing. "And you may just bleed to death if you don't quit arguing with me."

"Nonsense, it will stop soon," she insisted and once again attempted to free her hand.

"You're not going anywhere," he warned her. "Not until I make certain this wound is looked after properly."

"If you release my hand I will be able to do just that."

"It needs stitches," he insisted once again.

"You may be right," she relented, "but let me try the ointment and a bandage first. If it doesn't stop the bleeding then you can stitch the wound."

"You know you're wasting time, putting off the inevitable."

"Time will tell," she said and eased her hand out of his to turn away from him.

She sensed his hurt, and the strong emotion wounded her

more painfully than the cut itself. He assumed that she didn't trust him, and she realized that his hope had been that not only could *she* trust *him* but that *he* could trust *her*. Now he felt nothing but disappointment, an emotion he was all too familiar with.

"Drat," she whispered to herself.

"Something wrong?" he asked, hearing her mumble.

In the blink of an eye she could have her finger mended, and yet here she was contemplating stitches. Had she completely lost her mind? Or were her feelings for this man growing much too stronger and much too fast?

Michael moved up behind her. His broad body whispered against hers as his arms circled around her. His hand gently slipped beneath her injured one and when he spoke his warm breath fanned her cheek. "It's still bleeding."

They both watched the blood drip into the sink. "Let me help you."

What he really was saying was, *trust me*. And with a resigned sigh she said, "I'd be grateful if you did, Michael."

His relief and renewed hope flooded her senses and filled her with such pleasure that the stitches would almost be worth the brief pain. Almost. She could cast a numbing spell and pretend to flinch, but that wouldn't be honest, though she could look at it as protecting herself.

He kissed her temple as his one arm squeezed her waist. "Don't worry, it will be stitched before you know it."

She leaned back against him, surrendering completely. "I trust you."

He hugged her closer to him, and he whispered in her ear. "I would never hurt you, Tempest."

She hoped and prayed what he said was true—only time would tell.

"Let me get you the things you'll need," she said, but made no attempt to move away from him.

"I'll get them," he said, though he also made no attempt to move.

They both seemed content to stay as they were, pressed against each other, his arm around her waist, his lips beside her cheek.

It was when Michael felt her blood run over his hand that he went into action. He barked orders at her that warned he was to be obeyed and then with an agility that surprised her he set to gathering the items he needed.

The stained glass light that hung over the kitchen table wasn't sufficient lighting for Michael's work, and he set up a desk lamp from the sitting room on the kitchen table. He poured Tempest a shot of whisky and insisted she sip it slowly while he saw to cleansing his hands, then he prepared a fine needle and thread. He also packed her injured finger in ice, hoping to numb it as best as possible.

He prepared a bed out of a towel for a hand to rest on and just before he was ready to begin he started talking to her. He captured her attention with funny tales on the high seas, making himself and his shipmates sound more like rogue pirates than simple merchant seamen.

She sipped the whisky and listened to his stories while he dried her hand and prepared to stitch it. She was so engrossed with his comical tales that she didn't feel the needle prick her skin, and she only began to feel a slight pain when he was almost finished.

She flinched once and he held her hand more firmly.

She stared down at the small stitches, impressed. "You are rather good with a needle."

He finished off the last of the three stitches. "This type of stitching, yes, but don't ask me to hem a dress."

She laughed and handed him a jar. "Could you put a generous amount of this ointment on the wound before you bandage it?"

"Home remedy?" he asked.

She leaned forward. "A witch's remedy."

"Really?" he asked and opened the jar to sniff.

"Shhh," she said with a finger to her lip. "It's a secret, no one can know."

He realized the whisky had gone to her head. "Now, it's your turn to rest."

"I'm not tired," she insisted as she kept a watchful eye on his bandaging skills.

"A short nap will do you good."

"A snap of my fingers and I'll be as right as rain," she said, though she found snapping difficult.

Michael tried not to laugh, but failed to hide his smirk.

She wagged an unsteady finger in his face. "You best be careful or I'll turn you into a toad."

He played along. "Inherited your ancestor's magical skills, did you?"

"I possess my own skills," she said proudly.

"You can cast spells?"

"Hefty-duty ones."

He laughed; he couldn't help it.

She grew annoyed. "Foolish mortal."

He stood with a wobble. "Come on, witch, let's float into the living room together."

Tempest attempted to stand. "I'll float; *you*, foolish mortal, are reduced to walking."

She tilted precariously but Michael placed a firm hand on her. "Steady there."

"I can float on my own," she insisted as he came around by her, his arm circling her waist.

"But I can't." He smiled and her heart melted.

Her fingers went to the scars on his face. "These marks can't hide your beauty."

He looked into her pale-green eyes and they told him much too much. He was no fool—he knew when a woman wanted him, and right now Tempest had that look. And what made the situation even more difficult was that she spoke with sincerity. She actually thought him beautiful, perhaps not on a physical level but somewhere in him she saw his beauty. Her words touched him deeply.

"Kiss me," she said with a soft demand.

"I don't think that's a good idea right now," he said, attempting to balance her and himself as he directed them toward the living room.

She was most insistent. "I want you to kiss me."

He got her into the living room near the couch. "Later."

"Now," she persisted.

"Later," he argued gently.

"Right now!"

She turned so fast in his arms that he lost his balance, and frantically he reached out for her, afraid she would fall. She did the same with him and in a tumble of arms, legs and a complete loss of balance, they dropped down onto the couch.

Seven

~

"I behaved foolishly," Tempest said as she sipped her soup.

Michael smiled as he cut the ham and cheese sandwiches in half. He had heated the leftover soup, found the makings for the ham sandwiches and threw together a salad for supper, which they were presently enjoying.

"You behaved like anyone who is unaccustomed to drinking hard liquor."

"Poorly," she said with a shake of her head.

"Uninhibited," he corrected softly.

She lowered her face, attempting to hide her blush and the memories of her outrageous actions. She had all but attacked him, demanding he kiss her, and when he had fallen on top of her she had taken advantage of the moment, completely losing her senses and kissing him with a passion she had thought long since died.

"I apologize for my—"

"It's been a long time since you've kissed a man with that kind of passion, hasn't it?" he asked, not that he required an answer. He could tell by the way her hands had anxiously grabbed at him, the way her lips had met his with such a ferocious hunger, and the way her body had pressed against him as though she couldn't get close enough, couldn't feel enough of him. That type of intense hunger came either from love or a length of abstinence. Since she didn't know him long enough to be in love with him, it could only be abstinence that caused her need.

Her aggressiveness had heightened his own desire, no matter the reason for it, and his hands, mouth and body had become as eager as hers. But reality had intruded all too soon, and he had known that there was no way he would take advantage of her inebriated state. If they were to make love, and he hoped they would do so when she was fully aware of her actions and the consequences. So, like a gentlemen, he had disengaged their tangled limbs, though she didn't help his gallant efforts any, tucked a blanket around her and quickly exited the room.

He had not wanted to be lead into temptation, and one more look at her pouting lips would have sent him over the edge.

She broke the brief silence with an answer. "Yes, it has been a long time for me."

"Want to talk about it?" he asked, his dark eyes meeting hers to show that he actually cared.

"There's not much to talk about. I fell in love hard and fast, and it didn't work out."

He wanted to know more. "Why didn't it work out?"

The answer came easily. "He wasn't who I thought he was."

"He deceived you?"

She thought a moment. "He deceived himself. What he searched so hard for was in front of him, yet he was too blind to see it."

"And yet the memory of him lingers."

"As I said, I fell hard and fast."

"Which blinded you to his true nature."

"You're right," she agreed. "But love has a way of making the most intelligent person react stupidly. Haven't *you* ever been in love?"

"Only when it was convenient. I didn't have a lifestyle conductive to marriage and family, and I didn't exactly frequent places where I could meet Miss Right. Usually she was Miss Wrong, and it was a quick roll in the hay, and if I wasn't careful it was a quick roll of my money. Then there were the women who wanted marriage to American citizens so they could get into the United States."

"Didn't you ever take leave for yourself?"

He shrugged, reaching for another sandwich. "Once I did, I

spent a couple of months in my old hometown. I met a few
women, but every time they discovered that I was a simple
seaman they lost interest immediately. Most seemed to be
looking for the perfect guy. Good job, good money, good
spender. They wanted it all. Somehow to me they just didn't
give a damn about love. Then there were the women who had
it all and were only interested in a good night of sex, since
Mr. Perfect wasn't interesting enough in bed. But a rough seaman? He was a man of their fantasies."

Tempest suddenly felt guilty. "I'm sorry for my foolish actions, but I can honestly say I wasn't after a kiss because of
fantasies. I simply ached for you to kiss me."

He looked at her, his dark eyes compelling and trustworthy.
"I know, Tempest, and you don't know how good you made
me feel."

She reached her hand across to his, and he took it. "I like
when you kiss me."

"That's a dangerous admission, woman; it might just force
me to kiss you more often."

She smiled and threaded her fingers with his. "I'd like that."

He shook his head slowly. "Your honesty astonishes me."

"Why shouldn't I tell you that I like your kisses?"

He tightened their locked fingers. "Because I'll keep kissing
you, and kisses can lead to intimate touches, and . . ." He let
his words trail off, leaving her to imagine.

She didn't hesitate or grow flustered; she answered with her
usual honesty. "And to make love if we so choose."

"Are you leading me into temptation, Tempest, or casting a
spell over me?" he asked with a teasing smile.

"A spell can't force you to do something you don't want to
do."

"And if I want?"

"It can then expedite the desire," she informed him with her
own playful smile.

He released her hand so they both could return to their meal.
"Can you teach me about spells?"

His question both surprised and disturbed her. She had to
examine his past, his distant past, before she could take such
a dangerous chance. "Do you believe in witchcraft, Michael?"

"The book stirred my interest," he admitted.

"Then I suggest you learn more about it, and then we'll
discuss spells."

"What was your ancestor's name?" he asked.

She looked at him as if she didn't understand.

"The witch," he clarified.

She smiled. "Guess."

He laughed. "That's easy. Tempest. You're named after her?"

"I bear her name."

"Any particular reason why she was named Tempest?"

Her wide smile told him all he needed to know.

"Had a temper, did she?"

"At times her temper flared."

"A powerful witch with a soaring temper. She must have been a sight to behold," he said.

"I'm told she's had her moments."

"Tell me, Tempest," he asked curiously, "in the book I was reading it made mention of witches having second sight and of those who could fly. Exactly what powers does a witch possess?"

Tempest attempted to pour herself a cup of tea from the teapot on the table, but Michael beat her to it. He had warned her that he would take care of the meal and dishes this evening and that she wasn't to lift a finger, especially her wounded finger.

"You're too independent for your own good," he said with a smile and a shake of his head. "Now about my question."

Tempest relaxed in her chair, teacup in hand. "Not all witches are the same. Some are far more powerful than others. Most possess second sight to some degree or another. Most can cast spells, some more potent than others. The degree of power depends on the individual witch."

"How about flying powers? If someone thought that a witch could fly, then don't you think that somewhere in history there would be a basis in fact for that accusation?"

"Imagination."

Michael pushed his bowl and plate aside and leaned his arms on the table, intent on finding answers. "But in our imagination also lies the truth, so then couldn't it be possible that someone somewhere saw a person floating in midair? Or do witches— or anyone, for that matter—possess the power to transport their spirit or energy, if not their body?"

"You ask questions that have been continually examined

and debated over the years. And you will find a group of believers in one corner and debunkers in another."

"Do you believe that your ancestor possessed such powers?"

Tempest hesitated, uncertain how to answer. She chose her words wisely. "I believe she possessed a wisdom and understanding far beyond that of an ordinary soul."

"Is that what witchcraft is, then? An awareness that no one else possesses?"

She shook her head. "I think everyone possesses the awareness, but few nourish it."

"So if I nourished it, I could be a witch like your ancestor?"

Fear rose to tingle her flesh. If he nourished awareness, and he was who she thought he might be, then the spell would spin forward and seek a conclusion. "If your belief was strong enough, I imagine you could."

"Interesting idea," he said almost to himself. "You don't mind if I make use of your vast selection of books?"

"Please, feel free," she offered.

He poured her another cup of tea. "Relax and enjoy. I'll do the dishes."

"I should help," she protested.

His solid "No" kept her in her seat.

They shared conversation while he worked, common everyday chatter, and the remainder of the evening they spent in the sitting room, each engrossed in a book. Late evening found them saying good night upstairs, followed by a gentle kiss on the cheek and a whispered kiss across the lips.

Bear had made it a habit of sleeping in Michael's room, in his bed, curled up against him. He had to admit that he didn't mind the animal sharing his bunk. He was getting used to his presence and looked forward to his soft fur cuddled against him.

With an arm around Bear, his sleepy eyes drifted as they always did to the symbols on the wall. They intrigued him and now that he knew what they were he planned to read up on them and learn exactly what the symbols meant.

He fell asleep, mumbling words that were foreign to him.

He watched her every move from a distance and smiled. She was beautiful, more beautiful than he could ever have imagined. And her power radiated in a soft light around her. People were drawn to her light and he easily understood why. As soon as they entered the glowing sphere around her they were bathed in her love and hope.

Her skills had to be tremendous and for a moment he wondered if his own power, though substantial, was enough to match hers. But then what would it matter—once he joined with her their powers would unite, and he would not need to concern himself with trivial worries.

He continued to study her and her surroundings. She appeared a simple peasant woman at market, a basket partially filled with her arm. She took time to stop and chat with other villagers and anyone who spoke with her walked away with a smile. Children ran up to her, and she was patient with their grabbing hands and curious stares. She even stopped by an old, injured dog sprawled out in the dirt. She spoke softly to the animal, patting its head, and with the simple touch of her hand and a whispered spell, she healed its leg. The grateful dog licked her face until she laughed, a charming sound that reminded him of a favorite melody. The dog followed her, and he was certain she had gained herself a trusty companion.

She brushed her hair back from her face, the flaming color bright in the summer sun. She approached a market stall overflowing with vegetables and flowers. Her eyes sparkled, and she made her selections. The old portly man helping her beamed broadly, doing all he could to please her, and as she finished her purchases he placed a long-stemmed red rose in her basket, a gift from him.

She offered him a pat to his arm and a whispered blessing the man didn't hear though instantly felt, for his smile widened. She walked past the market stalls, coming toward him where he stood beneath a large old tree. She looked eager to touch the rose, and she did, pricking her finger on a thorn. She smiled at the painful stab and was about to touch her injured finger to her lips when he stepped forward.

"Allow me," he said to her and took her hand, bringing her finger to his lips and before she could protest he kissed her bleeding finger. He felt her body tingle and sensed her uncertainty, and he felt her erect a protective barrier around herself. He smiled and knew the hunt had begun.

"Tempest!" Michael woke with a shout, startling Bear, who hissed his disapproval over being disturbed.

He fought the urge to jump out of bed, as fast as his broken ankle would allow, and go check on Tempest. He feared for her safety, but why? Recalling bits and pieces of his dream made him think that her injury this evening was the cause of his strange dream. And his odd choice of reading material had helped to transport him to a different time period. Yet he couldn't shake his concern for Tempest.

With a damn, a hell and a few other choice oaths, he got out of bed, Bear not at all interested in where he was going. The cat chose to move to the warm pillow and curl itself up in a ball to sleep.

Michael slipped on his jeans, though he left the top button open. He only planned to take a quick peek in her room to make certain that she was safe and sound, then it was back to bed and hopefully no more odd dreams for the night.

He walked down the hall quietly, trying not to make a sound, though it wasn't an easy task with his cumbersome cast. He found her door ajar and eased it open, slipping soundlessly into her room. A small entrance area greeted him with an archway leading to the bedroom itself. The archway bore similar symbols to those in his room, and he grew all the more fascinated with them. His eyes remained steady on the symbols until he finally walked beneath the archway and into her room.

Shadows and light danced around her room from the flickering flames of the cornerstone fireplace. She lay asleep in her large bed, her thick, soft, blue quilt covering her though her one arm peeked out. He approached slowly and wasn't surprised to see the familiar symbols from his room carved in her headboard. He walked around to the side of the bed where she was turned on her side and looked to see her eyes closed and her breathing even.

She was safe and sound and relief washed over him. He turned to leave, and his eyes caught sight of her bandaged finger. He leaned over her and ran his own finger gently over the white bandage. "I wish you well," he whispered and leaned further down to kiss her cheek tenderly.

"Marcus," she whispered, her warm breath fanning his face.

A chill ran down his spine and he stiffened. She had loved another and had never forgotten that love. He straightened and left the room, annoyed by his own agitation. He climbed back in his own bed, talking to himself.

Bear once again hissed his disapproval at being disturbed

and cuddled against him when he finally settled down.

"Envious?" he asked himself. He had long ago given up on finding good, solid love with a woman. And yet perhaps he had always hoped. Hoped that one day he would find a special love, a forever love, a love that transcended time and reality and would exist for all eternity.

"You're crazy." He laughed at himself. His fantasies were foolish and impossible. Such a love didn't exist, never had and never would. He would be lucky if he found a brief love that was good and satisfying, never mind one that defied time.

But had Tempest? She couldn't seem to forget this man she once loved. He lingered in her mind and heart. And her dreams.

He ran his hand over his face and let out a hefty sigh. "I'm crazy. Definitely crazy."

And with a promise to himself to keep a level head, he drifted off to sleep.

By the end of a week and a half Michael realized his promise wasn't worth a hill of beans. There was no way, absolutely no way the two of them could deny the attraction they felt toward each other, though they tried damn hard enough.

And the more they tried the more they found themselves drawing closer and closer together. It was easy, especially in the kitchen when he helped her. They always managed to brush up against each other, place a hand on the other, brush cheeks and simply smile. Though the smile wasn't a simple one. It was suggestive and often much too seductive.

Then there were the conversations they shared. They seemed to find interest in any and all subjects. It was almost as if they had known each other forever, a strange yet exciting thought, and Michael looked forward to each day he spent with Tempest.

To Michael's surprise, the weather was beginning to change. The days grew slightly warmer and the snow began to melt. Not that the road appeared driveable, since he still couldn't determine where the roads were, but the mounds of snow grew smaller, and he knew it wouldn't be long before the first bud of spring peeked its head out of the ground. And the closer spring came, the closer he came to having his cast removed and the closer he came to his time here with Tempest coming to an end.

Then there were the strange dreams that continued to haunt his nights. He wondered who the mysterious man in his dreams was. He seemed almost familiar, and there was a power about him that fascinated Michael. Though he did think that his continuous dreams could possibly be caused by his growing interest in witchcraft.

He had been reading all the material he could on the subject, and the more he read the more his interest grew. Tempest had obliged him in his quest to learn more about her ancestor. She would answer his questions as best she could, though he always felt that she held something back, some small bit of information he felt would be worth knowing. Why, he couldn't say. He only knew that she kept something from him, and he wanted to find out her secret.

While her finger healed he had taken over the kitchen duties, and when the stitches were finally removed, leaving barely a trace of a scar, to his surprise, he remained helping in the kitchen. Tempest was a good and patient teacher in more ways than one.

One subject he persisted in learning more about was the man she had loved, but she usually found a way around the questions, not quite avoiding them, but not providing an answer.

He had decided that the direct approach was the best, especially since he wasn't a patient man. When he wanted to know something, he wanted to know it immediately. And he had waited long enough; he wanted some clear, defined answers. Not that it was really any of his business, but—he wanted answers anyway.

They were enjoying hot chocolate and oatmeal apple cookies in the living room one day when he asked, "Who is Marcus?"

Eight

Tempest was relieved that she had set her mug of hot chocolate on the end table only a moment before Michael asked his startling question. She appeared calm and indifferent to his query, though inside she quivered with nervous tension. "Marcus?" she repeated, leaving it up to him to explain where he had learned the name since she didn't recalling mentioning it to him.

"You mumbled it in your sleep."

She could very well have done that, but whatever was he doing in her bedroom? she wondered.

He seemed to read her thoughts, or he understood how odd his explanation sounded. "I don't make it a habit of visiting your bedroom. The night you injured your finger I felt the need to check on you, and you whispered the name. Was he the relationship that didn't work out?"

Tempest nodded, but offered no more information.

He looked at her. She appealed to all the senses. She made a stunning sight in a red turtleneck ankle-length knit dress, her fiery hair falling down around her shoulders in a stream of waves, and her red, sock-covered feet peeked out from under the hem. She smelled like freshly cut roses and her voice sounded as soft as the delicate petals. Her lips looked ripe for tasting and he damn well itched to touch her. Yup, all the senses—sight, smell, sound, taste, touch—she certainly had them all covered.

He sipped at the chocolate, staring at her over the rim of the mug, warning himself that now was not the time to be thinking of what she wore beneath that red dress. With much effort and his thoughts elsewhere, he asked, "The man's clothes in my room, do they belong to this Marcus?"

Since she had purposely produced them for him, she could answer honestly, "No."

"Brief with your responses, aren't you?"

"There's nothing more to add."

"Nothing?" he repeated. "Or you just don't want to talk about him?"

"I don't wish to discuss him," she said candidly. "But I get the feeling that doesn't matter to you."

He continued his questions, confirming her remark. "You said they belonged to a special friend."

"I have many friends, and several who are special to me. Don't you?"

"No," he said, discarding his empty mug to the coffee table. "In my profession you don't stay long enough in one port to make long-lasting friends. I had many acquaintances, but no one I could call a true friend." He realized she had once again successfully maneuvered the conversation away from herself, but not for long. "Was this Marcus a true friend?"

"I had thought so, but . . ." Her words drifted off.

"Showed his true colors after a while?"

Tempest recalled the darkness that had always surrounded Marcus. "I knew his true colors; I simply chose to ignore them."

He continued, needing to know more. "Blind to his faults?"

Her smile was sad. "Thinking, hoping I could change him."

Michael shook his head. "You can't change anyone; they can only change themselves."

She laughed softly and he was reminded of a light, heartfelt melody. "A fact I often remind others about."

"But never took it to heart yourself?"

"Unfortunately, no."

Curiosity continued to wage war on him. "Yet the relationship ended."

"I opened my eyes and—" She stopped abruptly, recalling

the dreadful feeling of closing her heart off to him.

Michael waited for her to finish, and when she hadn't decided that perhaps he had intruded enough for one evening. While she maintained a calm composure he could have sworn he sensed her sorrow, and that troubled him. He didn't wish to cause her unhappiness and evidently the memories had done just that.

He was about to change the subject when she did. "In all your travels, what place did you like the best?"

His answer came easily. "Here in Scotland. I felt a strange affinity with the land. It was almost as if I had returned home. The emotion was so strong, I had difficulty leaving, and I swore to myself that I would return someday to stay."

"So your plans are?"

"To move around the country until I find where I want to plant myself. What's your favorite place?"

She beamed with pride. "Scotland, of course. It has always been and always will be my home."

He was about to ask about her family when a cramp hit his toes that stuck out from the cast, and he raised his voice with a "damn."

Tempest saw his toes cramp and immediately took action. She went to her knees beside him on the couch. Her slim fingers carefully massaged his curled toes, attempting to coax the painful cramp out of them. A little magic helped, and within no time his toes relaxed and returned to normal.

Michael breathed in her rose-scented skin and touched his hand to her hair. The silky strands felt like silk, and he ran his fingers through them while he whispered, "Thank you."

She turned to look at him and he saw the flicker of passion, brief but bright, and he felt it stir in himself.

He patted the spot beside him. "Come up here by me. I want to kiss you."

She smiled. "I'd like that."

She joined him on the couch, cuddling next to him. He ran his hand around to the back of her neck and drew her mouth to his with an eagerness she matched. It was a kiss packed with a passion that had lain dormant far too long. And if they both were not careful it would spill over and demand more satisfaction, but for the moment they enjoyed themselves, impatiently tasting each other.

With a bittersweet reluctance they ended it, their lips returning for one last taste, one last touch until Tempest finally laid her head on his chest and sighed softly.

"That good, huh?"

She chuckled and patted his chest, impressed by the feel of muscles beneath his navy blue sweatshirt. "Exceptional."

He smiled, boyishly pleased by her praise, and slipped his arm around her to hold her close. She felt good nestled against him, as though she belonged there, as though it was a familiar feeling.

"It's strange," he said, "but this place and you feel so familiar to me."

His words concerned her and she knew she had to take heed and be careful. "We both offer comfort—perhaps a reminder of your mother and home."

"No," he said. "I don't believe so. At first I thought that possible, but it's different. Actually, so much more familiar and comforting than what I felt as a child, as strange as that may seem." He shrugged at his own remark. "Maybe another lifetime."

"You believe in past lives?"

"Never gave it a lot of thought, but part of it makes sense, so who knows what's true and what's not? Maybe I lived another life here in Scotland and that's why I'm so drawn to the place, and stranger still, perhaps we shared a life together here."

She lifted her head to look at him, and asked a question that she hoped would help solve her dilemma. "A good life, you think?"

He smiled, about to answer, when suddenly he frowned and shook his head. "Oddly enough, I don't think it was. Maybe we're back to give it another shot."

She rested her head back on his chest and didn't let him see her concern. "Hopefully this time will prove different."

His arm tightened around her. "We'll see that it does."

A short time later, Michael made his way to the sitting room to search for another book to take upstairs to bed to read. Tempest cleaned up the few dishes and returned to the living room to sit in the silence and contemplate.

Coincidence was part of the mortal world but not part of magic. Witches were aware and therefore understood the significance of signs, whether they warned or promised. Presently, many signs warned that she take cautious steps with Michael. While there were not enough warnings to portend results, there were enough to take notice and question more. And while she questioned, she could not take the chance of allowing their budding relationship to go any further. Intimacy was out of the question, though it was on her mind too often.

She liked Michael. There was so much more to him then he would allow people to see, and yet to her he was an open book, for her to read and study and learn about, and she enjoyed every interesting page. She only hoped the ending wouldn't disappoint her.

Michael returned to the living room, filled with excitement. "I found a book that pertains to those symbols in my room. Now I'll finally be able to find out what they say."

"Easier said than done," she said with an amused smile.

"Why?" His excitement faded.

"The meaning of ogam and rune symbols are debatable. No one actually knows for certain their true origin. And, of course, through the centuries various tribes changed their meaning to suit their existence. You would need to know who scripted the symbols and in what system they were taught." She hoped to discourage him for just a while longer, just long enough for her to be certain, to be safe.

"Tempest scripted them, didn't she?"

"It is believed so."

"Well, if not her, then who?" He seemed puzzled, as though he shouldn't even question the fact, and he shook his head. "No, it had to be Tempest. Did she keep a diary or journal?" he asked with a sudden excitement.

"Most witches didn't keep written accounts. The written word could be used against them, so they kept their knowledge safely tucked in their minds, trusting a rare few friends with their secrets."

"Will you tell me about Tempest, at least all you know?"

It wouldn't hurt to tell him a few tales, she thought, and besides, she rarely got to reminisce, only with a chosen few. "I think I could recall a few tales."

He yawned as he spoke. "Good. Tell me one."

"You're tired."

"Not too tired to listen," he insisted.

At that moment Bear made it known that he was ready for bed. He sat halfway up the staircase, meowing loudly while directing his intentions toward Michael.

"I think Bear disagrees with you," she said with a laugh.

Michael's laughter joined hers. "He seems to have attached himself to me."

"I'm impressed. He has never taken well to strangers."

Michael waved to Bear. "We're certainly pals now."

Bear agreed with a strong meow and planted himself on the step to wait.

Michael turned a smug smile on her. "Looks like he wants to hear a tale, too."

"A short one," she said, and silently berated Bear for being a traitor.

Michael moved to sit beside her on the couch, his arm going to rest behind her. "I'll take what I can get."

Tempest shared a memory she long enjoyed recalling. "This tale is before the 'burning times,' when witches were respected and their skills sought after. Tempest was kin to nature. She understood its unpredictability and its temper. And she advised the villagers accordingly."

"The villagers trusted witches?"

"You say that as if they were crazy."

He shrugged. "Spells, chants and charms can't do much."

"For the nonbeliever."

"There you go," he said, amused. "If you don't believe it doesn't work for you, so where, then, is the magic?"

"Within."

He grinned and shook his head. "I've heard that enough times. Search inward and you'll find your true self. What you usually find is more confusion. And, besides, how do you know when you do find yourself? Does a bell go off? Does someone tap you on your shoulder and say, 'Hey, pal, you've got it'?"

Tempest felt his doubt, and yet also sensed his need to believe. It lay dormant within him, and when it did finally spark to life, she wondered what the consequences would be.

"Are you searching, Michael?"

"Isn't everyone? Don't you think most everyone wonders over the real secret of life—even witches?"

Tempest smiled, recalling how many times her students

would ask her that very question, and her answer was always the same. *Open your eyes: it's right there before you.* Few understood and continued their search.

She provided him with the simplest answer. "Wise witches know the secret."

"Was Tempest a wise witch?"

"I would say she knew the secret."

"I wish I did," he said rather sadly. "And crazy as it sounds, I wish that I had the opportunity to know Tempest. Whether witches exist or not, she sounded like a remarkable woman."

"The basic belief of the Craft has existed in one fashion or another since time began. It is a simple belief, with its basis in nature. When studied and understood, secrets are then revealed, but only to those who possess the strongest belief. All power comes from within, Michael. No one can give it to you, and no one can rob you of it. It is yours to do with as you choose."

"That's the kicker—free choice."

She laughed. "Not an easy concept to be able to do exactly as you choose, is it?"

He shook his head in sad disgust. "You never make the right choice."

"Don't you? Perhaps you do and don't realize it."

He looked at her strangely and ran the back of his finger slowly down her cheek. "I bet you have some of your ancestor's best qualities in you."

He leaned closer and placed a gentle, loving kiss on her lips. The tenderness of it sent tingles down her body. Her own hand moved to his face, her fingers softly tracing the scars near his eye.

"Don't ask," he whispered. "You don't want to know."

She was tempted, for a brief moment, to intrude and discover the answer for herself, but intrusion was forbidden, and she would not break such an important rule. Healing, however, was encouraged. She touched her warm, faint wet lips to his scar and along with it went a silent spell.

He shivered from the sensation of her kiss, and his hand moved to her waist, his fingers aching for intimacy. His thumb drifted dangerously close to her full breast and while she was not overly large she certainly would spill over in his hand, and damned if he didn't want just that. But he remained a gentleman—not that he wanted to, but he felt it necessary. After all, she had been good to him, caring and generous. It wouldn't be polite to grab a feel, but then he wasn't looking to grab. He was looking for more, and suddenly the thought frightened him. How much did he really want from Tempest?

His silent question placed a distance between them, and he reluctantly drew away from her, needing to give his disturbing query complete thought.

"I think now would be a good time to tell me that tale."

She seemed confused herself, slowly shaking her head to clear it.

"Your ancestor," he clarified.

She recalled the tale she wished to tell him, and began. "As I mentioned, Tempest was akin with nature."

"She could tell when there was a storm brewing and such?"

Tempest spoke with the patience of a wise teacher. "That and more. The local villagers sought her help one day when one of the young boys failed to return from the nearby forest. His friends had explained that he just disappeared, vanished. One minute he was there and the next minute he was gone. They blamed his mysterious abduction on the forest fairies, which was utter nonsense."

"Why is that?" Michael asked.

"Forest fairies protect the forest from intruders and if they came upon a lost boy they would make certain he was promptly returned to his own kind."

"Okay," he said with a sigh. "Now we not only have witches, we have fairies as well."

"Only if you believe," she reminded him.

"So if I don't believe, I don't get to see the fairies?"

"You got it," she said with a grin.

"I'll remember that the next time I'm lost in the forest," he said with a trace of a smile. "So the villagers wanted Tempest to find the boy?"

She nodded. "They asked her to intercede with the fairies and arrange the boy's return."

"But the fairies didn't have him?"

Tempest shook her head. "No, they didn't. His friends had played a trick on him and hid away from him to frighten him, only they became separated and couldn't find the boy afterwards, and they were too frightened to admit the truth to their parents."

"Typical kids."

"The problem was that it was growing late and darkness would soon descend over the forest, making it impossible for anyone to find the boy."

"Except Tempest," Michael said with a certainty and pride that surprised her.

"That's where being close with nature helps."

"How? Signs can only be read if seen, and at night in the forest it's pitch black. How could she possibly find him?"

"She simply asked."

"Asked who?"

"The trees, the wind, the plants, the animals."

Michael looked a bit stunned. "You mean she could speak to them all?"

"As I said, she was akin with nature. She understood their ways and in turn they understood her. When she entered the forest at dusk she simply requested that she be directed to the lost child. And her request was granted. She was taken directly to the boy who sat huddled and crying against a broken stump."

"Was she able to get him home before dark?"

"No, darkness fell around them but Tempest asked an owl to guide them home."

"And the animal obliged?"

"Why wouldn't he? He knew Tempest meant him no harm and that if he should ever require help she would gladly give it."

"So the boy was safely returned to his parents?"

She nodded, though she wore no smile.

"What happened?"

Her answer was filled with sadness. "It was stories similar to that one that caused many innocent people to be burned for practicing the Craft. When young children vanished, especially in the forest, witches were blamed for the abductions. Yet the innocent were punished."

Michael spoke with a certainty that disturbed her. "Tempest was never punished. She was much too wise."

"You sound as if you knew her."

"I feel that I did." He shook his head. "Crazy, but she feels so familiar to me."

Bear meowed, alerting them that he had waited patiently long enough. It was now bedtime.

"My bedmate summons me," he said with a laugh and stood, reaching his hand out to Tempest. "Coming up?"

She shook her head. "I think I'll have a cup of tea before I retire."

His hand moved to his side and he nodded. "Good night then."

She looked up at him as if words waited anxiously on her lips.

He thought she would say something, and when no response came he leaned down over her, bracing his hands on the back of the couch along both sides of her head and kissed her.

It was a forceful kiss that warned he wanted more, much more, and not just intimacy. When he finished, he simply walked out of the room and up the steps, Bear at his heels.

Nine

~

Michael was in no mood to read by the time he got into bed. Thoughts cluttered his mind and disturbed him. In a little less than four weeks' time his cast would come off, and after making the few repairs to Tempest's house he would be on his way. The thought depressed him. For the first time in a very long time he felt comfortable, content as if he had come home, or had finally found a home.

He had never known a woman like Tempest. She gave without thought of receiving, and she cared with a sincerity that was hard to comprehend. And she reached out and touched with a touch he could have sworn healed. She was forever placing her hand to his arm, his face, his back, his chest, and he looked forward to every precious touch.

As of late he even found himself touching her without thought to what he was doing. He would simply find his hand on her arm or around her waist or stroking her cheek. She never pulled away from him; actually she seemed to welcome him, moving closer to rest against him. He liked this slow process of becoming familiar with her, though lately thoughts of intimacies had intruded all too often. He found himself considering what it would be like to undress her, intimately stroke her and make love to her. Strangely enough, he had the feeling her thoughts mirrored his own, and it was only a matter of time before they both acted upon their emotions.

Then there was this obsession with her ancestor. Why did the woman fascinate him? Why did he feel it was so necessary to find out about her? And why this sudden and inexplicable interest in witchcraft?

He had a feeling his bizarre dreams had something to do with it. He had considered discussing them with Tempest but he felt foolish. It was as though he was watching a series of events unfold, and the more he watched the more interested he became in the Craft. He couldn't seem to get enough information; he wanted more and more.

What disturbed him the most was that the dreams seemed to take on a darker side of the Craft. The recurring character seemed powerfully frightening and intent on having his way, especially with the woman who bore a remarkable resemblance to Tempest. Maybe that was why he was so reluctant to discuss the matter with her. His fantasies were turning dark, and he couldn't control them and at times he didn't want to. At times he enjoyed watching that dark character and feeling his power radiate through his sleeping body so that when the woke he felt somehow more alive than he had ever felt in his entire life.

"Crazy," he whispered to himself and placed his arm over his eyes, willing himself to go to sleep—and dream.

They sat by a stream, he clothed in dark garments, she in light. His dark hair hung down over his chest, and his dark eyes rested intently on her stunning face. His hand reached out to take hers but she drew away from him.

"You fear me?" he asked, though he knew the answer. He knew everything about her—her thoughts, her hopes, her desires, and that was the problem. She desired him.

"Don't play your games with me. You know what I feel."

"Then why do you fight it?"

"You want something from me that I cannot give."

His hand moved to rest lightly on her knee. "The choice is yours, I will not force you to submit to me."

"You couldn't."

He laughed and a chill ran over her. "You underestimate my powers."

"No," she said softly. "You underestimate mine."

He moved too fast for her to slip out of his reach. His hand grabbed hers firmly, but his dark eyes actually held her captive. "Join with me. Our powers combined could never be matched or challenged."

"You speak of joining for the sole purpose of power. What about love?"

"If love is what you wish, I will give it to you."

"Where does this love come from? Out of necessity? Or your heart?"

"I offer you unimaginable power, a far greater gift than love," he said with a hint of anger.

"You don't understand," she said sadly.

He laughed, and she braced herself for the chill that raced over her. "I understand all too well. You believe that love is power."

She touched his face, a face so handsome it could steal breaths and break hearts.

He rubbed his cheek against the palm of her hand. "I can feel your powerful energy race through me, and I want to taste it, savor it, drink deeply of it, and I want you to do the same with mine."

"But your energy would not be as strong as mine."

He gripped both her hands, and she winced. He softened his touch. "You speak foolishly."

"I speak with wisdom. My power comes from love. Where does yours come from?"

He released her and cupped her chin. "If you wish love, I will give it to you."

"You cannot give what you do not understand."

He smiled and it tingled her flesh. "Then make me understand, teach me about the power of love and perhaps then you will not deny our joining."

She attempted to protest and he stilled her words with a brief kiss. "You know it is inevitable. We will join."

"We will join. We will join. We will join."

Tempest stood at the bedroom door, listening to Michael repeat the words over and over and over, and tears came to her eyes. Had the spell been set in motion? Had he finally returned to settle their fate? She still couldn't be certain, though it seemed a strong possibility. And she was terribly attracted to him. She felt so comfortable with him and his touch felt familiar and his kisses drugged her senses, just as Marcus's had done so many years ago.

She quietly shut the door as she stepped back into the hall. She had to approach this situation with the utmost care. Just as she had set fate into motion when she joined with Marcus, she would do the same again if she joined with Michael.

She eagerly sought her bed and sleep, wanting to escape her haunting thoughts, if only for one night.

Michael woke early from a troubled sleep. He slipped on his jeans and grabbed for a sweatshirt from the drawer. He was surprised to find he had pulled on the red sweatshirt that didn't belong to him. He shrugged, not caring at the moment, and saw to getting on his socks. With the aid of the crutch which he had mastered near perfectly, he hobbled out of his room, intent on making himself a strong cup of coffee.

It was barely past dawn, and the rooms still hovered in near-darkness. He took quiet and careful steps so as not to wake Tempest. But as he approached the stairs, and her bedroom door that stood slightly ajar, he heard her soft cries.

She sounded upset, frightened, and he silently cursed whatever dream tormented her as he hurried into her bedroom.

Her blanket lay twisted down around her waist and legs and she struggled against it as if someone held her down. Her hair raged in glorious flames around her stunningly beautiful face and her troubled cries continued to spill from her trembling lips. He went to her side, resting the crutch against the headboard. He sat down beside her and gently gathered her in his arms.

She instantly responded, wrapping frantic arms around him and burying her face in his chest. He soothed her with slow, tender strokes up and down her back. He rested his chin on the top of her head and spoke softly, insisting that she was safe with him and that he would allow no one to harm her.

Her body trembled against his, and she attempted to move as close as possible to him. If he hadn't been braced against the wooden headboard she would have sent him toppling. Realizing she would not settle down until feeling completely safe he pulled her up and onto his lap where she cuddled herself contentedly against him.

He pressed comforting kisses to her forehead, stroked her slim neck and rested his one hand beneath her warm breast and continued reassuring her with his soft words yet firm promise that no one would harm her.

She gradually calmed and relaxed in his arms, falling into a peaceful slumber.

Damn, why did he have to feel so content like this with her wrapped safely in his embrace? A relationship with her just wasn't possible. A brief affair?

He shook his head. He wanted more.

Hell, he hadn't even made love to her yet, and he wanted more. Where did that insane feeling come from?

Need?

Did he need to love? To find something solid and trusting in his life? When he ran away at sixteen he thought one day he would stop. But he woke up at thirty-six and found he was still running. Why?

No answer came to him. He could make no sense of his life. It remained empty, devoid of any true emotions, hopes or dreams. It was as if he wandered the world searching for an answer to his existence.

Would he find his answers here in Scotland, or was it Tempest who would help him find the answers?

He sighed quietly and rested his head back. He didn't know what the next few weeks would bring. He only knew that he didn't look forward to his time with her coming to an end.

After making certain she slept peacefully, Michael tucked her safe and warm beneath the quilt and soundlessly left the room.

Tempest woke to the alluring scent of fresh coffee, eggs and bacon, and smiled, feeling more content than she had in a long time. She hurried to dress in a long purple knit skirt and a matching waist-length button-up purple sweater. She wore purple socks, minus shoes. She preferred her feet free from confinement and often went barefoot, though in the winter she wore socks to ward off the cold.

She twisted up her long reddish-gold hair and secured it to the back of her head with a gold clip as she eagerly made her way downstairs. The delicious scent was making her mouth water.

"Hungry?" Michael asked as she rushed into the kitchen.

She smiled as he turned away from the counter, coffeepot in hand, and she raced over to him, giving him a hug around his middle. "Starving," she said cheerfully and gave him a quick kiss on the lips before she abandoned him for the food on the kitchen table.

Her easygoing and undemanding nature never failed to startle him, and he found himself envious of her relaxed nature. He was always on guard, not trusting, waiting for the inevitable disappointment.

They talked, teased and laughed throughout the meal, and Tempest insisted that since he did the cooking it was only fair that she do the cleanup. He didn't argue with her. He liked watching her. She had a graceful yet sexy way she moved, though it was more like an orchestrated waltz. She swayed, dipped and bent in such provocative movements that he could have sworn she was dancing to entice him.

They both agreed there was work to be done in the greenhouse, but they could have agreed on any task as long as it was done together. A closeness had developed between them over the last few days that was hard to explain, and Michael didn't even want to attempt to try. He simply wanted to enjoy it.

They were about ready to make their way to the greenhouse, his arm around her waist and her contented smile fixed on him, when the doorbell sounded, startling them both.

Ten

Michael asked the obvious question. "How could anyone get through all that snow?"

Tempest could have kicked herself. She was so busy being content with Michael that her guard had slipped, allowing someone to approach her home without her knowledge. Of course, she knew who was at the door, but how to explain their visit to Michael?

Michael took a protective lead as they both went to the front door.

He was startled at the good-looking man who stood outside, elegantly tailored in solid black from his cashmere overcoat to his turtleneck and wool trousers. The stranger assessed him with an intensity that almost unnerved him, making him feel as if he had no business being in Tempest's house.

Michael suddenly wondered if this man was Tempest's special friend, but before he could comment a woman stepped around the man and Tempest stepped around Michael and the two quickly fell into each other's arms, happily chattering.

With the two women's endless chatter making introductions impossible, all four made their way into the living room, hanging coats in the hall closet along the way.

Michael was surprised at his own relief when he noticed that the woman was pregnant. She wore a matching gray knit skirt and oversized sweater that rested comfortably over her small, rounded stomach. They were obviously a couple, and on closer inspection he could see that the man was very much concerned with the woman's well-being and catered to her in the most loving manner.

"Michael," Tempest finally said, reaching out for his hand. "I want you to meet my sister Sarina and her husband Dagon Rasmus."

Michael offered a generous smile along with his hand to Dagon, and it was returned in the same manner, though he sensed that the brother-in-law was still taking stock of his character and reserving judgment until later.

Sarina, on the other hand, was much like her sister, though not in looks. She possessed a natural attractiveness, and her hair was dark where Tempest possessed a fiery beauty that set a man's heart to thundering. No, it was Tempest's easygoing nature that Sarina shared.

She took his hand, holding it with an affectionate friendliness as she spoke with him. "It is so nice to meet you, Michael. You're from the States, aren't you? Do you like Scotland? Do you plan to stay long? Whatever brought you here in the first place?"

Michael couldn't keep up with her questions, not because they ran into each other but because he wondered how she knew he was from the States when he hadn't opened his mouth, and he still wondered how they managed to make it through all that snow.

Dagon was just as curious as his wife and waited for his answers, but Tempest came to Michael's aid.

"Michael is exploring our fair land, though he requires a brief rest due to his injury."

Dagon and Sarina looked down at his cast-covered ankle, and before either could ask, he explained.

"An unfortunate accident, and Tempest was kind enough to offer me her home while I recover." His pause was brief before he asked, "Are the roads passable now?"

"We had no trouble getting here at all," Sarina said and sat on the chair to struggle with her boots.

Dagon went immediately to her side to assist her, and Michael couldn't help but notice that her black suede boots were barely touched by the inclement weather. For that matter, Dagon wasn't even wearing boots, and his expensive-looking leather shoes shined much too brightly for someone who supposedly had been outside in the snow. Something didn't seem right, but he chose not to pursue the strange matter. Tempest appeared pleased with her sister's visit, and he didn't want to put a damper on her happiness.

"Tea to warm you both," Tempest said as if confirming they were chilled from their extensive ride, and she reached her hand out to her sister. The two men followed the women, trailing behind their incessant chatter.

Tempest busied herself putting the kettle on and heating scones. Sarina set the table while Dagon and Michael sat at the table in silence.

The awkward pause allowed Michael time to actually feel the tension rise in the room, but why? Tempest obviously got along well with her sister, and Dagon and she had exchanged a sincere hug and kiss, so what was the problem?

Him?

He was the only outside interference in the family reunion, and he wondered if the couple actually objected to his presence here in her home. Did they think him a threat? And if so, why? Did they favor her *special friend* and think him an intruder?

Sarina broke the silence as she sat down beside her husband, their hands instantly locking together to rest on the table. "How do you like Scotland?"

"I feel at home here."

"And where is your home?" Dagon asked.

"New Jersey."

Dagon continued what sounded too much like an interrogation. "Returning anytime soon?"

"No, I like it here," Michael said with a curtness that caused the two sisters to exchange anxious glances.

It was obvious Dagon was protecting his sister-in-law, and Michael didn't care for his interference one bit. The man obviously was accustomed to having his own way. With his long, dark hair adding to his good looks and his arrogant manner, Michael didn't doubt that most didn't challenge his questions or authority. And while many might think his tall and lean build possessed insignificant physical strength, Michael had no doubt he could hold his own in a brawl—not that he intended to find out, but it was always wise to size up a possible opponent.

Tempest placed a platter of scones on the table and as she waved her hand toward the two men, Dagon rushed to say, "Don't you dare—"

Tempest waved her hand over them both. "Play nice, boys." She held her hand suspended over their immobile bodies to cast a playful look at her sister.

Sarina laughed softly. "You do know I will hear about this later."

"Your husband should have been more polite to my guest."

"He can be overprotective of those he cares for," Sarina said in defense of him.

"I appreciate Dagon's concern, but he is well aware that I am more than capable of taking care of myself."

"That doesn't mean he can't play the protective brother-in-law on occasion," Sarina said. "And besides, I have worried incessantly about you since last we talked, and my worry caused him to worry about me until he finally insisted we pay you an unexpected visit."

"I am pleased you are here."

"So am I, but we need to talk," Sarina insisted.

"We'll find time alone later; for now I must make certain these two get along, at least for a while." Before she lowered her suspended hand she directed the coffeepot with her finger to fill Michael's cup, and when the coffee was returned to rest in its holder, she reached for the teapot which had sat steeping with raspberry tea. She spoke as if in the middle of a conversation. "So Michael is going to do some repairs around the cottage for me when he has healed."

"That's generous of you. The place could use fixing here and there," Dagon said, reaching for a scone to put on his wife's plate, and then taking one for himself. "Though it does hold up quite nicely for its age."

"Old, is it?" Michael asked, noticing that his cup was filled with coffee. He hadn't remembered Tempest filling it, though she did know he preferred coffee in the morning and tea in the afternoon.

"The place has been in Tempest and Sarina's family for years," Dagon said.

Michael cast an appreciative eye around the now familiar

kitchen. "I like the place. It makes you feel welcome and comfortable."

Casual conversation continued until Sarina insisted that Tempest instruct her in making a batch of her soothing scented potpourri. Dagon knew his wife was skilled enough to produce a fragrant batch, and that what she really wanted was time alone with her sister.

Michael seemed to understand. "I'll clean up here."

"I'll help," Dagon offered.

"Appreciated," Michael said, and Tempest knew from the friendly exchange that they would survive being left on their own.

Tempest and Sarina went off to the greenhouse where together they worked on a batch of their favorite dried herbs and scented flowers while they talked.

Sarina didn't waste a minute, but got right to the root of her concern. "You know I am worried about my prediction, and now with meeting Michael, I am even more concerned. Michael could very well be Marcus returned."

Tempest nodded. "I know, I have thought about nothing else. And I must admit there is a strong possibility you are right." Tempest stopped crushing the dried leaves and sat with a sigh on the brightly painted stool, the sweet potent scent clinging to her fingers. "Oh, Sarina, I am ever so attracted to him. His kisses are like—" She stopped, abruptly shaking her head, realizing what she was about to say.

Sarina finished for her. "He kisses like Marcus, doesn't he?"

Tempest nodded, tears staining her green eyes. "I loved him so very much that at times I actually wish Michael was Marcus, and then I find myself liking Michael for who he is." Tempest turned a wide smile on her sister. "Michael is so caring, and he has survived many tragedies in his life and has grown stronger from them."

Sarina grew excited. "Then perhaps the spell is working."

Tempest's smile faded slowly. "There is much of the spell yet remaining for him to break. And he can still choose to return to who he once was."

"A powerful warlock," Sarina whispered.

"Marcus possessed remarkable powers."

"Evil powers," Sarina reminded.

"And yet he was never unkind or cruel to me."

"Why would he be?" Sarina asked. "He wanted something from you that you could only give willingly. Treating you cruelly would have served no purpose for him until he got what he wanted."

"He did get what he wanted, Sarina; I joined with him."

"I know, that one time, and then—"

Tempest shook her head. "We joined many times."

Sarina was speechless for several seconds before she asked, "How did you manage not to be devoured by his dark side?"

She laughed sadly. "He underestimated *my* powers."

"What happened?"

"He wanted a child, and I had taken precautions so that no child would be conceived of our joinings. When he discovered this he grew furious and we argued. I left, telling him our time together was over. He unleashed his fury on the innocent, and it was then that our powers were put to the ultimate test."

"And you cast the spell?"

Tempest wiped at the single tear that fell down her cheek. "I knew that I couldn't send him away forever. And memories of our time together led me to believe that he was not all evil and darkness, so I cast a spell that would give him another chance."

"Tell me it," Sarina said softly.

Tempest recited it in a mere whisper, though Sarina felt its power rush through her.

"With my love I send you away; for you to return on a future day; your life will be yours to create; choose wisely and repeat no mistakes; cherish life and hold it dear; fill no hearts and souls with fear; surround yourself with magic and light; and seek not to return to the dark night; if by chance you should lose your way; remember all these words I say; magical memories you will recall; and the choice will be yours to stand or to fall!"

Sarina wiped at her own tears. "You gave him a second chance."

"A final chance," Tempest said, "and if his choice proves unwise I will have no choice but to . . ." Tempest wept.

Sarina hurried to her sister's side, hugging her fiercely to her. "This time will be different."

Tempest looked at her through tear-filled eyes. "Do you see that?"

Sarina possessed an extraordinary gift of sight, but it was a sister's heartfelt wish that produced her prediction, not her skills. She was honest. "I wish I could say it was so, but you know yourself that the results of this spell are yet to be determined. It is in the hands of fate."

"I know that all too well," Tempest said and slipped off the stool to return to the workbench.

"And you know what will happen if you join with Michael, and he proves to be Marcus returned?"

"The reminder is appreciated, but not necessary. I know all too well that if I join with Michael and he is Marcus, his memory will begin to return, and the spell will carry out to its conclusion. I can only hope that Michael will have learned what Marcus never did, and perhaps he will finally become the immensely powerful witch he was always destined to be."

"Perhaps Dagon and I should remain for a few days," Sarina suggested.

"I appreciate the thought, but your presence here will only serve to delay the inevitable."

Sarina intended to protest, but the baby chose to do so for her and gave her a hardy kick. She laughed, her hand going to rub her stomach.

Tempest rushed to her side, eager to feel the child's movements, and their conversation was soon forgotten as the topic changed to babies, though it lingered in the back of both of their minds.

Dagon realized his sister-in-law had cast a brief spell over him when he took a seat in the living room with Michael. He decided this man proved important to her if she would do something that she knew would annoy him and cause him to complain to his wife; after all, it would do him little good to complain to Tempest herself. Her power far surpassed his, so he thought it best to learn more about this stranger.

"Do you find yourself feeling confined here after your sea adventures?" he asked, having learned a little about the man while they worked in the kitchen together.

Michael expected the third degree; actually, he thought he would finish questioning him, though he didn't remember that Dagon had ever started, and yet . . .

He ignored his confusion and answered, "No, I enjoy the change, and I enjoy the peace and quiet of this house. I've been doing a lot of reading."

"Anything of particular that interests you?"

"Oddly enough, witchcraft."

Dagon smiled, feeling he was about to learn something. "That's not odd; Scotland abounds with the tales, and witches play a large part of them."

"Then you know something about witchcraft?"

"Some," Dagon said, realizing most mortals were fools when it came to the Craft, but Michael didn't strike him as a fool, and he had no intentions of underestimating him.

"The subject never caught my interest before, though in my travels I must admit that I found local voodoo or shamanistic-type ceremonies fascinating."

"All cultures have their magical beliefs," Dagon said, relaxing back in the chair by the fireplace, eager to discuss more with Michael.

Michael was just as eager, and rested his injured ankle on the ottoman in front of the couch while Bear curled contentedly at his side. "Do you suppose that magic is the key to all such beliefs?"

"Belief is the key to magic."

"Simply believing allows you to fly a broom?" Michael asked confused.

Dagon laughed. "You sound like my friend Sebastian, believing that witches fly brooms."

"Well, if you believe they do, then don't they?"

"I suppose one could argue the point, since there were many accused of flying the night sky on brooms during the burning times."

"So what you're saying is that the accusers wished to believe what they saw, so therefore they convinced themselves they did."

"A more logical explanation, don't you agree?"

Michael nodded slowly. "Then you believe that any type of magic, voodoo or such, has to do with belief?"

"Belief is a powerful emotion," Dagon said. "It can cause fear, joy, pleasure and more. Think about the history of the topic. Witches were really a simple lot, believing in nature's way. They cherished the land, the sun, the passing seasons, and respected the continuous cycle that nourished life. They learned from it by making themselves aware and attuned to their environment. And from this their own skills grew. Grew to the point where they were knowledgeable in the properties of plants, they understood the planting seasons and the soil so their crop was always bountiful, and they prospered from their wisdom and were content."

Michael understood. "And those who weren't knowledgeable suffered and accused those simple people who were prosperous of being cohorts with evil."

"A reasonable explanation."

"Then you don't think witches ever possessed extraordinary powers?"

"That would bring us back to the beginning of our discussion and belief. If a witch believed she could fly on a broom through the night sky, then who is to say she couldn't."

"Aerodynamics?"

Dagon laughed.

"What about spells? Your theory would mean they can only work if you believe."

"Do you believe?" he asked, and waved his hand in front of Michael. "Rest."

Michael yawned, his hand rushing to cover his mouth.

"A spell, or suggestive thought?"

"If I believe, it works. If I don't?" he shrugged.

"But we also must remember that history tells us that witches were powerful spell-casters, so is it possible that their beliefs were so strong that they were able to make unsuspecting mortals believe?"

"An interesting thought."

"You must also have read that witches can never cause anyone harm."

"What if they did?" Michael asked curiously.

"Then they would be called a warlock."

A chill ran over Michael, a strange, discomforting chill. "I haven't read any material on warlocks."

"I'm sure Tempest has a book that makes reference to them."

"To whom?" Sarina asked, a white ceramic bowl filled with potpourri in hand and her sister coming up behind her.

Dagon and Michael answered in unison: "Warlocks."

The bowl crashed to the ground, and Sarina's hand flew to cover her rounded stomach protectively.

Dagon was by her side in a flash. Michael wasn't even certain that he saw him move. His arm went around her, and his hand covered hers.

"Are you all right?" he asked anxiously. "You look pale."

Her voice shook. "An unexpected kick caught me off guard."

Michael stood, leaving the couch free for them both to sit as Dagon helped his wife over to it.

Sarina rested back in her husband's arms and turned to her sister to offer an apology. "I'm sorry, Tempest, for breaking—"

Tempest never let her finish. She held up the white ceramic bowl, completely intact. "Not a nick; I caught it just before it could shatter."

Michael looked at the bowl as if he couldn't believe his eyes. He had heard the crash, he was certain of it. That bowl sounded as though it had shattered into a hundred pieces.

Sarina poked her husband gently in the ribs when she saw he was about to make a flippant remark. Dagon wisely remained quiet, his curious glance going from Tempest to Michael.

"Warlocks interest you, Michael?" she asked.

Michael sat in the single oversized chair that Dagon had occupied, and Bear jumped into his lap. "Dagon made mention of them."

Sarina gave her husband another jab to his ribs, but he was ready for her and magically deflected the poke before it reached him. He grinned at her, but her smile warned she would get him.

"We were speaking of witches and evil, so it was only natural that warlocks should be mentioned," Dagon said, sensing an explanation was necessary.

Michael stroked Bear, who had curled into a ball on his lap. "Dagon thought you might have a few books on warlocks."

"They're an evil lot," Sarina said curtly. "Not worth reading about."

Tempest walked over to the fireplace, moving the screen aside to add another log to the dwindling flames. Dagon and Michael moved to help her but she raised her hand. "I can manage, thank you."

Both men remained in their seats.

Tempest addressed Sarina's remark while she tended the

fire. "If Michael is interested in witches then he must also learn about warlocks."

"Think Tempest knew any?" Michael asked.

Dagon and Sarina stared at him so oddly that for a moment he thought he had grown two heads.

Tempest replaced the screen in front of the now blazing hearth and turned to answer him. "It's possible." She then looked at Sarina. "Michael was curious to know if we had an ancestor who was a witch."

"Oh, and you told him of Tempest?" Sarina asked casually, though her husband was the brunt of her true reaction; she squeezed his hand until he thought she would crack a bone or two.

"A tale or two that I could recall," Tempest said.

Dagon turned playful after extracting his hand from his wife's. "She was known for her fierce temper."

"She was not," Sarina said sharply in defense of her sister.

"I don't know," Dagon said with a slow shake of his head. "I recall a tale where she descended on a castle in a whirl of wind and light and had cast a spell that interfered with two lives."

Michael sat forward, his eyes wide with interest. "Tell me."

Sarina sent her husband a look that warned he was in for it, since the tale he was about to relate concerned the two of them. But Dagon ignored her, enjoying himself, though he kept his eyes off Tempest. "I heard that her entrance was a sight to behold, her astounding beauty radiating the entire area."

Sarina smiled, pleased by her husband's compliment to her sister.

Tempest did not smile. She simply listened, her expression vague.

"She was there to remind someone that her spell required her *best feat*."

Michael seemed confused and directed his concern to Dagon. "I don't understand. You told me that a witch can't cast a spell that harms."

"It wasn't a harmful spell," Dagon clarified and took his wife's hand. "The spell was cast out of love and actually brought two people together to join in a perfect union."

"Then why did Tempest descend on the castle with such power?"

"Showing off, I suppose," Dagon said with a teasing smile that he turned on his sister-in-law.

Tempest returned his smile. "I suppose that is a possibility."

Sarina spoke without thinking. "Why shouldn't she show off. Her powers and wisdom have survived centuries of censure."

"Centuries?" Michael asked.

Dagon and Tempest grinned pleasantly at Sarina and waited for her answer.

Sarina refused to be bullied by their smug smiles. "A tale persists regarding her age."

"But centuries?" Michael asked. "How could anyone live for centuries?"

"You know gossip," Sarina said with a soft laugh and looked to her husband for help. His hesitation did not disturb her. He had once promised her that he would always be there to help her, and she never doubted his word or his love.

Dagon didn't disappoint her as he spoke up. "Tales or facts, Michael. You will have to determine on your own what you believe and what you don't."

"Witches, spells, warlocks." Michael shook his head. "I have no idea why I suddenly find all this fascinating."

"Time on your hands with nothing to do can spark an unusual interest," Dagon said. "I think I recall a book or two you might enjoy on the subject. I'm sure Tempest has them in her vast library. Why don't we see if we can find them?"

Tempest scooped up Bear off Michael's lap. "A good idea. And I'll see to opening a bottle of wine for us and making tea for Sarina."

"And sandwiches—I'm starving," Sarina said.

The sisters went off to the kitchen, and Michael joined Dagon in the sitting room to hunt for the books. The remainder of the day was an enjoyable one. Good conversation, good wine and good food served to strengthen budding friendships, and it was with handshakes, hugs and kisses and a promise that Tempest would visit with them soon, Michael being welcomed of course, that Dagon and Sarina left the pair alone.

Tempest leaned against the closed door with a sigh and a smile.

"Tired?" Michael asked and brushed back a stray hair that had fallen along her cheek.

She nodded, her eyes suddenly fascinated with his face. Shadows played across it, giving the appearance of him being bathed partially in darkness and partially in light. One seemed to war with the other, each fighting for dominance—or was it wishful thinking on her part?

She placed her hand to his shadowed cheek and whispered, "Don't struggle so."

He appeared surprised by her words, and yet they made sense to him. He felt he had struggled his entire life and was still struggling, but with what? With life itself? Or with himself?

At the moment his immediate struggle was his overwhelming urge to hold her tightly to him and kiss her senseless. His other struggles could wait. He wanted Tempest now. Right now. Nothing else seemed to matter, not even his irrational thoughts. He only knew that he wanted her in his arms, and he reached out to take what he wanted, and what he was certain she wished to give.

Eleven

Michael reached out for her, his hand firm on the back of her neck as he urged her with a tug toward his waiting lips. Her eyes drifted shut, her lips began to ache for his taste and her body tingled in anticipation. He sensed it all with the suddenness of a wave crashing to shore, and when her lips were barely an inch from his, his mouth hurried toward hers eager to taste.

She felt as if his kiss united their souls. His lips demanded yet pleaded, and she simply surrendered. Time stood still, the air grew heavy and nothing could be heard but the beating of their hearts.

Tempest savored the taste of him; she thought of no one but Michael, and the way his lips fed hers, the way his tongue mated with hers, and the way he held her so tightly to him as though he never intended to let her go.

She returned the kiss full force, holding nothing of herself back, giving all she could and wanting all he could give her.

When his hand began to drift up her sweater she didn't resist; she wanted to feel his work-worn hand on her tender skin and drown in the pleasure. With one snap her bra came undone and his hand closed slowly over one breast, squeezing it ever so lightly.

She moaned in his mouth and he deepened their kiss, demanding more from her, and she gave it.

He took her nipple between his two fingers and played with it until it throbbed with a hardness that alarmed her and then his hand left her breast at the same moment his mouth released hers.

His fingers moved to frantically undo the buttons on her sweater and he did so with a speed that astonished her. In moments she had her purple sweater spread open and his mouth was descending to her breast. She cried out and wrapped her arms around him when his mouth fully settled over her nipple.

His teeth worked along with his lips, tormenting her until her moans reverberated through the small cottage, yet he didn't stop. He moved his mouth to her other nipple and she welcomed the intrusion, arching her back and offering herself to him.

Somewhere beneath this insanity reality intruded and cautioned her. With a soft whispered reminder, her sister's words floated up and into her mind, warning her of the danger of joining with Michael in haste.

But her emotions bordered on the uncontrollable, and she realized that if she didn't soon take command of the intense situation all would be lost, and she herself would forever regret it.

When his hand went to slip down in her skirt she stopped him. "Michael." Her breath was labored, his name shaky on her lips.

She knew he heard, and his hand halted briefly and then began to descend slowly. "Just one touch. Just one."

His own trembling voice betrayed his heated passion and Tempest understood without a doubt that if he touched her intimately that there would be no turning back.

His fingers grazed her flat stomach and dipped beneath the band of her lavender underwear when she whispered, "Another time."

He stopped, but not before his fingertips swept intimately across her and sent a shock of desire so strong racing through her that she gasped for air and gasped his shoulders.

"Another time," he promised and kissed her gently while her body shuddered against his. He kept an arm around her waist until she gave him a gentle shove, then he stepped away from her.

His eyes remained steady on her while she attempted to

rehook her bra and button her sweater. She fumbled with both and grew annoyed, though not annoyed enough to resort to magic.

His smile grew playful. "Want help?"

She shook her head. "I can manage."

His eyes suddenly took on a darker glow that sent a chill racing through her. "You do know we are going to finish this, don't you?"

Tempest wasn't certain what he meant. Was he speaking of what had just passed between them or was he talking of a time long ago?

She nodded, finding speech difficult.

Bear decided to interfere at that moment, to Tempest's relief. He wound his way around Michael's legs, alternating purrs and mcows for attention.

Michael picked him up. "Want a treat, big guy?"

The cat purred low and steady, and Michael tucked him in the crook of his arm and looked at Tempest. "Later."

The one word delivered with such confidence sent shivers down her spine, and she dropped back against the door for support. Whatever was she getting herself into? She liked Michael, respected him and admired his courage. He possessed a good soul. He was a good man. So where did her fear come from?

Marcus.

The name echoed in her mind. It wasn't Marcus she feared. She feared the fact that Marcus may not have learned his lesson, and if he hadn't then she would have no choice but to banish him forever. And that was what frightened her the most.

For now she would enjoy Michael and teach him what she could. When it came time for them to join, she would do so willingly and with an abandonment she had long waited for.

They shared a light supper and even lighter conversation, and they both sought the solitude of their bedrooms early.

The pile of books Michael had gathered in his room had been growing steadily. He had always enjoyed a good book but lately he found an unrelenting need to learn all he could about the strangest subjects. He simply could not understand his interest in warlocks. But ever since Dagon had mentioned them, he had this unexplainable desire to learn all he could about them.

He lay stretched out in his single bed, light burning brightly on the nightstand, and Bear curled comfortably in a ball against him as he read with interest about warlocks.

According to the old book he read, witches were defined as good and warlocks as evil. The latter practiced the darker side of magic and could cause complete chaos. Those who chose greed and arrogance as their creed became the warlocks' followers. A warlock's skill was infamous and many witches had difficulty combating them.

The book went on to explain that there was but one witch who could completely defeat a warlock, and that witch was referred to as the Ancient One. Her powers were limitless, her heart pure, her touch gentle. No warlock could defeat her. The only way her power could be threatened was if she completely surrendered her will and beliefs to a warlock.

Michael continued to read with growing interest.

It was believed that no warlock was ever captured or persecuted throughout history. Their numbers were kept limited due to the vigilance of the witches. A witch understood the warlocks' ways and did all they could to keep them from gaining any significant power. It is believed that they ceased to exist for some unknown reason. Some researchers believed that they never existed in the first place except in people's fantasies. Others believed that the Ancient One conquered their one true leader and without guidance their strength and numbers dwindled until none survived.

Any present-day practicing warlocks are considered poor examples of their forefathers and are considered harmless. But then many believed that the old ones were just as harmless or never existed. The book suggested that perhaps the truth lies somewhere in the middle.

Michael yawned, closed the book and turned off the light.

He wondered if both witches and warlocks were simply the product of fear. Had history actually produced the probability that such characters exist? Had those in power found a way to define evil in their eyes and place a name to it? Had a simple basic belief suffered because of ignorance?

And why did such questions intrigue him?

He relaxed and let sleep claim him, knowing he would once again be plunged into strange dreams that made no sense but somehow seemed familiar.

The nearly full moon cast the only light in the darkness where the couple walked along the riverbank.

The tall man garbed in all black stopped and walked to stand in front of the woman. "You are quiet tonight."

She was dressed in the palest blue gown and matching cloak, its hem embroidered with symbols of protection. Her reddish-blond hair fell in a mass of waves over her shoulders and to her waist. And her pale green eyes held a hint of sadness. "I sense your desire."

His long, lean fingers reached out to touch her face. "I wished you to."

"It cannot be the way you want it."

His laugh was low and arrogant. "I can feel your need for me."

"I won't deny that I want you," she said with a toss of her chin.

His hand cupped her defiant chin. "Good, then join me here and now."

She broke his hold with a shake of her head. "No, I am not ready."

His arm went around her waist, and he pulled her to him. His hand descended slowly down her stomach and came to rest between her legs. "I can feel you pulsate against my hand, and I can taste the sweetness of your passion. You are more than ready. You ache for the pleasure I can bring you."

She attempted to step away but he wouldn't allow her the distance. His grip remained firm and steady. "Not now." Her words sounded more like a plea than a refusal.

"You cannot deny me or yourself for much longer. Our joining is inevitable."

"Perhaps, but the choice remains mine."

He released her with a slight shove and stepped back. "You waste precious time."

It was her turn to laugh, though the light sound held no arrogance. "Be careful, your true character betrays you."

His hands balled into fists at his sides, and she watched him wage war with his temper. "I will have you."

She agreed with a simple nod. "Of that I have no doubt, but unless you can share your true self with me we will never truly unite."

He raised his hand, slowly bringing with it a twirling ball

of white energy that hovered in his palm. "You will surrender completely to me, and we will unite."

"We shall see." *She turned to leave.*

"Tempest!"

She turned, her hand up, ready to deflect the energy ball he threw her way. It shattered into a thousand sparkling lights.

His arrogant laugh filled the night sky. "I look forward to our joining."

Her soft smile silenced his laughter. "The choice remains mine."

Michael woke with a start, his room steeped in darkness. He sat up in bed, his breathing labored and feeling confused by the powerful rage running through him. She had denied him.

Him.

He shook his head and rubbed his face in an attempt to make sense of a senseless dream. It was as if he were the man in his dreams, sensing his emotions, knowing his thoughts, his feelings, his desires. And the strength of those emotions grew with each dream as though he was bringing the man to life.

Having learned to solve his own problems led him to depend on no one but himself, so the brief thought he had of discussing his dreams with Tempest was just that—a brief thought. And besides, when fully awake and rational he thought his dreams were nothing more than foolish fantasies conjured up by his choice of late-night reading material.

He dropped back against the pillow, Bear protesting his sleep being disturbed with a strong meow before the cat settled once again against his chest. He decided that a change in his reading material was necessary, especially his nighttime choices.

With a promise to himself of changing his reading habits he attempted to fall back to sleep. Two hours later he was still twisting and turning until he finally decided he had enough and got dressed in jeans and a gray sweatshirt and went down to the kitchen to make himself coffee. Not a good drink when you can't sleep, but a necessary beverage regardless.

He took his coffee into the sitting room, found a book on the powers of the mind and sat down to read.

Tempest found him asleep on the couch an hour after dawn. She placed a blanket over him and decided to let him sleep a couple of hours while she did some work in the greenhouse.

She protected her full-length gray knit dress with a colorful garden apron and quickly set to work filling peat pots with soil in preparation for the seeds. Spring wasn't far off, and seeds needed starting for her garden.

It had been a labor of love for centuries with her, and yet she never grew tired of the process. It forever impressed upon her the continuous cycle of life for all living things, and to be part of that never-ending process was nothing short of a miracle to Tempest that she cherished every day.

The task also helped her concentration. It allowed her to focus her mind and harness her energy for better protection and power. It was imperative that a witch protected her energy. Lost energy could be dangerous, leaving a witch vulnerable to all sorts of harms.

And with Michael being here, and her uncertainty as to his connection to her past, she felt it best to keep her energy at its optimum.

She sighed, recalling his kiss and his intimate touch. She had thought of nothing else all night, and it took her some time to fall asleep. When she woke her thoughts continued to drift to their intimate encounter, and as determined as she was she could not alter her thought pattern. Which was the main reason she had come to the greenhouse.

But even now, with her hands in the rich soil, her thoughts continued to return to Michael, and try as she might she could not force them elsewhere. So she decided to surrender briefly and give herself free reign to indulge in them.

She sighed, her fingers poking in the soil though accomplishing nothing. His face intrigued her, his many scars added a sense of mystery and danger about him. He was not a man who would back down from a fight, and he would definitely defend his honor and protect those he cared for. His dark eyes so deep in color and intensity warned any people who approached to keep their distance. And his lips wielded magic.

She had thought she had buried those potent emotions many, many years ago. The hurt of losing Marcus had been unbearable, and she had refused to give herself to anyone. She never thought, not even for a moment, that she could love with that much fervor ever again. Yet in the ensuring years she had made attempts to try and was always disappointed. All other kisses left her wanting—wanting Marcus.

He had left an indelible mark on her. His lips had been magic, his touch powerful and his lovemaking unforgettable. He had touched parts of her she was never aware of, and in doing so he had opened her own energy to incredible heights.

Michael's kiss, his intimate touch held the power to take her where once only Marcus had. And unlike Marcus there was a caring in Michael's eyes that bordered on love. Not that she had ever believed Marcus incapable of loving; he simply did not understand its magic.

And at the moment she wanted to explore the magic she felt with Michael. He was a good, caring soul and she wanted to touch that part of him and be touched. But patience was required at the moment, and things would progress all in good time. For now she would savor his kisses, take pleasure in his touches and simply get to know him.

She smiled. "Enough daydreaming."

She finished planting and returned to the kitchen to find Michael preparing breakfast.

"Pancakes," he said with a broad smile and flipped the one in the pan over.

"I'm impressed," Tempest said with her own welcoming smile and hurried to set the table.

They were soon both enjoying pancakes and conversing as comfortably as longtime friends.

"Tell me what you know about the symbols upstairs in my bedroom," he said, pouring maple syrup over his fat stack of cakes.

"You'll find them throughout the entire house."

"Where?" he asked with a curious eagerness.

"Above doorways, around windows, over beds, basically anywhere it was felt protection, luck, health and such were requested."

"So over the doorway the symbols would stand for what?"

"A barrier of protection against evil."

His curiosity grew. "Did this house belong to your ancestor who you're named after?"

Her answer was an honest one. "The house belongs to Tempest."

"She painted or engraved the symbols?"

She nodded slowly, and answered, "When a witch inscribes symbols she also inscribes her own power into them. The writing then becomes a powerful cast."

He appeared perplexed. "Do you think that Tempest feared something?"

It was her turn to look perplexed.

He explained. "You said the symbols were all over the house. Why did she inscribe them in so many places, if not out of fear?"

"If you recall the time you would understand. There was a witch-hunt going on. Scores of innocent people were being tortured and burned. Everyone feared even to speak the common word, frightened it would be misinterpreted."

"So she inscribed the symbols around her home to protect herself from the fanatics."

"From anyone who intended her harm."

He poured himself another cup of coffee from the pot on the table. "What about the symbols in my room? Protection also?"

"Yours are more in-depth."

"How so?"

She pushed her empty plate away from her to rest her arms on the table. "It's more a full cast than a brief inscription."

"A spell?"

"It would appear so."

"Do you know what it reads?"

She couldn't deny her knowledge. "Yes, I know."

"You worked it out?" he asked with a mounting excitement.

"Yes, I did."

"Tell me," he said with the eagerness of a little boy about to learn a much-desired secret.

Tempest responded the only way she could. "I think you should work it out on your own."

"Come on, that's not fair."

"The symbols interest you. What better way to learn about them then to work out an inscription?"

"I doubt there is time. I won't be here that much longer."

Tempest not only heard the disappointment in his voice, but she felt it and almost shivered from the overwhelming sense of loss. Hers or his, she wasn't certain. "You have at least two weeks before the cast comes off and then you mentioned repairs you would make to the cottage that should give you about a month. Enough time, I'm sure."

"And if I don't work it out within that time, will you tell me the spell?"

She hesitated, briefly considering her options. They were few, so her choice was simple. "Yes. I will recite the spell for you."

He looked pleased, and his pleasure made her smile.

"I promise I'll work hard to decipher it myself."

"I wish you success."

He leaned close to her. "When I want something I can be relentless in going after it."

His voice sounded dark—almost ominous—and memories of Marcus's hypnotic voice filled her mind. As did the spell she cast over him. The spell she had inscribed in the upstairs bedroom over countless nights and too many tears so that she would never forget.

Never.

And if he worked it out, recited it, what then?

He could only answer that question.

She spoke softly. "As I said, I wish you success, much success."

Twelve

The summons came just before dawn. The sweet whispering voices intruded on her sleep, and the anxious summons became all too clear as Tempest woke and hastily dressed.

White was the only acceptable color for this meeting, and she slipped on a long, flowing white wool dress, white leather boots and a white wool cloak with a hood that concealed most of her face when she pulled it up. Her hair was left free to fall naturally and as usual the flaming reds and gentle gold blended beautifully around her face.

She couldn't chance waking Michael, so with a whispered spell, a twirl of wind and spark of light she was off to the forest in a flash.

When the wind settled and the light faded around her she looked about her and took a deep breath. She loved this secluded place deep in the woods. Nature shined at its best here. The air was crisp as dawn peeked on the horizon, the trees and plants anxious for the birth of a new day and the sun that would nourish them. The weather had been warming slowly and the snow was melting away. Patches of bare earth covered the ground, giving notice that spring was close by. And a gentle mist hovered over the snow-covered hills in the distance.

She paid reverence to its splendor by extending her hands out and bidding the dawn welcome. The sun responded, instantly rising up and kissing her cheek with the first ray of morning light. She was one with her surroundings; she felt the energy, the power of the sun, and in reverence to her age and wisdom the sun bathed her in its brilliant rays as it ascended into the sky.

"Ancient One, it is an honor," came the soft respectful voice.

Tempest lowered her arms and turned with a smile. "Beatrice, how wonderful to see you again." She extended her hand out to the small fairy in welcome and for a place for her to light since she flitted in the air a short distance from her face. And of course it was a lopsided flit that kept her steady. "Damage your wing again?" she asked as Beatrice came to rest in the palm of her hand.

The small plump little fairy pushed at the green winter wreath that hung lopsided on her head and then adjusted her pale-blue cloak around her shoulders. "I'm forever bumping into the trees during flight."

"Allow me," Tempest said and reached out with gentle fingers to repair the delicate wing.

Beatrice blushed as she bowed her head. "That was gracious of you Ancient One, thank you."

"You're most welcome. Now why the urgent summons?"

Beatrice gathered her courage with a sigh and spoke. "The fairy community is concerned over the presence of the strange man in your cottage, and they requested that I speak to you on their behalf." She paused to look at Tempest wondering if she would comment before she finished. When she remained silent Beatrice continued. "They worry that this man is Marcus returned, and they fear the outcome of the spell."

"They assume Marcus will not conquer the spell, but return to his old ways?"

Beatrice nodded, her wreath tilting once again to the side. "They believe his dark side is stronger than even the smallest ray of light."

"And they expect repercussions for supporting me those many centuries ago."

"Marcus could never forgive. He will remember that the fairies stood beside you when you cast the spell that vanquished him, and he will see that we suffer."

"I would not allow that," she said sadly.

Beatrice spoke softly. "You still love him, don't you?"

Her smile reflected her sadness. "I will always love Marcus, but I know what must be done, and I will do it if necessary. The fairy community has nothing to fear."

"Is this stranger Marcus?"

"I do not know for certain. There are moments I think he is and there are moments I doubt they are one."

"Do you favor this mortal?"

Tempest sighed. "Very much."

"Is he a good mortal?"

A small smile broke free. "Good and caring."

"Then perhaps he is not Marcus, and there is no need for concern."

"There is always need for concern. If we do not stay aware, that is when darkness can once again descend on us."

"Then you are cautious with him?"

Tempest had to be honest. "Not as cautious as I should be, though aware enough to protect myself."

"Is there anything I can do to help you?" Beatrice asked.

Tempest shook her head. "No, though I appreciate the offer. This is between Marcus and me."

"And this man?"

"Michael," she said softly, and Beatrice smiled. "I will be patient and wait on the will of destiny."

"Many believed, and still do, that Marcus is your destiny."

"Yet destiny has a way of fooling the foolish."

"Do you feel you were foolish when it came to Marcus?"

Foolish?

One could be foolish in countless ways, and yet never realize she was a fool. So had she been foolish?

"I'm not sure, Beatrice. At times I felt very foolish for even thinking that I loved him, and other times I felt foolish for surrendering a tiny part of myself to him, but I don't think I was ever foolish enough to completely surrender myself to his will."

"If you had you would have lost yourself."

"I know, and that was unacceptable. My wisdom would never have allowed me to make such a mistake."

"But love affects people in strange ways," Beatrice reminded.

"Yes, everyone is different and reacts differently to love.

That is why so much is written on the elusive subject. Everyone is trying desperately to understand it, capture it and hold on to it."

Beatrice shook her head. "When will they all learn?"

"When they stop trying so hard and simply have faith in love; only then will they understand its true spirit."

"The lesson is too simple for them."

"But one well worth learning."

"Your love for Marcus, was it simple?" Beatrice asked.

"Nothing with Marcus was simple," Tempest said with a smile and a shake of her head. "Oddly enough, though I understood him, even enjoyed his company."

"You never feared him?"

"Never," she answered. "Fear makes one feel powerless and immobilizes when action is what is necessary. And of course, fear, greed, arrogance and such empowered Marcus."

"Many sought his skills for the wrong reasons."

"Which empowered him all the more."

"Then whatever did you find attractive about him?" Beatrice shook her head. "I should say 'interesting,' since Marcus possessed extraordinarily handsome features."

"His mind. It fascinated me. It possessed such potential, such power, such goodness to give to the world. I couldn't help but explore the possibilities."

"And you still think there is a chance for him?"

"There's always a chance," Tempest said. "All one has to do is take it."

Beatrice hesitated to ask, but understood she must. "If you love him, how then can you . . ." She couldn't continue, especially seeing and feeling the overwhelming rush of sorrow that washed over Tempest. She finally whispered, "You have no choice."

Tempest spoke softly, holding back her tears. "There's always a choice, Beatrice. We may not like it, but it is ours to make. Marcus must make his choice, and I mine. Hopefully his will be a wise one; I know mine will be."

The undeniable brought a brief moment of silence to the forest.

"Tell the fairies they have nothing to fear, I will protect them as always," Tempest said in a soft yet firm tone that signaled their meeting was at an end.

Beatrice bowed her head. "We never doubted you would. We only wished to be prepared and to protect you as well."

"Your thoughtfulness is appreciated, but this time I must face Marcus on my own."

Beatrice fluttered her wings and floated up off Tempest's hand. "I will be nearby if you need me."

Tempest smiled, nodded and then with a soft breath cast a protective spell around Beatrice. "Your flying skills will improve."

Beatrice grinned with delight. "How wonderful. No more bent wing. Thank you."

"You're welcome," Tempest said with a gentle laugh. "Now go and enjoy this beautiful day that smiles down upon us."

Beatrice flitted off with a quick wave.

Tempest took a moment to digest her own words. Choices weren't easy, but they were necessary. She had made many difficult choices in her long lifetime, but she couldn't bear to think of how difficult a choice it would be to send Marcus from her life forever.

There was still Michael, of course, but more and more she was beginning to come to the realization that Marcus lurked beneath his surface. Eventually he would emerge full force, his powers as strong as the day she had sent him away. What then?

Choices.

She raised her hand and with a gust of wind and light she transported herself back to the cottage, just outside the front door. A gentle twist of the handle and a soft push and the door opened quietly. She didn't want to disturb Michael if he still slept, and if not, she wanted to make a discreet entrance.

The door suddenly flew wide open and she almost tumbled in if it hadn't been for Michael's firm hand to her arm.

"Where the hell have you been?" he asked with an anger that surprised her since it was concern he actually was feeling.

He continued, giving her no chance to answer. "I've searched this entire house looking for you."

She couldn't take her eyes off him. He wore black jeans and a black knit sweater that defined his hard muscles, every one of them. And his hair fell unruly as usual and only added to that air of mystery and danger.

"Are you listening to me?" he snapped harshly. "Where did you go?"

She answered with the first thought that came into her head. "For a walk."

"What?"

She eased herself from his tight grasp and removed her cloak to hang in the hall closet. "I went for a walk."

He folded his arms over his chest, defining his arm muscles. They were impressive. "That must have been some walk, given that you've been gone since just before dawn."

"How did you know that?" she asked, walking past him and heading for the kitchen.

He followed without the support of the crutch, having mastered walking with the added weight of the cast. "I woke early and saw that your bedroom door was open, so I assumed you had gotten up. I came down here to help you fix breakfast. When I didn't find you here in the kitchen I returned upstairs, and when I didn't find you there I started searching the house."

Tempest made coffee and set to work gathering eggs, peppers, onions and ham to make omelets. "I felt the need for fresh air."

He shook his head. "At dawn? And that dress isn't exactly fit for walking in the woods."

She ignored the dress comment. "Dawn is the perfect time in the woods. The sun brings nature slowly to waking, and it is a beautiful sight to watch."

He grew so frustrated that he knew if he didn't do something, he was going to lose his temper. He got busy setting the table. "Sometimes, Tempest, you don't make sense."

She chopped the peppers and onions. "Sometimes, Michael, it isn't necessary for things to make sense."

He was about to respond when she turned a stunning smile on him that left him speechless.

"Thank you for worrying about me."

He felt as if he'd been sucker-punched. All he could do was stand there and gawk at her like an infatuated young boy. He had thought her beautiful, but with that soft, sincere smile, she was stunning.

No, he wasn't being honest with himself. He thought her sexy standing there in that white wool dress that accented every curve and mound of her shapely body. He even found the way her body swayed slightly as she beat the eggs in the mixing bowl sensuous.

Damn, but he was attracted to her, though it wasn't only an attraction. He had thought he'd go crazy when he couldn't find her. His heart pounded, his mind went wild with possibilities and he felt helpless to doing anything but wait.

Patience was not one of his stronger virtues, especially when he realized he cared for Tempest more than he wanted to admit. And he hadn't allowed himself to care for anyone in a very long time. Caring always seemed to lead to disappointment and pain, and he was tired of feeling both. Yet he couldn't ignore his emotions; they overwhelmed him and he could think little of anything else. Of course, being secluded here with her in the cottage didn't help, though it did allow for him to get to know her. And the more he did, the more he liked about her.

So where would all this lead?

Nowhere.

They were two different people from two different worlds.

"You seem preoccupied. Am I the cause?"

Her question shook him out of his reverie and he smiled at her perception. "That you are."

"I didn't mean to cause you worry. I'm truly sorry."

He shrugged. "It's really not your fault. You're entitled to come and go as you please and owe me no explanation."

"But you are a guest here, and I should have been more considerate."

"I don't think you know how not to be considerate, Tempest."

"I have my moments," she said with a gentle laugh.

"I can't see you getting angry."

Her laughter grew. "My name is Tempest."

"Can throw a tantrum, can you?"

She thought of the times she displayed her temper and the consequences, and her voice turned soft when she answered, "Only when necessary."

He saw how her own words affected her and felt her sense of regret. More and more he seemed to be attuned to her emotions and he had to admit that he liked the strange connection.

His eyes met hers and for a brief instant he felt as if they stepped within each other and touched souls. She appeared to sense the same, for her hands trembled and she hurried to place the plates she carried down on the table.

He stepped up behind her, slipping his arm around her waist and pressing himself against her. She tensed and he ran kisses along her slim neck to her ear and whispered, "Relax. I only want to hold you a moment."

Her body responded, leaning into his, and she rested her hand on his arm and surrendered to him with a sigh.

"I like the feel of you," he said, nibbling along her neck. "And your taste is magic." His nibbles turned to teasing bites that tormented her senses.

She warned herself to remain passive, not to respond too ardently, but her neck had always been extremely sensitive, and . . .

She shut her eyes tightly. Marcus always teased her neck with his lips and teeth. He knew the effect it had on her and used it to his advantage often. The thought sobered her senses.

"The omelets are getting cold," she said softly, though when he gave a gentle bite to the crook of her neck, she moaned.

"I don't care," he said, and turned her around in his arms. "I'd rather taste you."

His mouth was on hers as she opened it to respond, and he kissed her like a lover long denied. And she didn't deny him; she couldn't, she didn't want to. She wanted to taste him as badly as he wanted to taste her.

They savored each other, their kiss hard, then soft, then demanding, then surrendering until they both turned breathless from their passion and their foreheads came to rest against one another.

Silence reigned for several moments until they finally parted and quietly took their seats at the kitchen table. With the awkward silence continuing, they passed the plate of toast and butter back and forth and began to eat.

Michael broke the silence. "I've been working on deciphering those symbols in my room."

Relieved by the change of subject, her response sounded eager. "Tell me what you've learned."

"I did background work on the symbols, starting with their supposed origin, though I get the feeling that the books have missed something there." He shrugged. "But I'm working with what I have and the different variations. The one problem I faced was that I wasn't certain where on the wall the spell began and I didn't want to start at the end and work backwards."

"Did you determine the starting point?"

"I think I did; at least, I'm assuming it's the starting point and I intend to go from there."

Tempest understood the relevance of his deciphering the spell. That was one of the reasons she placed him in the room. "Interpret anything yet?"

He poured himself another cup of coffee. "Again, I can't be certain, but I think it begins, 'With my love'."

Tempest kept firm though trembling fingers gripped around her teacup. Michael had just spoken the first three words of the spell.

Thirteen

Michael lay in bed reading. The hour was late—almost two in the morning—but he was so engrossed in the book that he couldn't put it down. Bear, as usual, was curled against his chest. The cat had become his constant companion, following him wherever he went. He kept him company in the greenhouse while he tended his thriving group of plants. And Bear was careful in guiding his steps, running up in front of him when an object lay in his path or yawning loudly and as close to his face as he could possibly get when he felt it was time for them both to nap—a favorite pastime of his.

He stroked the sleeping cat as he continued reading about witches. It was amazing what witches were believed capable of doing and inflicting. If a person actually had such tremendous power at her disposal there wouldn't be anything that could stop her. It was believed that a witch could call down lightning and hail; that she could descend darkness over the earth at her whim and that she could destroy crops and farm animals. If a child was stillborn, the death was blamed on a witch who robbed the baby of his breath while in a mother's womb. A witch's curse was also known to make a man impotent or a woman infertile.

And, of course, a witch could fly the night skies on a broomstick, and she danced naked in the fields during a full moon and copulated with the devil. The sad part was that many learned people wrote books professing these foolish beliefs and instilling such nonsense in the masses—until it created hysteria and caused many innocent people to suffer.

Michael had learned through his numerous world travels that beliefs built on ignorance caused unnecessary suffering, and yet the practice continued to bring death and destruction along with it. That seemed far more evil than riding a broomstick or dancing naked in the moonlight.

He wondered how Tempest had faired during the burning times. Had she feared for her life? Had she attempted to help the innocent? Had she hid away from the awful chaos?

He had asked Tempest when her ancestor had lived and how old she was when she had passed on, but she couldn't answer. She insisted that any information would just be speculation since she had heard so many stories herself she couldn't determine fact from fiction.

Bear suddenly lifted his head, his eyes wide, his ears alert. He cocked his head as if listening and in a flash he flew off the bed. Michael didn't waste a minute, and followed, though not at the same speed.

Michael saw Bear's tail disappear into Tempest's bedroom as he hobbled into the hallway. Her soft anguished cries could be heard where he stood and he hurried along remarkably fast for a man with an ankle cast.

Bear was sitting on the bottom of the bed, his eyes intent on Tempest who turned and twisted and looked to be in the throes of a horrible nightmare. The cat glanced back at Michael and meowed as if demanding he help her. Bear didn't need to ask; Michael went instantly to her side, slipping under the quilt though resting his injured ankle on top of the quilt as he gathered her in his arms.

She grasped onto him, her arms wrapping tightly around him, her head pressing anxiously against his chest and her body trembling as she moved it firmly against his.

He kept her rooted to him with a solid embrace. She was going nowhere, nor did she seem to want to. He ran one hand in soothing strokes up and down her back against the purple silk pajama top she wore. The buttons had come undone during her fitful sleep and had partially exposed her full breasts. The peachy mounds lay firmly against his hard chest. Her bare legs straddled his one leg and he could feel the intimate heat of her spread over his warm flesh.

He warned himself to be good. Be a gentleman.

But damned if he wanted to be anything but that.

She whimpered and clung more tightly to him, and it was then that her fear invaded his senses and he suddenly turned protective. His whispered words soothed and reassured. "I'm here, Tempest, don't worry. I won't let anyone hurt you."

"Please, please." Her whisper was a pitiful plea and tore at his heart.

"Shhh," he soothed with a gentle voice. "I'll protect you. Always, Tempest, always."

She calmed, though her body continued to tremble against his.

He wondered what nightmare haunted her and attempted to chase it from her mind with reassuring words and a tender touch and as his eyes grew heavy and he drifted off to sleep he heard her whisper, "Marcus."

He hovered on the edge of darkness. One step and he would plunge forever into the dark, murky pit. And yet he sensed the power the darkness possessed and yearned to taste of it. It called to him like a lover in need and the urge to respond, to unite was like an intoxicant he found hard to resist.

A softer voice entered the darkness, calling to him, and while not as alluring, it possessed a strange tug that made him take notice and step back from the edge. The gentle voice tempted him to join her, to seek the pleasure that she and she alone could give him. An everlasting pleasure that knew no boundaries or restrictions and all he had to do was choose.

What choice did he make? And why did the choice seem so difficult?

The soft voice called out to him again, urging him to choose wisely, urging him not to repeat his mistakes, urging him to step forward.

Instead he stood his ground not moving to the darkness, not moving toward the light voice. He remained as he was, making no move in either direction, yet knowing a decision was necessary. And when the time came he would make one, but which one would he choose?

Tempest woke, wrapped around a sleeping Michael. Surprising as his presence was, it was also comforting and she cherished this quiet moment with him. He slept peacefully, at comfort with himself and his surroundings, which lead her to believe he found solace with her. A nice thought.

Her sigh was low, a mere whisper so as not to wake him, and she was surprised when he stirred.

"Nightmare gone?" he asked.

She looked up at him, his eyes fully alert. "Thanks to you."

"No problem," he said, his voice low and his body suddenly taut.

Tempest realized then that she lay near naked across him and that her legs were intimately straddling his, and that if she could feel herself growing moist, then he certainly could, too.

She attempted to move away from him gracefully, but his arms held her firm.

"Don't," he urged on a whisper. "I enjoy the feel of you."

It was too soon for intimacy, even though she ached for it herself. She didn't know enough, didn't understand enough about this man and his past. There were questions yet to be answered and discoveries yet to be made.

Yet she remained as he asked, in his arms, because she simply could not convince herself to leave his side.

"The feeling is mutual," she said and snuggled against him.

His hand traveled slowly down her back until it rested on her hip, and he eased the shirttail of her pajama top up so that his hand could feel her soft, silky skin. He caressed her with a methodical slowness that drove her insane.

"Tell me what you're thinking," he said.

Her answer was honest. "I'm thinking how much I like your touch."

"I like the feel of you. Somehow it's familiar, as strange as that may seem."

Her own fingers traced circles up and down his chest. "We've come to know one another."

His fingers skimmed her backside. "I want to know you better."

She could have surrendered right there and then but that wasn't possible so she reluctantly gave the only answer she could. "In time."

"Then I suggest we get out of this bed or that time will be now."

She wanted to offer some explanation. "Michael—"

"Don't, Tempest," he said firmly. "When you're ready."

He gently eased her off him, got out of bed and walked toward the door. "I'm going to wash up."

"I'll get breakfast started."

"I'll be down shortly to help."

She nodded and he left, and that's when a tear slipped down her cheek.

She battled with emotions she had thought were long since buried and feeling them surface now was a shock to her. She had forgotten how good falling in love could feel.

It felt simply delicious.

It warmed the heart and soul and ignited the senses.

And it frightened her.

She wiped the single teardrop away. She understood that fear was self-imposed and to rid herself of the destructive emotion she had to face the cause. She had to face her past and she wasn't certain she was prepared to do that just yet.

She decided action was better than feeling sorry for herself and she hurried out of bed to dress. Black tights, black socks and a hip-length black-knit sweater went on fast and she pulled her long, reddish-blond hair back with a black silk ribbon. Not that all the strands stayed in place; several fell freely around her face, particularly the deeper red strands. The flaming color added to her flawless peach complexion which required not an ounce of cosmetics.

After making her bed she glanced around the room for Bear and seeing he was nowhere in sight, hurried off to the kitchen. Her cat was a traitor. Ever since Michael's arrival and a quick assessment of the stranger Bear decided that he liked the man enough to make him his constant companion.

She entered the kitchen with a smile. She was glad the cat had befriended Michael. He needed a friend, and there was nothing like a feline forming an attachment to you.

Tempest went to work getting breakfast ready and found her day pretty much followed the same hectic pace. By late afternoon she and Michael found themselves relaxing in the living room with hot cider and oatmeal cookies.

"And I thought living a solitary life was boring," he said and munched on a cookie.

She reached for her own cookie. "I never lack for things to do and the village isn't as far away as you think."

"A walk?"

"A bicycle ride."

"And the village?"

She smiled after she finished munching. "A picture postcard place. You would love the small bookstore there. Mr. Hodges runs it and has for many years." She paused a moment, recalling that Mr. Hodges had recently turned 210 years old. He was a dear man and a powerful witch. "The shelves overflow with old, used and new books. The musty smell of old leather and aged pages adds to the wonderful atmosphere of the place. He travels and collects whatever strikes his fancy, and if I request a book on a subject he does his best to locate it for me."

"Sounds irresistible. I'd love to visit it."

"With the snow melting considerably and your cast coming off in less than two weeks, we should be able to visit the village soon."

Michael chose to ignore the issue of his impending departure. "Tell me more about the village."

Tempest loved the village of Cullen. It was a place where witches and mortals resided side by side and had for centuries. "You must visit the sweetshop. Mrs. Killcullen makes the best candy I have ever tasted."

"Sweet tooth?" he asked with a laugh as she reached for another cookie.

"Guilty," she admitted and bit into the soft, moist treat.

He liked talking with her like this. She was curled up in the overstuffed chair looking much like a contented feline. Her relaxed posture told him she was just as comfortable with him as he with her. They never lacked for conversation. There was always a subject to pursue or an interest they thought to share. It was as if they were good friends. Good friends who were on the verge of becoming lovers.

He directed his thoughts back to the conversation. "I must admit, I thought you were isolated here."

"In a sense I am, but I like my solitude and when I wish company I invite friends or family to visit. Otherwise I keep busy with my interests."

"Tell me of your interests, Tempest, the ones that I don't know of," he asked, eager to learn more about her.

"I am involved in several charities, the major one being

Wyrrd Foundation, run by a dear friend of mine, Sydney Wyrrd. We sponsor several charitable events throughout the year."

"Here in Scotland?"

"Scotland, the States, London, Paris—wherever is necessary."

"You travel frequently?"

"When necessary, and whenever I wish to visit with someone."

He had wondered at times what it would be like to have the money to do as he pleased. He had always had to work for every cent he had and presently he had few cents. "Did your family always have money?"

"My wealth dates back considerably," she answered, recalling the many centuries it had taken to build her wealth.

He looked around the unpretentious cottage. "You don't live like someone with means."

She placed her empty mug on the table. "I learned long ago the true value of things, like my home, which always comforts me when I return to it. And the friends I have in the village who are always happy to see me and special friends who are there when I need them. I am blessed with many riches, money being the least important of them."

He was honest with her. "I always had to struggle for money. The work was hard, the hours endless, the results unsatisfying. Friends were few and rarely lasted and I never had a permanent home to return to. I guess you could say I was poor in many ways."

"No longer," she said softly. "You have a special friend now—me. And, of course, Bear." She pointed at the sleeping feline curled beside him. "And this place will always be here for you to return to, Michael."

Return.

He never wanted to leave. He wanted to stay forever in this secluded little world with Tempest, not caring if he ever saw another solitary soul again. Here he felt as if he had come home, back where he belonged, and the thought of leaving tore at his heart.

Tempest sensed his distress and it disturbed her. She understood his misgivings, and she could offer no reassurance, for she wasn't certain of the future herself. But for now . . .

"Let's roast frankfurters and marshmallows in the fireplace for supper tonight."

"I've never done that before," he admitted eagerly.

"And we'll pop corn over the flames, too."

"Fresh popcorn?" he asked, sitting forward and disturbing Bear, whose ears had already perked up at the mention of roasted marshmallows.

She nodded. "And we'll spread it all out in front of the fireplace so it feels like a campfire meal."

"Sounds great to me," he said, his eagerness soaring. "Are you sure you have frankfurters?"

Michael had been in her refrigerator and large freezer on numerous occasions. He was familiar with her stock of supplies, and she herself wasn't certain she had frankfurters, though it wouldn't be a chore to get them. A simple snap of her fingers would produce what she needed. But how to explain that to Michael?

And there was that honesty factor.

She snapped her fingers. "I just remembered that there may be two packages of franks in the back of the freezer, bottom shelf."

He nodded. "Could be, that shelf is hard for me to get to. What about buns?"

Another snap of her fingers. "Probably with the franks."

"Marshmallows?" he asked with a steady eye on her fingers.

She snapped them again. "The pantry."

He stood up, dislodging an annoyed Bear, and walked around the coffee table to lean over her. He grabbed her fingers in his hand. "Can you produce the popcorn without a snap?"

His question startled her for a moment. Did he realize she used magic? She sensed he didn't, he was merely teasing her . . . and yet . . . She had an uncanny feeling that somewhere deep inside him lurked Marcus's memories. And in strange ways those memories would surface whether he understood them or not.

She was relieved that popcorn was one staple she refused to be without. "There's tons of it in the pantry."

"Sweet tooth and popcorn lover," he said, releasing her hand. "I'll have to remember that."

"And you?"

"Me?" he asked, offering his hand to her.

She took it and stood, keeping hold of her hand as they walked together to the kitchen. "Foods that you crave?"

He thought for a moment, wrapping his hand more firmly around hers. "Can't think of any."

She seemed surprised and stopped just inside the kitchen to stare at him in surprise. "Everyone craves something."

He searched his brain, furrowing his brow. "Nothing. I ate what I could get when I could get it and never gave it thought beyond that."

She sighed. "Impossible. You must have craved a type of food sometime in your life. Maybe when you were young you had a favorite."

He shook his head. "My mother was a great cook, and she'd try all sorts of recipes so my menus varied. One dish was as good as the next. Never had a favorite, though."

"That's impossible," she insisted. "Think. If you could taste anything at all right now, what would you want to taste?"

He knew he shouldn't. He warned himself to be a gentleman, but then he'd been a gentleman far too long and that devilish side of him was itching to escape.

So he had no choice, he gave it free rein with his answer. "You."

Fourteen

~

Michael didn't expect her smile or the playful response.

"Food, Michael, not pleasure."

"Sustenance," he said, as if correcting her. "That which man needs to survive."

"And the taste of a woman is necessary to a man's survival?" she asked, leaving his side, her destination the pantry.

He followed. "Imperative."

She reached for the bag of marshmallows and the popcorn on the lower shelf and seemed to give his answer thought.

Her response not only surprised him; it aroused him.

"I suppose I can understand how you feel since I do enjoy the taste of a man, and when deprived too long of such a satisfying experience it does seem to become a craving."

"Damn it, Tempest," he nearly shouted.

"What?" she asked so innocently that he almost believed her statement innocent.

"How do you expect a man to react to that remark?" he asked, grabbing at the bag of marshmallows and popcorn she shoved at his chest.

She searched the shelves for the skewers for roasting. "How did you expect me to react to yours?"

He attempted a response, but she continued. "Shyly? Perhaps blush?"

He gave a short burst of laughter. "Shy? Blush? Not you."

She turned a direct look on him. "Then what, Michael? What did you expect my response to be?"

He felt backed up against a wall and he figured he had put himself there.

She answered for him. "You expected the same reaction from me that I got from you. You grew aroused."

He was about to argue when instead he asked, "And did you?"

She stared at him with those beautiful pale-green eyes and her voice took on a softly sensuous tone. "How could I not when you placed such a seductive thought in my head?"

He stepped toward her. "You don't mince words, do you?"

She remained where she stood. "What purpose would it serve?"

"Some people like the chase, the cat-and-mouse game."

She stepped up to him and kissed him softly. "Isn't that the game we're playing now?"

He took another kiss from her, demanding a deeper taste. "Think the mouse will get caught?"

Her return kiss possessed its own demand and left them slightly breathless. "Caught? Never," she said. "Surrender?" She smiled. "A distinct possibility."

"Then the cat shouldn't stop chasing?" he asked on a laugh.

"I don't think the cat has any intentions of halting the chase."

"Perceptive."

She leaned up and caressed his cheek with a kiss. "Aroused."

"You're tempting me, Tempest," he said with a smile that was purely sinful.

"I hope so," she whispered and with a wink walked past him into the kitchen.

He followed yet again.

She decided it was wise to change the topic of conversation. She had heated her own passion considerably and required a cooling-off period. She really had no intention of taking their banter to the physical level, at least not presently, so her wisest choice was not to tempt.

"Tell me of your dreams, Michael."

He looked at her as if she had caught him off guard.

She clarified. "Your dreams of the future. What it is you look for in life?"

He had thought she meant his night dreams. Those dreams he was not ready to discuss with anyone, or for that matter face them himself. They haunted him nightly and were growing in intensity. What significance they possessed he didn't quite understand, but somehow he felt he would come to realize their importance. Until that time he intended to share them with no one.

He searched for an answer to her question, but then he had searched some time for that answer, the question having haunted him. "I can't honestly say."

"Yet you have given it significant thought," she said, busily preparing for their campfire meal.

He had placed the items he held on the counter and worked with a familiar ease beside her. He didn't understand how she so easily understood him or how comfortable they had become with each other in such a short time. But he also didn't wish to question their strange relationship or the fact that he even considered it a relationship.

And where to next? He didn't know and he didn't care. He only knew here with Tempest was where he wanted to be at this moment in time.

"Lately, it seems to be a constant thought."

"But one you have difficulty with."

He nodded, taking a wooden serving tray from the cabinet. "Confusion is more like it. I have all these questions and not one single solitary answer. And while my list of questions grows, my list of answers remain blank."

She probed, hoping for answers of her own. "Are you looking for a permanent home?"

"Is there such a thing as a permanent home?"

She realized he wasn't looking for an answer, so she remained silent and allowed him to continue.

"When I was young I thought my mother was permanent in my life, that she would always love me and be there for me. I never imagined her going away or being on my own. I think when I lost her I realized then that nothing was ever permanent. Not even a mother's love."

"Her love remains with you though she herself isn't here."

He shook his head in disgust. "I've heard it all before, but what good does her love do if she's not here. I have only memories and they fade with time."

Tempest thought of the memories she had shared with Marcus and how time had not dimmed a single one. "Memories remain as clear and constant as you choose."

He shrugged. "Then maybe I don't want to remember. Maybe it just hurts too damn much."

"And is the reason why you can't find the answers?"

"I don't even know the damn questions anymore."

She placed a gentle hand on his arm. "Perhaps it's time for new questions. The old ones grow worn and burdensome. If you discard them and search for new ones, perhaps then you'll find what you look for."

"You talk in riddles yet somehow make sense."

"A compliment," she said with a smile. "My thanks."

He shook his head. "You're unique, Tempest."

She laughed. "A nice way of saying you think I'm strange."

"Well, we are having a campfire cookout in the living room."

"And I can't wait," she said with excitement. "I love cooking over an open flame."

"I have to admit that I'm a novice when it comes to campfire cooking."

"I'll have you experienced in no time," she said with confidence.

Michael looked doubtful. "I don't know."

Her hand returned to his arm. "You must believe, Michael. Anything is possible if you simply believe."

At that moment, looking into the depths of her pale-green eyes, he felt as if he could believe in anything. The feeling so overwhelmed him, consumed him and frightened him that he stepped away from her, needing to place a distance between them.

The distance did not prevent her words from ringing in his head.

Believe. Simply believe.

By the time Michael roasted the marshmallows he was a pro and not only proud but insistent on demonstrating his newly acquired skill.

"I'm stuffed," Tempest said, holding her stomach that ached from the five marshmallows she had consumed and thoroughly enjoyed.

A flannel blanket had been turned into a makeshift picnic cloth. Empty plates, a near-empty bowl of popcorn and an empty bottle of wine attested to the fun time they had shared.

"This is really easy," Michael said and blew lightly on the roasted marshmallow he had just removed from the open flames. "And delicious, besides. Did your parents take you camping?"

Her parents.

How did she explain two entities beyond the scope of mortal understanding?

She chose her words carefully. "My parents made certain I was provided with a varied education."

"Are you close with them?"

"I only need to reach out and touch and they are always there for me."

"You're lucky you have a close family," he said with envy. "I could tell when I met your sister how much you meant to each other."

"Yes, I love my sister dearly and I was concerned that she would find the right man to share her life with."

"Dagon and her appear a good match."

She brought her legs up to hug her chest and she smiled. "I was instrumental in bringing them together. I think they were made for each other."

"They have a lot in common?"

Tempest laughed. "Not a bit. Actually I think she was completely opposite of what he was looking for in a wife."

"Whatever brought them together then?"

She looked at him oddly. "What usually does—love."

"Love isn't the answer to everything or all relationships," he insisted.

"Love can overcome many hurdles," she said, sounding like a teacher instructing a stubborn pupil.

Michael remained stubborn. "Love blinds."

"Love doesn't require sight."

"Love hurts."

"Love heals, people hurt," she argued.

"Love gives nothing."

"Love asks for nothing, but gives everything."

He was prepared to continue the debate when she pressed a finger to his lips. "Love is what two people make of it. There is no right way or wrong way to love. Love simply is simple."

He wouldn't give up. He moved her finger away from his mouth. "Which means any idiot can fall in love."

"You've never loved," she said sadly.

"Once or twice I thought there was a possibility." He shook his head. "I was wrong."

"So you closed your heart?"

"And opened my eyes."

She placed her hand to his chest, over his heart. "Then perhaps it's time to thaw it out."

His hand covered hers. "Think you can do that?" He didn't need an answer. His heart had begun to thaw when he'd met her. His problem now was knowing how to keep her from breaking it because he was damn sure he was falling in love with her.

What had he said about idiots?

She answered on a whisper. "I think I have the power."

He smiled; he couldn't help it—she was so beautiful and so sincere. "I think you may need *magic*."

"Let's see what I can conjure up."

He waited, his hand warm against hers.

And she took a deep breath and briefly gave thought to what she was about to do. The spell she was about to cast could evoke his memories, for she had recited the words to Marcus many, many years ago. But she cast it over Michael now and she hoped for a different reaction.

"Earth, wind, fire and ice; hear my wish for I ask it twice; free this soul of his tormented past; and send him a love that will forever last!"

He captured her eyes, and she watched in their depths how he warred with himself. Did he believe, or didn't he? Did he trust, or didn't he? Did he *love*, or didn't he?

No answer emerged from his inner battle; his private war raged on. And as with any true warrior there was no retreat, no surrender. And he advanced on her, bringing his lips down to faintly touch hers.

Her finger intercepted the kiss. "Believe, Michael, please believe."

He pushed her finger aside with a gentle annoyance. "I believe in this."

He yanked her up on his lap and kissed her like a man

consumed by lust. She didn't protest; she surrendered just like she had done with Marcus.

Michael couldn't get the kiss off his mind. He had turned his light off over an hour ago and he still couldn't fall asleep. His thoughts continued to center on that damn lusty kiss. He had no idea what had come over him. It was almost as if Tempest had conjured up magic, and it hit him full force in the gut. The desire to kiss her had been overwhelming and no amount of sane reasoning, or insane for that matter, would have deterred him.

He sighed, utterly confused by what he had felt, especially when he had kissed her. It was as if his senses were heightened to such a degree of awareness that he experienced her pleasure as well as his own. The two combined nearly drove him wild.

Her blood rushed and heated along with his, their hearts beat almost in the same rhythm and the taste of her was pleasure at its finest and in its purest form. He wanted to believe, ached to believe, that what he felt was love, and yet there was something else there he couldn't quite grasp, understand, make any sense of at all. And the strange sensation nagged at him relentlessly.

His dreams didn't help any, either. They haunted him night after night, and he found himself becoming more and more consumed by them. The man fascinated him; though dark in character and form, there was an appeal there that made him want to take a closer look, become more familiar, understand his power. And he certainly possessed a defined power. Michael could feel it radiate through him, and oddly enough, he felt as if his ankle was almost completely healed. He had thought about removing the cast in a day or two—that was how sure he was that the break had healed.

Of course, sane reason returned during the day, and he blamed his strange thoughts on his reading material. He spent a good portion of his time reading about witchcraft, warlocks, spells, potions and absolute nonsense, and yet . . .

He moaned. "Damn, but at times it makes sense."

How could magic make sense when magic didn't exist? And why did he feel an affinity with the Craft? Ancient rituals and practices had always fascinated him. It seemed every culture possessed some type of *magical* practice. Did that validate magic? Give it substance and therefore form? Did magic truly exist?

He placed his hand over his heart. Had her spell worked? Was his heart thawing or was it that she made him believe it to be so? Or did he *wish* to believe?

He began to grow sleepy, his lids drooping and a yawn escaping. He longed for sleep to grab hold and whisk him away where he wouldn't have to think, but then there were his dreams that waited.

The room was made of thick stone, beautifully crafted tapestries hung from the walls and a fire roared in a huge fireplace. Wooden chairs, a table and chests filled the stark space, yet added no warmth or welcome. Candles attempted to cast light on the dark, but darkness somehow seemed to prevail no matter how hard the numerous wicks flickered.

The man stepped from the shadows, though the shadows followed and lingered like sentinels around him. He reached out to the woman who stood a safe distance away from the blazing hearth, and she stepped out of his reach.

His laugh was low and chilling. "Why do you deny me when you ache for my touch?"

"Your heart is cold."

"Warm it," he challenged.

She cast him a skeptical glance. "How would you have me do that?"

"Cast one of your spells." Another challenge issued.

"I do not need to prove my powers."

He stepped closer to her. She stood as she was, her refusal to back down from him an obvious challenge.

He raised a hand to gently caress her face. "I can feel your power. It runs like a hot, burning river through me. It excites me and I ache for it to join with mine." He reached down to take her hand and place it against his chest, over his heart. "Thaw my heart if you dare."

"And what if I thaw it enough for love to flourish? What, then, will you do?"

"Love you, as you wish me to."

She shook her head and smiled with a sadness they both felt. "You don't believe me capable of thawing your heart and teaching you about love."

His smile held confidence. "I will give you love if that is what you wish."

"How can you give what you don't believe in?"

He grew annoyed and stepped away from her with an agitated groan. *"I believe in our powers."*

"You believe the opposite of me. I choose love, you choose power."

"Love or power—either would unite our extraordinary skills and create a bond of such superior strength that it could never be matched or broken."

"And all this if our powers unite?"

He approached her. *"Think of the possibilities."*

"I am," she said sadly.

He reached for her hand and once again placed it on his chest over his heart. *"Thaw it if you wish."*

She could feel the cold, and shivered.

His laugh challenged. *"Too great a task?"*

She issued her own challenge. *"What if I spark love in you."*

"Then it is yours. I give it to you freely."

She nodded, accepting his dare, and pressed her hand to his chest. A gentle heat radiated from her palm and penetrated his clothes and flesh to touch his icy heart. *"Earth, wind, fire and ice; hear my wish for I will ask it twice; free his soul of his tormented past; and send him a love that will forever last."*

His dark, brooding eyes reflected his admiration for her attempt.

"I have freed you to know love."

"Good, then it is yours; taste of it."

His movement was sudden and unexpected and he had her in his arms before she could protect herself. His lips claimed hers with such force that she trembled and yet in seconds he had her surrendering completely to his dominating kiss. Giving what he demanded and aching for what he gave.

She tasted not his love but his power—vibrant, potent and tempting. He forced it on her, wanting her to feel its thrill and excitement, and she did. It prickled her skin, heightened her pleasure and drenched her with an unrelenting passion that she ached to taste and that turned quickly to a quench so strong that nothing could satisfy it except—

She ripped herself from his grasp and distanced herself from him, attempting to calm her ragged breathing and control the rush of emotions that consumed her body. He purposely had brought her to the edge with intentions of forcing her to step *off, to take a plunge that would forever unite them.*

His cold smile made her shiver. "You will step with me into the darkness and enjoy it."

"Only if there is love in your heart."

"Thaw it and it is yours," he said on a laugh that echoed off the stone walls.

"I already have," she said, and with a snap of her fingers, disappeared.

The man stared at the empty space in front of him, his hand quickly moving to his chest in protection, rubbing at it over and over and over.

Michael twisted and turned in his sleep, rubbing at his chest repeatedly and trembling from the surge of power that rushed through him.

Fifteen

~

Tempest found him the next morning in the greenhouse sawing at his cast with the small tree saw. "Whatever are you doing?"

"Taking this damn cast off," he said adamantly and continued to saw.

"You can't," she said with alarm. "You have another week before it can come off."

He looked up at her with eyes that warned her he would have his way. "It's coming off *now*."

She attempted to reason with him. "And what if it hasn't completely healed?"

"It has." He worked diligently and with a precise rhythm.

"How can you be so sure?"

"I don't know," he answered curtly. "I just know that this damn cast is no longer necessary."

Tempest grew concerned. Was this Michael being his stubborn self? Or was Marcus in there somewhere regaining power and control?

"At least give it another day or two," she attempted to convince him.

"No!"

She jumped, startled by his forceful refusal. She heard the cast crack and realized her only alternative was to remain close by and use her healing powers if necessary.

The cast came off easily. Michael tossed the broken pieces to the ground and sat back in the chair. His foot remained propped on the low table.

His pause presented an opportunity for Tempest to run a gentle hand over his ankle and determine its condition.

"It feels fine," he said in defense of his rash actions, though he had to admit her warm hand felt awfully good against his pale flesh.

"You haven't stood on it yet," she warned him, her touch tender and her examination proving that the break was well-mended. Actually it had healed considerably well, and fast. He probably could have taken the cast off last week. Her determination surprised her and alerted her to the consequences of such news.

"I won't have a problem," he said with a confidence most would envy.

"Regardless, I would still be careful, at least for a day or two." Rest wasn't really necessary; he could probably dance a jig or two and it wouldn't bother him in the least. But then that would also mean he was well enough to leave, and she didn't want him to go.

The realization struck Michael as well and he suddenly wondered over his impulsive actions. He did tell her that he would make repairs around the cottage before he left, but there were no significant repairs that would detain him for more than a week or two at the most and that was working at a snail's pace.

"Maybe you're right," he finally said, deciding that even if his ankle felt as good as new, it would be wiser to be cautious. "I'll do as you suggest."

"Good," she said with relief, and stood. "I'll get you a sock and your other slipper and then you can attempt to stand, though not for long."

He smiled at the way she took over his care and the sincere sound of concern in her voice. She actually worried over him, and that knowledge made him feel awfully good.

He expressed his appreciation simply. "You've been good to me, Tempest."

She shook her head, though she smiled. "I ran into you with my car."

"You didn't mean to; the snowstorm blinded your vision."

"I have menial driving skills at best." She protested his defense of her, though the thought that he chose to defend her warmed her heart.

"Your driving can't be that bad. You got me here, didn't you?"

She snapped her fingers. "With a snap."

He looked at her oddly for a brief instant and she felt a shiver run down her spine. Had her action stirred a memory? She had to be cautious and more diligent in her efforts to discover whether Marcus lurked in the depths of Michael's soul.

"Hurry with that sock and slipper, I'm anxious to walk normally again," he said sitting forward in the chair.

"Don't you dare attempt to move until I return," she demanded with a pointed finger.

"Casting spells again?" he teased.

She kept a pointed finger at him and returned his playful banter, though her remark did hold credence. "One that will certainly keep you in place."

His deep laughter filled the greenhouse. "I'm too strong for you, Tempest."

A shiver ran down her spine again. For a brief moment he sounded like Marcus and his laugh chilled just as deeply as Marcus's once had. Why did she question the validity of his identity? If she was completely honest with herself, she would accept the obvious, and yet . . .

Michael was completely opposite from the man she had once loved. He appeared to actually care for his fellow man and was concerned by the injustices of the world. Would that spark of humanity benefit him when his old self surfaced? Would he discover the true magic in his soul and refuse to return to darkness?

Time.

She had precious little of it, and she had to use it wisely if she was to help Michael. And what of Marcus? Only time would tell.

Michael took it slow the remainder of the day. As soon as he stood on his foot he could tell that his ankle was fully healed and that it presented no problem. But he kept his remarkable recovery to himself. He didn't want Tempest to know, and for a very selfish reason. He wanted more time with her.

He tried to remind himself that they were opposites that could never be together. She came from one world he from another, and like oil and vinegar they would never mix. And yet he couldn't quite bring himself to accept that. Somewhere he hoped magic would intervene.

And that was another reason he found himself wanting to stay with her. He found himself engrossed in witchcraft and magic, and of course fascinated with the symbols in his room. So far he had deciphered the spell to read, "With my love I send you away."

He hadn't told Tempest of his discovery, and he didn't know why. He only knew he wished to keep it a secret and in time he would speak of it to her. At the moment he felt he needed to gather all the ancient knowledge he could and digest it. Again, he couldn't say why. But it was necessary; he absolutely knew it was necessary to him.

Supper that evening was a quiet affair; it seemed both of them had much on their minds and they worked in relative silence side by side. Lamb stew was served along with hot, crusty bread and a good red wine.

Tempest was the first to break the silence. "I think we need to escape this solitude, if only for a short time."

Michael seemed eager by her suggestion. "What do you have in mind?"

"A visit to the village, a browse through the bookshop, lunch at Swan Inn and chocolate from Mrs. Killcullen's sweet-shop."

"Yes, yes, yes and yes," he agreed with several nods.

"We'll go tomorrow—that is, if you don't mind driving with me?" She would have to ring Sarina and ask if she could transport the car here, but she didn't think that would be a problem.

"I can drive if you prefer," he offered.

"I think I can manage. Only patches of snow remain, and I think I might have spied a bud on one of the trees."

"I can't believe the turn in the weather. It's almost as if spring is demanding her entrance."

Tempest agreed. "If you watch the signs, they all point to her early arrival. The birds are beginning to sing and look for prospective homes for their nests. The animals are venturing out of their winter lairs and a crocus poked its face through a snow patch the other day."

"And here I expected the snow to keep us captured for a while."

She sensed his disappointment. It matched her own.

"The weather is unpredictable in this area. That's why it pays to watch nature's signs; they never misguide. Now what do you say we take our coffee, tea and dessert into the living room and enjoy the fire's warmth? Spring may be on the way, but winter still chills the air."

They settled comfortably in the big overstuffed sofa, Tempest with her sock-covered feet tucked beneath her and Michael close by with his arm resting along the back, his fingers only inches from her slim neck.

"It may sound crazy, but sometimes you feel so familiar to me."

Now was her chance to discover. "How so?"

His fingers moved to stroke the soft column of her neck. "When I touch you I feel as though—" He paused and shook his head slowly. "That I've touched you before." His fingers lingered at her throat. "I remember the warmth of you and the vein that pulsed in a steady rhythm at your throat and how that throb felt against my tongue. Hot and vibrant." He stopped, shut his eyes and then slowly opened them. "And how I ached to taste the very essence of you."

Tempest was speechless. She could do nothing but stare at him and in the depths of his dark eyes she thought she recognized the determined fierceness of Marcus. Or was it her imagination? Did Michael's words suggest or speak of old memories?

"Let me taste you, Tempest."

Michael's voice rang clear in her mind and at that moment she wanted Michael and only Michael.

She made no move; it wasn't necessary. He moved toward her and with a tilt of her head his lips touched her throat. It was a gentle kiss, as if he was familiarizing himself with her or perhaps recalling the taste of her. With the tip of his tongue he traced a line over the pulsing vein in her neck and it fired her blood.

She moaned softly and grabbed hold of his shoulders, needing a solid mass to steady her wild emotions. It did little good, especially when his teeth followed nipping sensuously along her sensitive skin until she thought she would lose all sane reasoning.

"I love the taste of you," he whispered, working his way up her neck, over her chin and to her mouth.

She greeted him eagerly, devouring him with her own hungry need.

His hand slipped beneath her red sweater, and finding her braless he cupped her full breast in his hand and squeezed lightly. Their kiss deepened and he teased her nipple with his fingers, pinching it with a pressure that had her moaning in his mouth.

He wasted no time in pulling off her sweater, tossing it aside, lowering her to the couch and taking her nipple in his mouth like a hungry man long in need. She tasted so damn good and so damn familiar that he felt as if he had come home after a long, endless voyage. And the sense of relief so overwhelmed him that he slipped his arm around her waist and hugged her to him as if he would never let her go.

His mouth alternated from her lips to her breasts and his hands explored with an urgency that was hard to deny.

His fingers eased beneath the waistband of her leggings and while his intentions were to explore slowly, her soft moans and the gentle arching of her hips expedited his intentions. When he touched her moistness it was his own moans that rang in his ear and with a gentle haste he slipped a finger inside her.

"Damn, you're so hot and wet," he groaned near her mouth and kissed her fast and furiously.

She arched against his finger, taking him deeper inside her and shutting her eyes to lose herself in the magic of his touch. Sane reasoning vanished and in its place was a simple primal need to mate, to become one, to join.

"Damn, Tempest. Keep moving like that against me and I won't be able to stop."

"Don't," she whispered in his ear. "Please don't."

He was lost, his senses gone, and he was so hard he thought he'd burst right there and then. His fingers continued to probe, his lips to kiss and his intentions clear.

Tempest was lost in a maze of pure pleasure and she couldn't think clearly, couldn't control her passion, couldn't stop from crying out his name, "Marcus!"

In an instant everything stopped and they lay in an awkward silence. He slowly moved his hand away from her and with eyes that blazed with contained fury he looked down at her. "You're still in love with Marcus?"

She scrambled to get out from under him, to reach for her sweater, to cover up and explain. He wouldn't allow her to move. He held her firm where she was beneath him and his dark eyes warned she was going nowhere until she answered his question.

Tempest shivered, feeling much too vulnerable.

"Answer me," he said, his agitation visible.

Honesty was her only choice, but then she would have it no other way. "I loved him many, many years ago."

"What happened?"

Her reply was a mere whisper. "I sent him away."

"You regret your decision?"

"It was necessary."

"You didn't want him to go?"

"No," she said, her eyes holding his.

One question haunted Michael, but he feared he already knew her response. So he kept the nagging thought to himself, wondering over and over whether she would take Marcus back if he returned.

She attempted an apology. "I'm so sorry, Michael."

"So am I," he said and moved off her.

She sat up, reaching for her sweater and yanking it over her head. "I didn't mean—"

"Don't," he said before she could finish.

"But you remind me of him," she hurried on.

He shook his head and laughed. "Great."

She realized her words hurt, and she didn't mean them to. "Please, Michael," she said with a gentle touch to his arm. When he didn't pull away she continued. "There are subtle likenesses I can't deny but you have qualities he never had and a gentleness to your soul that I admire. I'd like to explore these feelings I have for you if you would let me."

He feared the hurt and disappointment of a lost relationship, but he thought he would probably fear more never taking the chance. He had to let her explore just as he had to explore, and in the end . . . ?

He shrugged. "Why not?"

No more was said on the subject. They talked and ate their dessert and shared a brief good-night kiss before retiring, and it was with a silent prayer on both their lips that they fell asleep in separate rooms.

His lips touched her neck and they both shivered at the unexpected jolt of pleasure that rushed over them.

His arms tightened around her waist, and he pulled her back to rest against him. "If a simple kiss creates this much passion, can you imagine what our joining would create?"

He kissed her neck again, his long, lean fingers stroking just beneath where his lips tasted her.

She relaxed against him, relishing the play of his lips and fingers along her sensitive skin.

His hands began to roam her body and his kisses became more impassioned, demanding more of a response from her, which she gave.

"Join with me," he said with a heavy whisper in her ear.

"Too soon," she managed to respond as his hand slipped down in the folds of her gown to tease her unmercifully.

If he didn't support her with his one arm around her waist she would have collapsed to the floor. Her body felt as if it had turned fluid, melting against him and into him and feeling—she moaned.

Feeling so much more than she should.

"Join with me," he insisted once more, his whisper harsh near her ear.

"No," she answered much too softly.

He placed his mouth against her ear. "You want me."

His hot breath sent a tingle of pleasure racing through her body and she shuddered.

He laughed and hugged her tighter. "I can smell the scent of you and feel your dampness. You ache for me to pleasure you."

She attempted to deny the obvious. "No."

"Yes!"

She tried to pull away from him and he held her firm.

"Yes," he whispered, and with deliberate slowness kissed at her neck again.

Her pitiful objection could barely be heard and her struggles soon ceased, and the crackle and pop of the burning log in the hearth mingled with her anguished moans of pleasure.

"Join with me," he coaxed between kisses.

"No."

His laughter rippled over her. "Yes."

"No." She sounded more adamant.

"You will," he warned.

"No!"

His laughter grew louder and louder and louder—

"No, Marcus, no." Tempest bolted up in bed, perspiring, though she shivered.

She placed a trembling hand to her neck and shut her eyes against the tingle between her legs.

"What now?" she asked herself.

She received no answer and she wasn't certain she wanted one.

She opened her eyes and dropped back against her pillow. She didn't want to think about her dream. Didn't want to know if—

She shook her head, attempting to shake away her concern but knowing in her heart it wasn't possible. She could not run or hide. She must face the inevitable.

The question persisted. *What now?*

How did she deal with the present problem at hand?

The answer came easily.

She didn't.

She couldn't.

It was impossible.

She had not woken from *her* dream. She had woken from *Michael's*.

Marcus was here.

And he was getting ready to emerge.

Sixteen

~

Tempest spoke with Sarina early in the morning, receiving permission to transport the compact car back to the cottage. She inquired as to Michael's recovery and she asked that her sister visit soon.

She promised she would, and ended the call quickly, not wanting her sister to sense her concern—an unlikely objective, since Sarina was highly attuned to her feelings and probably picked up on her worry as soon as they spoke. If she did, Sarina chose not to mention it and Tempest was grateful. She wasn't in the mood to discuss her present dilemma. She wanted, for one day, to forget her mounting problems and enjoy.

She dressed in a deep green sweater and matching column skirt, added black leather boots, left her hair free and hurried downstairs.

Michael was already in the kitchen and she smiled at his appearance. He had availed himself of the clothes, the use of which he had previously protested. He looked absolutely wonderful in black wool trousers and a gray cashmere sweater. Even his usually unruly hair seemed to behave and added credence to his new sophisticated style.

But then Marcus always did appreciate fine clothing.

Her thought troubled her but she refused to give it life. She walked over to him, her smile brighter. "You look great."

He ran a quick, appreciative glance over her. "You don't look bad yourself."

She took the mug of tea he handed her. "Thanks twice."

They had decided to forego breakfast, especially after Tempest had detailed the menu at Swan Inn. Lunch would certainly prove an experience.

"You sure you don't want me to drive?" he asked when he climbed in the car and watched the way she looked with confusion at the dashboard.

She shook her head almost reluctantly. "I think I recall how this works."

"Think?" he asked, knowing they were in trouble. "How long have you been driving?"

She thought about that and counted on her hand, proudly holding up two fingers. "Two days."

"When you ran into me, your experience on the road had been two days?"

A proud smile preceded her answer. "Yes."

"And you've had no other experience?"

"Dagon demonstrated how the vehicle worked. It doesn't appear difficult."

"Demonstrated? He didn't give you lessons?"

She realized her mistake too late and attempted to make the best of it. "There wasn't much time, and I was insistent about driving myself home."

"This is Dagon's car?"

"Yes, he was kind enough to lend it to me. I'm sure I'll get the hang of it in no time."

Michael looked around him at the patches of snow and the narrow muddy road and shook his head. "Get out. I'm driving."

She sent him an indignant look. "I beg your pardon."

"You can beg it all you want. I'm driving." He was out of the car before he finished and around on her side opening her door before she could manage a protest. "Out."

"But—"

She never finished; he took her arm. "No arguments. I'm driving."

The determined look in his eye told her it would be useless to argue. She got out of the car and into the passenger's side.

"This isn't necessary. I am capable of driving."

Michael fastened his seat belt. "I'll give you lessons. When I'm sure you can handle the car without picking up any road-kill along the way, then you can drive."

She wasn't one to take orders lightly. She had spent too many independent years to be told what to do now. "I—"

"Save it," he said firmly. "You're just wasting your breath. I don't intend to see anything happen to you because you're too stubborn to learn how to drive properly."

She calmed instantly. He was concerned for her. She smiled and almost hugged herself. *How charming.*

He turned the key and popped the car into drive. "Directions," he reminded her.

She pointed to the narrow road that appeared to head straight into woods. "That road is the only way in and the only way out."

He raised a curious brow as he headed for it. "You got us through there in a blinding snowstorm?"

"A wish and a prayer," she reminded.

He shook his head as he traveled down the narrow, bumpy road. "Someone must've heard you."

She almost laughed. "I have confidence."

"You've got guts," he said with what sounded like admiration.

"Thank you."

Their conversation turned to the surrounding countryside and Michael was surprised when suddenly the woods gave way to meadows and another narrow road that with just two turns brought them to the small village of Cullen.

It was tucked away between hills and woods as if it wanted to remain a secret from the world. Stone cottages with thatched roofs and buildings of which the brick had weathered many years greeted them and for a moment before he caught sight of the people dressed in modern-day attire, he thought they had stepped back in time.

They parked the car along the narrow street that was sur-prisingly busy with shoppers. He zipped up his bomber-style jacket and she buttoned her black wool coat up to her neck and slipped on her leather gloves.

The air held a sharp chill to it today and the gray skies didn't look promising.

She took his hand without a second thought and he smiled, holding firm to it. "We'll visit the bookshop first."

He really didn't care where they went. He felt so good being out with her, walking without the cast, feeling the bite of the cold air, finally feeling alive. It was strange, but he was feeling more and more alive lately, as if he had woken from a long sleep and was just beginning to live.

William Hodges, the proprietor, greeted Tempest warmly when they entered.

"Tempest, how delightful to see you again," he said and gave her an affectionate hug.

She, in turn, kissed his cheek. "I've come to browse and discover treasures, William, and I've brought a special friend, Michael."

Michael noticed he eyed him skeptically and was more formal in his greeting. "It is always a pleasure to meet a friend of Tempest's." He held his hand out.

Michael accepted his cordial acknowledgment with a handshake, though he could feel the man was uncertain of him. Michael, on the other hand, sized the man up immediately. Tall, handsome features, with pure white hair that added to his dignified posture, and well-educated and well-traveled. He was a seasoned man, though ageless, his face lacking the lines and wrinkles one would expect to see. He also seemed protective of Tempest, but he sensed it was more from being a truly close friend than a lover.

"Are you also looking for treasures?"

He stepped up behind Tempest. "I think I've found what I'm looking for." His own words surprised him, though he didn't regret them. It was the truth and he was glad he spoke it.

William Hodges smiled upon hearing that and simply nodded. "What interests you, Michael?"

"Witchcraft and warlocks," he said without thought.

William and Tempest exchanged a brief glance. "Let me show you where that subject would be located. In the meantime, Tempest, would you be so kind as to set the kettle?"

"You have a new blend of tea," she said with excitement.

"A blend of rare herbs you will love," he assured her and proceeded to show Michael the way.

Over an hour had gone by and Michael remained where he

sat at the small wooden table and chair in the back corner of the shop, a solitary light growing brighter as the shop grew darker with the onset of clouds and rain outside.

A teacup and saucer made of fine china and filled for the third time with an herb tea that Michael could not get enough of sat beside his arm, and a stack of books a good foot high sat on the corner's edge of the table. His leather jacket hung on the back of the chair and the sleeves of his gray sweater were pushed up to his elbows. He was having the time of his life with the reading material in front of him, and while he wished he could purchase all his finds he knew he would be lucky if he could afford one.

Tempest had wandered back by him from time to time and had refilled his cup without asking if he cared for more. He heard her chattering with William Hodges and he had heard the tiny bell over the shop's door ring several times, but the small distractions didn't bother him. He continued his reading and searching through the stacks of books, finding countless bits of information that fascinated him and kept him enthralled.

One book in particular caught his attention and he found himself unable to stop reading. It was an old book, the pages worn from endless reading, and he assumed the price out of his reach, so he read what he could.

It pertained to warlocks and their creed and to a myth that many believed in. It was believed that one warlock had risen in strength and abilities to use his power to unite all warlocks. Under him warlocks became a force to be feared and there weren't many who could oppose them. Witches could, though they needed to be powerful in their abilities to even think of confronting a warlock. There was, however, one witch whose powers were tremendous, and she was made mention of before in his readings.

The Ancient One.

He wondered if she existed, or was she a myth?

"Find what you were looking for?" William asked as he approached with an armful of books.

"The Ancient One," Michael asked anxiously.

William appeared startled almost dropping the books he held.

Michael barely noticed his reaction. "Do you have any books that make reference to the Ancient One? I have read bits and pieces on her, but have found no solid information, and I guess I'm wondering if she's fact or fiction."

William seemed to give his query thought.

Tempest came up behind William and answered Michael's question. "No one knows for certain about the Ancient One. It's been a debatable issue for years and many scholars disregard even the suggestion of her existence." She placed a gentle hand on William's arm. "Don't you have one or two books that at least make mention of her?"

He seemed relieved, as if a troubling decision had been taken out of his hands. "I think I just might. Let me have a look."

He disappeared around the corner of the six-foot-high shelving.

"Find any books you want to buy?" she asked, looking over his selection.

He laughed softly. "Plenty."

"Make your choices, then. I have sold many of my books I feel I no longer want or need to William for credit. This way I can purchase a book whenever I wish and not worry about money."

"I do worry about money," Michael said. "And I don't expect other people to pay for me."

She placed her hand on his shoulder. "Then think of it as a gift. I have enjoyed your company and wish to thank you."

"I should be repaying you."

"You forget," she said with a smile. "I ran into you. I owe you."

He laughed. "That you did, but you have more than repaid me."

Their debate was left to settle later since William appeared from around the shelf with two books in hand. "These might be what you're looking for."

Michael accepted them eagerly, opening them to peruse the pages.

"We'll take both of them," Tempest said to William. "And I think Michael favors the book in front of him, and this one as well."

She picked up the one he would have liked to purchase, but thought too expensive. He attempted to protest, but her gentle glance asked him not to do so in front of Mr. Hodges. He acquiesced to her silent request, intending on speaking to her later.

"Excellent choices," William said with a smile and gathered up the selected books to take to the front and wrap, though Michael was reluctant to let go of his new finds.

"There are a few more shops I would like to stop at before lunch," Tempest said.

Michael stood, grabbing his jacket. "I guess we've spent enough time here."

"I sometimes spend an entire afternoon here."

He slipped his jacket on and ran a gentle hand over the books on the shelf. "I can understand why. There's so much knowledge here."

"We can return another day, if you'd like."

He spied her coat draped on a nearby chair and scooped it up, holding it open for her. "Any time you want to come here, I'm ready."

Tempest slipped into her coat. "Wait until you taste the food at the inn, and then the chocolates at Mrs. Killcullen's shop. The bookshop isn't the only shop you'll want to return to."

Michael carried the two packages of books Mr. Hodges handed him after another cordial handshake, and with reminders to visit soon he and Tempest were out the door and into another shop before the light rain could dampen their clothing.

It was a shop of scents, and at first Michael wasn't the least bit interested until Tempest began to explain how different scents affect people differently. He was then lifting jar lids, sniffing oils and dabbing lotions on Tempest. By the time they left, Tempest had a small brown shopping bag full of various items that Michael insisted smelled great on her, and like a woman complimented, she bought every one.

The stationery shop was next and Michael found himself fascinated by the selection of items ranging from notepads to letters to of course pens and pencils. He couldn't resist getting a pencil with a Highlander bagpiper on the top. Tempest purchased notepads, letter paper and matching envelopes in white linen imprinted with her initial in gold.

They wandered out of that shop and into the wool shop where Highland plaids abounded and Tempest insisted on buying him a green-and-blue plaid scarf that were the common colors for Scotland. She wrapped it around his neck tucking it inside his jacket and giving him a kiss on the cheek.

He laughed, grabbed her around the waist and pulled her to him. "Let me thank you properly."

His kiss left her breathless and red-faced and she found it difficult to say good-bye to Mrs. MacFadden who owned the shop. The woman simply smiled and nodded her approval.

They ran the short distance to the Swan Inn, attempting to outrun the rain that began to fall in earnest from the darkening sky.

The old inn greeted customers with a friendly warmth that chased any chill away. A huge stone fireplace in the entrance room welcomed with a blazing fire. Scents that tempted the nostril and the stomach drifted overhead and a short, round woman with gray curls piled high on her head and a smile that was contagious rushed to welcome them.

"Tempest, how wonderful to see you."

Tempest hugged the woman. Michael noticed that everyone who greeted Tempest had thrown their arms around her and hugged her as if they couldn't get enough of her. If he didn't know any better he would swear they treated her like royalty or at least someone befitting a royal status.

"I've come for your carrot and leek soup and your mutton pie, Mrs. MaClaren," she said with a lick of her lips. "And I was hoping you made your rum bread pudding."

"Cooling as we speak," she said proudly.

"My lucky day," Tempest said with a smile. "And I've brought along a special friend to share it with. Mrs. MaClaren, this is Michael."

The short woman ran a suspicious eye over him before extending her hand. "Pleased to meet you."

Michael had the feeling she didn't quite mean it, and was saving her opinion of him until later. He seemed to receive similar greetings from all the shop owners and it puzzled him. He greeted her as cordially as possible since she frowned from beneath gray bushy brows at him.

Mrs. MaClaren sat them by a window, a ecru lace valance its only covering. Pots of green foliage crowded the wide windowsill, the healthy, vibrant leaves spilling over the edges of the pots and sill. A lace tablecloth covered the old worn wooden table and a candle with a glass shade sat in the center, its flame softly flickering.

Michael decided he would have what Tempest was having; the only difference was that he selected coffee while she chose tea.

Rain pelted the windowpanes and the wind whipped at shop signs, swinging them precariously and sending shoppers scurrying for shelter. Another large fireplace warmed the dining area and the lighting was soft, adding a cozy atmosphere to the room.

"You're well known around the village," he said after his coffee and a small teapot were placed on the table.

"I've known most of the shopkeepers for many years," Tempest said, wondering how he would react if he discovered that Cullen was a village of witches and had existed for nearly eight hundred years.

"They seem protective of you."

"We share a special bond and I help sustain the village in hard times."

He looked out on the cobbled streets and the quaint buildings and the mist-covered hills in the distance. "It certainly has charm and character. I don't blame you for remaining here."

She glanced with a smile out the window. "I couldn't live anyplace else. My richest and fondest memories are here."

"Was Marcus from around here?"

She turned a surprised glance on him.

He shrugged. "I'm curious."

She sensed his curiosity and chose to satisfy it. "He didn't live far from here."

"How did you meet him?"

She leaned forward, resting her arms on the table and lowering her voice. "Do you really want to know?"

He pushed his coffee cup to the side and copied her position, though his voice was firm. "I really want to know." And he did. He felt the need to understand her previous relationship. Why now, he couldn't say. He only knew it was necessary.

It was time. She understood that, and she told him what he needed to hear. Of course, she did omit the fact that their meeting took place over four hundred years ago. "I had finished shopping in the village one day and was headed home when one of the merchants I knew gave me a rose. A thorn accidentally stabbed my finger, and Marcus, who had been standing under a large tree away from the heat of the day took notice and offered his help."

Michael listened with a keen interest to what sounded like a familiar story.

"He startled me at first. I hadn't seen him standing nearby and his sudden appearance caught me off guard. We began to talk, and . . ." She shrugged. "Our relationship developed."

Their introduction sounded far too similar to his dream, and he thought himself crazy for comparing the two. Why did she always stop at a certain point when she spoke of Marcus, and never go any further?

He pursued his curiosity. "What did he look like?"

Her answer waited while their soup and homemade rye bread was served, though the wide smile that surfaced gave Michael his answer.

"He was quite handsome."

"How handsome?" he asked, irritated with himself for feeling jealous.

She could feel his annoyance, and the fact that it disturbed him upset her. Marcus had been an exceptionally handsome man, but Michael's face intrigued her. The scars, the defined structure, the sharp angles and lines gave him a strength of character and an air of mystery. He was two men in one and she liked the man whose face she looked into.

Her answer therefore was sincere. "Not as handsome as you."

Her remark shocked him speechless.

"I love your face. It fascinates me and tells me there are exciting stories yet for you to share with me." She ran a finger along his chin and over a scar. "It hints at strength and courage"—she skimmed his cheek—"and compassion." She smiled when she ran her finger over his lips. "Passion, too."

He grinned and enjoyed her playful antics.

She rested her finger in the middle of his chin. "I want to know you better."

"The feeling is mutual," he said, and brought her finger to his lips.

The subject of Marcus was dropped as they dug into the delicious soup and chatted endlessly about endless things. The subject matter didn't matter; they merely wished to talk and share, and they did.

Mrs. MaClaren fussed over them as if they were her children, ordering them to rest between servings so they wouldn't be too stuffed to enjoy dessert and of course brandy along with their tea.

Michael relished every moment, refusing to think that his time with Tempest would soon come to an end. Even the thought of never seeing the village of Cullen again upset him. He felt as if this was his home, and he hadn't felt at home anywhere in a very long time.

They were having a delightful time when Michael suddenly felt a coldness descend on him and with a slow turn of his head and his dark eyes intent he focused on the man who entered the dining room.

He was tall, slim and worldly-looking and he carried himself with an air of arrogance that annoyed. His eyes were dark, his complexion pale and his hair black with streaks of silver running through it. His clothes and posture spoke of wealth—old wealth—and Michael grew disturbed by his presence.

So did Tempest.

She recognized him immediately and understood his presence. He was one of the old dark ones. One of the warlocks who had followed Marcus and one of the few who had retained his old ways. He was here for one reason. He had come in search of Marcus.

"Do you know him?" Michael asked, his eyes remaining on the man.

"I have seen him around but I don't know his name." An honest enough remark, since she wasn't aware of his present-day surname. She had known him simply as Tobias.

He was shown to a table clear across the dining room from them. Michael turned his attention back to Tempest, though he would glance every now and then out of the corner of his eye at the man. He seemed vaguely familiar, and yet he was certain he had never met him.

Tempest sensed Michael's unease and thought it best for them to leave. She found the perfect excuse. "I think we should visit the sweetshop."

His smile pleased her. "After the amount of food we just consumed, you want sweets?"

She gave an emphatic nod. "I want sweets for later this evening."

He stood, placing his white linen napkin on his empty dessert plate. "Then it's sweets you'll have."

Tempest moved out of her chair, purposely blocking the man from Michael's view. It would be best for all if they avoided eye contact. She didn't want either man recognizing the other. Marcus would emerge in time, his power fully restored, but it was Michael's strength of character that she hoped would prevail.

They left the dining room arm in arm, completely ignoring the man. After a hug and kiss from Mrs. MaClaren for Tempest and a firm handshake for Michael they headed back out into the rain that had tempered to a steady drizzle. They hurried a few stores down to the sweetshop and announced their arrival by ringing the bell over the door.

The shop was small and smelled like only a candy shop could—delicious. Glass and wood display cases showcased a variety of chocolates, and baskets of colorful candy occupied much of the remaining space along with an old, worn rocking chair that held a collection of worn teddy bears.

Mrs. Killcullen was a tall, large woman with a beautiful pale complexion and soft red curly hair. She was very much in command and very pleasant. She was the only one of the shopkeepers who actually greeted him with enthusiasm and seemed pleased to meet him, which endeared her to him.

Mrs. Killcullen talked incessantly as they made their choices and Michael smiled when he noticed that Tempest sampled most of their selections. She looked like a kid having a grand time in a candy shop and it pleased him to watch her.

He drifted around the shop, selecting a peppermint stick, not having had one since he was a kid, and admiring the collection of bears when he suddenly felt compelled to turn around and walked toward the window.

He looked out at the light rain drizzling against the large window, and saw the mysterious man standing across the street staring at the sweetshop. He wore a raincoat, no hat and no umbrella, and he simply stood there staring.

Michael stared back.

His eyes were cold, bitter cold, devoid of emotion, and yet Michael could not glance away. He felt compelled to keep eye contact with the man, as if he was in a contest of wills in which he intended to be the victor.

Michael began to feel warm and that warmth grew and radiated throughout his body, flooding him with a surge of energy so powerful he felt as if he was invincible.

That's when the thunder roared and a shaft of lightning struck the ground near the man.

Michael didn't blink an eye and the man simply smiled, turned and walked away.

And Michael recalled the words he had read: *Witches can call lightning down.*

Seventeen

~

Michael drove home with too many haunting questions in his mind. Life had suddenly turned crazy for him. Why would he think that witches could call down lightning? And why did he even believe witches existed at all? Was he going completely insane? And yet the question haunted him, and he couldn't make sense of it.

"Is something troubling you, Michael?" Tempest asked. She had seen him approach the window, had seen the flash of lightning and had wondered.

He didn't take his eyes off the road. The drizzle had turned to a downpour and visibility was poor. "Do you believe witches exist? I mean, real witches. The kind that can perform real magic."

"What is real magic?"

"You tell me," he said seriously.

"Why would I know?"

"Witchcraft is part of your heritage. I can't believe that some of that knowledge wasn't passed down from generation to generation. Stories, at least."

"But how does one determine the difference between fact and fiction?"

He turned a quick glance on her. "You mean like the Ancient One. Was she real or wasn't she?"

"Tales, myths, legends. Are they true or simply fables created to entertain or to frighten?"

"Or are these fables based on a thread of fact that was woven into a complete fabrication?"

"A debatable issue that has been argued for many years."

He stole another glance. "True, but witchcraft is being practiced today."

"But in its original form? Or has the passage of time and modern society altered it to accommodate its own ideals and beliefs?"

"Which returns us to the question what is real magic?"

"Magic is what you believe."

"Back to if I believe, then I can do anything—like fly."

"If you believe strongly enough, why would you think you couldn't?"

"Reality and aerodynamics."

She smiled. "The Wright brothers believed they could fly and obviously conquered both your objections."

He returned her smile. "Good answer, but that's solid reasoning and determination. Mortal qualities that are not usually associated with witches."

"Belief is associated with both mortals and witches. It's just that a witch's power to believe far exceeds a mortal. She accepts her inherent abilities without qualms, embraces her heritage and practices her remarkable skills daily. She never once doubts."

"And that's a witch's magic?" He seemed disappointed by her explanation.

Tempest remained patient as only a wise teacher could. "It is the essence of magic, the very core of its existence."

"You sound so sure of such beliefs. Do you practice magic?"

"To a degree everyone does in one way or another."

Michael continued searching for answers. "But can anyone call down lightning, or is that a witch's magic?"

"According to myth, only a powerful witch can call down lightning, and—" she paused, causing him to glance at her. "There really would be no reason to do so except perhaps because of anger or to demonstrate power."

"To prove one's ability, is what you're saying."

"Proving one's abilities would be more of a mortal trait, and . . ."

"And?" he asked, waiting anxiously for her to finish and not understanding her reluctance.

She hesitated. "A warlock trait."

He raked his hand through his hair in frustration. "Witches, warlocks, Ancient Ones. Next thing you know I'll be seeing fairies."

Tempest had to laugh. "Well, this is a mystical, magical land."

He turned a smile on her. "And magic is simply believing."

"Now you're getting the hang of it."

He pulled up to the house and shut off the motor. He leaned over toward her. "Then, my dear Tempest, I believe I'm going to kiss you."

She laughed softly, her lips reaching for his. "I believe, too."

They kissed softly, testing and tasting each other until their emotions took control and Michael reached out to slip his hand around her neck and draw her closer. Their kiss turned to passion and their passion to impatience.

"Inside," Michael ordered abruptly.

Tempest didn't think, she merely responded, running from the car to the front door and fumbling in her purse for her keys.

Michael rushed up behind her, grabbing her around the waist and raining kisses along the back of her neck. She leaned into him, enjoying the play of intimacy they shared and wishing it would never end.

When her fingers fumbled with the keys, he laughed and grabbed them from her hand to insert into the lock. "I don't want to wait forever," he whispered with a laugh in her ear. In wanton playfulness, he nibbled down the side of her neck as he worked the door open.

He walked her along with him into the cottage and slipped her out of her coat and himself out of his jacket. With firm hands around her waist he directed her into the living room and lowered her to the couch. He followed her down.

Time stood still for Tempest and magic took over.

Michael's magic.

He kissed her long and easy, fast and hard, gently and lovingly. And that was all he did. Kiss her.

Tempest lost herself in the taste of him. It had been so long, and she had always been on guard, but with Michael she didn't feel the need to defend—only to surrender. And she was dangerously close to completely surrendering to this man who appeared to be stealing her heart.

The telephone rang and Tempest knew it was her sister calling. Had she sensed her complete surrender and wished to protect her? But then, who was she surrendering to? Michael or Marcus?

Michael moved off her reluctantly and as she hurried into the kitchen to answer the phone he called after her. "We will finish this."

She shivered as she answered the phone, recalling those very same words that were said to her hundreds of years ago.

"Are you all right?" Sarina asked before Tempest could issue a greeting.

Tempest was honest. "I'm not sure."

"Then come visit us, and do bring Michael. He is still there, isn't he?"

"You know he is, Sarina, or you wouldn't have called."

"I thought he was, but my pregnancy has been playing havoc with my abilities and I worried I could have been wrong," she admitted with concern.

"You are well and so is the child, so do not worry," Tempest reassured her.

"I worry about you; please come visit."

Tempest could plainly hear her concern. "Right now would not be a good time and right now is no time for you to be worrying."

"I worry about everything," she admitted tearfully.

Tempest laughed, which caused Sarina to cry. That brought Dagon to the phone.

"Why is she upset," he demanded to know.

"Because she is carrying your son," Tempest said, laughter still evident in her voice.

He grew annoyed. "And you find this funny?"

She heard Sarina crying softly in the background and insisting that Dagon return the phone to her.

"No, I am speaking to your sister and she will explain herself."

Tempest laughed again. "Is that a demand or a request?"

He remained agitated. "A demand, if it must be."

Tempest chose to be patient. "Then I will attempt to respond to your demand and alleviate your worry."

Dagon's tone changed considerably. "I would appreciate your help."

Tempest explained. "Sarina is reacting to her pregnancy the exact way our mother responded to hers. She was emotional the entire time she carried Sarina and she all but drove Father out of his mind."

"But he survived, right?" Dagon asked hopefully.

"And was a better man for it," Tempest said with a laugh.

That brought a laugh from Dagon, a much relieved laugh. "If you were here I would kiss you. You have just saved me endless worry."

Sarina continued to sob softly in the background.

Dagon interpreted. "Your sister insists that you visit with us and you're to bring that mortal—Michael, if I recall his name correctly—with you."

"Perhaps in a week or two."

"She says you are to come now." Dagon chuckled.

"Do I need to respond to that, Dagon?"

"I never once thought you would. You will visit when you visit."

"Thank you," Tempest said most graciously.

"No, thank you. Now I must go and take care of your tearful sister."

"And how do you intend to do that?" Tempest asked, a protective tone to her query.

"With much love and patience. See you soon." And with a click he was gone.

Tempest smiled at the phone. She was pleased and so very relieved that Sarina had found Dagon to love and be loved. They were perfect for each other.

And she was beginning to think that Michael was perfect for her. That the life he had lived had taught him many things and instilled qualities in him that had been lacking in Marcus. At least, that was what she wanted to believe.

Magic.

If she believed strongly enough, would it be so? Would Michael have taught Marcus what he needed to know to emerge a powerful witch instead of a dreaded warlock?

She had to believe in Michael with all her heart and soul, but then that would be easy, since she loved him with all her heart and soul.

She rested her head against the phone on the wall. Why hadn't she realized this sooner? Why hadn't she prepared better? But then who can prepare themselves for falling in love? It strikes without warning and leaves one numb and vulnerable. Nothing makes sense, nor at times does one want it to.

"Are you all right?" Michael asked, coming up behind her and slipping his arm around her waist.

She felt his concern so deep and pure, so honest, and she leaned back against him. "I'm fine." And she was. He was here with her now—Michael, not Marcus—and she would love and help him all she could.

"I was thinking," he whispered in her ear.

"About what?" she whispered back.

He gave a short laugh. "About chocolate."

She remembered then. "We left all the packages in the car."

"I retrieved them while you were on the phone. The chocolate awaits us in the living room."

"You're tempting me," she teased.

"Indulge," he said softly.

Another familiar remark from the past that Tempest chose to ignore. She turned, took his hand and hurried off with him to do as he suggested.

The hour was late and Michael attempted to yawn away sleep for the third time, but this time it refused to cooperate. He reluctantly closed the book and placed it on the small table beside his bed.

He wasn't sure what was real anymore and what was myth. He had been digesting information for several weeks now. Some things made sense and others seemed impossible to believe, and yet . . .

He wanted to believe.

Why? Why did he want to believe in the power of a myth?

His eyes drifted shut and he fought sleep, knowing he would dream, but not wanting to.

The long, wooden table was brimming with a variety of food and sweets, the rich scents tempting the senses. It was a display for gluttony at its finest.

"Indulge," the man said on a whisper to the fiery-haired beauty.

She looked the delicious and abundant fare over and slowly shook her head.

He picked up a sugar-coated red grape and offered it to her. "Just a taste?"

"I'm not hungry."

"What does that matter?" He slowly licked at the sugar on the grape. "It tastes good, sweet and"—he paused and bit into the fat grape, a drop of juice catching on his chin—"succulent."

"I am not hungry," she repeated.

"Indulge anyway," he said, offering her the other half of the grape. "It feels good; come taste."

She held her hand up at his approach. "Don't test me."

"I am not testing, sweet. I'm tempting." He finished the grape and wiped away the drop of juice, licking it from his finger.

She shook her head, her tolerance fading. "You think to tempt me with this display of gluttony?"

"I offer you a feast."

"You offer me famine."

His voice filled with anger. "You speak in riddles."

"That you should understand."

"Do not play teacher with me," he demanded.

"Then do not act like a neophyte."

He threw his hands up and wide, causing thunder to crack loudly outside the thick stone walls of the castle. "You tempt my patience."

Her smile purposely teased. "When did you learn patience?"

He was quick to respond. "The day I decided you would share my bed."

They stood face-to-face, he having moved rapidly to her side in an attempt to intimidate. She raised a hand to his handsome face. "Patience takes practice. I shall see that you have much of it."

His arm went around her slim waist. "And I will continue to tempt you to indulge, to taste the forbidden, to surrender."

He kissed her softly, their lips barely touching, a faint teasing kiss that tempted her senses. When he felt her shiver he brushed a rough kiss across her lips and then took complete command.

They were soon locked in an embrace and between kisses he urged her to indulge her desires and taste fully of life.

Indulge. Indulge. Indulge.

Michael twisted and turned, mumbling the word over and over and over in his sleep.

Tempest, however, had bolted up in bed, the distinct taste of Marcus on her lips. His power was growing and he wanted her to know it.

Michael set to work over the next few days to attending to the minor repairs that the cottage needed. There weren't many, and he thought to take his time with them, giving him more time with Tempest. But the more he thought about it the more he decided that perhaps his decision wasn't a wise one.

He foolishly had fallen in love with Tempest. It was a crazy thought, but then love was none too sane. She fascinated him in more ways than one. Sure, she was beautiful, but beautiful women were a dime a dozen. Her wealth made little difference to him. He could live in this small cottage with her for the rest of his days, work at a menial job and be content. It was sharing everyday life with her that was so important, so necessary to him.

They could talk endlessly and never grow bored and they could share silence and never feel awkward. He loved the feel of her, the taste of her, the scent of her. She was familiar to him and he felt he had come home when he held her in his arms.

The one major obstacle appeared to be an old love in her life she simply could not forget. He supposed she could forget him, given time, and perhaps if he made love to her he could *make* her forget him.

But being honest with himself he knew that he wanted her to love him for himself and not for any other reason, because his love was the only real and solid thing he had to offer her.

The more he worked the more he thought and the more he decided that by prolonging his departure he prolonged the inevitable disappointment and hurt that was certain to follow. With that thought weighing heavily on his mind, he made a decision.

He would leave tomorrow and spare them both the pain.

He hesitated about approaching her with the news, or perhaps it was his own reluctance to follow through with his decision that made him delay speaking with her.

It was late afternoon when he finished the last of the repair work and returned the tools to their cabinet. He had worked slowly, cleaned up slowly and now he walked slowly to the kitchen where he knew Tempest would be busy preparing the evening meal.

As usual, the kitchen smelled delicious, and he was certain he sniffed pot roast, which meant mashed potatoes and gravy. His mouth was already watering. Then there was the sight of her in a long, pale-blue column dress with a deep purple and blue fringed shawl draped around her waist and dark purple socks on her feet. Her hair was piled on her head though several strands fell free along her neck and down her cheeks. Rosy cheeks from cooking over the stove.

"Supper will be ready in thirty minutes if you want to wash up first," she said with a smile.

He nodded. "I'll take a shower."

She stopped snapping string beans and stared at him. "Is something wrong?"

He plunged right in, afraid he would lose his courage. "I've decided that since the repair work is finished and I'm healed that I shouldn't impose on you any longer, so I'll be leaving early tomorrow morning."

Eighteen

~

Tempest was struck speechless, her heart beating wildly and her lungs fighting for air.

And Michael simply turned and walked out of the room.

She grabbed the edge of the counter, needing something to hang on to, an anchor to keep her in place, or else she would sink in a pitiful heap to the floor.

Leave? How could he?

She didn't expect this from him. No, she didn't expect this from Marcus, but he wasn't Marcus, or he didn't know that he was or didn't care that he was. He was reacting as Michael would. The man who had suffered many hurts and disappoints in his life and was attempting not to suffer another.

This was the man she loved.

Could she let him leave, walk out of her life?

Would Marcus let him, or would Michael be the stronger of the two?

Or did any of it matter?

She shook her head. Nothing mattered to her at the moment but Michael and how she felt about him. She could not deny her love for him.

Him.

Not Marcus.

She loved Michael with all his physical and emotional scars.

He was an exceptional man who accepted people for their own worth. Who had the courage to face adversities and emerge stronger because of them. He had a good, kind soul and she could not let him simply walk out of her life. She had waited too long for him.

Michael.

Not Marcus.

Tempest approached a chair on shaky legs, her hand not leaving the counter until she could plant it firmly on the back of a chair by the table. She sat to give her decision thought. It was one that was necessary and one she had known was inevitable, but with this joining there was one difference.

With Marcus she understood she could never really surrender herself completely to him. To do so would be surrendering her powers to his and forging a bond so powerful nothing could destroy it.

With Michael?

She shook her head. Could she join with him and not completely surrender herself? She didn't know and not knowing gave her reason to pause and consider the consequences.

Joining with Michael could cause Marcus to emerge full force with all his powers, abilities and memories, but then there was the spell. It had to be fulfilled one way or another.

And a portion of it already had been. Michael had created a life for himself that had taught him invaluable lessons and had strengthened his character. From their many talks she had discovered how he had learned to cherish life not only for himself but for others. And she understood that his scars represented the battles he had fought to protect others. He had surrounded himself with magic and light without realizing it and it had served him well. Which brought him to the point in the spell where he might feel as though he were losing his way and instinctively he had sought her out.

Whether or not he recalled all the words, she had said something had driven him to find her and that something was the force of the spell. It was in his dreams that he recalled magical memories, and the way in which he responded to them would be a deciding factor in his choice.

She shook her head slowly, her thoughts troubling her.

What if he chose unwisely?

Would she have the courage to look Michael in the eyes and send him away forever?

Her question produced a moment of fear that startled her. Fear was an emotion she rarely experienced, since she understood its conception. One had to believe in it to give it life. Which meant that she feared losing Michael more than she cared to admit.

Witches were wise women. They understood the variables and rhythms of life and worked with them. They forever sought knowledge and the understanding that came with it. Their steps were taken with purpose and awareness.

And Tempest could do no differently now.

She was aware, fully aware, of how much she loved Michael, so her purpose was clear. She wished to join with him out of love. She understood the consequences and chose to accept them, whatever they may be.

And fear?

She smiled. She would not allow the wasteful emotion to interfere.

She stood and saw to covering the cooked food so that it would remain hot. She laughed to herself, knowing that she would reheat the dishes later, much later this evening.

With purpose and awareness that gave her courage, she calmly climbed the steps.

Michael walked out of the bathroom shirtless and shoeless, wearing his worn blue jeans. His wet hair dripped water onto his naked chest, the tiny beads sliding slowly down over his hard muscles.

Tempest walked directly to him ready to tell him how she felt, how much she wanted him to stay here with her when instead she did what seemed the most natural. She leaned forward and with an eager tongue began to lick the beads of water off his chest.

Her actions stunned him and for a moment he froze, shutting his eyes against the exquisite pleasure, knowing he had to stop her and knowing he damn well didn't want to.

Her tongue licked softly and gently, like a kitten slowly drinking herself full. With the tip of her tongue she flicked at the tiny drop caught on his nipple and before she could rush her tongue over the sensitive dark orb he grabbed her by the shoulders and held her a safe distance away from him.

He fought to control his raging emotions and took several seconds to calm himself, though he doubted the brief cooling period would help. At that moment he wanted nothing more than to scoop her up, carry her to her bed and make love with her until they both were exhausted. But he wanted them making love because of love, and that was a dream, this was reality. Tomorrow he was leaving and he wanted no one-night stand between them.

He was about to tell her when she pressed a finger to his lips. "Let me say what I must."

He nodded, his heart beating madly and his body anticipating.

Tempest thought of all the things she wanted to say to him and said the most simple. "I love you. I don't want you to leave. I want you in my life forever."

He smiled and it grew into a gentle laugh. "I'm dreaming, right?"

She laughed, stepped out of his grasp and with deliberate slowness licked from his nipple, along his neck, up to his ear and whispered, "Welcome to *my* dream."

He turned his face to capture her lips with a gentle tug. "Do you really love me?"

She tugged back at him with more of a demand. "With my heart and soul."

Her demand faded as he took command of his own. "I have a condition."

"Anything," she agreed, melting against him.

He laughed, feeding her raging desire with his own. "Our love must be forever. I can't love you any other way. I don't want to."

She pulled away from him so she could look into his eyes and see to his soul and know the truth. "You love me, Michael." And he did, she saw it, felt it, understood it.

Michael loved her.

"Always," he admitted candidly. "Since that day in the snowstorm when you appeared out of nowhere and kissed my pain away I've loved you. I feel as if I've loved you forever."

She threw her arms around him. "Oh, Michael, I love you so very much."

He scooped her up in his arms, holding her tightly to him. "Pinch me so I know I'm not dreaming."

She nibbled at his ear. "Take me to bed and I'll prove to you this isn't a dream."

They were in her bedroom in no time. Clothes were discarded in haste and they collasped on the bed, he coming down gently on top of her.

Maybe it was weeks of controlling his passion or years of waiting to find love. He didn't know and he didn't care.

"Later we can take our time. I want you right now," he said and kissed her senseless.

She felt his need and the impressive size of him pressed hard against her and she grew wet with desire.

He ran a firm hand over her breast, squeezing the plump mound as his mouth took pleasure in tasting her hard nipple. His hand moved on, while his mouth remained pleasuring them both.

His work-worn hands skimmed over her, anxiously moving down along her waist, over her hips, across her belly and easing down into the tangle of soft curls between her legs.

He moved his mouth to hers and brushed a kiss over her lips as he said, "Open for me."

Her body turned liquid and she did as he asked, his fingers slipping in with a suddenness that excited and surprised. He rested his forehead to hers. "Damn, you're so wet and ready."

Her need was as urgent as his and she arched her back and whispered, "Now, Michael, I want you now."

He didn't need coaxing. He had contained himself for far too long, and besides, he had the rest of their lives to take his time with her and that thought made him all the more hard and anxious.

He entered her quickly and she cried out from the sheer joy of his much-wanted invasion.

He stilled, looking down at her in question, and she smiled. "Don't stop. You feel so good."

He grinned, pleased by her encouragement, and once again moved to bury himself deeper inside her. She moved to accept him, thrust after thrust, until they set a rhythm that captivated them both.

Tempest wanted it to go on and on forever, but it had been so very long and she knew her climax would come fast and furious.

Michael looked down at her, sensing her fight to prolong her release and feeling her need to surrender to herself. "Don't fight it, Tempest. Don't," he urged and drove harder into her. "Let go. Let go."

She shook her head. "Not without you."

He laughed. "Damn, you're stubborn—but I'm in control here, sweetheart."

And with that he thrust into her fast and furiously, rushing her to a climax that had her throwing her head back and screaming.

He joined her without a problem, his own release as explosive as hers.

They shuddered against each other and remained joined for several silent moments, each reluctant to part. And when they finally did it was to lay wrapped in each other's arms.

With his breathing finally calmed, Michael said, "Damn, it's real."

She playfully pinched him in the side. "Very real."

He laughed and hugged her to him. "And magical."

"Love is magic at its best."

"Did it take my leaving for you to realize your love for me?"

He questioned almost as much as she did, but she understood his need to know. "Not really. I found myself attracted to you from the beginning and the more I came to know you the more I cared and the more I fell in love."

"No love at first sight?" He didn't sound disappointed—only curious.

She was honest. "I definitely felt something when we first met, and I felt the need to explore it, examine it and enjoy it. And in doing so I discovered love at its best."

He kissed her, soft and gentle. "Damn, I'm lucky."

"We both are."

His next question sounded anxious. "What now?"

Her precise thoughts, and not an easy question to answer, but her years of wisdom provided one. "Let nature take its course."

He seemed skeptical. "And what course might that be?"

"Time, so we may come to know one another better."

"I feel as if I've known you a lifetime, and I feel anxious for our life together to begin. I want all of you completely and fully. I want your total surrender and yet somehow that isn't even enough." He shook his head. "It's crazy how I feel about you. I don't even understand it at times. There are moments I feel the need to protect you, and then there are moments I want your complete capitulation. The one constant in my warring emotions is that you remain a part of me, an intricate part, or else life simply wouldn't be worth living."

She understood better than he how he felt and why, and yet she could provide no explanation. He had to discover on his own. He had to emerge in his own time and in his own way. Her hands were tied. The only thing she could do was love him.

And she did.

Later that evening Tempest reheated the cold food and they took their plates to eat before the warmth of the fireplace in the living room.

"This food tastes too good to be leftovers," he said, scooping up a mound of mashed potatoes and gravy.

"Magic," she said with a smile. "It comes in handy when cooking."

"Is your interest in magic because of your ancestor?"

"I must admit that she has a distinct bearing on my life." She poured them each another glass of merlot from the bottle that sat on the coffee table.

"When did you learn of her existence?"

Tempest sipped at her wine and took time answering. "I can't recall." She then decided to turn the question back on him. "You have a fascination with her, don't you?"

He almost looked embarrassed. "I don't understand why. Don't know what I find so interesting about witches and such."

"It's the unexplainable."

"What do you mean?"

"The concept of witches has fascinated society for centuries. Today it is a practiced craft, though not totally accepted by society. There are still those who believe it to be the work of the devil, and then there are those who abuse the craft and hurt the very nature of it. And there are those who wish to believe in the power or magic of witches."

"Which is why myths and tales pop up from time to time."

"Again, the unexplainable. People are thrilled and excited by the idea and the possibility that magic could be real. When if they would only believe in themselves, that is when they would discover true magic."

He laughed, dropping his napkin to his empty plate. "Back to belief, are we?" He finished the wine in his glass and poured himself another. "Do you *believe* that your ancestor's powers came from her simply believing?"

"If she were a true witch her magic wouldn't work if she didn't believe."

"Okay," he said, leaning forward. "Let's put this theory of yours to a test. You claim that if I believe strongly enough I could perform magic, right?"

She worried where this questioning would take them. Michael might not believe, but Marcus had no difficulty in believing in himself. "Right."

"So a little hocus-pocus and I could raise that wine bottle off the table, right?"

She smiled and nodded. Marcus detested wasting his talent on menial magic—perhaps her concern was for nothing.

He flexed his fingers and blinked his eyes a few times as if preparing himself. "Okay, here goes." He concentrated on the near-empty wine bottle, focusing all his attention on it, but then it wasn't his attention that was needed; it was his energy.

Tempest couldn't help but giggle, he looked so serious in his concentration and determination to prove her wrong.

Suddenly the wine bottle shot across the table and crashed into the flaming logs in the fireplace and for an instant, a sheer fraction of a second, Tempest caught the fury of Marcus in Michael's dark eyes.

He was there waiting, growing stronger, more powerful with each passing day and she by joining with Michael had just increased his strength considerably.

"Damn," Michael muttered. "Did I do that?"

"Do you believe you did?" she asked, hiding her concern with a smile.

He looked perplexed. "Part of me wants to believe and part of me looks for sound reasoning."

"The choice is yours."

"What do you think?" he asked as if she had the right answer.

She spoke words she hoped would help him. "I think you're a good witch who needs practice."

He laughed, shook his head briefly, then stared at her with a sudden passion that instantly heated her body. "Since I'm a good witch, let's make some good magic." He didn't wait for her response; he crawled on hands and knees around to her side.

Her eyes widened from the look of pure carnal lust in his eyes. "Don't you want to go upstairs?"

"No," he said firmly, sitting back on his haunches and grabbing her by the ankles to yank her toward him.

His swift action caught her off guard, and she was unable to grab hold of anything or do anything to stop her sudden momentum.

He pushed her gray knit dress up to her waist and grinned when he saw that she wore no panties. His grin grew as he grabbed her bottom and raised her up to meet his descending mouth.

She gasped and grabbed at the rug on the floor beneath her. His tongue was quick and skillful, and she was mindless in mere seconds, begging him like a fool for more and more and more.

When he stopped she almost cried out her disappointment, but then she heard his zipper and moaned with anticipation. He grabbed her around the waist and brought her down on him fast and hard, so fast that she climaxed, immediately crying out his name.

Her body grew limp, but he would have none of her lethargy.

"Ride me," he demanded. "Ride me hard."

His hands on her waist set the rhythm and bracing her hands on his broad shoulders for support she picked up the tempo and rode him harder than she thought possible. She thought, with what little reasoning she had left, to make him cry out her name, but it was she who screamed and he who captured her mouth with a crushing kiss as they exploded in a blinding climax together.

They finally made it up to her bedroom after cleaning up the living room and leaving the dishes in the sink. She insisted she needed a shower and he insisted on joining her, tormenting her unmercifully with his hands and lips.

And once back in the bedroom he proceeded with his intimate torture until she thought she would completely surrender to him, but she didn't. She held a small part of herself back and kept her eyes from directly meeting his. She didn't want to see Marcus there. This was her time with Michael. Marcus would return soon enough, but for now she wanted Michael and only Michael.

And he wanted her. She could feel his raging desire as strongly as her own and met his demands with those of her own. This time was theirs. How long it would last she didn't know and at the moment she didn't care.

With a tiredness born of pleasure they lay wrapped in each other's arms and drifted off to sleep.

Nineteen

~

Tempest. Tempest. You know I am here, answer me."

She shook her head. If she ignored his insistent voice he would go away.

"I will not go away," *the familiar voice said with a harsh laugh.* "I have come back and you will help to make me grow stronger and stronger."

"I will not," *she argued.*

"But you will. You want to. You miss me."

"I have Michael now."

"Foolish witch, I am Michael."

She shook her head, attempting to deny his words. "No, Michael is different. He is good and kind—"

"He is me. We are one and I am the stronger."

"No," *she said adamantly.* "Michael has learned what you never did and he will choose wisely when the time comes."

His voice held anger. "I will conquer your spell, Tempest, and you will surrender completely to me."

"Not to you, to Michael."

"Not Michael. Me, Marcus. Marcus. Marcus."

"No!" Tempest shot up in bed, Michael bolting upright beside her, his arms going instantly around her.

"It's all right. It's all right," he said, holding her tightly.

She pressed her head to his chest and tried to calm her rapid breathing.

Michael rocked her back and forth in his arms. "It's only a dream. It can't hurt you."

She wished she believed that but she knew better. Marcus had the strength to come to her and let her know that soon he would emerge, blend with Michael and regain full power.

But she believed in Michael.

But Michael was Marcus.

Once she had also believed in Marcus. She had seen a brief light shine in his soul and that had given her hope for him and given her the courage to cast her spell. Now she must have patience and do the only thing she could to help.

Love.

The strongest of all magic.

Michael sat at the kitchen table stroking Bear who sat contentedly in his lap. He kept a steady and concerned eye on Tempest who was fixing lunch. Early morning had found them not very hungry, so they skipped breakfast. It was already well past noon and if he hadn't mentioned his hunger he doubted she would have considered eating. She had been preoccupied all morning, and he was certain it had to do with her dream.

He thought he had heard her call out for Marcus when she woke from her dream, or perhaps he had heard the name in his own dream, he just couldn't be certain and that disturbed him. He didn't want their relationship starting off with her still haunted by an old flame. He preferred her thoughts focused solely on him since he couldn't think of anything but her.

Love sure could drive a person crazy, but then crazy didn't seem so bad all of a sudden.

She chopped the celery and onions and mixed them with the tuna as if she was a mechanical robot. It was obvious her thoughts were miles away and he intended to bring her back right fast.

"Tell me about Marcus."

Bear raised his head, hissed and spit and then settled down.

Tempest on the other hand dropped the bowl of tuna she was mixing, spilling the contents all over the countertop.

She sighed and with trembling hands began to clean up the mess with paper toweling.

Michael came up behind her, having deposited an annoyed Bear on the chair. He reached out, slipping his hand over hers. "What's wrong, Tempest?"

He was afraid to ask if she had had a change of heart. He thought she might have dreamed of her old love and decided she had made a mistake in declaring her love for him. That frightening thought tore at his gut.

Tempest turned, wrapped her arms around his waist and rested her head on his chest. "I don't want to lose you, Michael."

Her remark stunned him and he wrapped strong arms around her. "You're not going to lose me."

"Promise me," she said, looking up at him through misty eyes.

His kiss was possessive. "I promise. You have me forever and ever."

She sighed, though she didn't sound relieved and placed her head back on his chest.

"Do you want to talk about this, and be honest with me, does this have something to do with this Marcus character?"

She laughed lightly. "You're perceptive."

He admitted the truth. "No, jealous."

She looked at him with surprise. "Really?"

"Really. The thought that you actually loved another man drives me crazy and I'm feeling crazy enough as it is. Crazy in love, to be exact." He kissed her again to prove his point.

"I'm feeling just as crazy," she said after regaining the breath his kiss had stolen. "In love."

"Then the problem is?"

"Losing you. The thought frightens me to the depths of my soul."

He could relate to her fears. The idea that he could lose her twisted at his gut and made him want to tremble. But life had its risk and there was nothing either of them could do about that. He had learned that at an early age. The only thing they could do was love each other and face life together.

"I don't plan on going anywhere. I'm staying right here with you."

She looked as if she still didn't believe him.

He cupped her chin firmly. "I'm not Marcus. You have to believe in me. *Me*, Tempest."

She asked him the strangest question. "Do you believe in you, Michael?"

He looked at her oddly for a moment and then smiled. "Yeah, I do."

She kissed him softly. "I believe in you, Michael. Remember always that I believe in *you*."

He gently returned her kiss and was concerned by the sadness he sensed she felt. He wanted her happy right now. "Ham," he said, nodding slowly. "I knew we should have had ham for lunch. It would have survived the fall."

She laughed shaking her head. "Perceptive again. Are you sure you're not a witch?"

"If I was I would clean this mess up with the snap of my fingers." He snapped his fingers to prove his point.

They both laughed but Bear hissed and spat once again, alarming them both, but for different reasons. Michael looked his way and Tempest turned to see that the turned-over bowl of tuna was now upright, its contents intact. Michael's magic had worked and it had upset Bear.

She blocked his view of the counter, turning and giving him a slight shove. "See to Bear. I'll clean this up and make ham sandwiches."

He didn't argue, his concern for the disgruntled cat catching his full attention. He picked up Bear and soothed him with gentle strokes, and the agitated cat settled instantly.

Tempest had no choice but to toss the tuna salad in the garbage.

Michael pulled a chair out from beneath the table and settled down with Bear in his lap. "Tell me about Marcus."

Bear hissed, slightly content with Michael's attention.

"It's obvious Bear didn't like him."

Memories recalled just how true his remark was. Bear had entered her life when she was about five hundred years old. She rarely went anyplace without him. He had attended Sarina's wedding but had refused to join her in the car for the return trip home. He hissed and spat and protested until she had no choice but to transport him home with a snap of her fingers. He had always been a temperamental feline but she loved him dearly and wouldn't have him any other way.

The few times Marcus had come to her cottage Bear made it known that he did not like him. The two kept a safe distance from each other. Bear was confident that Tempest would not allow Marcus to harm him, which allowed him to continue his antics, and Marcus was aware of Tempest's attachment to the cat, therefore he attempted to ignore the temperamental beast, as he often referred to him.

"Tempest."

She shook her head, looking to Michael and attempting to recall his question. She smiled after a brief hesitation and her shaking head turned to a confirming nod. "The two didn't get along."

"You get a treat for that, pal," he whispered to Bear.

"What was that?" she asked, having heard only a mumble.

He cleared his throat. "How did he treat you?"

She stared at him, lost in her thoughts once again wondering over the wisdom of the conversation and the sanity of it. He was Marcus and he was asking about himself. But then she did need to take responsibility for this situation since she had cast the spell.

He waved his hand at her. "Tempest, are you here with me?"

She shook her head, returning her to reality. "Sorry, my thoughts keep wandering today."

"Where do they wander?"

"To memories."

"Good ones?" he asked.

"Aren't the good memories the ones that are always remembered when a relationship ends?"

He recalled his childhood memories and nodded. "I suppose you're right."

She realized then that she wanted to answer his question. "I have good memories of Marcus. He was a complex man, and demanding, and yet . . ." She paused as if searching. "He understood me and in his own way respected me"—she smiled—"even at times admired me."

Michael didn't care for the loving way she spoke of him. "What happened?"

"I couldn't give him what he—" She stopped abruptly and then softly said, "Wanted. I couldn't give him what he wanted."

He saw the pain in her eyes and his heart ached for her and at that moment he wished that he had the bastard here in front of him so he could cause him some real physical pain. "What did he want that you couldn't give him?"

"My soul," she whispered.

A sudden chill ran down his spine and he stared mindlessly at her. "I don't understand."

"He wanted my complete surrender, everything I am, the

whole of me, what gives me purpose, my very being. My soul."

Her explanation made him shudder and he shook his head, still not understanding. "Why?"

She walked over to the table with a plate full of ham sandwiches and pickles and a bowl of potato chips. She sat them down and took a chair across the table from Michael.

"Because he offered the same to me."

"Now I'm really confused," he said, reaching for a sandwich to place on his plate. "If he was willing to give you the same, to commit that strongly, what was the problem?"

Tempest filled her own plate. "Love."

He stopped before taking a bite of a chip. "Love?"

Her smile was sad. "He didn't love me. He didn't believe in love."

Michael dropped the chip to his plate and sat back in his chair. "What did he believe in if not love?"

"The power of two souls."

Michael was about to shake his head again when he stopped and stared at her, stunned. "God lord, he was a witch."

She remained silent and watched his eyes widen. "No—he was a warlock."

Tempest simply nodded.

"And he sought you out because of your ancestor," he said as if memories rushed back at him but interpreting them didn't prove easy.

She nodded, again waiting to see how far this would take him.

He grew anxious. "Is that why you have so many books on witches and such? Did you want to understand his beliefs better? Did he come from a line of witches?" He grinned. "Did he possess magical powers?"

"He believed."

Her simple answer stunned him and words failed him.

Tempest munched on a chip, waiting.

How did he respond? How did he even feel? The man she had loved had believed himself a warlock. He didn't even know if he believed in witches, warlocks and things that go bump in the night.

Damn, the guy could be a nut, a raving lunatic, or . . .

A warlock.

But in today's day and age? He could very well practice the Craft, but a warlock with magical powers? There was no such thing. And yet Tempest said he believed.

Damn. He had to go fall in love with a woman who had an ancestor that was a witch and who had once loved a man who claimed to be a warlock. Next thing you know he'd be seeing fairies.

"Do you believe, Michael?" she asked.

"I believe you were right in ending the relationship. Whatever attracted you to him? Besides his looks, since I recall you mentioning how handsome he was."

"It wasn't his looks that attracted me; it was his interests. We had much in common."

"Your interest in the bizarre?" he teased.

"Are you bizarre?" she asked with a smile. "You find the history of witches interesting."

"It does fascinate me. But tell me, do you really believe that witches possess magical powers or that at one time they did?"

"When we close our minds to possibilities we no longer believe, and belief encourages growth and sustains life. Without belief nothing can exist. Therefore, I believe in possibilities."

He shook his head. "Remind me not to ask you a complex question."

She laughed softly. "You've opened your mind, Michael, to possibilities. Do you believe Marcus possessed magical powers?"

He gave her question serious thought. "This may sound strange, but I think your ancestor outshined this guy Marcus."

"Possibilities, Michael, possibilities," she said and raised her water glass in a toast.

He clinked his with hers. "Possibilities and—" He paused and smiled. "I believe in the possibility of a walk in the woods after lunch. . . ."

She had walked in the woods with Marcus many times. Now she would walk in them with Michael. "I believe that's possible."

They laughed, talked and ate their ham sandwiches and Bear slept contentedly in Michael's lap.

The woods seemed quiet to Michael. It was a beautiful prespring day. Winter's chill remained in the air but the burst of sunshine added a degree of warmth that reminded that spring was around the corner. Small buds peeked from tree branches. The green foliage stretched anxiously toward the sun, gaining nourishment for new sprouts. And patches of stubborn snow melted slowly away.

He held Tempest's hand as they walked a well-worn path into the woods that surrounded a good portion of her cottage. He wore workboots, black jeans and a black sweatshirt. He didn't feel the need for a jacket. Actually he felt warm even though the air was brisk.

Tempest wore dark-green leggings with a matching hip-length cable-knit sweater. Black leather boots made the trail easy for her to walk and a dark-green blanket jacket sprinkled with tiny gold stars added extra warmth. Her fiery hair was free and her creamy cheeks were tinged pink by the bite of cold air.

Michael held firm to her hand, keeping it warm in his. "I love the outdoors."

"Is that why you decided to backpack through Scotland?"

"I felt a need to see this land," he attempted to explain. "We docked at Glasgow a few years back and due to unexpected repairs we were stuck there for a couple of weeks. I took off for a week and discovered I loved the land and the people, and when the ship left dock I promised myself I'd be back to explore."

He didn't tell her that the need to return was so great he had just picked up and left one day, catching rides on ships that finally brought him back to Scotland. He couldn't understand the relentless urge that drove him, he only he knew he had to satisfy it. He had to return to Scotland. He had been away too long, far too long.

"Then you won't mind living here, making this place your home?"

He stopped walking, bringing her to a halt beside him. He brought her hand up to meet his lips. "I love you, Tempest. Wherever you are is home for me."

She wore a smile that teased. "You won't get bored isolated here with me in this place?"

She caught the glint of mischief in his dark eyes and admired his slim lips as they came down on hers and kissed her senseless.

He moved off her mouth to nibble at her ear. "I can think of things that will keep us both busy."

Her sigh was part moan as she leaned into him, and he in turn wrapped her arms behind her back so that he could feel the length of her pressed against him.

"Those kind of sighs are going to get you in trouble," he warned playfully.

"Promises promises," she teased, nipping at his neck. "The ground is wet, there's no place for a romp."

"Sweetheart, you just challenged me," he said with a deep laugh and held her arms firm behind her back as he walked her backwards toward a thickly based tree.

She giggled and squirmed to free herself, though not whole-heartedly.

He nipped at her neck and mouth and all but carried her over to the tree as she continued her useless struggle. Her giggles didn't help her any, and they echoed eerily throughout the woods.

The first light sting to his face caught Michael by surprise. He thought it a bug and shook his head, attempting to shake the pesky pest away. But two more followed and he thought he caught a sparkle of light out of the corner of his eye. He freed one hand and swatted at the tiny shaft of light.

"Don't!" Tempest yelled and was out of his grasp in a flash, dropping to her hands and knees.

"What's wrong?"

"You just knocked out a fairy."

Twenty

"I what?" Michael asked, stunned, swatting more carefully at the tiny sparkling pests that descended down around him.

"Leave him be," Tempest said with a shout and a wave of her hand.

The tiny sparkling lights moved away from him and hovered over Tempest.

He watched her reach down and pluck something off the wet ground and place it gently in the palm of her hand.

"Beatrice," she said with concern.

"What the hell is going on?" Michael demanded.

Tempest shot him a lethal look and with a pointed finger ordered, "Silence!"

He and his senses froze into a silent rest.

Tempest turned her attention back to the tiny unconscious fairy. "Beatrice." She held her hand over the plump little body, allowing her healing energy to rain down over the fairy.

The other fairies gathered around her, casting a soft glow from the sparkle of their wings. Whispers of concern sounded more like the buzzing of bees and they waited impatiently to see if the Ancient One could heal Beatrice.

Tempest continued radiating energy over the prone little body while keeping a careful eye on Michael. With Marcus regaining his strength her spell would not last long on him.

She had to hurry and she had to rectify this unfortunate situation.

A hint of a moan sounded from Beatrice and all the fairies breathed a sigh of relief and buzzed about how they were confident that the Ancient One would make Beatrice well.

"Easy," Tempest warned softly when Beatrice attempted to sit up fast.

Beatrice held her head. "I feel as though I've had too many fruit nectars."

Tempest laughed. "You took a whopping blow."

"The only thing I remember is going into a flying dive to protect you."

"Protect me?"

Beatrice sat up slowly, straightening her crooked head wreath before pointing at Michael. "From him."

Tempest finally understood and smiled. "He wasn't harming me, we were being playful."

Beatrice looked at her oddly until she comprehended her remark. Then her face turned bright red. "Oh my gosh!"

Tempest attempted to contain her laughter. "I appreciate the thought."

Beatrice stood with help from Tempest. "My deepest apologizes, Ancient One."

"Accepted, but not necessary, and I want you all to know that Michael is a truly good soul," she said, looking around her.

A soft buzz filled the air and Beatrice flew up to join her friends, though she flitted for a moment in front of Tempest's face. "We trust your word, but we will remain close in case you should require our help."

"Thank you," Tempest said. "But you must go now; the spell cannot hold Michael much longer. And he is not ready to be introduced to fairies just yet."

Beatrice smiled, waved and with a rapid flutter ascended up and away, the other fairies following close behind her.

Michael began to move and Tempest had mere minutes to come up with a reasonable explanation. She chose confusion as her defense.

"What the hell is going on?" Michael asked and shook his head, expecting something to fly at him.

She bounced up to swat at him playfully. "You don't play fair."

He raised a brow. "Fair or fairy?"

"Fairy?" she repeated and then clapped her hands like an excited child. "Oh, you've seen a fairy! It's said the woods are full of them."

Michael felt confused and took a moment to think. "You said fairy."

"I said fair."

He shook his head adamantly. "Something about a fairy and a knockout."

"You saw a fairy that was a knockout?"

He pointed an accusing finger at her but found he lacked words of reason.

She playfully grabbed his finger, covering it completely with her hand. There had been enough excitement for one day. "I prefer where we were about you not being fair."

His thoughts drifted back to his previous intentions and the tree. Unfortunately he couldn't shake the fairy dilemma. "Do you think there are fairies in these woods?"

"Belief, Michael," she reminded him.

The sun suddenly vanished behind a cloud and the wind picked up.

Tempest released his finger and stepped in close to him.

His arms instantly circled her protectively. "We better get back to the house. It looks like the weather may change."

Tempest agreed, not liking the look of the ominous overhead cloud.

Fat raindrops fell just as they entered the house and the sudden weather change disturbed Tempest. It had been a beautiful day with no rain predicted. Where had the cloud come from?

Tempest had barely slipped out of her jacket when Michael slid eager arms around her. "About that challenge."

"That was in the woods," she teased

"A challenge is a challenge, sweetheart."

"There is the bed upstairs," she offered with a smile.

He shook his head slowly and his eyes darkened the same moment the afternoon light faded and a chilling darkness descended followed by a powerful clap of thunder and a sharp bolt of lightning.

Tempest felt a rush of heat enter the room and she instantly erected a guard around herself.

Michael stepped away from her, stripping off his sweatshirt.

She tried to ignore his muscled chest and the impressive width of his shoulders but it wasn't working. She had wrapped her arms around him too many times not to think about how good he felt. Marcus had been tall, lean and slim of build and his strength remarkable. She had felt a hint of that strength in Michael and knew it would grow.

Michael looked as if he rushed toward her, and she took several hasty steps back.

"Keep going," he said, his voice deeply commanding.

She had the distinct feeling Marcus was making himself known to her, due probably to the fact that she wrapped a silent spell around him. He had hated when she demonstrated her skills and he was incapable of deflecting them.

There was, however, one place he always remained in control, and that was when they joined.

Tempest continued to take careful and slow steps backwards into the kitchen.

"Turn," he ordered sharply and pointed his finger toward the sitting room.

She cast a quick glance over her shoulder. Did he intend their destination to be the couch?

He shook his head and gave a deep, chilling laugh. "You're so easy to read. The couch doesn't interest me; the greenhouse is our destination."

She tripped over her own feet and righted herself before he could reach out and touch her. She was right—Marcus was tormenting her. They had shared a memorable moment in the greenhouse and she supposed he intended to remind her of it.

But what of Michael? He was still part of him. How would he react?

She took cautious steps and once at the greenhouse door she turned around, opened it and entered in a rush.

Michael proved just as fast coming up behind her, slipping a possessive arm around her waist and whispering near her ear. "I want to taste you."

Her knees grew weak and if he hadn't been holding her she would have collapsed. It wasn't only his suggestive remark that caused her reaction; it was the intensity of his feelings when he spoke. She could sense the strength of his desire to do just as he said and it fired her own passion.

She knew their destination; she had gone there with Marcus. It was a small, tucked-away area abundant with blossoming plants and the surrounding pathways were heavy with mulch, providing the area with a decidedly woodsy atmosphere. And the overhead glass offered a spectacular view of the sky, dark and ominous as it was.

Michael stopped exactly where she had expected him to, though she hadn't expected the kisses he rained along her sensitive neck or for her knees to turn to complete jelly.

"I'm going to start at the top and work my way down."

That was it; her legs refused to hold her any longer. He laughed softly in her ear and tightened his hold on her waist.

She hadn't known he had grabbed the throw from the chair in the sitting room until he tossed it on the ground in front of her. It appeared to float down and spread perfectly over the mulch. She couldn't help but recall how Marcus had performed a similar feat, tossing down his cloak to spread evenly on the ground.

He rested his lips next to her cheek. "Now to rid you of these clothes."

He was purposely tormenting her. But who—Marcus or Michael?

We are one.

The problem was that she was attempting to separate the two and that was impossible. They were one and until one dominated the other there was nothing she could do.

Michael settled the dilemma for her by bringing her attention back to him and the matter at hand. He was slipping her sweater up, his hands roaming beneath the bulky wool to tease her warm flesh.

His fingers roamed slowly along her rib cage, lingering here and there as he made his way to her breasts. His hand moved over her black lace bra and teased the nipple beneath until it was rock hard and aching.

She waited impatiently for him to continue, pressing her body back against his, but he surprised her by suddenly pulling the sweater over her head and tossing it aside, then yanking her back against him and holding her firmly to him with the weight of his arm.

His free hand resumed in tormenting her nipples while his mouth feed feverishly at her neck and she moaned from the double pleasure he was creating for them both.

She felt his own readiness rubbing against her, and she relished the thought that he desired her with as much passion as she did him.

His own impatience won out over his methodical assault and with a rush he freed her of her bra. He spun her around and he dipped his head to capture a hard nipple in his mouth and feast. Her hands went to his broad shoulders for support and her head fell back with a small, low moan slipping from her lips.

She could feel his impatience grow along with her own. She wanted more and she wanted it now. He stepped back and hurried out of the rest of his clothing. Her breath caught when she viewed him completely naked—not that she hadn't before, but now in the shadowed light his body looked even more impressive in size and strength, and added to that was an air of danger and mystery. As he approached her she wondered who was about to intimately touch her—Michael or Marcus?

He immediately saw to removing the rest of her clothes and tossed them carelessly to the side, his hands eager to return to her. He held her for a moment at arm's length, his eyes taking their time to roam over her with appreciation.

He chose simple words to enflame her, though they came from his heart and that made all the difference. "You're beautiful."

He walked her slowly toward the throw on the ground and when her feet felt the soft knit she shivered, knowing he had finally had her where he wanted her.

He smiled, understanding her emotions, and then with a playful wink he lowered his lips to her breasts. She lost all sense of time and reason as he did as he had promised. He worked his way slowly down her body and when her legs began to turn weak he ordered her to stand.

He would not be denied; he would have her his way.

When his mouth finally touched his intended target she thought she would faint, but he ordered her yet again to stand still and she found herself obeying, though with great difficulty.

His tongue and fingers alternated in pleasuring her and she moaned and pleaded with him that she was about to collapse and still he would not relent. He simply continued having her his own way.

She was senseless with passion by the time he lowered her to the soft throw and she could do nothing but moan, "Please, Michael, please."

He laughed softly as he covered her with his body and took her gentle pleas into his mouth to taste and devour.

He pulled his mouth from hers and as he positioned himself to enter her he ordered on a whisper, "Surrender."

The word startled her and she looked into his eyes, dark brooding eyes that always insisted on having his way. She shook her head.

His entered her with deliberate slowness. "Surrender."

"No," she said, though her body arched eagerly against him.

He slipped further into her only to slip back out. "Surrender to me, Tempest."

"No." Her response sounded more like a plea.

He laughed and entered her full force, only to draw back yet again.

A moan of disappointment escaped her lips and she bit at them, angry with herself for giving him satisfaction in knowing that his little game was working.

His laugh turned hardy and his tormenting more thorough as he continued his game.

She called on her own strength and power and wisely began to repeat his name. "Michael. Michael. Michael."

It was a litany in his head and he shut his eyes and listened. His name sounded so good on her lips and he felt so good being inside her, loving her. And damn, but he loved her. She was part of him and he part of her, and he couldn't bear life without her.

She was a necessity to his soul.

And there was no need for surrender—only a merging. A merging of two souls into one, which was what he wanted from her. He wanted to merge with her. Lose himself within her. Forget the world existed. There would be only the two of them, stepping from the darkness into the light.

He opened his eyes and looked down at her, felt his body moving slowly, felt her body responding in kind, and he smiled. She smiled back and they began to move together, increasing their pace, moving with a more dominating force and riding on a love so pure it startled them both.

Michael took command then and Tempest obeyed without

question. He took them soaring to new heights and as they spiraled back down in an all-consuming heat their hearts caught, their souls touched and they burst together in a blinding light.

After waiting for his breathing to calm, Michael moved off her to draw her into his arms. She snuggled against him with a contented sigh and they lay in silence, watching the dark overhead cloud disappear and dusk cover the land.

"First night star," Tempest said, pointing her finger at the tiny glow in the far distance. "You must make a wish and hold it strong to your heart and silent on your lips."

Michael watched her reach out as if plucking the tiny twinkling brightness from the night sky and brought her fist to rest over her heart.

"Now you."

"The heavens have granted me my wish; I have you. I don't want anything else." He kissed the tip of her nose.

"Oh, Michael," she said on a sigh and moved her clenched fist to rest over his heart. "Then I'll share my wish with you."

"I want us to share everything, Tempest. Everything."

His kiss was solid and firm, as if his intention was to seal their fate.

But their fate had yet to be sealed by the completion of the spell and Tempest held her wish firm to his heart and wished with all her power and might that when the time came he would be wise and choose wisely.

She wanted so badly to do more, to help him more, to make him understand the consequences more, but she couldn't. She had cast a spell that would give him a chance, a strong second chance at life. The rest remained up to him.

She opened her clenched hand and placed her palm against his chest, the warmth of her healing touch penetrating his skin and she silently repeated her wish.

Give us both the courage to choose wisely.

Twenty-one

A sudden storm late that night pounded the cottage and Michael's sleep turned restless. He fought the dream that began to haunt him, but the force it possessed was like an intoxicating drug he was powerless to resist. And though he made an attempt to fight, he always managed in the end to surrender. Surrender to an energy that all but consumed him.

The man's hand ran over the naked woman's damp flesh. Their joining had been fast and furious, neither able to wait to join, but yet there was a tension in the air that was heavy and troubling.

They lay in a large bed draped with velvet curtains and a fire crackled in a large stone hearth, keeping the room warm.

The man's hand finally rested on the woman's stomach. "Why do you fight your surrender?"

"I cannot give you what you want."

"Yet I feel you want to give it."

The woman spoke softly. "What I want to give and what is right proves difficult."

"You deny yourself needlessly. Every time we join I can feel you on the verge of surrender, so close and so tempting and just when I think you will let go, give yourself to me completely, you pull back and deny yourself."

"It is necessary," she insisted.

"Why? You fear being touched by darkness?"

She smiled with confidence. "Do you fear being touched by light?"

"I can manage the light," he answered with equal confidence.

"Can you," she challenged. "In the light there is love, an emotion you seem to have difficulty with."

"Love makes no sense, it serves no purpose but to entrap and cause heartache and pain. Why subject myself to a useless emotion?"

"Know the essence of love and know the truth. Is it truth that you fear?"

He grew annoyed. "I fear nothing, yet I have the power of fear behind me."

She shook her head. "Fear holds no power over those who believe and know the truth."

He challenged her. "You do not fear darkness, then?"

"Somewhere in darkness there is light if one but looks with wise eyes."

He leaned over her to stare directly into her green eyes. "Surrender to my darkness and see if you can find a shred of light within me."

She placed a hand on his lean, hard chest. "I do not need to surrender to find light. You do."

A challenge he could not refuse. "I, unlike you, am confident in my powers and do not fear surrender."

"Then surrender to me," she said on a whisper.

"Gladly," he said and dropped back on the bed, spreading his arms out and offering his naked body in surrender.

"You will submit?" she asked seriously.

"I submit and will do nothing to stop you from having your way with me."

She could feel his confidence—it pulsated with strength—and she simply smiled and began to touch him.

They were both drenched with sweat by the time she climbed on top of him, and he took charge of their joining. She didn't protest; she let him have his way.

It was necessary.

And as they neared climax she whispered, "I found that shred of light in the darkness."

Michael bolted up in bed.

He was sweating, he was hard as a rock and he felt an invincible power stirring within him.

He looked down at Tempest, who slept peacefully. He wanted her with an urgency that he was certain the man in his dreams had felt. He told himself not to disturb her. He told himself to deal with these damn dreams. He told himself to ignore this raging force growing inside him.

He laughed beneath his breath and reached his hands out for Tempest.

Michael sat on the floor in his room, half a dozen books spread out before him and his eyes fixed on the symbols on the wall. A soft rain drizzled against the window and in the distance he heard the sound of classical music and knew Tempest was relaxing with a cup of tea and possibly readying for an afternoon nap.

Sleep eluded them after he had woken her early this morning. She had responded most willingly to his urgent demands, though for the first time he had felt a small part of her had maintained control and refused to surrender completely. He had never noticed the small bit of reluctance before, and he wondered if his dream had made him more aware, more sensitive to her emotions. The thought that she held even a tiny part of herself in reserve annoyed and disturbed him.

If she loved him, why the reluctance?

He shook his head, not understanding but intending to find out.

He returned his full attention to the symbols on the wall. He had realized that a protective symbol was placed before the spell, as if holding it firmly in place. And he couldn't help but shake the idea that he knew these symbols—somehow, somewhere he had seen them before and understood their meaning.

And lately he couldn't understand why he grew so annoyed every time he walked in this room and looked over the symbols. It was as if a quiet rage took hold of him until he finally had to leave the room. Today, however, he was determined at least to decipher a few more symbols.

He poured through the books in front of him, writing down different symbols and their meanings and attempting to make sense of them. Bear seemed to have different ideas, walking back and forth on top of the books and demanding more attention than usual. If Michael didn't know any better he would swear the cat was intentionally interfering with his work.

He picked him up for the fourth time and moved him off the books, telling him firmly to stay put on the rug beside him, when in the distance he heard the phone ring. After three rings he realized Tempest must have fallen into a deep sleep and with Bear on his heels he went downstairs to answer the phone.

"Michael," Sarina said, surprised when he picked up. "How is your ankle?"

"Completely mended thanks to your sister's care and generosity."

"She has a good and caring heart."

"Yes, she does," Michael agreed and felt that her remark was meant to remind.

"I'm actually glad you answered," Sarina said. "I've been trying to get Tempest to come visit with me and Dagon, and now our friends from the States have come for a visit and they would like to see Tempest again. Do you think you can convince her to come visit? And, of course, we would love for you to join us."

"Thank you for the invitation. I'll speak with Tempest about it."

"Is she there?" Sarina asked.

Michael sensed the caution in her question and wondered over it. "She's napping, but I can wake her if you'd like."

"No, no that won't be necessary," she said anxiously. "She is feeling well, though, isn't she?"

She gave Michael no time to respond. "A silly question. I've never known Tempest to be ill."

"Never?" Michael asked curiously.

"She takes excellent care of herself," Sarina said as if that explained all. "Though she does tire herself out at times."

Since he was the one who had recently exhausted Tempest he wanted Sarina to clarify her remark. "And how does she do that?"

"She's overly generous to those who seek her help."

"Is that my sister?" Tempest asked, entering the kitchen and rubbing the last remnant of sleep from her eyes.

Michael nodded. "Hold on, Sarina, your sister woke and wants to speak with you. It was nice talking with you."

"And you, Michael, and please come visit."

"We'll see," Michael said and handed the phone to Tempest.

She looked half asleep to him, and after she took the phone from him he stepped behind her, slipped his arm around her waist and drew her back to rest against him. She didn't protest, but relaxed against him while she spoke to her sister.

"Really, Sebastian and Ali are visiting, and Sydney, how wonderful. Yes, I would love to see them again."

"Sebastian says to tell you that he's practicing and getting better every day."

Tempest laughed, recalling how the mortal recently turned witch had delighted her with tales of his travesties and triumphs while learning his newly acquired craft. "I would love to talk with him again; he was so delightful."

Michael gave her waist a gentle squeeze and her neck a soft kiss and she smiled at the twinge of jealousy she felt in him.

"Then you must come visit," Sarina insisted. "I've invited Michael, as well."

"You say Sydney is also visiting?"

"Yes, and she wishes to talk with you. You must come visit, Tempest, you must."

Tempest heard the alarm in her sister's voice and didn't want her to upset herself. "Yes, I think a visit is a good idea."

"Then you'll come visit soon?" Sarina asked anxiously.

"Within the week," Tempest promised.

"Wonderful," Sarina said. "I can't wait to tell everyone."

"I'll call you before we come," Tempest said.

"Good, I can't wait," Sarina said with excitement. "Hold on a minute. Dagon wants to speak with you. I'm going to tell everyone right now that you'll be visiting soon. Take care, Tempest."

Tempest smiled, pleased her sister was feeling so good.

"Tempest, thank you," Dagon said. "She's been quite concerned about you and worrying herself senseless."

"I know," Tempest said, having felt her sister's distress. And confided in her brother-in-law what she suspected. "It's time, Dagon."

His voice filled with a protective strength. "Is there anything I can do to help?"

"Being who you are will be enough."

"We will all be here to offer our strength to you." He paused briefly. "And to Michael."

"Thank you from my heart," she said, grateful that he understood her feelings and offered his support.

"See you soon, Tempest."

She hung up the phone and Michael turned her around in his arms. "Is everything all right?"

She smiled and nodded. "My sister, her pregnancy and needless worry."

"What does she worry over?"

"Me."

"Why?" he asked.

She stepped out of his arms and went over to the counter to take two wineglasses from the cabinet. "She wants me to find love."

He walked over to meet her at the table, picking up the bottle of merlot to pour in each glass. "Then she will be happy and relieved to know that you have found love."

She raised her glass in a toast. "She will be thrilled."

He clinked his glass with hers. "I'm glad. I like Sarina."

"How about Dagon?"

"I suppose he'll grow on me."

She laughed. "Wait until you meet Sebastian and Ali Wainwright. And then, of course, there's Sydney Wyrrd."

She spoke the name with such fondness that Michael grew curious. "Who is Sydney Wyrrd?"

Tempest went to the refrigerator. "A very dear and old friend of mine, and a very wise woman."

While she arranged cheese and grapes on a plate Michael saw to getting the crackers. "I just might want to talk with her."

"I'm sure Sydney will find time to talk with you. Many seek her counsel. She is generous with her wisdom, as it should be."

He looked at her oddly as he followed her, platter in hand, she carrying the wine bottle and glasses. They sat on the couch in the sitting room and continued their conversation.

"Your sister commented on you being generous with those who seek your help. What help do they seek from you?"

"Friendship," she said without hesitation.

He shook his head. "I don't understand. The help they require is friendship?"

Tempest reached for a slice of cheddar cheese. "Think of

what true friendship requires. It is being there when someone needs to talk, to laugh, to cry. It's not being judgmental, but equally accepting your friend's faults and qualities. Friendship expects nothing, yet gives everything, and in so doing, a bond is forged that can never be broken."

"That's not true friendship; that's a rare friendship."

"And one worth having, though many people find it difficult not only to give but to find."

He shook his head as if understanding but realizing his discovery difficult to comprehend. "And you give it freely."

"Of course."

"I'm surprised you don't have a hoard of people at your door." He took a sip of his wine.

"Those in true need of friendship find their way here."

"Like me?" he said and raised his glass in a mock salute.

She leaned over and kissed his lips. "You not only found friendship; you found love."

"You do know you're not like other people, Tempest."

"I've been told that many times over the years."

He suddenly grew curious. "How old are you? I'm thirty-six," he said, realizing the question was on the tip of her tongue.

She couldn't lie and she couldn't tell him the truth. She chose diversion. "More wine?"

He smiled and held out his glass. "You're older than I am and you don't want to tell me."

She could answer that honestly. "That's right."

"But I want to know," he persisted.

"Does age really matter?"

"Evidently it does, since you don't want to tell me," he said with a laugh. "It doesn't matter if you're older than me."

She wanted to laugh but restrained herself. "Good, then we haven't got a problem."

"No, we don't," he agreed. "So how old are you?"

"Could we save this discussion for another day?" she asked much too sweetly.

He grinned. "Are you that much older than me that you're afraid to tell me?"

"You might say my age would surprise you."

He leaned over and gave her a quick kiss. "You look great, whatever your age."

"Wise words," she said with a smile.

His hand went around the back of her neck, and his lips came down on her for a more thorough kiss. When he finished stirring both their passions, he placed his forehead to hers and whispered, "I don't care how old you are, Tempest, I love you."

"And I don't care how young you are, I love you," she teased and tempted his lips with her own eager ones.

The topic was soon forgotten when their kisses turned lustful. Clothes were discarded, food and drink forgotten and magic was made.

Much later, wrapped in a blanket on the couch and finishing their wine and cheese, they discussed a visit to Sarina and Dagon's.

"I'm driving," Michael insisted.

She much preferred to transport them there, given that the trip was at least five hours, but how to do it without him realizing it was the problem. "It would be good practice for me to drive."

"You can practice right around here, where there are almost no cars. On the roadways I'll drive. And since you want to leave by the end of the week, that doesn't give you much practice time. So I drive."

She scrunched her face at him.

He laughed. "I'm not taking any chances with your safety or mine. I drive."

"That's not fair," she protested.

"I don't care," he said, laughter still evident in his voice. "I drive."

She was losing her temper, especially every time he said *"I drive."*

"You're getting angry," he said, amazed that he could sense her emotions so easily and amused by the fact that she felt he was dictating to her.

Laughter still edged his voice and irritated her all the more. "I'll drive if I wish."

He laughed again. "Oh, no you won't."

She sat up and away from him, attempting to cover herself with part of the blanket. "You can't tell me what to do."

"Oh, yes I can." His eyes twinkled with merriment.

She poked at his hard chest with her finger and pronounced each word firmly. "No, you can not."

He grabbed her finger. "Spells won't work, witch. I'll have my way in this."

She looked at him with surprise, a spell resting on the tip of her tongue, ready to cast. He had stepped into her mind and read her intentions. And while he couldn't interpret them correctly, he soon would.

Time was drawing near.

She gave him this small victory, knowing a more important battle was yet to be fought. "All right. You can drive."

"That's what I've been telling you, I drive. When do we leave, and Bear does come with us, doesn't he?"

She looked toward the sleeping cat cuddled in a nearby chair and knew instinctively that the temperamental feline would climb in the car without a problem if Michael was driving. "Yes, he'll come with us."

"Afraid to drive with you, is he?"

She yanked her finger out of his grasp. "Watch it, buster, or I'll zap you back to the States."

He rocked with laughter, and Tempest had to keep a firm lid on her temper.

His laughter subsided and he said, "You've read too many books on witches."

"You forget, I'm a descendent of a witch," she said with pride.

"Then show me your magic," he challenged.

She grinned, threw the blanket off her, pushed the rest of it off him and slowly moved over him to taste.

Twenty-two

Michael lay wrapped around Tempest in bed. Sleep had already claimed her and was about to sneak up on him, but his jumbled thoughts fought surrender. His mind seemed consumed by the future and possibilities they hadn't discussed. He wanted a long-term commitment with marriage and children. What did she want? And why hadn't he asked her? Did he fear the answer?

Sleep weighted his eyes, and fight as he might he couldn't keep them open. As soon as they closed he slipped into a deep slumber to dream once again.

The man paced in front of the riverbank, casting an angry glare at the woman who stood under the large tree a few feet away.

"Tell me why after these many months my seed has not taken root," he asked with an accusing tone.

"My children will be born of love."

He stopped pacing and all but flew at her, his face twisted in rage. "You take precautions to prevent conception?"

She showed no fear of him and spoke calmly. "My answer remains the same. My children will be born of love."

He grabbed her roughly by the arms. "Why do you join with me?"

She spoke the only way she could, truthfully. "I foolishly love you."

His touch softened. "Then our children would be born of your love and my strength."

She shook her head. "I know there is love in your heart; I have touched it. Why do you deny it?"

"You answer that question yourself when you say you foolishly love me. Love is a foolish emotion and I am no fool."

She stepped away from him, his hands letting her go. "I prefer you to be foolish—perhaps then you would understand the true power of life."

"Surrender to me and give me a child and you will learn what true power is," he argued.

She looked at him through misty eyes. "I cannot give you what you want."

His dark eyes glared with anger. "You refuse me?"

"I foolishly thought I could reach that small shred of light and teach you to love."

He floated toward her. "In time perhaps you can. For now our power will sustain us."

She raised her hand and along with it a protective shield preventing him from getting closer. "I cannot give you what you want."

He couldn't penetrate the energy shield she had easily erected, and the strength of her power infuriated him. "Cannot or will not?"

"Cannot, will not, does it matter? It will never be."

"It will be. I command it," he said with a force that caused thunder to rumble in the clear afternoon sky.

"No," she said, her voice soft and filled with sorrow. "It will never be."

"Do not force my hand," he warned. "You will be sorry."

"Do not test my power," she cautioned with tears in her eyes. "You will regret it."

"Surrender!" he ordered, attempting to step closer to her and being forced to keep his distance by her protective barrier.

The tears came then and her strong voice belied the ache in her heart. "I cannot. I cannot. I cannot."

Michael woke slowly, the words ringing repeatedly in his head. He turned toward Tempest who was sleeping soundly on her side beside him and he snuggled against her, resting his hand on her stomach.

His dream had caused him to consider the fact that he had

not taken precautions to prevent a pregnancy and he wondered if she had. He had always been vigilant about protection and yet with Tempest the thought had not crossed his mind. Not that he would mind her becoming pregnant, though he would much prefer they marry first.

Actually, marriage hadn't been discussed at all, so he was getting far ahead of himself. But then again if precautions weren't taken it was a strong possibility that she could already be pregnant. They had made love often since that first time, but then it took only once.

These were matters that needed discussing and the sooner the better, especially with them going to visit her sister. He wanted their relationship known, and he wanted to know her intention regarding their relationship because he certainly knew his intention.

They had a long drive ahead of them when they went to visit her sister. A perfect time and place to discuss such matters. No interferences, captive attentions and no place to run if the topic annoyed or the answers disappointed.

He drifted off to sleep, pleased by his decision.

"You've taken precautions against pregnancy?" Michael sounded disappointed to his own ears.

They had left her cottage only about an hour before, rising at dawn to get an early start. With their bags in the trunk, Bear sleeping comfortably in the backseat on a pillow surrounded by his favorite toys, and fresh coffee in a thermos and blueberry muffins to fuel them they had set off in pleasant moods.

That was, until Michael began his questions.

Tempest, on the other hand, seemed to expect his displeasure, though made no reference to it. "I thought it best."

He told himself she was being responsible and sensible, so why the hell did it disturb him so? "Do you want children?"

"Very much," she admitted. "When the time is right."

"When is the time right?"

"When I know without a doubt that they will be conceived from love."

Her remark near infuriated him. "You doubt my love?"

Her hand went out to touch him gently on the shoulder. "No, I don't doubt your love."

"Then do you doubt your love for me?" he was quick to ask.

"No, Michael, I love you."

"Then what's the problem?"

She turned the question on him. "Do you wish a child now?"

"That isn't the point."

"But it is. We've just begun to love, and that love needs nurturing. How can we nurture a child with love if we haven't nurtured our own love?"

Why did she always make sense? And why had he been irrational about her being responsible? They hadn't even discussed marriage yet and here he was arguing over a child. Whatever was his problem?

"You're right, I'm putting the old cart before the horse. It's marriage I should be discussing with you."

"Are you proposing to me?" she asked with a smile.

"Damn," he said, "I just keep sticking my foot in my mouth every time I open it." He sent her a wicked little quirk of a smile. "I guess you can tell I'm not the most romantic guy."

"So then that was a proposal?" she teased.

"Sweetheart, you're challenging me again."

She sighed, dramatically recalling how he had handled her last challenge. "You're so good with challenges."

She grabbed the door handle when he suddenly swerved the car off the road and brought it to an abrupt stop. He leaned across the console, grabbed her chin, squeezing her face in his rough-worn hand and puckering her lips.

"Listen well, sweetheart, I never thought I would find love, never thought I was the type of guy that could give love or receive it. When we first met I thought you were a beautiful but crazy broad, and I thought I was nuts for even thinking that I could fall in love with you and crazier still for thinking *you* would love me. It was all the stuff of fairy tales and I damn well didn't believe in fairy tales, but then something strange happened. You taught me to believe, to believe in possibilities. And I did. I believed I loved you and that you loved me and damned if it didn't work."

He kissed her puckered lips awkwardly and laughed. "I love you, Tempest, and I want you to be my wife—no," he said with a huge smile. "I believe you're *going* to be my wife forever."

Her hand ran up his arm gently to remove his hand from her face and she held it firmly in hers. "I believe, Michael, that you are right." She phrased her acceptance carefully. "I love you, and I want to be your wife. *Michael's wife*," she emphasized.

He was about to kiss her when he felt a rush of heat engulf him and he jolted back away from her. He closed his eyes against a wave of dizziness and placed a firm hand on the steering wheel.

"Michael!"

He heard her call to him but she sounded so far away and the distance frightened him. She was too far, too far out of his reach and he fought to return, to come back to her, fought with every ounce of strength he possessed.

"Michael, please, Michael."

Her anxious pleas grew louder and he finally opened his eyes to her worried face.

"Damn," he said, "that was strange."

Tempest realized that Michael's proposal of love made Marcus attempt to surface and fight for dominance. But Michael had been the victor and she was thrilled.

She threw her arms around him and kissed him with serious intent, her hand slipping into his jacket.

He grabbed her hand and tugged playfully at her bottom lip with his teeth as he reluctantly pulled away from her. "Keep that up and we'll never make it to your sister's."

"We could stop along the way at one of the small inns."

"Don't tempt me, Tempest," he said with a shake of his head. "Or it will be well into tomorrow before you see your sister."

Her free hand slipped to his lap and covered the hard length of him. "There's a small, quaint inn up the road."

"Tempest!" he warned, going for her hand that was causing him havoc.

Her lips moved to torment his ear with nips, kisses and a whispered, "I'm hungry to taste you."

"Damn," he muttered, pushed her away from him and pulled the car onto the road. "We're going to that inn."

They were two hours behind schedule when they rode into a rainstorm. With the windshield wipers on full speed, the thermos filled with hot chocolate and their passion well satisfied they settled in for the remainder of the long drive.

"How do you think your sister and Dagon will feel about us?"

"They will be happy, but cautious," she said honestly.

Michael could understand that. Here he was a stranger who had entered Tempest's life only about eight weeks ago and now all of a sudden he was to be her husband. "I don't blame them—it's a reasonable reaction. I am, after all, pretty much of a stranger. They know nothing about me."

Tempest hid her smile. Sarina knew much about him when they first met, though she could only read his present life. Prevented from seeing any more about him only made her more suspicious.

"And I don't have much to offer you."

Her temper flared. "You offer me love, the richest of all gifts."

"But is love really enough?" He wanted to believe, Lord how he wanted to believe the truth of her words. But being a cautious man, he had to ask, "Won't your family be concerned by my lack of finances, and aren't you?"

"They're not marrying you, I am. And I have enough money for us both."

"You are nuts," he said, sounding annoyed.

"Why? Because I choose to share my wealth with the man I love?"

"You really know nothing about me, and yet you accept my proposal of marriage. I could be a lunatic."

"Then we'd make a perfect pair," she said with a laugh.

"You don't have a lick of sense," he said with a shake of his finger at her face.

"Do you love me?" she snapped at him, though she smiled.

"Damn right I do," he snapped back.

"The problem, then?"

He looked about to tell her when he grumbled beneath his breath, "Crazy."

"Crazy in love," she said sweetly.

"Are there anymore crazies in your family I should know about?"

She almost laughed out loud. "You may find a few of my family and friends *eccentric*."

"I guess being eccentric is better than being crazy."

"There's Rasmus Castle in the distance," Tempest said with pride and a point of her finger, ending their debate.

Michael stared at the awesome sight. It imposed, impressed

and intimidated all in one glance, and that was from a distance. Woods surrounded the stone edifice, giving the impression that there was no entrance or exit to the castle. A light mist hovered over the top towers and drifted down to enshroud a turret or two.

He found himself anxious to see it up close. Castles had always fascinated him and he had visited many during his travels. There were those that had seen modernization over the years, but it was the ones that had retained their bleak, dark character which had caught his interest. They possessed a strength that had survived centuries of progress while retaining their integrity and secrets. Castles always had secrets and he had often touched the cold stone walls to see if they would share them with him.

Warlock.

The word rushed into his thoughts with strength and conviction.

He shook his head to chase the fragmented thought away and he grew annoyed with himself, though he couldn't understand why.

Tempest sensed his unease and attempted to distract him. "Sarina should have tea ready when we arrive. Though spring has barely arrived, the chill of winter persists." She slipped her arms into her black wool coat that lay over her shoulders. She had worn a pale gray knit column dress that buttoned down the entire front with black pearl buttons and she had been pleased to see that Michael had dressed in black wool trousers, a gray cashmere sweater and a black wool sports jacket. His fine toned-muscled body did his attire justice.

"I could go with something stronger," he admitted, feeling strange and yet not understanding why.

"Dagon has some good Scots whisky I'm sure you'd enjoy." She grew concerned herself when as they approached the private road that led to the castle she felt a surge of energy swirl in the air.

Something was wrong.

Michael felt it, too, she could tell, though he didn't understand its source and he simply picked up speed.

Tempest wished she could transport herself to the castle immediately. Something was terribly wrong and Sarina was involved.

Michael brought the car to a sudden stop and hurried out of the car, joining Tempest who was already on a run up the front steps. The castle appeared to quake and shake as if hit by an earthquake and yet the surrounding area was completely still.

They didn't knock at the door. Michael grabbed the door handle and flung the thick wooden door wide open.

Chaos greeted them.

Michael stared with shock at what looked like a tornado whirling in the center of the foyer, its force sounding as if it was about to crumble the entire castle. And within the center of the whirling funnel was Sarina and a man who firmly held on to her.

Dagon rushed up to Tempest while two other women held hands and cast anxious eyes at her.

"You must help them," Dagon insisted, grabbing Tempest by the arms.

Michael watched with a keen interest, feeling a strong sense of power emanating from the funnel and feeling an odd kinship with the whirling force. It was almost as if it nourished him, made him whole, gave him life. And he took a deep breath, drinking from the power it offered.

Tempest was too busy attempting to calm Dagon to notice Michael's reaction. "Tell me what happened. I must know the source to help them."

Dagon hurried to explain. "Sarina was helping Sebastian practice his magic when something went wrong. Whatever happened is too powerful for any of us to correct."

"What type of magic?"

"Floating, moving, emerging," he said, trying frantically to recall.

Tempest grew alarmed, casting an anxious glance at Michael and what she saw in the depths of his dark eyes frightened her even more. Raw power ready to burst free.

She hurried forward to break the spell but she wasn't fast enough.

Michael took two firm strides forward, shooting a light of energy from his extended hand and with a force that rivaled the swirling funnel he shouted, "Cease!"

Twenty-three

~

The whirlwind died away as if obeying a master and brought the swirling couple to a gentle rest on the marble tile floor.

Dagon rushed to his wife's side, his arms wrapping around her, and Ali and Sydney hurried over to Sebastian.

Michael turned furious eyes on Tempest, reaching out to grab her by the wrist. "We need to talk." He yanked her toward him but before he could leave the foyer Dagon and Sebastian were in front of him.

"You can talk with her here."

Michael shot a vehement look at the stranger.

"Michael," Tempest said as calmly as possible. "This is Sebastian Wainwright and the beautiful blond-haired woman is his wife Ali. The gracious lady beside her is Sydney Wyrrd."

He nodded, though kept warning eyes on the two men. "Under the circumstances, you will understand the need for Tempest and me to have privacy."

Dagon reiterated Sebastian's remark. "You can talk with Tempest here."

Michael was an impressive man, standing an inch or two over both other men, and the scope of his shoulders and chest hinted at his strength; but then physical size mattered little where witches were concerned, and that was what worried Tempest. She was certain Michael had regained Marcus's powers and neither Sebastian nor Dagon could come close to or combat his skills.

She took command of the situation, as was her way. "I think it would be wise for Michael and me to talk privately."

"Are you certain?" Sebastian asked, his obvious concern and courage endearing him to her.

"It's time," she said and they all seemed to understand.

Dagon offered them his study, assuring Tempest they would all be close by if needed.

Michael kept a firm grip on her wrist as they proceeded to the study, Tempest knowing her way.

Once alone in the room that smelled of aged leather and lemon polish, he released her and got directly to the point. "Explain."

There was so much to be discussed, only where did she start? She slipped out of her coat and draped it over a chair near the fireplace. She rubbed her hands together and then rubbed at her arms, taking a moment to glance out the window and see that the rain had turned heavy and the skies foreboding, appropriate weather for her current dilemma.

Her pause gave Michael time to calm down, and he slipped out of his sports jacket, dumping it on top of Tempest's coat. He caught sight of a crystal liquor decanter on the table in front of the window and walked over to pour himself a glass of what he hoped was whisky.

He wasn't disappointed when he took a gulp; it was whisky at its best. He looked to Tempest, his glass raised.

She understood his silent question. "No, thank you."

"Let's talk," he said more calmly, and she nodded.

They sat at opposite ends of the settee in front of the fireplace, the burning log casting just enough heat to make the room comfortable.

"Where to begin?" she asked of herself, though Michael answered.

"At the beginning."

"That was a long, long time ago."

"For us?" His question was strange to his own ears.

She nodded and told him what she knew she must. "Michael, I'm a witch."

He didn't seem surprised. "I figured as much. All those books on the subject, your knowledge of the Craft, your ancestor being one. I had a feeling you were a practicing witch."

She realized that he wasn't aware of the depth of her powers. "I'm a real witch and I perform real magic . . . " She took a deep breath and continued. "Just like you."

He took a large gulp of whisky before he responded. "You're telling me that I'm a witch, too."

"A witch most definitely, though possibly—" she paused, gathered her courage and said, "a warlock."

He stood then and shook his head. "But warlocks are evil, and I'm not evil."

"Let me attempt to explain what I think is happening."

"Please do, because this whole thing is making me feel like I'm nuts." He raked his fingers through his dark hair. "Did you see what I did out there? I have no idea how I did it, and the damnedest thing about it is that it made me feel good and strong, and I damn well want to feel that surge of power again."

"That force of power is a witch's natural ability. It can be developed and made stronger but it takes time, concentration and work. Every witch possesses it to some degree or another. It is meant for good and must never be used in a harmful manner."

"And I take it warlocks use that power to their own advantage."

"For their own advantage and to take advantage of others."

"I don't feel the need to harm, but let's forget about warlocks for the moment," he said with a wave of his hand as if dismissing the disturbing subject. "Why do you say that I'm a witch?"

"You have the power, have always had the power, in this life and in another."

He downed another gulp of whisky. "You're saying I've lived before and as a witch?"

"There's a strong possibility that you have and that I have known you before."

He finished the whisky in his glass. "Tell me the whole thing through, Tempest."

She obliged him, knowing it was time, though not for the entire truth. "I've lived many centuries and in one of those centuries I met a warlock who was eager to join with me and combine our powers to form a formidable force that could not be destroyed. I foolishly fell in love with him, though he felt love was foolish. I thought I could teach him the true power of love, but I was wrong. When I refused to give him what he wanted most he went into a rage, causing others to suffer. I could not stand by and watch him harm others. I had no choice but to do something about it."

She took a breath and looked directly at him. "That warlock was Marcus."

Michael instantly understood the implication. "The man you spoke of, the one you loved so deeply." He shook his head slowly. "Is that why you love me—because you believe me to be him?"

She heard and felt his disappointment and his painful emotions tore at her heart. "No, Michael. You are who you are. Marcus can be a part of you, but he isn't the whole of you. I fell in love with *you*, Michael. The man who I ran into with my car because I can't drive. The man who thought I was crazy and who constantly warned me about my lack of common sense. The man who has a good soul and deeply cares about people. The man who has led a good, decent life and wishes to marry and have children. And the man who believes in love."

He went to her, his arms instantly going around her and drawing her as close as he could get her. He had the need to feel her firmly up against him, hear her heart beat, feel the heat of her, smell the scent of her and know she was his and his alone.

"The dreams," he whispered.

"What?" she asked, her face resting against his chest.

"Since the first night I arrived at your cottage I've been haunted by strange dreams. Now they're beginning to make sense. It's Marcus's life I've been dreaming about." He thought a moment and reluctantly added, "His life with you."

"Learn from those dreams, Michael," she urged. "They can teach you much."

His arms tightened around her and he sounded concerned. "I couldn't have been that much of a fool, though the strength of power, a witch's power, can corrupt. It makes me feel invincible and I must admit that at times I like the feeling."

"Power can corrupt if it is used for anything but good," she said as if reminding a pupil. "And power used for good is the mightiest of powers."

"So you really think that I'm this Marcus guy who used his power unwisely and has returned to mend his evil ways?"

"Yes, I do and I think that soon his power will surface full force and you will recall everything."

"Then what?"

"The choice will be yours."

His frustration showed in his weary expression. "Any sane person would hightail it out of here and never look back. And yet I find myself believing everything you've told me." He shook his head. "I must be crazy. No, I know I'm crazy. And on top of that, I'm in love with a crazy witch."

Tempest giggled.

"Find it funny, do you?" he asked, though he smiled himself.

She kissed him, happy his frustration had faded so easily.

A sudden thought dawned on him. "They're all witches. This castle is full of them."

She nodded. "Yes, they are all witches, though Sebastian is a novice. He recently acquired his skills when he joined with Ali."

"Is that common?"

"No, when a mortal marries a witch he doesn't automatically become one. Sebastian offered a special cast to the heavens along with Ali and in doing so earned his own power. Unfortunately he doesn't quite have it under control yet."

"Which is the reason why he and Sarina were caught in that nasty whirlwind."

They walked holding hands to the settee and sat down. "Sarina understands Sebastian's need to practice the Craft. She herself had a problem with her own skills recently."

"I assume then that they are all aware of this situation, which would explain why Dagon and Sebastian came to your defense." He raised their joined hands and kissed hers. "I can't blame them, though at the time I felt like snapping—"

She quickly clamped her hand over his fingers that were in motion to snap. "Don't! A simple snap can cause problems."

"You mean if I had snapped my fingers at the two I would have moved them out of the way?"

"You would have sent them on their way, far away," she warned, gently pushing his hand down to rest on his lap. "I suggest you don't try anything until we've had more time to talk about this and more time for you to understand the consequences better."

He removed his hand from beneath hers and stared at it, turning it back and forth as if expecting it to look different somehow. She didn't care for the awe she heard in his remark.

"What power."

"Keep it in perspective," she warned firmly.

He looked at her strangely and for a moment she could have sworn she had seen that look of arrogance that was so familiar to Marcus.

"You've used your powers several times on me, haven't you?"

He sounded more intrigued than angry, which made his question easier to answer. "Only when actually necessary."

"When was necessary?" He laughed and answered his own question. "Getting me to your cottage and into bed?"

She nodded. "Yes, I definitely needed my skills for that task."

"If you had used your skills to drive we would have never met," he said teasingly. "Whyever did you attempt to drive in a snowstorm?"

She shrugged. "I felt a need to experience a mortal challenge."

He reached out to run a finger down along her cheek. "It was destiny. We have much to settle, you and I."

She felt a chill descend around her and Michael stood abruptly, dragging her up along with him.

"Let's return to the cottage right now and discuss this."

"I don't think that's a good idea."

"Why?" he asked, annoyed by her refusal.

"It would be good for you to talk with others with like skills besides me. And I really do wish to visit with my sister. I think a few days here would do us both good."

Michael reluctantly agreed.

She all but fell against him dramatically. "I don't know about you but I'm starving and Magaret is the world's best cook."

He kissed her pouty lips once, then twice, realizing how much he liked the taste of her. "Is that because she's a witch?"

"No, though she is a witch, as is the entire staff here at Rasmus Castle. Margaret uses no magic to prepare her meals though you would swear she did, her meals are so delicious. You're in for a treat."

A sound knock at the closed door drew their attention.

"Tempest," Dagon called. "Afternoon tea is being served and your sister felt you wouldn't want to miss Margaret's blueberry crumb cake."

Tempest sighed. "We'll be right there."

"That good, is it?" Michael asked, her sigh reminding him of the sounds she made when she climaxed and making him look forward to their next time alone.

"Heavenly," she said and began to tug him eagerly toward the door.

He in turn yanked her back toward him and she collided with his chest. He grabbed her face with a gentle hand, but kissed her none to gently. His kiss spoke of promises and passion simmering just beneath the surface and she felt a sudden chill again.

"Later."

Did he warn or did he promise? Tempest wasn't certain, but she looked forward to discovering the answer.

They joined the others in the sitting room where tea was being served. Michael was relieved to see Bear sharing a large pillow near the fireplace with a white cat who looked to be as temperamental as him, since she occupied most of the pillow.

Tension was thick and nerves were on edge when Michael took a seat next to Tempest on the couch. Their hands remained clasped, their bodies close and their intentions clear. They stood together.

Sydney took matters in hand and broke the silence. "I think, my dear Michael, that you could use a spot of brandy with your tea."

She was not only a gracious woman, but a beautiful one, and dressed elegantly in a white knit dress that spoke of one much too shapely for six hundred years. And her dark hair held not a hint of gray and was worn twisted and pinned to the back of her head with a gold clip. Michael relaxed instantly in her peaceful presence. "Yes, ma'am, I certainly could."

"Sydney, my dear boy. Ma'am sounds too old and though I am six hundred years old I don't feel a day over two hundred."

Her comment brought a round of laughter from all and an

easing of the tension, though it didn't totally dissolve it. It did, however, open communication.

Sarina started with, "Thank you for saving Sebastian and me."

Michael was honest in his response. "I'm not sure how I did it, but I was glad I could help."

His unpretentious response won over Dagon and Sebastian.

"I'm grateful," Dagon said and sent a nod toward Sebastian. "This one just can't seem to get the hang of magic."

Sebastian immediately defended himself with a smile. "One minute there, I'm doing the best I can for a mortal recently turned witch. It isn't easy learning all the spells, commands and chants, and of course there is the simple point of a finger that can get you into trouble."

"Not to mention a snap," Michael said, agreeing with the man's frustration.

"It's all in the practice, darling," Ali said, patting her husband's shoulder as she stepped around his chair to help herself to a piece of blueberry crumb cake.

Michael realized then that both Sarina and Ali were pregnant and both looked radiant and nearly the same size, leaving him to surmise that they were due around the same time.

Ali was a gorgeous woman, though at the moment she looked like a little girl who had just received a favorite treat. Her long, blond braid that ran down her back added to her childish delight.

"Sarina, I think we should try baking a cherry pie for tomorrow's dessert," Ali said with fork in hand, ready to devour.

"No!" Both men nearly shouted.

Michael laughed as he accepted the teacup and saucer Tempest handed him. She had poured a liberal amount of brandy into it.

"Your kitchen skills haven't improved?" Tempest asked, eagerly reaching for a piece of the cake to share with Michael.

"No," Sebastian answered for her. "Our kitchen resembles a battlefield when she finishes."

"Do you cook, Sebastian?" Michael asked.

"I'm an excellent cook."

"Are you an excellent witch, Ali?" Michael asked, turning his attention to her.

"Positively wonderful."

"That's debatable," Dagon teased.

"It seems to me your solution is obvious," Michael said and all eyes turned on him as if he was about to deliver a prophetic statement. "You each possess a developed skill the other wishes to improve on. Why not take the time to teach each other?"

Tempest beamed with pride over his accurate advice. She saw admiration in Sydney's eyes and a pleased look on Sarina's face, and even Dagon appeared impressed. Sebastian and Ali looked stunned.

"That's too simple," Ali said, as if it seemed impossible.

"The simplest solution is usually the best, though sometimes the hardest to achieve," Michael informed her.

Sebastian leaned forward on the ottoman where he sat with Ali, plopping down in the chair behind him. "You know I think you've got something there. It makes perfect sense."

"My husband is sensible," Ali said with pride before taking a bite of the cake.

"Someone in your family has to be," Dagon remarked, snatching a fat crumb from his wife's piece of cake from where he sat on the arm of the chair beside her.

Ali stuck her tongue out at him. "I'll have everyone know that I won the forest fairies mud pie contest."

"You cheated," Dagon said with a laugh. "You stole my mud pie and I got stuck with your mess."

Michael leaned over and whispered to Tempest, "Fairies?"

"Later," she whispered back.

He shook his head, turned it to a nod, and looking confused, held his head still while he picked at her cake.

Sydney seeing his reaction smiled. "We take some getting used to. Just think of us as eccentric."

Sebastian laughed. "That was my mistake, thinking them eccentric."

Michael liked Sebastian, perhaps because he had been a mortal and could relate to him. "Did you have trouble accepting the fact that witches actually existed?"

Ali giggled. "I think he still has trouble believing."

Sarina, who had remained quiet, spoke up. "He believes, and you should believe in him."

Tempest noticed for the first time how tired her sister looked. Ali must have noticed, too, for her concern showed.

Tempest voiced her worry. "You look tired, Sarina."

Dagon moved off the arm of the chair to squat down in front of his wife. He didn't like what he saw. "You should have told me you were tired. That little mishap took more out of you than you've admitted."

"I am tired but I wanted to visit with my sister," Sarina said.

"Then we'll go to your room where you can stretch out on your bed while we talk," Tempest suggested and stood as if her word was a command.

"Excellent idea," Dagon said and took his wife's hand to help her up.

"Your bags have been sent to your rooms," Sarina said, leaning against her husband after she stood.

"Rooms?" Michael asked.

"I placed you in a suite with two bedrooms, thinking you both may want time alone," Sarina explained.

Michael was about to protest the intended separation but a firm hand from Tempest to his arm warned him to keep silent. He ignored it. "We appreciate the thought, but we will be sleeping together."

Tempest realized he was staking his territory and waiting for someone to object.

Sarina spoke. "I'll have you both moved to a single bedroom."

"Don't trouble yourself, Sarina," Michael said, suddenly feeling her weariness. "We'll just make use of one bed."

"Man after my own heart," Sebastian said, causing everyone to laugh and his wife to jab him in the ribs.

Sebastian stood rubbing his side. "Come on, Michael," he said, placing a hand on his shoulder. "I know where Dagon keeps his private stock of the good stuff, and have I got stories of witches to tell you."

Dagon scooped his wife up into his arms. "I'll join you after I make certain Sarina is settled."

"That's not necessary, Tempest, can—"

"Follow us," Dagon said in a tone that warned he'd have his way.

Sarina rested her head on her husband's shoulder, too tired to protest.

"Take your time, Dagon," Sebastian said. "I'll begin with stories about you."

"All lies," Dagon said with a laugh as he left the room.

"Not likely," Ali said, helping herself to another piece of cake.

"You two will forever bicker," Sydney said, pouring herself and Ali another cup of tea and moving to the couch beside Ali.

Tempest gave him a quick kiss on the cheek and whispered, "See you later."

Michael followed Sebastian, overwhelmed by the amount of love and caring that swarmed in the room. It seeped into his heart and tore at his gut and reminded him just how great it was to have a family who loves.

Twenty-four

Supper proved a festive affair, with much talk and laughter. Sarina was feeling refreshed after a much-needed nap. And the food proved the best Michael had ever tasted. Tempest had been right about Margaret. She was the world's best cook.

One thing Michael did notice that hadn't caught his attention before was the way all of them treated Tempest. It was almost with a reverence and deep sense of respect. When they had entered the dining room for supper he had watched as each of them went to take their seats. It was obvious that Tempest was being given the place of honor at the head of the table until she whispered something in Sydney's ear and the woman took the seat as if it was intended for her.

He realized that she was asked many questions during the meal on a variety of topics, when her advice was sought she answered with an aged wisdom that startled him. There was more to her than just being a witch. She possessed a degree of knowledge that far surpassed the others, and he wondered at its origin.

Michael began to grow restless by the end of the meal, wanting, perhaps needing time alone with Tempest, and she seemed to understand or feel the same way. Immediately following dessert she made apologies for wishing to retire early, blaming her weariness on the long, tiring day.

No one objected and everyone offered their good nights to them both.

Michael slipped beneath the covers of the double bed, eager to talk with Tempest and make love. He didn't count on the day finally catching up to them both and within minutes of them resting in each other's arms they fell into a heavy slumber.

"Join with me," Marcus said, his arms reaching out to Tempest.

There was a full moon shining down on the flowing stream, the rushing waters creating a soothing melody in the late summer night air.

"A perfect setting," Tempest said, glancing up at the star-filled sky and down around at the meadow and woods that surrounded them.

"I wanted our first time together to be perfect." Marcus took off his black cloak and spread it on the ground. "It is only appropriate that our first joining be completed in the beauty of nature."

"You tempt me much too much, Marcus."

He removed his tunic to expose a lean, hard chest. "You knew this time would come. It was inevitable. It is our destiny."

Tempest stood in her pale-yellow tunic that covered a white linen shift, her fiery hair flowing in hundreds of waves down her back to her slim waist. She appeared an ethereal beauty in the moonlight, and Marcus walked up to her, his intentions obvious, his patience gone.

She held up her hand and he stopped. "What of love, Marcus?"

He contained his annoyance. "I know not of love, Tempest. What I do know is that when we are apart, I miss you. When we are together my heart beats faster, my blood heats and I grow heavy with the want of you. I would protect you with all my powers and never let harm touch you. This I can offer you."

"It is a start," she said with a smile, and lowered her hand.

Marcus approached her slowly, his hand going to gently stroke her face. "You will not be sorry. I will give you more than you ever thought possible."

"I simply want you."

"Then you shall have me."

He disrobed her with a slowness that titillated, and his hands explored her naked flesh with a magical touch that had her body quaking.

She had expected a demanding joining from him, not deliberate tenderness. His surprising derision succeeded in melting her doubts and causing her to respond completely to his touch.

"I knew you would be responsive to the magic of my touch. It is an ache inside you that must be satisfied."

He lowered her to his cloak, his naked body moving over hers, his mouth seeking her breasts, his hands seeking her moist heat. He took her hard nipple in his mouth the same moment his finger entered her and she cried out, her hands stretching out to the sides, grasping the blades of grass in a frantic attempt to anchor herself in reality.

"Let go," she heard him say. "Let go."

The words echoed in her head and as he continued his sensuous assault on her body and mind she began to obey his every word. And when he entered her much later she heard his command that penetrated the sensual fog. "Surrender."

Her response echoed in his head. "No. No. No."

They climaxed together for what seemed like forever, her cries echoing in the night. Marcus threw back his head and looked to the heavens and at that moment a shocking thought hit him.

Michael bolted up in bed, shaking. "Good God, Tempest," he said on a whisper, looking down at her sleeping peacefully. "I loved you."

Tempest stirred from her slumber, her sleepy eyes fighting to open and not knowing why. A glance at the bedside clock told her it was three in the morning and the empty spot beside her in bed was the reason her sleep had been disturbed.

Michael was in the room; she could feel his presence. It was strong and palpable. It took only seconds for her eyes to adjust to the darkness and with a quick glance around the room she found him standing at the window.

He was completely naked, his back to her, and she admired the strength of his body. He had broad shoulders she loved to wrap her arms around, a tapered waist and a firm buttocks that led to muscular legs.

Her glance darted up to his head and its dark layered hair

that never managed to look neat yet appealed to her anyway.

He appeared to be deep in thought, his arms crossed in front of him. The rain continued pelting the window and a chill filled the air though a fire roared in the hearth.

His disturbed mood had awakened her, penetrated her sleep, and called to her for solace.

She slipped from the bed, her body bare, feeling perfectly comfortable with their shared nakedness. She approached almost in flight, her feet lifting slightly off the carpet. She thought to surprise him but just as she reached out to touch him he turned on a spin and locked her in his arms, her back pinned to the front of him.

"Gotcha," he whispered and kissed the side of her neck where he knew she was the most sensitive.

She shivered in his arms, gooseflesh running over her, and he wrapped his arms more tightly around her. She rested her head back against his chest and placed her arms over his.

"You couldn't sleep?" she asked, concerned.

"A dream," he admitted.

She felt his body tense against hers and she realized that the dream had disturbed him. "Want to talk about it?"

He kissed her neck again. "I have something else in mind."

"You have much on your mind."

He nibbled all the way up to her ear. "A witch's intuition?"

"A lover's familiarity."

He moved so suddenly she had no time but to respond to his demand. He spun her around, hoisted her up and insisted, "Wrap your legs around me."

She did so without thought.

He clamped firm hands on her bottom and walked her to the bed, dropping down on it and easing himself into her. He was hard and thick, and he filled her with a quickness that thrilled and excited. His thrusts were deep, hard and fast and she welcomed the repeated rhythm that raced her to the edge of complete surrender.

She had been near the edge so many times before. She had almost toppled off it more than once but she had managed to hang on. She had always hung on and never let go. Never surrendered herself completely.

"Let go," he ordered sharply.

She shook her head.

"Let go." His voice was a deep growl. "Damn it, let go."

"No. No. No."

He rested his forehead against hers. "I love you, Tempest. I've always loved you." He shook his head, his rhythm remaining constant. "Michael, Marcus, me. *Me*. Me loves you always. Always. Always."

Could she trust him? God, she wanted to trust him. She wanted so badly to take a step off that edge and know he would catch her.

But there was the spell. There was more yet for him to remember, and how then would he feel?

"I love you, Michael. God, how I love you."

Her words did him in. He exploded in a flash, groaning until he thought his throat was raw and silently swearing over his power not being equal to hers.

Her climax came after—he saw to that—but then she let him and the thought annoyed him.

He would have her surrender.

Damned if he wouldn't.

Twenty-five

⌒

"You have to see Dagon's tower room," Sebastian said, digging into the fat waffle on his plate.

Ali disagreed, while reaching for the spiced apples to coat her second waffle. "I think he should visit with the fairies in the woods."

"The grounds may be wet after yesterday's soaking, but they are magnificent," Tempest offered, pouring herself another cup of English breakfast tea.

"Or they could tour Edinburgh for the day," Sarina suggested, helping herself to a second serving of scrambled eggs.

Sydney spoke up. "I think Michael should be left to decide what he would like to do since Tempest will be busy visiting with the women."

Michael was quick to decide. "I want to tour the castle from top to bottom."

"Bottom to top," Sebastian said. "We end with the tower room."

Ali shook her head and reached for a fat sausage. "I still think the fairies are the better choice. He'd love meeting Beatrice."

"He knocked Beatrice out cold," Tempest said, and all eyes turned on Michael.

"Then it was a fairy I knocked out," Michael said with relief. "I thought I was going—" He turned an accusing glare on Tempest. "You put a spell on me."

She had no time to defend her actions, because Ali interrupted with, "Explain, buddy."

Michael obliged her, her tone too sharp to be ignored. "I didn't know she was a fairy when I swatted at her."

They all waited for further details.

Tempest explained. "A misunderstanding that was cleared up quickly."

"Is Beatrice upset?" Dagon asked with concern.

"No, quite the opposite, but I'm sure she'll explain herself when you see her. You know how she loves to tell a tale."

"You're forgiven," Ali said, pointing her fork at Michael.

"He didn't mean it," Sarina said in his defense.

"You're too empathetic," Ali accused, turning her fork on Sarina.

"And you're too judgmental," Sarina snapped.

Tempest was surprised by their bickering.

"Time for that tour," Dagon said and stood.

"Not going to defend your wife?" Ali asked with an attitude.

Dagon bent over and kissed Sarina's cheek. "I've made that mistake on several occasions since your arrival. I don't intend to make it again."

Sebastian also stood, depositing a hasty kiss on his wife's cheek.

"Call that a kiss, buddy," Ali said, her fork giving him a quick but harmless poke in the arm.

"Don't poke your husband, he's a good man," Sarina said with a shake of her finger at Ali.

"He's my husband and I'll do as I please to him," Ali said, "and watch that finger."

"You're a shrew," Sarina accused.

"And you whine," Ali shot back.

"Come on, Michael, hurry," Dagon said, walking briskly toward the door with Sebastian in quick pursuit. "The tears are going to start any minute."

Michael rushed out of his chair and stopped to give Tempest a sound kiss.

"Now that's a kiss," Ali said. "Can you teach my husband how to do that, Michael?"

That stopped Sebastian in his tracks and he turned, ready to pounce on his wife.

Dagon grabbed his arm and smiled at Ali. "I'm sure Michael will be only too happy."

"Sure I will," Michael said with a grin that faded fast when Ali stared at him.

"My husband is the best kisser in the whole world. He doesn't need lessons from you."

Michael looked stunned, as did Tempest.

"Hormones," Sydney mouthed to Tempest and she smiled and nodded in understanding.

"He is not, Dagon is," Sarina said, her finger up and shaking.

"Run," Sydney warned with a laugh, and the men beat a hasty retreat.

It was late afternoon by the time the three men entered the tower room. Michael was awed by the collection of historical artifacts displayed so artfully in the cylindrical room. He took his time examining piece after piece, a glass of Scots whisky in his hand that got refilled every time it was near to empty.

Dagon and Sebastian relaxed in the circle of chairs in the center of the room talking and drinking, their glasses being refilled frequently with a snap of the fingers.

"I'm telling you, this magic stuff isn't easy," Sebastian said.

The word "magic" had Michael fast joining them. "I agree," he said, taking the chair between the two.

"At least you've always been a witch," Sebastian said with envy.

"It doesn't do me much good when I haven't got the slightest idea how to use my skills, and besides—"

"You're still having trouble believing in magic," Dagon finished.

Sebastian nodded. "I agree with you there. I still pinch myself at times just to remind myself that I'm in the real world."

"And I always thought that I was in the real world," Michael said.

Dagon grinned and raised his glass in a salute. "The world of magic is much better."

"Because it's always been a part of you," Sebastian said, refilling all their glasses.

"It's a part of both of you now," Dagon explained. "And it's a craft that can be learned and perfected to the highest level if you so choose."

"I don't know," Sebastian said doubtfully. "I watch you and Ali and then there's Sydney's skills." He shook his head. "And then there's Tempest. Wow. She's remarkable."

Dagon shot him a warning look but it was too late.

"Why is she so remarkable?" Michael asked.

Dagon answered. "She's worked on her skills."

Michael asked a question that surprised him. "Can you match her powers?"

"No."

"Can Sydney?"

Dagon shook his head.

Michael paused in thought a moment then asked, "Is there any witch that can match her skills?"

"More whisky?" Sebastian asked and reached for the crystal decanter, but Michael shook his head.

He was insistent. "Is there?"

Sebastian looked to Dagon and he reluctantly answered. "None that I know of."

Michael reached for the decanter of whisky. "She must be quite old."

"Ancient," Sebastian said and regretted his remark as soon as he heard it slip from his mouth.

Michael appeared not to have heard, he was so lost in his thoughts, and Dagon breathed a quiet sigh of relief.

Dagon attempted a bit of levity. "Magic is much like a woman."

Both men's eyes widened at his remark.

"Just when you think you begin to fully comprehend magic, you realize you haven't understood it at all."

"That's the truth." Sebastian nodded.

Michael agreed with his own nod. "You can never really understand a woman."

"Amen," Sebastian said with a salute of his glass.

Dagon threw in another opinion. "I think the trick is not to try."

Michael added his own bit of wisdom. "I think you need to believe."

"Believe what?" Sebastian asked.

"Believe in love," he explained. "If you love a woman, I think that makes a difference. I think love opens a door between her and you and allows you to understand, if only a little."

"You may be right," Sebastian said. "Realizing how much I loved Ali opened up a flood of emotions I never expected and helped me to truly understand how I felt and how she felt."

Dagon agreed. "That's true. When I admitted to myself that I loved Sarina, something changed, and I understood what had to be done to make certain that I never lost her love."

"But love can be damn painful," Sebastian said. "When I thought that I had lost Ali I thought my heart was literally breaking, and I got this twisting knot in my gut that wouldn't go away. I couldn't eat, I couldn't sleep, I couldn't do my work. I felt as if I was going insane."

"Join the club," Dagon said. "I was damned frightened that I didn't possess the power to save Sarina from that damned spell. And I hate that gut-wrenching feeling that won't go away and won't let you eat and makes you totally senseless."

The two men looked to Michael.

"Okay, so I've experienced the same thing. Only I didn't think I had a chance in hell with Tempest. I was out of work and out of money, and her telling me she's wealthy—" He took a gulp of whisky. "What chance did I have? And yet my heat ached and yes, my gut wrenched until I realized I had no choice but to leave. Thing was, though, I admitted to myself I loved her but never told her of my feelings. She confessed her love when I told her of my intentions to leave. I was so damned relieved when she told me." He shook his head. "But now it's become more complicated."

"Not if you believe," Sebastian reminded him.

Dagon also spoke up. "If your love is strong, it will survive chaos."

Michael thought that a strange remark, and yet somehow appropriate. "I can't imagine life without her."

"I know, I feel the same way," Sebastian agreed. "Ali is so much a part of me, I miss her when I'm at work and I can't wait to get home to her."

Dagon laughed. "I'm surprised Sarina isn't tired of my constant presence. I hunt her down throughout the day and yet she never seems to mind."

"I miss being alone at the cottage with Tempest. It was like no one else in the world existed but the two of us and that was just fine with me."

"Damn, look what love does to you," Sebastian said with a grin and raised his glass.

Dagon and Michael raised theirs.

"I wouldn't have it any other way," Dagon said.

"Damn right," Michael said, and they toasted their words with a clink of glasses.

"What do you suppose our women are up to?" Dagon asked.

"Probably in the kitchen talking like we are," Sebastian said and stood quickly. "Maybe we better check with them."

Dagon stood with haste. "Definitely."

"What's wrong?" Michael asked, standing along with them.

"Ali in the kitchen can only mean trouble," Sebastian said.

Michael laughed. "How much trouble could she possibly get into?"

"Don't ask," the two men said in unison and shoved Michael in front of them to be the first out the door, and the first one to enter the kitchen just in case Ali was at the electric mixer again and they required a shield.

"I'm sorry, Sarina," Ali apologized, setting the teapot on the hot pad in the center of the kitchen table and sitting in the chair beside Tempest. "No one warned me about hormones raging out of control during pregnancy."

"I do whine lately," Sarina admitted.

Sydney poured the tea, her pointing finger doing the work. "A woman's body changes; it can't be helped."

Sarina sighed dramatically and ran a loving hand over her rounded stomach. "I enjoy carrying our son."

"I bet Dagon enjoys the improved size of your breasts," Ali said with a squirt of lemon into her tea. The squirt missed and almost caught Tempest in the eye, but she was quick enough to deflect the juice with her finger and send it back to the cup.

Sydney shook her head slowly.

Sarina giggled. "Actually, he does." A frown replaced her faded giggle. "I worry though that my increased sexuality might be too much for him to handle."

Ali almost spit her tea out. "Oh, I can't wait for Dagon to hear that one."

"Your desire for sex hasn't increased?" Sarina asked curiously.

Tempest listened with acute interest while sipping her tea.

"Of course it has, and Sebastian handles it without a problem," Ali said proudly and turned to Tempest. "So how is Michael in bed?"

"Ali," Sydney scolded. "Apologize. Do you forget who you speak to?"

Ali glanced Tempest up and down. "Looks like I'm talking to a woman."

"Alisande Wainwright—"

Tempest interrupted. "Ali's right, Sydney, I am a woman. A woman who enjoys being part of this conversation."

"So the answer is?" Ali asked, reaching for a shortbread cookie.

Tempest beamed. "Fantastic."

"Nothing like a man who knows what he's doing in bed," Ali said.

"Yes," Sarina agreed, "too many of them don't know how to use their equipment."

Ali laughed. "You have a way with words, Sarina. I would have been more blunt."

"I was being polite." Sarina smiled.

Ali turned to Sydney. "Your turn, dear Aunt. Which man fine-tuned your fiddle the best?"

"There's only one man who can fine-tune a woman's fiddle the best, dear heart," Sydney said. "And he's the man that woman loves. Without love, it's merely sex."

The three women nodded in agreement.

"Love takes sex to a different level," Tempest said. "It defines the depth and consciousness of the act. It joins souls."

Ali looked at Tempest, impressed. "You make it sound magical."

"It is magical," Tempest said. "Magical to all those who open their hearts and souls to it."

"And you don't need to be a witch to perform the magic of love," Sarina added.

"But you need to believe in magic," Sydney said.

"To believe is magic," Tempest corrected gently as only a wise teacher could.

Sarina sighed like a lovesick girl. "Dagon and I believe."

Ali even sighed, though it was more sensual. "Sebastian and I certainly believe."

They both looked to Tempest.

She held her tongue. Did Michael truly believe? And what of Marcus? Did he ever believe? She spoke from her heart. "I believe in Michael."

Tears clouded Sarina's eyes and Ali sniffed to keep hers from falling. Sydney laid a comforting hand over Tempest's.

"Pudding," Ali said with the delight of a mischievous child. "Let's make chocolate pudding."

Sarina reacted just as eagerly. "I want vanilla."

Tempest raised her hand and waved like a pupil eager to be heard. "I want butterscotch."

Sydney got caught up in the moment herself. "Strawberry."

"Let's prepare it ourselves like mortals do," Ali said, rushing out of her seat and heading for the electric mixer.

"Don't touch that," Sebastian warned, rushing around Michael who had been forced to enter the kitchen in front of the two men. "It's a lethal weapon in your hands." He slipped a firm arm around her waist and guided her the opposite way.

Sarina came to her defense. "Ali has learned how to deal with the electric mixer so that no mishaps occur."

Dagon came up behind his wife, slipping his hands around her waist to rest over her rounded stomach. "Which means she's learned not to touch it."

Tempest voiced her disappointment. "But I was looking forward to butterscotch pudding."

Michael went to her side and with a firm hand drew her up against him. "I'll make you butterscotch pudding." He kissed her then and it was no light peck.

"Oh, how sweet," Ali said. "He'll cook for her."

Dagon and Sebastian sent Michael a look that accused, and Michael laughed. "I'm certain Dagon and Sebastian were just about to volunteer their help."

Sarina looked up at her husband and Ali turned a questioning glance on hers.

"You want chocolate?" Sebastian asked and kissed the tip of Ali's nose.

"Vanilla?" Dagon asked of Sarina and nibbled at her ear.

"What kind would you like, Sydney?" Michael asked.

"My favorite, strawberry," she answered with a smile that told him she appreciated his thoughtfulness. She then announced, "Ladies to the sitting room, the men now have the kitchen."

The three women gave their husbands pecks on their cheeks and followed Sydney out of the kitchen.

Michael pushed the sleeves of his gray sweater up. "Let's get started."

"You're going to pay for this, pal," Sebastian said with a laugh as he pushed the sleeves of his white sweatshirt up.

Dagon reached for an apron on the wall hook by the door and slipped it over his head to protect his black cashmere sweater. "He most definitely is."

Tempest and Sarina left Sydney and Ali in the sitting room with Sydney attempting to teach Ali how to knit. The lesson was not going particularly well, but then Sydney had patience.

The sisters strolled the castle halls arm in arm, talking.

"Michael seems so nice," Sarina said.

"He has a good, caring soul," Tempest assured her.

"And Marcus?"

Tempest expected the question, though the answer troubled her. "He's there waiting, and I think impatiently."

Sarina squeezed her sister's hand. "He was so powerful and so reckless with his power. Do you suspect he has changed?"

"I suspect Michael will have a struggle on his hands, but as I said before, I believe in him, and I feel he will make a wise choice when the time comes."

"You have no doubts?"

"Doubts will not help him," Tempest said wisely. "I must keep my belief and faith in him strong if he is to succeed."

Sarina stopped and looked into her sister's eyes. "You love him more now than you did those many years ago."

Tears glistened in Tempest's eyes. "I would have never thought that possible, but Marcus has matured into Michael. And I find Michael's qualities hard to resist."

"How do you think Michael will react when he recalls the spell? Do you think he will blame you for his difficult life?"

"If he has learned his lessons, then he will know that his path was his to choose, his life and his choice."

Sarina held tight to her sister's hand. "I worry about you."

"I am the stronger," Tempest said with confidence.

"But love can weaken the strongest soul."

"No, love strengthens the weakest soul."

Sarina smiled. "You've strengthened Michael's soul. He will have no choice but to succeed."

"Time will tell," Tempest said. "But enough of my problem. I want to hear about you."

They began walking again as they talked about the impending birth, her wonderful husband and how happy she truly was.

By the time supper was over Michael was feeling caged and uncomfortable. He couldn't explain it to himself so he didn't attempt to explain it to anyone else. But as the evening wore on, the odd sensation grew more disturbing and he felt an overwhelming need to return to the cottage.

They were all gathered in the large living room, though Michael had wandered off by himself to stand in front of a row of windows that looked out across the castle grounds. He couldn't make sense of his strange emotions and yet oddly enough, he welcomed them.

The chatter in the background began to disturb him more and more and his need to isolate himself with Tempest grew into an uncontrollable urge.

He turned fast on his heels and came up behind Tempest where she stood next to her sister's chair. "I want to return to the cottage now," he whispered in her ear.

Tempest felt his power rush over her like a tumultuous wave crashing hard on shore. It was going to be difficult to deny his request and yet she felt now was not the time to be alone with him. "In a day or two," she murmured.

"Now!" he persisted.

His agitation was sensed by all and the room grew quiet.

Tempest spoke calmly. "We'll leave tomorrow."

"We'll leave now," he corrected her firmly, his arm tightening around her waist, and with a raise of his hand and whispered words in an ancient language that had long died away, he wrapped them in a spell. A white mist rose up around their feet to spiral up, completely encasing their bodies.

Dagon and Sebastian hurried forward but there was nothing they could do. Tempest herself realized that when she felt the powerful force of the spell she worked around them.

This was Marcus's doing. He was making his presence known. He was recalling memories, increasing in strength.

The mist grew thick and Tempest could barely make out her sister's worried face. She could break the spell if she chose to but she felt it was better not to. Time was fast approaching when they would face the consequences of her spell and it was better that they did it alone.

So she watched as they all faded from view and in a sudden gust of wind she and Michael were off and deposited safely in the living room of the cottage.

The rush of power had sent his passion soaring and when the mist evaporated around them he scooped her up in his arms and headed for the bedroom.

Twenty-six

~

With impatient hands Michael undressed her and with hasty hands he shed his clothes. He scooped her up once again and tumbled down on the bed with her, his hands reaching out to touch intimately.

"I want you to feel my love," Michael said, his hands exploring her body with an eager tenderness. "All of it and all that I've ever possessed."

His touch was magical and as he explored her with a loving hand she drifted into a haze of sexual pleasure that was beyond anything she had ever experienced. His mouth trailed his hands and his lips fired her skin, leaving a tingling wake in their path.

His tongue entered her with a defined precision that made her cry out and arch her body and when she felt completely mindless he entered her with a sharp quickness and set a rhythm that in seconds had her ready to tumble over the edge.

"Let go," he urged. "Trust me."

The pleasurable pain was so exquisite, she groaned and teetered on the edge, ready and willing but holding on to that last shred of sanity.

"Let go," he urged again. "Trust me. Me, Michael."

Hearing his name, knowing it was Michael, the soul who truly loved her, forced her surrender, and she took that step off the edge. She spiraled down and down and down into the darkness and yet she refused to lose her faith in Michael. And at that moment she felt him wrap around her and soar up and up and up like a majestic bird until they burst into the light together and exploded in a sparkle of brilliant showers.

With labored breathing he whispered, "I love you, Tempest—now, then and forever."

She held him tightly to her, silent tears slipping down her cheeks and with hope that she had surrendered wisely clinging desperately in her heart.

Michael woke early, surprised no dream had haunted his sleep. It was just past dawn and Tempest lay contentedly beside him in a deep slumber. Their joining last night had been a powerful one. She had finally surrendered her last ounce of will to him and her energy had raged through him with such force that he had experienced a climax he had not thought possible. It felt as if he had been reborn. And even now he could feel the residue of that energy.

He was much too wide awake and energized to return to sleep, and he didn't wish to disturb Tempest so he quietly slipped out of bed and went off to get dressed.

He took a quick shower and shaved and hurried into jeans, a red sweatshirt and workboots, then headed to the kitchen for a much needed cup of coffee. He thought about working in the greenhouse or doing a bit of reading when he was struck with the sudden urge to take a walk.

He slipped on his bomber-style jacket, and headed out the door into the brisk early-morning spring air. He didn't know where he was going, didn't even realize he was familiar with the well-worn path. He only knew he had a destination, wherever that may be.

He wasn't surprised to see that he stopped in the same spot where the fairy incident had occurred, though he was startled when Sydney stepped from behind the large tree with a tiny, plump fairy sitting on her shoulder.

"Fancy meeting you here," he said with a smile.

Sydney stepped forward, dressed in a pale-blue knit ankle-length dress, not attire you would find appropriate for the woods, yet somehow Sydney seemed to blend perfectly with her surroundings.

"How gracious of you to respond to my request on such short notice."

"At least that explains my sudden need to take a walk."

"A silent, but powerful invitation," Sydney explained. "I wished to talk with you."

"You could have called."

"No, I wished to speak with you in person, and to introduce you to a friend." She held her hand up to her shoulder and the tiny fairy stepped onto her finger and into her palm. Sydney then extended her hand out to Michael. "Michael, may I present Beatrice, a dear, dear friend."

Michael found the little creature enchanting. "My pleasure," he said with a nod of his head. "And my apologizes for having knocked you out. I was not aware of the fairy population in the woods."

Beatrice pushed at her tilted head wreath. "A misunderstanding I have taken no offense to."

"What can I do for you ladies?"

"Listen," Sydney said.

"What am I suppose to hear?" he asked.

"The truth," Beatrice said.

Michael nodded and took the arm Sydney held out to him. He escorted her to a nearby felled tree and with a snap of her fingers she covered it with a soft cushion before sitting down.

Michael joined her and waited impatiently for her to speak.

"Patience is a true virtue, Michael," Sydney informed him gently, and lifted Beatrice to return to her shoulder.

He smiled. "I'm still working on that one."

"Work harder; it will serve you well."

Beatrice paced impatiently along Sydney's shoulder. "Let's get to the matter at hand."

"Patience," he said with a pointed finger at Beatrice.

"Pish posh," Beatrice said, stopping on the edge of Sydney's shoulder and pointing her own finger at Michael. "You need a talking-to."

He couldn't help but laugh. She was a gusty little bundle and he liked her. "I'm all ears."

"About time," Beatrice said. "Sydney, talk to him."

"I have no business interfering, Michael."

"Oh, yes, we do," Beatrice said.

Sydney ignored her. "The past has dictated the future and choices made then come to fruition now. How much has been learned is the key to wise or foolish choices."

Michael shook his head. "I'm no good with riddles."

Sydney laid a comforting hand on his arm. "Many years ago I met a man full of arrogance and pride, a Scottish laird. He knew me to be a witch and warned me about casting any spells over him. The past had taught me to follow my beliefs and trust in myself, but I allowed my love for this man to foolishly cloud my judgment. It cost me the love of that man. To this day I regret my decision. I regret having not followed my beliefs, for in their strengths lay my strengths. I have had many years to ponder my actions and I often wish I had another chance. Second chances are marvelous gifts that should never be denied. And a second chance allows us to choose wisely."

"Got that?" Beatrice asked him, shaking her tiny finger at him.

What he got was the sorrow and heartache Sydney felt, and it troubled him. She had truly loved this man, and to lose a cherished love is devastating. He could never bear the thought of losing Tempest. He simply could not live without her.

"I'm attempting to comprehend," he said, and placed a comforting hand over Sydney's.

She smiled her gratitude.

"My turn," Beatrice said.

"Another story?" Michael asked with excitement and winked at the tiny winged creature. "Is your wing crooked?" He looked closer at her, and sure enough, her wing was bent. He extended his finger to repair it and was stunned when the tiny fairy dropped flat to Sydney's shoulder, her hands covering her head.

His voice was gentle. "I mean you no harm."

Her head came up slowly and she looked with wide eyes at him. "What did you say?"

He glanced from Beatrice to Sydney and back again at their expressions of surprise, which were curious to him. "I mean you no harm," he repeated.

Beatrice stood, pushing her crooked head wreath away from her eye. "Remember those words; they will serve you well. Remember Sydney's words, for love sometimes forces difficult choices. And remember in the end, love is always the victor."

Michael understood that there were many messages in their words and yet he still felt there was a missing piece and that was the piece he needed to find.

With hugs, kisses and encouraging words to Michael, Sydney and Beatrice took off in a whirlwind of light and Michael took his time returning to the cottage. He had to clear his head and attempt to make some sense of all that had been happening to him of late.

He walked in the woods, their natural melody soothing to his ears and the fresh scent of earth and pine invigorating to the senses. He felt a rush of wonder run through him. This was magic at its finest.

He took a deep breath and without warning a sudden rush of power raced through him, filling him with such force and presence that he felt the urge to scream out to the heavens.

He remained silent, attempting to harness the force, draw it in and contain it. He instinctively knew that he must contain it. He did so with little difficulty and that surprised him.

Two solid steps took him to a large rock that he sat down on and he shook his head, not really understanding a lick of what was happening to him. How did he make sense of witches, warlocks and fairies? And yet how did he not, when the proof was there before his own eyes? Since there was solid truth in it all, how and where did he even begin to understand who he actually was?

If the man in his dreams was part of him then it would be best to understand that man and understand what had happened to him.

He returned to the cottage with much on his mind.

They sat snuggled on the couch. A night shower drenched the land and a low fire burned in the fireplace.

"I apologize for being rude and pulling you away so abruptly from your family," Michael said. "But I felt an overwhelming urge to be alone with you. And I need to know more."

Tempest expected this, and offered her help. "What do you need to know, Michael?"

"Tell me about Marcus."

He knew much himself already and she wanted him to realize that. "Recall your dreams and you will know Marcus."

He shook his head. "I want *you* to tell me about him."

She ran a tender touch over his arm, which held her. "There was a good in Marcus, though he favored the darker side.

Power was everything to him and he sought it without thought or consequence. And as his power escalated, so did his thirst for more power. It was unquenchable."

He heard the sorrow in her soft voice and kissed her temple to show that he, Michael, was there for her now.

She continued. "Love was foolish to him. It was a senseless and useless emotion that served no purpose. Power was the ultimate union to him and the power generated from two highly skillful witches would create an indestructible force."

"Did you feel he ever loved you?"

Her soft laughter was filled with sadness. "There was a moment, a brief fleeting moment, when I looked deep into his soul and thought I saw a shred of light. Small but significant. I hoped that given time he might discover it himself, but time ran out."

Marcus had kept the love he felt for Tempest locked tightly away, out of fear or foolishness he wasn't certain. He only knew that love had existed and it was a deep binding love that could never, ever be broken.

"What happened between you and Marcus to finally end it?"

Tempest turned her head to look into his dark eyes that no longer seemed mysterious to her. "That is a memory for you to recall."

"And what do you expect to happen when I do?"

"Only you will be able to answer that."

"I feel his power stirring impatiently inside me," he whispered in her ear. "And I can almost feel the ache for it to rush forward and consume me."

"Marcus's power is a formidable force. Be careful."

He gave her a strange look. "If his power is a formidable force, and he was searching for someone with equal skills, then your power must be just as formidable."

"I can impress," she said with a smile, feeling now was not the time for him to recall the true extent of her skills or remember that she was called the Ancient One.

He brought his head down to kiss her slow and easy before saying, "Show me how you impress."

She turned around in his arms. "I love a challenge," she said and licked her lips slowly while her hand began to tease his body.

• • •

Michael tossed restlessly in his sleep. He fought the darkness that suddenly wrapped around him and pulled at him. He didn't want to go. He didn't want to know. He wanted to remain Michael and only Michael. He wanted Marcus to go away, but he wouldn't go away, and they struggled until the darkness swallowed him.

The door to the castle blew open in a rush of whirling wind, sending Marcus crashing back against the stone wall. He watched as the swirling funnel came to an abrupt halt only a few feet in front of him and settled to reveal Tempest in all her glorious anger.

He smiled. "I have heard about that temper of yours but never realized the power it manifests. Magnificent, absolutely magnificent."

She wore white, the power of light, and her reddish blond hair raged in all its fiery splendor, matching her ignited temper. She pointed an accusing finger at him, its force keeping him locked against the stone wall. "How dare you hurt those less fortunate because you were angry with me."

His own temper surfaced, though it remained useless against her immense power. "Release me, Tempest," he warned in a voice that chilled to the bone.

"When I am ready."

"Release me," he bellowed at her.

"Silence, Marcus, or I will take your voice."

This time his raging bellow reverberated off the stone walls. "Release me now!"

"You dictate to the Ancient One?" she said, her fury sending a whirl of wind wrapping around her. "Your power is nothing compared to mine."

"It equals yours," he insisted.

"It is menial in its use and substance."

He smiled slowly. "Care to prove that?"

"You issue me a challenge?" she glared at him as if he were a witless child.

Marcus grew irritated and spoke foolishly. "Afraid to accept?"

His release was so instant, he fell to the floor on his hands and knees.

"I expected better of you, Marcus," she said and turned her back on him to walk a few steps away, making it clear that she considered him no threat.

The insult had its desired effect and he flew at her.

She turned and simply raised her hand. He slammed to a dead stop.

He took several steps back and sent a forceful spew of energy from his hand. It bounced off the protective shield Tempest had erected.

"You're wasting your time and energy, Marcus."

He used the force of his anger to combat her, but it did little good. She deflected his power time after time until Marcus dropped to his knees, drained.

She stood over him, her chin high, her power strong. "I give you a choice. You behave or I will have no alternative but to send you away."

He raised himself slowly, his breath labored, his knees barely able to hold him. "Behave? You tell me I must behave? How dare you dictate to me!"

"How dare you force my hand!"

"You brought us to this point," he accused.

"Your arrogance brought us here. Now tell me your choice. Do you cease your hurtful behavior? Or do I send you away?"

He spoke with arrogance. "You are powerful, Tempest, but not that powerful."

"Don't underestimate my abilities. You will regret it."

"I am well aware of your abilities, Tempest," he said, his arrogance mounting. "But I am also well aware of your love for me. And that love will not allow you to send me away."

Tears filled her eyes. "No, my love will not allow me to send you away forever. My love for you will give you another chance."

His eyes widened. "Think of what you say, Tempest."

"I have thought," she said sadly. "And you give me no other choice." She lowered the protective field and as he stepped forward she extended a pointed finger at him and along with her words a mist rose up from his feet and began encircling him.

"With my love I send you away; for you to return on a future day; your life will be yours to create; choose wisely and repeat no mistakes; cherish life and hold it dear; fill no hearts and souls with fear; surround yourself with magic and light; and seek not to return to the dark night; if by chance you should lose your way; remember all these words I say; magical

*memories you will recall; and the choice will be yours to stand
or to fall!"*

Michael bolted out of bed in a fury. His dark, angry eyes
swept the room to find it empty. He grabbed for his jeans,
slipped them on and went in search of Tempest.

Tempest waited in the kitchen. She had woken early, had
known Michael was in the throes of a dream that would seal
their fate. She had left him alone, needing her own time to
reflect on the possibilities.

Would she actually be able to cast him away when she had
fallen so deeply in love with Michael? And how did she explain Michael's words of love?

Then, now and forever.

He had made it sound as if Marcus had loved her and yet
Marcus had never once declared his love for her. What was
she to think?

Rain viciously pelted the windows and the dark gray skies
made it seem closer to dusk than to dawn.

Tempest hugged herself. The moment was at hand; she
could feel his anger fill the house, feel his heartbeat thunder
in his chest and feel his power rush down to descend over her.

Marcus was here.

Twenty-seven

~

Michael rushed into the kitchen and though he looked as he always did—dark hair, dark, penetrating eyes and lingering scars—he wasn't the Michael she had come to know and love. She saw Marcus in all his arrogant splendor.

She raised her head high and stood with confidence. She had known she would one day face the man she had loved and had banished. And she would face him with strength—and with a love that had never died.

Michael circled her slowly, glaring at her with accusing eyes. "You banished me for centuries."

"You gave me no choice."

"And you gave me this," he said bitterly, pounding his chest with angry fists. "You gave me this miserable existence, and expected what?"

"I expected you to grow and to learn," she said, her own temper increasing. "And I did not give you this life. You chose it yourself, and it was a wise choice."

"This pitiful existence I chose, and wisely?" he asked with his familiar chilling laugh. "Never. You forced it on me."

"If you recall the spell then you know that you created your own life."

He laughed again, harshly this time. "The spell. To think all this time the spell was right in front of me. Tell me, did you purposely place me in that bedroom where the spell surrounds the wall to torment me?"

"The spell was meant to protect," she said, her voice filling with anger.

"Protect who?" he shouted. "Certainly not me; or perhaps this was for your amusement."

"You still speak foolishly after all this time," she said. "You know I am incapable of harming anyone."

He pointed an accusing finger at her. "You don't look at what you did to me as harm; you yourself called it growth."

"Growth was necessary for you," she argued. "Necessary for your continuation."

His chilled laughter turned the room cold. "You call this foolishness continuation?"

"Have you learned nothing?" she all but screamed at him.

"I have learned that your precious love for me meant nothing."

His words pierced her heart and she spoke what she knew to be the truth. "My love saved you."

He threw his hands up in the air and lightning flashed and struck the ground outside the window. "Your love robbed me of my true existence."

Ever the wise one, she spoke. "Your true existence is within you. Find it and you find the truth."

"Within me," he said with a fist to his chest, "resides my power, that is my truth."

She shook her head. "Will you forever remain a fool?"

Thunder cracked overhead and lightning pierced the earth with a blinding light. Michael drew the power down within him and smiled. "No, I will never be a fool again."

"You never stopped," she accused, feeling hurt and disappointed for him.

"You took everything from me," he shouted with a fury.

"I gave you everything," she cried, her heart feeling as if it were being torn in two.

"You banished me." Anger, resentment and bitterness filled his voice and swelled within him. The combined emotions joining with his power rocked the foundation of the small cottage.

Tempest's own fury mounted and she knew the power raging between them was a formidable force and must be contained. And yet her own disappointment fueled the fury, giving it greater life.

Tempest, therefore, was not surprised to see Dagon and Sebastian materialize in the kitchen. They immediately walked to position themselves protectively beside her.

"Reinforcements, Tempest?" Michael asked snidely. "Has your power diminished that much over the years that you need assistance?"

Dagon spoke with a force of his own. "Tempest is returning with us."

Michael laughed and shook his head. "Tempest is staying here and finishing this with me once and for all."

Sebastian made his presence known. "Don't think so, pal. She's coming back to Rasmus Castle with us."

An eerie silence filled the room, causing the hair on the back of everyone's neck to stand up and a chilling shiver to race down their spines.

"She goes nowhere," Michael warned with a strength that rattled the windowpanes.

Dagon bravely made an attempt to step forward, but a touch from Tempest cautioned him against such a rash action.

"Time apart might serve us well," Tempest said.

Michael's laughter sent goose bumps racing over everyone. "We have already had too much time apart. Parting again would serve no purpose and only postpone the inevitable. You will remain here."

Dagon took Tempest's hand. "We'll stay."

"Not necessary," Michael said firmly.

"Necessary," Sebastian insisted and moved closer to Tempest.

She appreciated their show of support and protection, but there was nothing they could do. Neither of their powers were sufficient enough to offer any type of defense. "Thank you for your concern, but it's best you leave."

Dagon refused to listen. "Absolutely not. We're staying."

Tempest tried again. "Really, Dagon, it isn't necessary."

"Necessary or not, we're staying," he reiterated and Sebastian nodded to confirm his support of the decision.

"You both will leave now," Michael ordered.

Dagon attempted to protest when Michael simply snapped his fingers and sent them on their way. He raised his hand in a circular motion and smiled. "Now no one will be able to disturb us."

Tempest felt the thickness of the heavy shield he had wrapped around the cottage and decided not to remove it. It was time they talked and the only person who she could talk with, who would understand, was Michael.

Michael. Not Marcus.

Marcus's past may have surfaced but Michael was who he was here and now and that made a difference, a significant difference. He would need time to deal with past memories, past powers and past desires. In the meantime she had to have patience and help guide him wisely. The spell needed fulfilling and she wanted him prepared no matter how difficult of a task it seemed.

Bear entered the kitchen at that moment, looked at Michael and hissed. The cat did what *she* had hoped to do; he touched Michael deeply enough that he responded.

He scooped up the hissing cat with a tender touch, calmed him with a few strokes and soft words until he had him purring contentedly. Bear had worked his magic, too—he had instantly calmed Michael.

"Hungry?" she asked, feeling starved herself. They had used an enormous amount of their power and she knew he had to feel drained.

"Famished," he said and a hint of a smile, Michael's smile, touched his lips.

Michael sat at the kitchen table while Tempest got busy with breakfast.

"Now I know why I was so interested in the Ancient One," he said. "I knew her personally for a very long time."

"Part of you did, not all of you," Tempest attempted to explain.

"Tell me more," he said with a frustrated sigh. "I need to understand. I feel as though there's a part of me I don't understand. I've always felt that way."

Tempest talked while she prepared pancakes. "You created this life, though hard at times, to help you learn from your past mistakes. In so doing you've allowed yourself the opportunity to experience your power at its best."

He listened with interest. "You mean I've always possessed magical powers?"

She nodded, pouring the batter on the hot skillet. "You never lost those powers; they simply lay dormant, waiting for you to call them forth."

"And I've been living this spell you placed on me?" he asked with an hint of anger.

"Yes, but you need to listen to the spell to make sense of it and to understand its intentions. Every word holds magic."

"It repeats and repeats in my head. I feel it is attempting to tell me something." He shook his head as if shaking out the confusion.

"Listen to its litany and you will learn."

"What will I learn?"

"The essence of the spell itself."

"And will I understand why you placed it on me? Because I must tell you, Tempest, I'm having a hard time with the fact that you sent me—" He shook his head again. "Marcus—away."

"You are Marcus," she reminded him.

"I don't know who the hell I am anymore. Michael, Marcus, me. Where the hell is me? I thought I knew me and now I don't know anything. I don't even know if my life was my own. You cast the spell, you forced issues."

It was Tempest's turn to shake her head. "I cast the spell, but you created your life. Think on it and examine it and perhaps then you will understand."

Marcus placed a sleeping Bear on the cushioned chair and walked over to her. His arms slipped around her waist, his mouth came down on hers and he kissed her as if for the first time.

Time stood still and souls touched.

"I love you, Tempest, always remember that," Michael whispered and kissed her again.

"I love you," she murmured against his lips. "I've always loved you then, now and forever."

"I need time," he said his forehead pressed to hers. "I need time to understand this and deal with it."

"Time is yours, but the spell must be satisfied before long. And you must remember your power has returned full force. I advise you to feel it, embrace it and practice it before it begins to consume you."

"Consume me?"

"Power is energy and unless focused and restrained it can cause yourself and others damage."

"I like the feel of it," he admitted.

"It rages and swirls and can make you feel invincible. That is not the best part of your power. The real part, the true essence of it is the calm and peace that penetrate the soul. When that is learned and experienced you move beyond invincible."

"And I thought this magic stuff was easy." He almost laughed but couldn't.

She placed her hand to his cheek. "It is, Michael, it is simple and therein lies its secret."

"You possess a rare wisdom."

"That comes with a price."

He looked at her strangely before realization struck. "Everyone wants from you—even I wanted to join with you for the sake of your power."

"People, even witches, don't realize they possess their own power."

"But yours is immense and that's where the envy comes in."

She shook her head. "A senseless waste of energy. It serves no purpose and only manages to blind the truth."

"How do I find the truth?"

She kissed his cheek. "Look within your soul. All the answers you need are there."

He sniffed the air with a smile. "Pancakes smell great."

She laughed, hugged him and together they hurried to set the table.

Michael spent the afternoon in the small upstairs bedroom, staring at the spell written in an ancient language that he now understood. He wanted to make sense of all this, but most of all he wanted to understand his love for Tempest and her love for him.

Had it always been there? Is that why he had felt so strongly about her when they first met? Was he remembering what they once had together? He stared at the symbols.

With my love I send you away.

She had wrapped him in the spell with her love, never to be alone and never to forget. She had unselfishly sacrificed a part of herself for him. And what had it taught him? She had given freely of her love without any reservations. Was she a fool or wiser for it? More questions, not always answers.

For you to return on a future day.

She had given him a second chance. She hadn't just banished him for all eternity; she'd given him another opportunity at life. To learn and to grow. Why? Love? Love started the spell—would it wind its way through its entirety?

Your life will be yours to create.

She had left his life in his hands, had given him an empty canvas to paint as he chose. Had he painted in drab, lifeless colors or vibrant hues that would offer him challenges and growth? His life hadn't been easy; it had in fact been hard and many times lonely. Had he created this? If so, why? What had he learned? He had seen many harsh things in his travels and had felt disheartened for the misfortune of the oppressed and poor. His eyes had been open to the injustices of the world and the need for hope and love. Love again. Always love.

Choose wisely and repeat no mistakes.

She had offered him caution in his choices and reminded him not to repeat past actions that had caused his downfall. Unknowingly he had seemed to heed her warning. Had she placed those words there out of protection? Out of concern? Out of love?

Cherish life and hold it dear.

She had reminded him how important it was that life be valued and held close to one's heart. Another place one found love.

Fill no hearts and souls with fear.

She had warned him of using fear to intimidate and he certainly understood fear. He had experienced it many times when he watched those who felt stronger impose their will on the weak. Greed took precedence over love when fear was present.

Love.

One way or another it always managed to show up in the spell.

Surround yourself with magic and light.

Here she reminded him of his power, the power of good, the power of magic and light. The power to offer hope and love to all those who sought magic. Not only a witch's power, but everyone's power.

And seek not to return to the dark night.

She cautioned him not to return to his past ways. Not to

step into the darkness and forget that light and magic existed. In the dark there was no hope or love—only fear. It was a stark reminder of how easily darkness can invade the soul.

If by chance you should lose your way; remember all these words I say.

She had even placed a safety precaution within the spell, unselfishly offering him her help if he had trouble keeping on his path. Had she done that out of love?

Magical memories you will recall.

Magic. She had made certain that they were magical memories so that they returned to him in a magical manner. His dreams. She had allowed him to recall his past through his dreams. She had carefully planned this spell, covering all areas she felt he would have difficulty with. She had protected him with her love.

The choice will be yours; to stand or to fall.

And in the end she had given him a choice. To stand or to fall. But which one was the wise choice? Which one would be done for love?

He rubbed his weary eyes, tired of looking at the symbols and tired of trying to make sense of the spell. Tempest had certainly worked her magic magnificently.

He shook his head. That was a thought Marcus would have. Tempest had worked her magic, all right, but it was the magic of love. An endless love, an all-forgiving love, a love that gave hope and possibility. A love that gave him a second chance.

Michael understood that, cherished the thought, but deep inside him he felt his power stir, swell and rise majestically to the surface. It was an overwhelming force that made him feel unconquerable.

The question now was, What choice did he make?

Twenty-eight

The dreams stopped. They were no longer necessary. Michael recalled more and more of his past every day. There were days that he liked what he remembered, and there were other days that he found the memories difficult. But he dealt with them; he wanted to. He wanted to make sense of who he was because he suddenly didn't know himself.

And he needed to understand Tempest better. The idea that she was a witch didn't disturb him. The idea that she was the Ancient One was another matter. He sat in the living room reading the few books that made reference to the Ancient One and he made mental notes.

She was constantly referred to as ageless or born at the dawn of time. Her power is believed to be uncommon and to come from light and love. With her aged wisdom she attempts to enlighten and unite the world for the betterment of humankind, and she does so unselfishly.

She teaches her work to those she feels who are worthy and she herself never stops learning, gaining a higher knowledge or sharing her wisdom. According to the writings there is no other witch as powerful as the Ancient One.

Michael could understand Marcus wishing to unite their powers. It would be an awesome joining of forces and together they would be indomitable. There would be nothing they wouldn't be able to accomplish.

That could be a frightening or enlightening thought. If used harmfully it could cause massive destruction and yet if used for the betterment of humanity it could bring hope and love to millions.

The thought was sobering and made Michael understand the tremendous responsibility that Tempest had to face when casting the spell. She had all of humankind to think about. Her love for Marcus was minor compared to her responsibility to humanity. And her choices in a way were not her own.

He suddenly wanted her in his arms and he tossed the book and his mental notes aside and went in search of her.

Tempest stood in a small clearing, her arms hugging her waist. It was a beautiful spring day. The sky was clear, the air fresh, the flowers bursting in glorious color and the trees magnificent with new growth.

She took a deep breath, breathing in the very essence of her being—life. It surrounded her in all its magical splendor. And seeing its beauty and wonder, she knew she would always do what she must to protect it.

She had made difficult decisions before; she would make them again at any cost.

Her tears started then and flowed down her cheeks. She needed this cleansing of her soul. She needed to shed tears for what could have been and all that may never be.

Her sobs began to echo through the woods and it sounded as if the forest wept for her.

Michael walked up behind her, his arms going around her, his hands grabbing hold of her crossed arms, and he drew her back against his strength and into the arms of his love.

She went without reluctance, needing him, wanting him and aching for him. She had known centuries ago that it would be only him who could soothe her heart and soul, that there would be no other. That destiny was theirs to share no matter the years that had separated them.

He placed his cheek next to hers. "I loved you then, Tempest, though I never admitted it to you or to myself. My need for you was uncommon, unbearable and unquenchable. The more I took from you the more I wanted, and the more I wanted the more I took."

She listened with closed eyes and an open heart.

He kissed her cheek. "Now I want to give to you." He

turned her around in his arms and her eyes drifted open. "I love you. Then, now and forever."

Her eager lips met her anxious ones and they fed like starving children who did not know when to stop. And they didn't. Their kiss lingered until building to a passion that required more nourishment, and they continued to feed their hunger.

Their arms remained wrapped around each other. There was no need for touch; only the quenching of a long-lost love.

Slowly their lips eased and Michael rested his forehead to hers. "I've missed you, Tempest; I can feel it down into the depths of my soul how very much I've missed you."

Her tears began again, soft and slowly. "I like who you've become. So far you have made wise choices."

He wiped at her tears with his finger. "You wrapped me in a spell that allowed me the wisdom to grow."

She shook her head. "You made your own choices."

He would not allow her to deny the truth. "Choices that could never have been made wisely without your guidance. You wove part of yourself into that spell to protect and guide me. You sacrificed for me."

"I did what was necessary," she insisted, her tears subsiding.

"No," he said firmly. "It wasn't necessary. You did it out of love."

"I know no other way."

"And you love no other. Not the way you love me."

Her tears started once again. "You, Michael, you. I love you."

He kissed at her tears. "Marcus remains a part of me. A part I must face and deal with. He will never go away, but he must grow. He must learn. It is what you wanted for him. It is why you cast the spell the way you did. You gave him all he needed to choose wisely and to make no mistakes."

She smiled at him. "And he has done an admirable job thus far."

"Thus far," he repeated. "The spell still must be completed."

She placed a hand to his chest. "I have confidence in you. In the man you've become and the witch you have grown to be."

"The witch I once was seems foreign to me, but my warlock days haunt me."

"They were not good times," she said sadly. "You abused

your power and hurt others, and all for your own selfish needs."

He released her and took a step away from her. "That power overwhelms me at times and I can feel the urge to embrace it."

"A dangerous thought," she warned.

"But one I must face."

"Do so with strength and courage," she cautioned. "That power can corrupt the strongest of souls and once released it is difficult to control."

"I've controlled it before."

"You gave it life, you fed it and nourished it."

He nodded. "I remember. I catch glimpses of my old life, old ways, old places. They were around this area, weren't they?"

He sensed her reluctance to answer and stepped forward to take her hand.

She held it out to him and grasped his hand firmly in hers.

"I need to know me, or perhaps find me," he said softly.

"I can take you if you'd like."

"Where?"

"To the cave where you performed your magic."

His eyes widened. "It's around here?"

She nodded. "Close by and sealed."

"Would I be able to unseal it?"

"I sealed it the day I sent you away."

"And my power still doesn't match yours, does it?"

She shook her head.

He placed his finger under her chin to raise her head higher. "Will my power ever equal yours?"

Her eyes held many truths that tore at his heart. "There is a possibility."

"Always possibilities," he said softly.

"If you allow them, if you face what must be faced, if—"

"If I make a wise choice."

Her silence told him he spoke the truth.

"Take me to the cave," he said adamantly. "I must learn about me."

She took his hand. "A wise choice to help you make a wise choice."

He smiled and the Michael she knew and loved spoke up.

"Sweetheart, I'm always wise." He kissed her soundly and stepped forward, leading the way.

Tempest followed dutifully, knowing he instinctively knew where to go.

The cave was in a remote area of the woods where humans rarely ventured. They were not knowledgeable enough about the woods to see the natural trails to take. They always had to chop and cut down trees, stamp on foliage and destroy life as they made what they called "progress."

If they opened their eyes they would see that nature had already cleared a path for them exactly where they needed to place their feet.

Michael knew this, as did Tempest. They walked the woods with confidence, familiar with the natural pathway. They ducked under low-hanging tree branches, instinctively stepped around new ground growth and were careful not to disturb any nests.

Their feet walked lightly upon the earth, disturbing as little as possible, and it wasn't long before they reached their destination.

They stopped and stood hand in hand before a large rock that was braced against a hill. Michael made no move, nor did Tempest; they simply remained as they were, staring and listening.

"It's too silent. No animals stir, no birds chirp, no breeze blows," Michael commented softly.

"The woods know of your return. They can feel it."

He released her hand then and turned around to stare at the multitude of trees and dense foliage that stretched out endlessly before him. "I mean no harm."

The silence remained.

"They don't trust me."

Tempest took his hand. "They don't know you."

He squeezed her hand. "They think of me as Marcus and fear his old ways. I can feel their fear. The years have not diminished their memories."

"Give them time. They will come to understand how different you are from him."

He laughed softly. "I am him."

"You're who you choose to be."

"Then it's time for me to discover me." He kept a firm hold

on her hand and walked toward the large rock. "Can you move this?"

She nodded, slipped her hand out of his and with a simple gesture of her hands the rock vanished.

"An illusion," he said, shaking his head. "You created a mere illusion."

"Many things are mere illusions if one would only look and see."

"You were always the teacher," he said teasingly.

"And you always required teaching." She waited for his response and was pleased when he laughed at her remark. Marcus would have grown angry at what he assumed was an insult, but Michael had learned and would learn more. She only hoped the knowledge he gained would be enough in the end.

They entered the cave and as they proceeded in and the darkness grew, thick torches began to spark to life, lighting their way.

"Another illusion?" he asked with a turn of his head over his shoulder to where she walked behind him. The pathway was narrow and could only be walked single file.

"I didn't do anything," she said, her voice faintly echoing off the stone walls. "That's your doing."

He stopped and she almost collided with him. "My doing?"

Tempest talked to his broad back, surprised he hadn't remembered. "You would have arranged for light either to guide your way or to guard you."

"Guard me?"

She explained. "You would have been familiar and comfortable in the dark. The light was probably a guard against intruders. Light being an intrusion to you."

"So the torches light as you pass them, not me."

"Right, and not a bad concept."

"Makes sense," he said with pride for his own idea. He kept walking, not realizing he instinctively knew his way.

They soon turned a corner and entered a large room that filled with a muted light. They both stopped and started at the stone slab altar in the middle of the room.

"This place was in my dreams," Michael said and approached the altar that held candles, wooden bowls and a dagger.

Tempest contained her excitement. He was responding to the cave as if he didn't recall it and that was a good sign. It meant Michael possessed the stronger character, had built it over the years and made it superior to that of Marcus.

He ran a slow, examining hand over the cold slab and touched the half-burned black candles. He walked around the altar to the other side and dipped his fingers into the wooden bowl that held black stones etched with symbols.

He closed his eyes and let his power radiate down his arm and into his hand, empowering the dormant stones.

Tempest watched and felt the rush of power that swept into the room. The darkness of it chilled her to the bone, but she remained as she was, confident of her own abilities.

With a shuffle of the stones between his fingers, he grabbed a handful and cast them down onto the black scarf that lay draped over the altar. They spilled slowly from his hands as if reluctant to leave, clattering against the hard stone and sending a chilling echo throughout the cave.

He braced both hands on the edge of the altar and with a bowed head examined the stones. He recalled long, black hair hanging past his shoulders and a black tunic and robes and fingers long and lean with no scars of calluses. And he recalled his knowledge of the stones.

"They spoke once of our joining," he said, addressing her yet keeping his eyes on the cast. "They spoke of possibilities and the blending of magical forces." He raised his head slowly, his eyes looking darker as he settled a cold stare on her. "They spoke of us."

Tempest wisely chose silence. Marcus had made himself known and she could do nothing. It was up to Michael and the strength and courage he had wisely built over the years.

Michael suddenly stepped back, his hands falling away from the stone altar. "Damn, what power."

Tempest shivered from the force of energy that filled the cave. She raised her own defense shields and waited. Would Michael succumb to a power that enticed?

He walked over to her. "I've never felt such a force of power. It's remarkable."

"Know it for what's it's for," she warned.

He looked at her oddly and then smiled like a schoolboy about to play a trick on the teacher. He rubbed his hands together until a ball of energy began to form, and he tossed it up into the air for it to burst over their heads, causing a sprinkle of shattering light to descend over them. "It's simply power."

She shook her head. "You are wrong. Power comes from different sources; those sources determine its strength and weaknesses."

"And can your power outdo my power?" he asked like a teasing child.

She smiled and couldn't help herself; she had to show off. She rotated her hands as Michael had done, but more slowly building and building the energy between her palms. The glowing sphere grew larger and larger, along with Michael's eyes.

When it all but consumed Tempest she cast it up to float to the top of the cave and with a sudden snap of her fingers the sphere burst into a shower of light that rained down upon them like brilliant fireworks.

Michael stood with his finger to his lips. "There's a lesson in here somewhere, I know there is."

She smiled, pleased he had paid attention. "Learn it and you will know the source of true power."

He cast a quick glance around the cave before reaching for her hand. "Its starkness leaves me cold."

She hung on tightly to his hand. "Then let's step out into the light."

He followed closely behind her as they retraced their steps and on hurried feet they rushed out of the cave to the bright afternoon sun and the chirping of birds.

"Listen," he said with excitement. "The birds are talking."

"About you," she said and ran up to fling herself in his arms.

His well-toned body took the impact with nothing more than a mere flinch and his arms swung around her, holding her tight. "What do they say?"

Tempest wrapped her arms around his neck and kissed him quickly. "They tell the woods to watch and wait."

"For what?" he asked and kissed her back.

"For you."

"Me?"

She wiggled herself out of his arms and he reluctantly let her go. "They talk of your progress and yet they caution that you are who you are."

"You understand them?" he asked, surprised.

"They are part of me," she answered with pride. "Good witches and nature are one."

"So can you tell me if they've waited to pass judgment on me?"

"They pass no judgment; it's not in their nature. They wait, they watch and they learn. Then they see the flow of things."

"Flow?"

"Life," she said with a laugh, realizing he was like a newborn babe that required learning. While Marcus and his memories were a part of him, there was a stronger part of him that was Michael. What happened when the two completely merged as one would be the ultimate test.

"Flow," he said, testing the rhythm of it. "I like that."

She hooked her arm in his. "And they like what they see in you."

He walked with her. "Yet they continue to wait."

She nodded. "They watch and learn."

"They watch me?"

She nodded again.

"They will learn about me?"

Her head nodded once more.

"Then they see the flow of things, as you said."

She looked at him with a tenderness in her eyes that could only be from love. "Life, Michael, what will you do with it?"

He stopped walking and took her in his arms. "What you're saying is that life is a choice and soon the time will come for me to make a choice."

She smiled at his wisdom.

He kissed her softly and from the heart. "The choice is mine."

She raised gentle hands to cup his face. "It always was."

Twenty-nine

~

Early the next morning Michael and Tempest decided to explore the woods once again. They both were aware that time
was drawing short and soon, very soon, Michael would have
to make a choice. But for now they wanted to make magical
memories to always have to remember.

They were dressed comfortably for the crisp spring day,
Michael in blue jeans and a white sweatshirt and Tempest in
black knit pants and an oversized sweater.

They were about to set out when a commotion sounded at
the front door. Michael immediately went to the door, Tempest
close on his heels.

He swung it open.

"I told you that you miscalculated the distance," Sarina said,
annoyed, and brushed wood chips from her pale-yellow knit
dress which flowed softly over her rounded stomach.

"So I landed us outside the house instead of inside," Ali
said with an indifferent shrug. "Big deal. We're here, aren't
we?" She chased a couple of spiders off her bright pink oversized sweater that hugged her protruding stomach.

"You landed us in the woodpile," Sarina said, hands on hips,
glaring at her.

Tempest quickly stepped around a startled Michael. "Are
you two all right?"

Ali spoke up. "We're fine. Your sister just happens to be in a complaining mood."

"I am not," Sarina said defensively.

"Come in," Tempest insisted, hoping to calm the bickering women.

"I'm starving," Ali said and kept walking toward the kitchen though she paused a moment to say, "Hi, Michael."

"Good idea," Sarina said following her, "as long as you don't cook. Hi, Michael."

Tempest plucked a fat little spider off her sister's back as she passed and placed it outside before giving Michael a quick kiss on the cheek and then catching up with the warring pair.

Michael wisely chose retreat, hurrying outside and into the woods.

The two were already setting the kettle to boil and looking for food when Tempest entered the kitchen. "Sit, both of you, I'll see to conjuring up food."

Ali rubbed her hands together like a joyous child and took a seat at the table. "I love conjured food; it's fast and delicious."

Sarina joined her at the table. "You better watch your weight, you know you've put on more than me."

"One pound, one lousy pound," Ali said, waving a finger in her face.

Tempest shook her head and snapped her fingers, setting the table with a choice of biscuits, buns and fresh fruit. "Eat so you will both stop arguing."

"We're not arguing," Sarina snapped.

"Right," Ali said, though the word was barely distinguishable, her mouth being full.

Tempest joined them at the table after setting a pot of tea to steep. "Do your husbands know you're here?"

They both laughed and Sarina answered, "Are you kidding?"

"They forbade us from coming here," Ali said. "Can you imagine being forbidden from going someplace? What would you do?"

Tempest smiled. "I'd go."

"That's one of the reasons we're here," Sarina said, reaching her hand out to offer a comforting touch to her sister. "Though the main reason is to see how you are."

Ali pointed her finger at the teapot and proceeded to serve tea. "How are you? And how are things with Michael?"

Tempest sighed. "I'm fine."

"Liar," Sarina said with a weak smile.

"All right," she admitted. "I'm concerned, but there really isn't much I can do about anything. The spell was cast; it was allowed to unfold and it now seeks fulfillment. How it will be fulfilled is the true question."

"Does Michael understand who he once was?" Ali asked, reaching for a biscuit.

"Yes," Tempest said. "He is gaining insight to his past deeds and attempting to understand himself. But Marcus's power intoxicates, and it's a hard force to ignore."

"Does he understand he fights himself?" Sarina asked.

"He fights a part of himself he once was," Tempest corrected. "The spell helped him to make changes, to see things differently and to want to be different himself. His old ways no longer suit him and yet he can create new ways that would serve Marcus well in this world."

"Or serve his new self well," Ali said, still munching.

"I think something disturbs you," Sarina said, holding her sister's hand.

Tempest wore a strained smile. "I love Michael so very much. He is everything and more than Marcus ever was and I fear losing him forever."

Tears clouded Ali's eyes. "Michael is a good guy; he'll know what to do."

Sarina offered her own encouragement. "When I first met Michael I could feel the goodness in him. He cared about people, genuinely cared, and I could tell that he cared about you, though his feelings confused him."

Tempest smiled and recalled happy memories. "He thought me crazy. When I ran into him with the car—"

"You ran into him with your car?" Ali asked in disbelief. "No wonder he thought you were crazy."

"He didn't think I was crazy for running him down with my car in the snowstorm," Tempest explained. "He thought I was crazy for kissing a stranger."

"Let me get this straight," Ali said, waving a honey bun in her face. "You run him down with your car and then you kiss him in the middle of a snowstorm."

"Well, he mentioned something about kissing it and making it all better," Tempest said, as if that explained it.

Ali waved the bun in the air. "There you go, now I've got it. You kissed a stranger to make his boo-boo all better." She shook her head. "You are crazy."

"Ali," Sarina scolded.

"Oh, don't tell me she's the Ancient One again. She's a woman plain and simple." Ali looked at Tempest, her creamy complexion flawless, her pale-green eyes stunning and her fiery hair raging in glorious waves. "Well maybe not plain and simple to the eye, but inside she's a woman with a woman's needs. Which means she makes stupid mistakes as only women can."

Tempest laughed. "There's a lesson in that statement somewhere."

"Men are simple creatures," Ali continued with her lesson. "Give them food and give them sex and they're satisfied. Throw in love and it's mass confusion. They have no idea how to deal with it within themselves or with the woman they love."

Sarina giggled. "You do have a point. They think they know, they attempt to know and they often brag about love, but they haven't got a clue."

"I think Michael knows about love," Tempest said softly. "The life he chose taught him much about it through hard-won lessons. He sees the truth in people and he seeks the truth. His path hasn't been easy but he has walked it with pride and determination and in the end I think his strength of character will help him choose wisely."

"Do you think he understands the spell enough for him to make the right choice?" Ali asked, dusting crumbs from her hands over her empty plate.

"I can only hope," she answered.

Ali turned to Sarina. "Can't you see the outcome?"

"It is not for anyone to see," Sarina said.

"Then what good is all of our hocus-pocus if we can't do anything to help?" Ali asked, frustrated.

Sarina and Ali turned to Tempest for the answer.

Her answer was a wise one. "We always help. It is how that help is put to use or if it is used at all that matters. I wrapped Marcus in a powerful spell and added much love to it. That

love followed him throughout the spell. What he does with it—
recognizes it or disregards it—is entirely up to him. But never
doubt we help. We can do no less. It is who we are."

"You *are* a wise teacher," Ali said with much respect.

"We are all teachers, if we but listen," Tempest advised.

"What do you think we should have for lunch?" Sarina
asked with a grin.

"Tuna salad," Ali said. "I definitely want tuna salad."

Tempest shook her head and laughed.

Michael couldn't wait any longer to return to the cottage. His
stomach was growling for food and his tired feet were protesting their extensive walk. He hoped Sarina and Ali would
be gone when he returned. He didn't understand why he
wished to be alone with Tempest, he only knew that he did.
And besides, he wasn't good with two hormonally raging
women.

The smell of fresh baking cookies and laughing voices told
him he wasn't going to get his way. He thought at first to go
straight upstairs to wait out their visit, but instead his nose
followed the delicious scent of chocolate chip cookies straight
into the kitchen.

"Michael," Ali called out in welcome. "Have a cookie."

Michael wasn't certain he was in the right kitchen. He had
never seen it such a mess before and he had never seen three
women who looked as if they had been through a battle with
cookie dough. He cautiously approached Ali's outstretched
hand.

"Want to help us finish?" Sarina asked, licking her dough-
covered fingers.

Michael took the offered cookie and stepped around the two
women to get to Tempest's side and safety. Though when he
noticed her dough-splattered face and clothes he wondered if
he had made a wise choice.

"What happened?" he whispered as he kissed her cheek.

Tempest smiled with delight. "We played mortals."

He stared at the cookie in his hand.

"It's good; try it," Sarina urged.

With three women, two of them pregnant and eagerly await-
ing his verdict, he wisely popped the cookie into his mouth.
Surprisingly, it tasted better than good. "Wow, it's delicious."

Ali squealed. "Wait until Sebastian learns that I can make delicious chocolate chip cookies just as a mortal does."

Michael couldn't help but smile at her sense of accomplishment and he praised them all. "Good work, ladies."

They beamed like prized students.

His stomach chose to growl at that moment and before he knew it all three women had him sitting at the kitchen table and were fussing over him. He had to laugh; the scene appeared so comical to him and yet so heartwarming. They cared about him, actually cared for his well-being. He could feel their concern, Tempest's being the most prevalent. And he had to admit it felt awfully good to be fussed over. He actually felt that he was part of a family, an honest-to-goodness family. Witches though they were, they were still family.

"I'll make him a tuna salad sandwich," Ali said.

"No!" the other two shouted.

Michael grew alarmed.

"He doesn't like chopped pickles and hot peppers in his tuna salad," Tempest said. "I'll make him a ham sandwich."

"Chopped pickles and hot peppers?" he said.

Tempest placed a hand on his shoulder. "I'll make you a ham sandwich."

"I don't know," Michael said. "Ali's tuna salad sounds pretty good to me."

Ali grinned and went to the refrigerator. "One tuna salad coming right up."

Michael ate two sandwiches, chips and half a dozen chocolate chip cookies while the women finished baking and cleaning. They laughed and teased each other and talked of family, friends and babies. He watched the way Tempest looked at them with warmth, love and a touch of envy.

She wanted a child.

And he wanted to give her one.

The realization struck him hard. He wanted a full life with Tempest, babies and all.

"Look at the time," Sarina said, glancing at the clock. "We better get back home."

Ali half filled a paper bag with cookies.

"You can't take that bag with you," Sarina warned. "We're supposed to be in Edinburgh shopping. How are you going to explain cookies?"

"How are we going to explain that we didn't buy a single solitary thing?" Ali asked.

Michael laughed. "She's got you there, Sarina."

Sarina wasn't one to accept defeat. "We'll pop down to the village and buy a few things before we go home."

"Candy!" Ali said, her eyes going wide.

Sarina wagged a finger in her face. "You better watch your wei—" She stopped abruptly, chewed on her lower lip and said, "Pecan rolls."

"Fudge with nuts," Ali said, her eyes gleaming.

"Let's go," Sarina said, "but this time I cast the travel spell."

"I can get it right," Ali insisted.

"I am not being deposited in another woodpile, or heaven forbid a rooftop," Sarina said and hurried over to Tempest to give her a kiss. "Be well and take care. I love you."

While Ali said her good-bye to Tempest, Sarina walked over to Michael. She leaned down and kissed his cheek. "Love my sister as she has loved you, unselfishly."

He nodded, knowing he would have no problem with her request.

Ali hurried over to him and kissed his other cheek. "There's some of my tuna salad left. Enjoy and take care, sweetie."

"Put your finger down Ali, I'm casting the spell," Sarina ordered.

"I can do it," Ali insisted.

"Let me," Michael offered and with a snap of his fingers the two women disappeared.

Tempest looked at him with concern.

"I sent them directly to the sweetshop," he said and held his hand out to her.

She walked over to where he sat at the kitchen table, her hand reaching out for him. He grasped it and pulled her to him, his arms wrapping around her waist and his face pressing firmly to her tummy. She ran her hands through his hair and held him close to her.

They remained that way for several silent moments and then Michael drew his head away from her and looked up to say, "If we made a baby now it would be conceived of love."

Tempest thought on his words. He was right; any child conceived now would definitely be born of love. She loved him and he loved her—it was plain and simple yet deeply truthful.

And if now she conceived a child and she lost him to the spell she would at least have a part of him with her forever.

A selfish thought.

An honest thought.

A difficult decision.

"You fight what you want. Why?"

"There is much for us to settle before we can think of a child."

He pressed his hand to her stomach. "We have settled many things already. Why not solidify our love by creating a child from that love?"

She had to keep things in perspective. She couldn't be selfish now after all these years. After he fulfilled the spell there would be time to think of a child. Now was not the time, no matter how much she wished to conceive a baby with him.

"There is time for a child; there is no need to rush."

His annoyance rippled over her and she braced herself against the chilled shiver that rushed her skin. She closed her eyes and was reminded of Marcus.

"Look at me," he demanded.

She slowly opened her eyes.

"Who am I, Tempest? Who do you see when you look at me?"

She traced the scar by his eye, caressed his cheek, ran a tender finger down his nose and over his chin. With her touch came his emotions and she allowed herself to feel one and all of them and she knew without a doubt who he was. "I see Michael, the man I love and the man who loves me."

"You don't doubt my love, do you?"

She shook her head. "No, I am confident of your love."

"Do you doubt who I am?"

That question caused her to pause in thought.

He answered. "Your hesitation tells me you doubt."

Her hand cupped his cheek. "I don't doubt you, Michael."

"You doubt the me that's Marcus?"

She shut her eyes again.

"Don't," he said softly. "Look at me, please."

She opened them. "You must face the you that is Marcus."

"And you worry whether or not I can do that?"

"His power entices and is hard to ignore."

"Your power is hard to ignore."

"My power is based on light, his on darkness."

He smiled. "I can tell the difference."

That impressed her. "I am pleased; that means you have learned."

"I've learned more than you think."

"But tell me," she said, her hand falling softly to his shoulder. "Can you control his power? Keep it in hand?"

"I have a good teacher."

"And you are an apt pupil."

His smile faded. "Trust in me, Tempest."

"I trust you, Michael," she said softly. "I truly do."

He stood and kissed her gently, tasting her as if for the first time, and she responded as if kissed for the first time, hesitantly, nervously and cautiously.

"Trust me," he whispered again and his kiss turned more demanding.

She attempted to withdraw, but he wouldn't let her.

"Trust me," he said again and scooped her up into his arms and carried her out of the kitchen.

Thirty

~

They undressed each other with haste and fell on the bed together just as hastily. But Michael took control, capturing her hands in one of his and exploring her body with his free hand.

"Not fair," she said on a harsh whisper.

He laughed and slipped his fingers between her legs. "I know."

She moaned when he began to pleasure her.

He leaned down and took the erotic sounds into his mouth. He kissed her deeply and drank his full of her, quenching her thirst along with his own. He finished with a brush of his lips across hers. "I love the sounds you make when I touch you."

And with a smile he ran the tip of his tongue over her hard nipple.

She let out a sensual moan that sent shivers racing over him.

He continued to torment her with a skillful tongue and she responded, arching her back, moaning her pleasure and begging him not to stop.

He didn't. He made love to her with the intensity of a madman and she responded madly.

Suddenly they could stand the wait no longer and he moved over her and into her with a sharp entrance that had them both moaning their pleasure.

It was a quick and explosive climax for them both and they

clung tightly to each other as wave after wave of pure, endless pleasure rushed over them.

"I love you, Tempest, then, now and forever," he whispered breathlessly in her ear.

Tears filled her eyes and a lump kept her from speaking. She could only hug him fiercely to her to show him how much she cared and wanted never to let him go.

They slept peacefully that night. No haunting dreams, no reminders of the past, just a calm slumber before the inevitable storm.

Morning brought spring sunshine and the promise of a new day but then that was the continuous cycle of life—always a new day, a new start, a new beginning.

They began with a walk in the woods, surrounding themselves with the purity and magic of nature. And when Tempest disposed of her shoes and socks, Michael joined right in doing the same. His actions startled her.

He ran around like a young boy who had only discovered the joy of going barefoot. "Damn, this feels good."

"Energy," she explained, watching him act like a child.

He grinned. "I can feel it run up my legs. People should do this more often."

"Mortals don't understand the importance of such a simple act."

He looked at her, his smile gone. "I never did."

She smiled. "That's because you never understood magic."

His grin returned. "But I'm learning."

"And doing a good job."

"Teach me more," he said like an eager student.

"I've taught you all I can and given you all you need to know. The rest is up to you."

His expression was again changed, only this time he looked uncertain and a little fearful. "I'm not certain what to do."

She took his hand and felt the strength of him. "Continue to search for who you once were so you know who you've become."

"I catch glimpses of him and—" He stopped and shook his head. "I don't understand why Marcus hasn't fully returned. His power is tremendous. Why doesn't he just become who he once was? Why do I interfere?"

Tempest realized that Michael continued to speak as though Marcus and he were separate entities. He had yet to realize that he was Marcus and that he would need to merge the two. Only then could the choice be made and the spell completed.

"The spell gave you an opportunity to rectify your past and build a new future, a new day, a new beginning. You chose that new beginning, you built a new you, yet—" she said with a brief pause, "your past lives within you. All that you were, good or bad. That doesn't just disappear. It may lay dormant, but eventually it must be faced and dealt with. Therefore, you must know who you truly are here and now."

They walked hand in hand to a fallen tree to sit, their feet remaining bare.

"Tell me about you," he said.

She laughed softly and it sounded like tinkling chimes. "You know me. You know me better than most."

"No, I don't think I do," he said seriously. "I know you're the Ancient One, a wise woman who many seek to learn from and wish to emulate. I know you're a woman who cares deeply for family and friends. I know you're a woman who gives much of herself for the benefit of others and yet seeks no compensation. And I know you're a woman who loves deeply and forever."

"What else, then, is there for you to know about me?"

"Much," he said with a tender kiss to her cheek. "Tell me what you wish for yourself."

"For myself?" she asked as if the question were too odd to understand.

He nodded and smiled. "You, yourself, Tempest."

She thought a moment. "I have what I want for myself. I have accomplished much, have aided many—"

"For yourself," he repeated.

This time she didn't hesitate. "For myself I wish love and I have been granted my wish. You have been sent to me."

He kissed her hand. "It is you who have been *returned* to me."

She was surprised by his remark, though didn't show it. Was he beginning to understand? She hoped so.

"And is that all you wish?"

"That is everything," she said. "Love, true love when understood and given freely is everything anyone could ever hope for and yet most have no idea of its power. They take it for granted, abuse it and disregard it as if it meant nothing. And then they search for what they feel is missing in their lives when it is there if they would only reach out, grasp it and hold on to it."

"Love isn't easy to understand."

"Love is simple; people make it difficult."

"You're wise, you know more than the average person," he said.

She shook her head. "No, I just seek to understand."

"Did Marcus seek understanding?" he asked.

"Marcus thought he possessed it."

"But he didn't?"

"He sought a side of the Craft that defied understanding, though he never fully realized its nature, and that was his mistake."

"And yet his power was tremendous."

"The base of his power was weak," she said.

Michael became defensive. "How can you say that? I know what I feel. The power that surges through me is far from weak. It possesses a force of strength that is undeniable."

"A foundation must be solid and dependable or else the structure is weak. When power is built on greed, jealousy and hate it makes for a faulty foundation that could never truly sustain the structure. It is bound to crumble."

"So what you're telling me is that Marcus was doomed to fail."

"It was inevitable," she said sadly.

"And he never realized this?"

"His arrogance and pride got in the way, more parts to a faulty structure."

"But he loved, he loved you. I felt it," he said adamantly.

She nodded, slowly fighting the tears that threatened to fall. "Yes, I felt his love, if only briefly."

"Then why didn't his love for you help strengthen the structure?"

She took a moment to contain her tears. "Because he never told me that he loved me."

"That's all he had to do?"

"That and renounce his warlock beliefs."

"Instead he went up against you."

She nodded. "He threatened and mistreated those I protect. I could not stand by and watch harm come to the helpless."

"He forced your hand."

"I would not give him what he wanted. He thought lust was enough to hold me and I thought love was enough to change him. We were both wrong."

"Were you?"

She looked at him strangely.

"You never gave up on him. When you cast the spell you wrapped it securely with your love. You sacrificed a part of yourself for him to have another chance to prove himself worthy."

She let her tears fall then. "And you have."

He wiped her tears away with his finger. "Your love carried me through many difficult times. Even when you allowed me to create my own life, you did so with an unselfish love and that love nourished and sustained me."

"You did the work, not I," she said softly.

"You started me off on a firm foundation."

She smiled and cuddled close in his arms. "And you built a sturdy structure."

He lifted her chin to deposit a kiss on her soft lips. "This time it won't crumble."

Tempest prayed he spoke the truth.

Michael sent Tempest back to the cottage, insisting he needed time alone to explore not the woods, but himself. He found he could think better when he was alone and he found he could access Marcus's power more easily and keep it more controlled.

He found his abilities much more powerful inside the cave surrounding the altar. The cave became like a second home to him. He felt comfortable there and in control of himself and his power.

And he felt the need to feel his power. It nourished and sustained, but in a different way from love. A way that he had no business exploring and yet it fascinated him and he couldn't deny its existence. It was part of him, a forceful part of him.

If he didn't explore it, how would he ever understand it? Or understand himself.

At least that was his sane reasoning for an insane act. He knew damn well what he was doing. He was exploring the dark side of magic.

And in so doing, exploring Marcus.

He entered the dark cave and as he passed the torches they remained lifeless, no flames burned to light the way. He didn't need light to guide him. His dark eyes could see clearly and his feet instinctively knew the direction to go.

He snapped his fingers when he entered the room and torches came to attention, as did the candles on the altar.

He was drawn to the stones in the bowl and their raw energy. They almost spoke to him when he touched them and when he threw out a cast on the altar top his eyes rounded in anticipation.

It was a good one, he could tell. How he wasn't certain, but he understood the results and that's what mattered. He felt a surge of energy swirl around him and race up his body, filling him with intense power.

"Damn," he muttered, the strange sensation making him feel invincible and capable of anything he chose to do.

So this was how Marcus had felt—how he had felt.

He had to begin to acknowledge that he was Marcus. That he had lived the life of a warlock centuries ago—a powerful warlock. One who had many followers and believers and one who controlled through his power.

What did he do with it? How did he compatibly merge the two sides of himself without destroying the qualities of each one?

Those were questions he had no answers for and ones that needed addressing.

You are me, I am you.

The words echoed through his head and caused him to grab tightly to the stone altar to steady himself.

Marcus was the strongest in this cave. His magic was here, the power that sustained him and each time Michael came here he felt himself grow stronger and stronger. He had warned himself to be careful and to approach Marcus's power with caution, but the more he experienced its essence, the more he wanted.

It was who he was.

If he kept things in perspective and caused no one harm perhaps he could understand and make use of his remarkable power. Tempest possessed immense power and Michael wished to equal hers.

And he didn't want to fail her.

He deeply loved her. He hadn't known a love like theirs could exist. He didn't know a love like theirs was possible. But then Tempest always reminded him of possibilities in life.

Whoever thought he would fall in love with an ancient witch and that he was a warlock who had lived centuries ago?

Insanity.

That would have been his first thought, but now everything seemed to be making sense to him. He had never felt comfortable in all the places he'd traveled. He had always felt something had been missing in his life, a part of him he couldn't find.

He had found that part of himself here in Scotland. He had felt it when the ship had first docked and he touched ground. He felt as if he had come home; the overwhelming sensation almost made him shed a tear.

This was his home and would always be.

He felt it here, now—that sensation of coming home. It filled him with sheer joy and pleasure. He finally knew where he belonged and he would never leave.

He looked at the stones he had cast on the altar and recalled that he had thrown numerous casts over the years that had foretold many fortuitous events. He thought to throw another cast but something warned him that now was not a good time, perhaps it was actually time for no casts.

He felt a cold shiver race through him and knew that his own thoughts disturbed him, but that was all right because he understood. He understood that Marcus was part of him and would protest some decisions he made. He would be tolerant of Marcus, and the time would finally come that Marcus merged with Michael and they became one.

Suddenly he felt anxious to be with Tempest, to touch her warmth and to love her. He never wanted to stop loving her. He wanted to give her as much love as possible.

Fool.

The word echoed like thunder in his head.

Marcus had to remind him of his presence.

But if Michael felt a fool, it was because he was a fool in love.

He didn't bother to replace the stones in the bowl. He left them spread out, hurried out of the room and out the cave and went in search of Tempest.

Thirty-one

~

Tempest wasn't surprised when Sydney materialized in her kitchen. Actually she had been expecting her. She had set the steeping teapot on the table, added a plate of shortbread cookies and arranged two settings for tea.

"I see I was expected," Sydney said. And before joining Tempest at the table, asked, "I don't intrude, do I?"

"Never," Tempest said with a warm smile. "Please sit. I could use a wise woman to talk with."

"I am flattered that you think of me as such."

"I taught you, you could be nothing less and now you are here to help teach me."

Sydney was stunned. "Teach you? What could I teach you?"

Tears pooled in Tempest's eyes. "How to live without the man I love."

Sydney reached a comforting hand out to her. "You fear Michael will make the wrong choice?"

She let her tears fall. Crying was a good way to cleanse her emotions, to rid herself of doubt and fear, to rebuild her strength and to face tomorrow. "I feel Marcus grow stronger. And I know his power intoxicates."

"You don't think Michael has learned enough to combat that power?"

She wiped at her tears. "It's not that. His power must be

understood and dealt with. It must be turned from darkness into light."

"And is that difficult to do?"

Tempest shook her head. "No, it is simple, though most would not know that."

"Michael would?"

"Marcus would."

Sydney understood. "The decision must be made by Marcus, then, not Michael."

"Actually they both must decide. They must unite as one, understand that and accept or deny this existence."

"So Michael presently wars with himself?"

Tempest nodded.

"And you fear his choice."

Again she nodded. "I know most would think me foolish for reacting this way. I am the Ancient One. The wise woman with all the answers. The one who offers hope and love to all those who seek her. The one who knows."

Sydney squeezed her hand and Tempest grasped onto her, needing her strength. "But you're also a woman in love. And love can hurt, as you well know."

"My heart broke the day I sent Marcus away." She shook her head and brought her hands to cover her face for a moment, then wiped at her tears. "My heart didn't break; it shattered into a million pieces and it took me a very, very long time to deal with the pain."

"I understand," Sydney said, her own tears threatening to spill.

"I remember when you lost Duncan. I remember your pain and your tears."

"You helped me through it and I was forever grateful. You also told me to examine and understand what had happened and to learn and I did."

"What did you learn?" she asked, as if the answer could help her.

"I learned that love is the strongest and most powerful emotion we possess and that it possesses true magic. I learned that love doesn't hurt, but that we hurt love. I learned that unselfish love is the rarest of all and that you seldom find it or possess it. But if found it is truly magical. And I learned that *you* define unselfish love."

Tempest couldn't stop her tears. They ran down her cheeks and she let them have their freedom.

Sydney reached for her hand and held it tightly. "Even when Marcus proved himself unworthy, you remained unselfish. You gave him another chance at life and at love and you did it by sacrificing a part of yourself. Not a small part but a very large part. I don't think anyone truly understands what you did."

Tempest was grateful for Sydney's comforting touch and she clung to her. "The hurt was unbearable that day I faced him. I knew I had no choice. I knew what must be done, what I had to do. I told myself that I had to separate myself from it. That the Ancient One must handle it and that the woman inside me who loved him had to step aside." She shook her head, her tears falling.

"But that wasn't what was necessary, was it?"

"No, I realized as I fought with him that I could never separate the two. The two made me whole, made me who I was and who I would always be."

"And you used that wisdom to save Marcus, didn't you?"

She nodded slowly. "I realized if I could instill that wisdom within him that he might have a second chance."

"And you gave it to him at a high price to yourself. Unselfish love, what a beautiful gift."

"A costly gift, but one well worth giving."

"I admire you," Sydney said, a tear falling from her eye. "And understand why you are the Ancient One and the price you pay for it."

Tempest smiled. "It isn't a burden to me. It is simply who I am. Right now it is the woman within me that hurts, and if I keep her separate from the whole of me I will never fully comprehend the wisdom of this situation."

"And must you always? Can't you just allow yourself time to be a woman?"

"I am always a woman, but I am also always wisdom. One isn't really whole without the other."

"Which is how Michael is feeling right now?"

She nodded. "Yes, he must merge both sides of himself, and in so doing finally understand who he is and what he feels."

"And you wait on this?"

"Yes, I can do nothing until he is ready." She smiled. "That's not true. I can do much, I can love him with my heart and soul."

"Unselfish love—so very difficult and yet I wish myself capable of it."

"But you already possess it, Sydney, and it is why you lost the man you loved."

Sydney disagreed. "I lost him for lack of courage."

"It took courage for you to walk away."

"But if my beliefs were strong, I would have—"

Tempest stopped her. "No, your beliefs were strong and you did what was necessary for him and for yourself."

"I can't help but wonder, though, that if—"

"*If* is a small word that people give too much credence to and in doing so give it tremendous power. If is only as big as you make it and the passing years have a way of making small ifs gigantic. Deal with the real issue, not what you made of it."

"You mean as you're doing with Michael," Sydney said with concern. "You're dealing with the issue of love."

"Yes," Tempest admitted. "Most would think that the issue is Marcus and his warlock ways. But his true test is discovering his origin of power."

"And you don't think he understands this."

"I can't be certain what he understands right now. He is still attempting to understand who he is."

"There is time, isn't there?" Sydney asked anxiously.

"It grows shorter as he grows stronger."

"Does he know this?"

"Instinctively he does, though he doesn't admit it. It will not be easy for either of us, though it is necessary."

"And you will face it with your usual strength," Sydney said.

"There is no other way for me."

"I never fully realized the scope of your power and the sacrifices you make. You must be lonely at times."

"Loneliness can be a good friend. It is how you embrace that loneliness that makes the difference," Tempest said, teaching as only a good teacher could.

"Then you embraced your loneliness all these years?"

"I embraced it with open arms and I learned from it," Tempest explained. "I learned to cherish the silence and hear the secrets it holds."

"The silence has secrets."

Tempest laughed softly. "More secrets than you know."

"I have often wondered," Sydney said curiously. "You teach, but who has taught you? Where does your knowledge come from?"

Tempest was fast to explain. "From all that surrounds me. There are answers in the sky, the earth, life itself. They all teach, if one would listen and see."

Sydney smiled knowingly. "You have taught me this before and I listened."

"You were one of my best students. I am proud of you."

"I'm grateful for all you taught me, but mostly I'm grateful for your friendship."

"I have few good friends, Sydney, and you're one of them."

Sydney beamed with pride. "I am honored. But tell me what can I do now to help you."

"You have done more than you know," she answered. "You gave me a shoulder to lean on and a friendly ear that listened without judging. You are a true friend."

Sydney struggled to keep her tears at bay. "I am here for you always."

"As I will be for you."

"Tempest!"

The two women smiled upon hearing Michael call out eagerly for Tempest.

"I should go," Sydney said.

A hand to her arm stopped Sydney from rising. "Stay, visit with us."

"Michael doesn't sound as if he'd like company."

"Tea," Tempest said. "Stay at least for tea. He can be patient for teatime."

Michael rushed into the kitchen and came to an abrupt halt when he caught sight of Sydney. "Oh, company."

"Hello, Michael," Sydney said.

Michael returned the greeting, though disappointment accented his voice. "Hi, Sydney."

"I'm here for tea," she explained and reached for the pot to pour herself a cup.

Michael turned cordial after hearing she didn't plan on staying long. "Mind if I join you?"

"Please do," Sydney said.

They spent the next hour in a friendly conversation and

Michael found himself enjoying the company. They laughed, talked and reminisced about other times and places and it helped Michael to better understand his heritage.

Witches were truly unique people.

No sooner than Sydney bid them good-bye and Michael joined Tempest by the sink, his arms going around her waist, than Dagon and Sebastian dropped right into the kitchen.

"Damn," Michael muttered and received a poke to the ribs from Tempest.

"We thought we'd see how things were going," Sebastian said.

Dagon walked directly to Tempest and gave her a peck on the cheek even though he had to step around Michael to do so.

Tempest felt the tension crackle in the air.

Men.

They were all the same. Protective and territorial.

"Things are going fine," Michael informed them both and tightened his hold on Tempest's waist.

"A drink?" she asked and all three men nodded.

She left Michael's side, though not before he gave her a quick kiss and she went to the pantry to get the good scotch. If anything would soothe their manly feathers it was good scotch.

She placed the full bottle and glasses on the table and then decided there was something urgent she had to see to upstairs and left the three men at the kitchen table. To fight or to talk. It was up to them, and she had no intention of interfering. She was certain they would use no magic. They were too aware that they were no match for each other, and they were aware that she was more powerful than any of them and would settle any dispute her way.

She grabbed a mystery book she had been reading off the table in the living room before going upstairs to relax on the bed and read, leaving the men to mend fences.

Michael poured the scotch the mortal way. He still hadn't gotten used to pointing his finger and having magic do his work. He preferred to do his own work.

Dagon raised his glass. "To friends."

Sebastian joined in and looked to Michael.

Michael didn't hesitate. Dagon was offering a truce and he

took it. He raised his glass. "To *good* friends."

Glasses clinked and smiles surfaced; the tension had been broken.

Sebastian spoke first. "So how's magic treating you?"

Michael liked Sebastian; maybe it was because he was mortal and he could relate to him, or maybe it was because he could sense he was a regular guy, unpretentious and honest. Dagon was a different matter.

"As well as I can figure it out."

"It isn't that difficult. It's actually simple," Dagon said with his usual air of arrogance.

"You were born a witch," Sebastian reminded.

"So was Michael."

The air suddenly crackled with tension again.

"True," Sebastian said, "though he didn't know he was a witch."

"Warlock," Michael corrected and the two looked at him. "I'm just beginning to realize what that means."

The air quieted again.

"Anything I can help you with?" Dagon offered with much less arrogance and more empathy.

"Did you know Marcus?"

Dagon shook his head. "No, it was before my time."

Michael took a generous gulp of scotch. "It would help me to know more about him."

"I'd like to hear more about warlocks," Sebastian said, taking a drink that emptied his glass.

"I know tales and legends and those today who think themselves warlocks but have no idea what it means to truly be one," Dagon said.

"Tell me what you know," Michael said. "Any information might benefit me."

"Evil lot," Sebastian said. "At least that's what I've heard."

Michael stiffened at his remark.

"No harm meant," Sebastian said and refilled his glass.

Michael relaxed. "None taken, especially when I really can't comprehend this whole warlock thing."

"The easiest way to explain it," Dagon said, "is that a warlock is basically an evil witch. Someone who practices the Craft from the dark side."

"Now are we talking demons and such?" Sebastian asked.

Dagon shook his head. "No, evil is more simple than people think. Greed, hate, jealousy—those things constitute evil. And when promoted to their full potential their power is substantial. A warlock feeds and grows off that power."

"Does a warlock love?" Michael asked.

Dagon looked at him oddly, as if he himself found the question puzzling. "I would have to say that a warlock thinks more of lust than of love."

"What if a warlock found love?" Michael asked, with a relentless need to have answers to his disturbing questions.

"Wouldn't the question be can a warlock actually love?" Sebastian asked.

Dagon rubbed his chin, giving both questions thought. " 'Love' and 'warlock' are two words that are definitely not synonymous. I can't see the two being compatible."

Sebastian offered his own opinion. "Since you love Tempest, Michael, then it must mean that you've freed yourself of your warlock traits."

Dagon's opinion differed. "Or he hasn't fully embraced that part of his past."

"Marcus's power entices," Michael said. "It's like a siren's song that's impossible to ignore."

"Be careful," Dagon warned. "The dark side is easy to fall prey to."

"But if love exists, can't it rescue?" Sebastian asked.

Michael looked to Dagon and waited for his answer.

"I'd like to believe that love could rescue the darkest heart, but I can't say for certain. The stories I've heard of Marcus paint him to be ruthless and uncaring, and yet Sarina has told me things that make me believe that perhaps Marcus did have the capacity to love."

"What has she told you?" Michael asked anxiously.

"She remembers Marcus treating her sister with respect. A strange concept for a warlock."

"Perhaps he respected her power," Sebastian said.

"Or feared it," Dagon offered.

"Or underestimated it," Michael added, his expression reflective. "Maybe he never fully understood what she offered him. Maybe he was too busy thinking of his own selfish needs."

"That's insightful," Sebastian said.

Michael smiled. "I'm trying, though I can't say it's easy."

"Where love is concerned, nothing is ever easy," Dagon said with a shake of his head. "Add to that being a warlock and you don't have a difficult situation, but an impossible one."

"Tempest taught me that there are always possibilities," Michael said. "And I'd like to think that I have numerous possibilities that will lead me to making a wise choice."

"Ever the teacher," Dagon said with a sadness to his voice that startled the other two.

"You sound as though you feel sorry for her," Sebastian said.

Dagon looked at Sebastian with surprise. "Of course I do. Think of how it must be for her. Everyone always seeking her skills, her knowledge, her power. It is seldom that someone doesn't want something from her. She is forever in demand, and does she turn anyone down when they request her help?"

Sebastian shook his head along with Dagon. "She gives it."

"Damn right," Michael agreed. "She always takes time for people. Even now she thinks more of helping me than of her own feelings."

"Hell, this must be tearing her apart," Sebastian said. "Helping you, loving you and yet knowing there's always the possibility that she may have to let you go." He shook his head. "I don't know where she gets the strength."

"Sarina told me that she never remembers her sister not having strength," Dagon said. "She often speaks of her sister's endless acts of compassion and her ability to deal with them as though they were everyday chores that simply needed tending."

"Tempest is a rare woman," Sebastian said.

"Witch," Dagon corrected.

"Woman," Michael insisted. "Tempest is very much a woman and needs to be a woman. Too many think of her only as the Ancient One. She has a right to live her life and I intend to see that she does just that."

Sebastian slapped Michael on the back. "You certainly don't sound like a warlock. You sound like a man in love."

Dagon agreed with a nod. "That you do."

"I have to tell you both," Michael said, sounding like he was about to confess a secret. "I really think that Marcus loved Tempest. I know he was a warlock and lust was in his blood, but I sense there was love in his heart for her. Does that sound strange?"

Dagon shook his head. "I would never have thought it."

"But there are possibilities," Sebastian said. "Which means anything is possible, even a warlock in love."

Michael ran his fingers through his hair in frustration. "Maybe it's just wishful thinking on my part."

"Maybe it's a memory so strong that it haunts you," Dagon suggested.

Michael looked at him with hope. "You think that's possible?"

"There are those possibilities again," Sebastian said with a laugh.

"And where there are possibilities, there is also hope," Dagon said.

"I tell myself that," Michael said though sounded doubtful. "But there are times I feel confused and unable to think straight."

Sebastian laughed. "Why wouldn't you feel that way? You find out that you're not only a witch with special powers, but a warlock with immense powers at his disposal. How would any man react to that news?"

"He's not any man," Dagon said seriously. "And you must remember that, Michael."

Michael nodded. "I can't forget it. I feel it, see it, know it in everything I do."

"Have you practiced your magic?" Dagon asked.

Michael shook his head. "Not really."

Dagon understood. "You fear it."

"Yes, I do," Michael admitted without hesitation.

Dagon placed a firm hand on his shoulder. "Embrace it, or you will never fully understand yourself."

"I sometimes wonder if I do want to understand who I am."

"Fear the consequences?" Sebastian asked.

Michael nodded.

Dagon voiced what Michael couldn't. "You fear losing Tempest."

Michael released a heavy sigh and rubbed at the back of his aching neck. "I love her so damn much. I want to be with her all the time. I want to touch her, hold her, kiss her until I drink my fill of her and yet it's never enough. Never. I always want more. Always more. It's a never-ending need that I don't want to end. I want it to go on forever and ever and ever."

"Then make certain that it does," Dagon advised.

"But I'm not sure how to do that. I'm not sure what's expected of me or if there's something expected only of Marcus. I'm not sure and I don't want to make a mistake. I made one already, and look where it got me."

"It got you love," Sebastian said. "An unselfish love that never ends."

"He's right," Dagon said. "Look to that love—maybe that's where you'll find your answers."

"And what if I don't?"

"Then you lose," Dagon said. "You lose yourself and you lose Tempest."

"Not again!" Michael said adamantly. "Never again."

Thirty-two

~

Michael woke with a start to discover the spot beside him in the bed was empty, and he grew irritated. He found himself wanting Tempest beside him more and more. It was as though she had become a need to him, an endless need that could never be satisfied. And to feel that dependent on someone surprised him. He had lived a good portion of his life alone, never really needing anyone. But now that he'd found Tempest he couldn't comprehend living life without her.

He almost thought of them as one soul, neither being able to survive without the other. The thought actually filled him with joy. To think that two were one seemed the very essence of love, and something that was rarely found.

But he had found it.

Why?

That was an odd question and one he felt he hadn't asked, and yet it was there for him to comprehend.

Why should he even question it?

He instinctively knew that if he did question it, it would help him understand many things. He hopped out of bed, determined to pursue the thought.

He took a quick shower and slipped on black jeans and a black sweatshirt.

The knock at the door came as he left the bedroom and by

the time he was descending the stairs Tempest had answered it.

He came up behind her, his arm wrapping protectively around her waist. He pulled her back firmly against him. "What do you want?" he said to the man outside. He recognized him immediately. He was the man who had stared at him when they had lunch at Swan Inn. He didn't care for him then and he cared for him even less now.

"I think it is time we talk."

He had an emotionless voice and Michael instinctively knew that he possessed no compassion.

"I know you?" Michael asked, though he knew the answer and the thought that he once was connected with this pitiful man disturbed him.

Tempest remained silent, understanding this was for Michael to handle.

"You know me," the man said with a single nod of his head. "And the time has come for us to talk."

"There's nothing for us to discuss," Michael said with a firmness that Tempest felt rush over her.

"There is much to discuss," the man persisted. "Time draws near."

Michael wondered briefly if this man could provide answers to some of his troubling questions. If he could it would be worth a talk with him, and since he felt superior to the man he saw no harm in talking with him.

"Come in," he offered, and the man shook his head adamantly.

"I cannot cross the threshold of the Ancient One. She has too strong of a protection around her home."

The symbols. Michael recalled the symbols and understood. They kept evil away and the man standing outside was evil and had once been a part of Michael's life. The thought unnerved him and made him angry.

"Join me out here," he offered and took several steps back, his eyes focused on Tempest.

Michael tightened his hold around her waist until he realized she felt no fear from this man. It was he who feared her.

"Go to him if you wish," she said softly and for his ears alone.

He hesitated, wondering if it was wise to speak with this

man, this stranger who wasn't a stranger. And yet he felt a need. A need to know more, and if he could satisfy that need then it was necessary for him to speak with him.

"I won't be long," he said and kissed her sensitive neck.

She shivered and pressed herself back against him. "Be safe with my love."

He felt a surge of power race through him and realized she had wrapped him in the protection of her love.

Unselfish love.

He kissed her again and squeezed her waist before stepping around her and out the door.

Tempest closed the door after him, resting her forehead against it. "Keep him safe. Please keep him safe."

The man walked with a pride and arrogance that irritated Michael. He thought himself superior to others and cared nothing for the common man. But Michael had been and remained a common man. He could not forget his youth and the many hardships that followed. He could not forget the struggle to survive and the loneliness of having no one who cared and no one to love him. His past was very much a part of him. It made him who he was today, but then had he chosen it to help him build character? To help him understand what he had never understood in his previous life?

"It is good to see you again," the man said, stopping beneath a large spruce tree. "You would remember me as—"

"Roland," Michael finished, the name suddenly rolling off his tongue.

He smiled. "You do remember. I am relieved. I thought perhaps we had lost you."

"We?" Michael asked, standing to the side of him to look him over and realizing he presented a more powerful image than he actually possessed.

"The other warlocks who survived after your untimely demise. We have waited patiently for your return. We have remained away, concealed for safety sake. But with your return we will be able to once again regain our former power and glory. We will once again rule."

"I am no longer Marcus."

"No," Roland said with pride. "You are more. Your power has sustained you and it has grown. You are near to invincible by now." His voice turned to a whisper. "Even the Ancient

One would have difficulty going up against you."

"I repeat," Michael said, curtly, "I am no longer Marcus."

Roland retreated a few steps. "You are Michael, I understand this."

He wished he did. "You understand nothing." His irritation grew and he paced in front of the man whose eyes suddenly widened with fear.

"Whatever you wish me to understand I will and whatever you wish me to do you have only to ask."

Michael felt his feet leave the ground and found himself planted directly in front of the startled man. He towered over him in strength and character. "What do you want from me?"

"Only to serve you," he said nervously.

"You served me well once, many, many years ago," Michael said as though suddenly remembering.

"You had only to command and I did it."

"You never questioned me?"

Roland shook his head. "Never. Why would I? My job was to serve."

"What did I give you in return?"

Roland smiled with the pleasure of his memories. "Everything I ever desired and more. I wanted for nothing. I had everything."

"Did you have love?" Michael asked.

Roland laughed. "Why would I want such a foolish thing? It serves no purpose and causes nothing but problems."

"You never desired it?"

Another laugh and a smirk answered his question. "Why would I when I had so much?"

"And do you still possess such wealth?"

Roland held his head high. "My wealth has grown over the years. I possess much, unlike the Ancient One who lives in nothing more than this menial cottage. I have everything, where she has nothing. I have achieved where she has failed."

Michael felt his anger rise, though suddenly cool. He could almost feel Tempest touch his arm and warn him that the man before him deserved his sympathy, not his anger. He calmed considerably, and smiled. "You measure your achievements by your possessions?"

"Of course," he said as though the question was foolish.

"And friends?" Michael asked. "Do you have many?"

"I need none."

"The other warlocks you speak of. Are they not your friends?"

"I would not trust them," Roland said. "They are jealous of me and desire what I have."

Michael began to walk around the man, his dark eyes assessing him slowly. "You tell me that you have much, and yet I feel that you wish me to give you more."

"Your protection will afford me more wealth," Roland said greedily. "I have waited long for your return and feel I deserve a reward for my patience."

Michael smiled. "You deserve a reward?" His temper mounted. There was no controlling it. "*I* have suffered these many years and *you* deserve a reward?"

The man began to shake. "I have remained faithful to our ways."

"And for this I owe you?" His voice rose and echoed through the trees and over the land, causing the birds to fly in fright and the animals to scurry off to safety.

Roland retreated several more feet, though Michael advanced on him as he did so. "I will serve you well again."

"What will you do for me?" Michael demanded to know.

"Whatever you ask of me," the man offered, bowing his head.

"There is nothing you won't do for me? Nothing? I have only to ask and you will do my bidding without objection?"

"As I always have done," Roland said without hesitation.

Michael's words shocked both Roland and himself. "Find me love."

"What?" Roland asked, confused.

"Find me love," Michael repeated, clearly and calmly.

"You wish to love?" Roland asked as though Michael had asked something disgusting of him.

"Do you not wish its power, Roland?"

"Love has no power. It is a foolish and worthless emotion."

"Love possesses the strongest powers."

Roland shrugged indifferently. "If you wish love then I will attempt to find it for you."

"You think it's that simple?" Michael asked with a chilling laugh.

Roland shivered.

"If love possesses the strongest of powers, what makes you think it would be easy to find? What makes you think you could find it at all?"

Roland remained silent, fear of giving the wrong answer evident on his perspiring face.

"You disgust me. Leave," Michael ordered with a wave of his hand.

"But there is much for us to do," Roland objected.

Michael's raised voice chilled the air. "There is nothing I wish from you. Leave!"

Thunder rumbled overhead and caused Roland to jump and scan the suddenly darkening sky. He hurried off without another word and without glancing back at Michael.

Michael paced beneath the tree, his emotions running strong. *Love.*

It always came back to love.

But there was something missing. Something he couldn't quite grasp hold of and understand, and he felt if he could understand it he would have all the answers he needed to make a wise choice.

Thunder continued to rumble overhead and the skies grew darker along with his mood. He could go to the cave and cast the stones, he could walk the woods and feel the earth's energy, he could bury himself in books and look for answers.

The front door to the cottage opened as the first drop of rain fell on him.

Tempest stood in the doorway, watching as the rainstorm soaked Michael. He made no attempt to move. He simply stood there and let the rain fall on him.

It was a torrential downpour and it cleansed the earth, the trees, the plants, the animals and Michael.

She felt the urge to step out in the rain and join him, though she didn't wish only to join him—she wished to join with him. To love under the rain, to feel it soak her skin along with his touch.

She shivered at the thought and Michael noticed. He held his hand out to her and without thought she went running in the rain to him.

His arms captured her, her arms wrapped around his neck and she whispered in his ear, "I want you."

Her words startled him and raced his blood and his lips took instant action, coming down on hers. His tongue entered her mouth with a swiftness that surprised though welcomed, and they kissed as though their souls were blending.

He lifted her up so her feet dangled above the ground and began walking toward the cottage.

She reluctantly tore her mouth from his. "No, here in the rain. I want to make love here in the rain."

He laughed and found her mouth again. "Damn, but I love you," he said before kissing her with an urgency that had them both eager and impatient.

He walked her under the tree, letting her feet touch the ground while he continued to kiss her. His hands unbuttoned her sweater and he was pleased to find her breasts bare. His hands roamed them with a tender roughness and her nipples hardened, more from the stinging rain than from his touch, he suspected. But he didn't care. Her wet nipples felt so good that he couldn't wait another minute to taste them.

His mouth captured her fast and hard and she cried out, grabbing hold of his shoulders, dropping her head back and closing her eyes against the rain and the exquisite feel of his mouth feeding on her nipple.

He tormented her with pleasure but then she wished to torment back and she ran her hand down his arm and dropped it to reach between his legs and intimately caress him.

His mouth left her but only for a moment, only to warn her that she was playing a dangerous game with him and she laughed, her touch turning forceful.

He groaned and dropped his head to rest against her forehead and feeling empowered by his response she opened his zipper and slipped her hand inside his jeans.

"Tempest," he said on a moan.

She laughed softly in his ear and her warm breath tickled his skin, made him shiver and grow even harder. She felt the change and laughed again.

"You'll pay for this," he whispered on a groan.

"Promise?" she asked with a teasing laugh.

He raised his head and his dark eyes locked with hers. "Oh, I promise, sweetheart."

He locked her lips with his and she continued to touch him, explore him, excite him. And when she thought herself completely in control he took charge, his hands doing to her what she had done to him—touch, explore and excite.

The rain continued to fall, soaking them completely and adding to the sensuality of the moment. Their wet flesh became highly sensitized, and it was with hurried hands that they reached out to each other, he pulling up her skirt and she releasing him from his jeans.

He braced her against the tree, his hands on her backside, and he entered her with a forcefulness that had her crying out and wrapping her legs firmly around him. Theirs was a hungry joining, an aching need, and the heavens opened up, drenching them as they moved together in a precious rhythm that united souls.

They clung to each other as climax after climax racked both their bodies and though thunder rumbled overhead and lightning sparked the sky they remained together, not wanting to part, not wanting ever to part.

Michael finally turned sensible and he scooped her up into his arms and carried her into the cottage. He carried her straight to the bathroom and stripped her and himself of their wet clothes. He ran a shower and joined her under the hot spray.

They continued to cling to each other and Michael reached for the soap and began to wash her. She, in turn, took the soap from him and followed suit. Calm and gentle touches turned to passion and they were once again caught up in desires that raged out of control.

This time Michael made certain that they finished making love in bed and as the rain continued to pound the earth and cottage Tempest cuddled in Michael's arms and they both drifted into an exhausted sleep.

They woke later that afternoon, hungry.

Bear greeted them when they entered the kitchen, though his greeting was more of a protest. They had not fed him and he was perturbed that they had forgotten about him. Michael saw to feeding him while Tempest saw to feeding them.

When they finished a simple meal of turkey sandwiches and chips they moved to the living room to cuddle on the couch. The rainy day had turned them lazy and loving and that's what they continued to do as night fell on the earth.

"Did you know Roland?" Michael asked as they lay wrapped in each other's arms on the couch, a fire in the hearth chasing an evening chill from the room.

"I knew him as Tobias," she answered, resting her head comfortably on his strong shoulder.

"Tell me about him."

She didn't wish for such a perfect day to end on talk of warlocks but she understood his need to know. "He was close to Marcus."

"To me," Michael said.

She was pleased he acknowledged the fact, though she understood that his acknowledgment could also draw the time for a choice nearer. "He served Marcus, providing him with whatever he required or desired. In return Marcus provided him with an exceptional material life."

"He gave him whatever he desired?"

"Whatever he desired," she repeated. "And Tobias or Roland was a greedy man. Money, women, power—he wanted it all, and Marcus gave it to him in return for more greedy souls. And the more Tobias gave Marcus the more his wealth grew."

"So Roland feels now that Marcus has returned he will resume his old ways and in doing so provide himself with more wealth."

Tempest nodded. "Once one possesses material riches, one wants more and more and more. Roland wants more."

"You have wealth, Tempest," he said as though he questioned her.

She smiled and traced circles on his chest. "Yes, I am rich. I have a loving family and good friends. What more could I want?"

"But you do have money that helps provide you with a good life."

"It assists me in helping others, but it is not my primary concern. It is who I am and what I can do for others that concerns me. If I lived my life with only myself in mind, what would I have to show for my life? Nothing but selfishness."

"Do you ever think of yourself?"

She laughed. "I have my moments, and today was one long moment."

He found her response amusing, but he felt the need to learn more about her. "You puzzle me at times."

"Why?"

"You give without asking for anything in return. You never demand, never stamp your foot and complain. You merely accept."

Her laughter was strong. "Untrue. I have a temper and I attempt to contain it, though I am not always successful at doing so."

He hugged her. "But your temper flares for others, never for yourself."

"I detest injustices and try my best to help those souls in need."

"Marcus was a soul in need, wasn't he?"

Her voice held a hint of sadness. "He was a soul rich in power and possibilities. His potential went far beyond anything he could ever imagine and yet he surrendered it all for a false power."

Michael stroked her arm and wrapped his leg around hers. "I think I'm beginning to understand about the power of magic."

"What do you understand?" she asked hopefully.

"That magic is based on love."

She smiled. "You grow wise."

"You gave me the tools I needed to gain wisdom."

"You possessed the tools, you just didn't know how to use them."

Michael refused to accept credit for his achievement. "No, if it wasn't for your—" He stopped suddenly and stared at her. "It's so simple. It's been in front of me all this time and I didn't see it. I was too busy concentrating on myself."

He released her and moved off the couch to pace the floor in front of her. "I know I needed to accept that I am Marcus and Marcus is me, but I always felt there was something more to it all than just that. Something deeper that Marcus understood that I as Michael didn't. And my mistake was in assuming that Marcus was attempting to remind me of his beliefs."

Tempest listened in silence, wondering over his discovery.

Michael ran his fingers through his hair in excitement. "But his beliefs also contain knowledge he had learned and yet refused to accept. That knowledge he had learned was why he turned with such desperation to you. He understood its power and what it could do once combined with his."

Tempest fought back tears, feeling that Michael had uncovered the truth and what he needed to know to bring the spell to completion. She stood and waited for him to finish.

"And that power had begun to work its magic on him, didn't it?"

She nodded.

"He finally understood the essence of your power, but found it difficult to deal with, to surrender to."

She nodded again.

He walked over to her and took her face in his hands. "I've known all along; I just needed to remember, didn't I?"

She couldn't nod and couldn't speak; she answered with the slow closing and opening of her eyes.

He spoke softly, almost in reverence. "He knew—I knew all along."

"What did you know?" she managed to ask.

He kissed her lips gently and whispered, "That you're love in its purest form."

Thirty-three

Tempest reluctantly stepped away from him. "Now you will recall everything."

"I have recalled much already," Michael said. "The memories offer me little. It is now that concerns me. This time spent with you has taught me more than I could ever have hoped to learn. In the past my arrogance interfered, and I never truly understood the depth of the love you so unselfishly offered me. It is easy for me now to blend my past with my present. I understand what Marcus searched for and I understand what I have searched for. And I understand that *now* is the time I must make my choice."

"I can do no more for you," she said, though wished she could.

He walked over to her and reached out to take her hands. "The rest I must do on my own."

"The dark side may still tempt," she warned.

He laughed and raised her hands to kiss each one. "The dark side tempts mortals every day."

"You aren't mortal," she reminded him and stepped closer to him.

"I am a witch," he said, raising his chin with pride.

"Welcome home," she said and pressed her cheek to his.

"What now?" he asked with a sense of eagerness.

She took a calming breath, preparing herself for what she had waited centuries for. "The spell must be completed. You must make a choice."

"We must meet in a circle of light to accomplish this," he said, amazed that he was beginning to remember so many things. Spells and chants filled his head and memories of magical feats astounded him.

She smiled. "You've just realized the extent of your magic, haven't you?"

His grin held a touch of arrogance. "Yes, I was very good."

"You were a show-off," she said with a poke to his ribs.

"But I showed off well, sweetheart."

She laughed, hearing Marcus's arrogance and Michael's confidence. They had merged well and she was happy.

He hugged her to him, rocking them back and forth. "Do you trust me?"

She suddenly realized that she did and she nodded. "Very much."

"Then know all will be well for us."

Tempest didn't respond; she simply slipped her arms around his waist and rested her head to his hard chest. She wanted to believe him. But she was aware that pride and arrogance might block his path and his choice might not be the wisest one.

She could do no more than trust and love him and if her own beliefs were strong she would know that was enough. And if by chance his choice proved wrong she would do what was necessary no matter the heartache and pain it would cause her.

"When does this meeting take place?" he asked.

She would not delay it. "Tomorrow evening. After this rain the sky should be clear, the stars brilliant. A perfect night to end a cast."

"I look forward to it."

She hugged him tightly. "Choose wisely, Michael, please choose wisely."

The phone didn't stop ringing the next morning. Sarina called first, insisting on knowing what was happening since she sensed something was going on.

"Tell me," she insisted. "I must know; I'm worried senseless here."

Tempest didn't want her pregnant sister worrying and she didn't want her to know that she was worried herself. But how to hide her feelings from someone who can see so much? Being wise definitely came in handy. "I can feel your concern, Sarina; it's making me feel the same way."

"Tell me if I have something to concern myself with."

Tempest thought to fudge the truth but realized she cherished her sister's advice and wished to speak with her about the situation. "Michael and I will complete the spell this evening."

"I knew it, I knew it."

"What did you know?" Tempest heard Ali say in the background.

Sarina repeated what Tempest had told her.

"Let me talk to her," she heard Ali say.

"No, I'm talking," Sarina said.

Tempest could almost see them fighting over the phone.

"Fine, I'll go pick up one of the other phones and . . . Tempest," Ali shouted in the background. "Don't say a word until I pick up the phone."

"How long are Ali and Sebastian visiting with you?" Tempest asked.

"Too long," Sarina said with a laugh.

"I heard that," Ali said on another phone.

"Good, now be quiet and let Tempest talk," Sarina ordered.

There was an eager silence as they waited for Tempest to speak.

Tempest shared her fears. "Michael and I meet tonight to finish the cast and while I trust in him to choose wisely, a part of me worries that he could fail, leaving me with the possibility of losing him forever. A thought I find unbearable."

"You have to trust him," Ali said with confidence. "There's really not much else you can do, and besides, you gave him all he needs to make a wise choice."

"She's right," Sarina said. "Michael came to you like a newborn babe, knowing nothing, understanding little of his past. Look how much he has learned and grown. He will know what to do."

"I tell myself he will and not to worry, but I love him so much," Tempest said with tears threatening to spill. "He's become an important part of my world and I want him with me now and forever."

"And I'm sure he feels the same way," Ali assured her. "Which means he will think twice before making a decision."

"Or know instinctively which choice to make," Sarina said.

"She's got a point," Ali agreed. "He's just as much in love as you are and his instincts should be good and sharp."

"Especially between the two of you," Sarina pointed out. "If anyone has a strong connection, it would be you and Michael. Your many years, your combined wisdom and knowledge will probably serve you well this evening."

"True," Tempest said, feeling better.

"We'll be thinking of you tonight," Sarina said.

"Strong, good, successful thoughts," Ali added.

"I appreciate it," Tempest said, grateful for having such a wonderful sister and a special friend.

"Let's have ice cream, Sarina," Ali said.

"It's barely ten in the morning."

"Fudge swirl—and I know I saw whipped cream in the fridge," Ali tempted.

"Whipped cream, you say?" Sarina said. "Call me later, Tempest."

"Enjoy the ice cream," Tempest said and hung up the phone, only to have it ring again. "Hello."

"I called to wish you well," Sydney said.

She and Tempest talked for a few minutes and when she hung up, the phone rang again. This time she spent a few minutes hearing encouraging words from Dagon. When he finished Sebastian called and offered his advice, which Tempest was grateful for.

When she thought herself done she received a summons from the fairies, and knew they were concerned. She wasted no time in going to them.

She grabbed a jacket and headed out the door and into the woods.

Beatrice paced along a fallen tree, her cockeyed head wreath nearly covering her eye and her wing crooked as usual.

Tempest shook her head at the sight of her and smiled. She was a constant she could count on, right down to the crooked wing. No matter how many times she fixed it or placed a protective spell around her, she managed to crook the wing. But then that was Beatrice.

"Good, you've come," Beatrice said, patting the log for her to sit.

Tempest took the offered seat and waited for the tiny fairy to express her concern.

Her words surprised Tempest. "We're concerned for Michael."

"Michael?"

"Yes, the fairies have come to respect him and all he has achieved in his new life. He has grown to be wise and fair and we think him good for you."

Tempest smiled. "I think him good for me, too."

"How do you think he will fare tonight?"

Tempest had gone over and over this in her head and with everyone who called, but she had no answer and would find none, not until this evening when Michael made his choice.

"We will have to wait and see."

Beatrice climbed on Tempest's leg to sit. "The fairies have confidence in him. They believe he will make the right choice, though the warlocks whisper of his successful return."

"Everyone waits for tonight."

"Everyone wishes you and Michael well," Beatrice said with a pat of her hand.

"It is all up to Michael."

Beatrice shook her head. "It is up to love."

Tempest smiled at her wise words and added her own. "Love never fails."

"We fail love," Beatrice finished.

Tempest felt confident. "Then tonight can only be successful."

Tempest dressed in a gown of pure white. Yards and yards of gossamer material flowed around her, her feet were bare, her reddish-blond hair wild and free. She waited in a clearing in the woods for Michael. It was near to midnight, the sky overhead clear and bright with thousands of twinkling stars. The warm spring night air reminded one of summer and the sounds of the night insects and nocturnal animals provided a soothing symphony.

It was a perfect night for love.

She had prepared the large circle that surrounded her, securing it with magic and light and when the moment was right the protective circle would burst into light, wrapping Michael and her in the heart of its power.

While the woman in her waited with nervous anticipation, the Ancient One waited with a serene calmness that most would never understand. What was done was done and nothing could change that. It was here and now that mattered and nothing else, not the past, the present or the future. Only this moment was important.

Tempest heard his approach. She knew the trees' branches bent in respect for him and the animals moved silently out of his way and the owls followed him with their wide knowledgeable eyes and the fairies offered their blessings to him.

She held herself tall as only the Ancient One could, with all the love and wisdom she possessed.

Her breath caught when he stepped out of the darkness and stopped just outside the circle. He was dressed in the ancient style, the style of the wise ones long ago. Black and purple robes gave him the appearance of a mighty ruler born of wisdom. His dark hair had grown longer, falling carelessly past his shoulders, and his scars added a sense of strength. He made an impressive sight.

She smiled when she looked into his dark eyes; they held the eagerness of a young boy who was about to begin a grand adventure.

"It is time," she said and invited him into the circle.

Michael entered with eager and confident steps and when he did the earth circle surrounding them burst into a brilliant light that shot several feet up to the sky before settling down to a low light that burned steadily.

He waited, knowing he must follow the Ancient One's lead.

"Tell me what you have learned from this spell," she said, her tone calm, her manner peaceful.

He answered quickly. "I learned that trust is earned and love is given."

She smiled, thinking him finished, but he continued.

"And I learned that patience is the wisest gift one can give to himself."

She almost cried. It was so rare for anyone, even a witch, to understand the importance of patience. She continued her questions. "Tell me what you learned from your past."

He answered eagerly. "That power based on greed, hate, fear and indifference can corrupt, hurt and cause endless pain and suffering. And that is a weak power born of the ego."

"You answer me wisely, but now tell me what is truly in your heart, past, present and future."

He took a breath as though he had much to say and was preparing for it. "Once I wanted the ultimate power. I wanted to capture pure love and combine it with my power to give life to a force that would be invincible. Instead it captured me and I didn't understand the importance of that union until it was too late. I was lucky that the love I had thought I'd foolishly lost forever actually saved me and gave me a chance to redeem myself."

Tempest felt her heart swell with pride and her eyes fill with tears for the man she loved.

"I thought to repay that love." He shook his head. "But I realized no payment is required; that it was given freely and that is how I will give my love in return—freely and from my heart and soul. And for the future?" He shrugged. "As long as we love, it doesn't matter."

The time was here for his choice, and she hoped with all her heart that he understood what he must do and hoped he had the courage to do it.

Tempest stepped toward him. "I will repeat the spell to you and then the choice will be yours to make."

With a nod he whispered, "I love you."

She held back her tears, attempted to ignore the ache in her heart and the wrenching in her stomach and wished, wished on all the heavenly stars that he chose wisely.

With her hands raised to the heavens she repeated the words that had once shattered her heart. "With my love I send you away; for you to return on a future day; your life will be yours to create; choose wisely and repeat no mistakes; cherish life and hold it dear; fill no hearts and souls with fear; surround yourself with magic and light; and seek not to return to the dark night; if by chance you should lose your way; remember all these words I say; magical memories you will recall; and the choice will be yours to stand or to fall!"

Tempest lowered her hands and looked at Michael and wished, wished with all her heart that he would do what he must.

He smiled, then laughed not a chilling laugh but a knowing one and he slowly went down on his knees before her, wrapping his arms around her waist and pressing his face firmly to her stomach. "I love you, Tempest, and I wish to share a life of magic and light with you. I renounce all that I was and ask you to accept me for who I now am, the man and witch who loves you. *Now, then and forever*."

Her tears fell—she couldn't stop them—and her heart burst with joy as she went down on her knees in front of him, cupping his face and raining kisses on him. "I love you, Michael. You're the breath I take, you're my heart that beats—" She paused and kissed him softly. "Your soul and mine are one."

He hugged her fiercely to him. "Then let's unite our souls forever. We've been separated far too long."

They fell together to the soft carpet of earth beneath them and with unhurried hands they touched each other; with gentle lips they savored each other and with an age-old love two old souls united forever.

The heavenly winds whispered in song, the fairies rejoiced and Mother Sky smiled down upon her children.

Epilogue

~

Six months later

"Stop worrying, Sebastian," Dagon said for the third time. "Your daughter Jade will not develop her magical skills for several months."

Sebastian looked down into the bassinet at his beautiful, smiling, gurgling daughter whose tiny fist clung tightly to his finger. "So you tell me, but I have this uneasy feeling."

"Nonsense," Ali said, her arm going around her husband's waist. "She's a normal, healthy, little girl."

"She's a witch," Sebastian said, as though it explained his concern.

The little girl seemed to agree with a gurgling laugh.

"See," Sebastian said, confirming his worry.

Everyone in the sitting room in Rasmus Castle laughed.

Dagon and Sarina stood with their arms around each other, looking down at their smiling son, Alexander.

Sydney sat with Lady Lily and Bear curled contentedly on her lap.

Beatrice fluttered back and forth between the two bassinets, keeping a careful watch over the three-month-old babies.

Tempest and Michael stood off to the side, watching the

happy couples with their newborn babies with thoughts of their own future children in mind.

Sarina and Dagon drifted away to sit on the couch.

"In the summer you'll have twin sons," Sarina said to her sister with excitement.

"Twins?" Michael asked in disbelief but with joy.

"Twins," Sarina repeated, thrilled with the prospect.

Michael hugged his wife to him and gave her a kiss. They had married right after the completion of the spell. It was a small ceremony with family and close friends in attendance. And of course a score of fairies highlighted the dusk ceremony.

It was a day Michael would never forget and he would never forget the sight of Tempest when she joined him in the ceremony circle that joined them together forever. He never imagined her looking more beautiful than she already was, but that day she took his breath away, walking toward him in pure white, a wreath of white wildflowers circling her head and a multitude of fairies fluttering behind her as they held her long, white veil.

Now Sarina predicted not just one child but two, and the thought thrilled him. He hugged Tempest closely to him. Life was good and he was grateful.

Sebastian looked to Michael. "At least you needn't worry about your children being more skilled than you. Your powers are more than sufficient."

Dagon attempted to further alleviate Sebastian's fears. "It will be months before Jade can do any magical feats. You have nothing to worry about."

Tempest didn't wish to worry him, but she had the distinct feeling that Jade was much more powerful than anyone gave her credit for, and then there was Alexander. The children's powers were definitely being underestimated.

"I don't know," Sebastian said with a shake of his head. "I have this strange feeling that—"

Ali laughed at his worry. "Don't be silly. Jade's only three months old, she has no skills; and even if she did she wouldn't know how to handle them."

"Ali's right," Dagon assured him again. "The babies just wouldn't know wh—"

He stopped dead and his eyes widened in shock.

Everyone followed his eyes and stared with amazement at the rattle that floated above Jade's bassinet. Cooing and gurgling and what sounded distinctly like laughter joined the floating rattle as it spinned and dipped and spinned again directly over Jade.

"No, skills?" Sebastian asked, though watched his daughter's magical antics with pride.

"Damn," Dagon said. "I never would have believed it."

"Oh, you haven't seen anything yet," Tempest warned and Michael smiled in understanding.

All eyes focused on the floating rattle and with a gurgle of laughter from Jade, the rattle was sent in a furious spin to Alexander's bassinet.

Dagon raised a fast finger to deflect the projectile rattle when suddenly the rattle was sent hurdling away from Alexander's bassinet to land with a crash on the floor.

Jade laughed as only a young little girl could and a sigh could be heard from Alexander.

"History repeats itself," Sydney said with a laugh, and all joined in.

"History can be changed," Michael said and all eyes turned to him.

"Only if love is strong," Sydney said, "as you well know."

Hand in hand, Tempest and Michael walked over to Sydney.

"We have a special gift for you," Tempest said, holding her hand out to her.

Sarina and Dagon took their son from the bassinet and Sebastian picked his daughter Jade from her bassinet and joined his wife who stood beside Dagon and Sarina. Beatrice flitted in front of the two couples, a wide smile spreading across her tiny face.

Sydney realized something was going on, something had been planned. She accepted Tempest's hand with a brief hesitation.

"You have done much for many," Tempest said.

"Not nearly as much as you have done," Sydney argued.

"It matters not, your time is now," Tempest said and walked her over near the row of windows. "Stay here."

Tempest moved to Sydney's one side and Michael stood on the other. Together they extended their hands toward the windows in a slow circular motion. A swirling mist began to appear, growing larger and larger and larger until it consumed the entire row of windows and wall.

Michael stepped in front of the swirling fog. "You offered me wise words that helped me to make a wise choice. And I wish to thank you for your help by offering you another chance at love."

Sydney's breath caught, her heart raced and for a moment she felt that time stood still. "What do you mean?"

Michael explained. "Tempest and I wish to send you back in time to the man you once loved and lost, so you have another chance to love again."

Sydney was speechless.

"You do want to go, don't you?" Michael asked with a teasing laugh as his hand went out to take hers.

Sydney nodded. "Yes, yes, I want to go." And she grabbed for his offered hand.

"Say your good-byes," he said with a kiss to her cheek.

Sydney hurried over to Dagon and Sarina and kissed each one, along with baby Alexander. Sebastian was next, and a tender peck to baby Jade's cheek had her turning to Ali. They hugged each other fiercely as tears streamed down their cheeks.

"I will miss you," Ali said, "but I wish you to find your love as I found mine."

Sydney turned to Michael. "Will I be able to return?"

"Anything is possible," he answered with a smile.

"Then I will see you again," Sydney said and gave her one last hug, reluctant to leave her. "Take care of her," she said to Sebastian and turned away with tear filled eyes to join Michael.

"It's time," Tempest said.

Sydney kissed her cheek. "I don't know how to thank you for this."

Tempest hugged her. "Love, Sydney, love with all your heart."

"A wise choice," Michael said, coming up beside her.

"You both should know," Sydney said.

"Now it's time for you to know," Michael said and extended his hand to the swirling portal in time and winked. "We thought you might need a guide."

Beatrice flew over to her fluttering next to her cheek. "Mind the company?"

"I'd love the company," she said truthfully and with relief of making this exciting journey with a friend.

"Time to go," Tempest said.

With one last smile and a handful of kisses to those she loved Sydney, with Beatrice by her side, stepped into the portal.

The swirling mist swallowed her up and slowly disappeared.

Michael took Tempest into his arms, held her tight, kissed her gently and whispered, "It's time to make new magical memories."